Song of Stars

Other Books by Rae D. Magdon

Amendyr Series
The Second Sister - Book 1
Wolf's Eyes - Book 2
The Witch's Daughter - Book 3
Wolf Eyes – Book 4

Lucky Breaks Series
Lucky 7
Lucky 8

Devil Wears Yellow Garters

Fur and Fangs

Tengoku

And with Michelle Magly

All the Pretty Things

Dark Horizons Series
Dark Horizons – Book 1
Starless Night – Book 2
Eclipse – Book 3

Song of Stars

Rae D. Magdon

Desert Palm Press

Song of Stars

By Rae D. Magdon

©2022 Rae D. Magdon

ISBN (book): 9781954213470
ISBN (epub): 9781954213487

Desert Palm Press
1961 Main Street, Suite 220
Watsonville, California 95076
www.desertpalmpress.com

Editor: Toni Kelley
Cover Design: Rachel George

Printed in the United States of America
First Edition December 2022

Acknowledgement

Special thanks to Hannah, Yeager, and Ayaka for reading my initial manuscript.

Thanks to Lee and Toni from Desert Palm Press for putting the shine on my story.

Rachel, your work on this cover is astounding.

Dedication

With love to Tory, my other half and best friend.

Mirae — Firstday

DAWNBELL TOLLS THE LOW, melodic notes of morning. Mirae stands upon a beach of black sand, gazing across a vast ocean of stars. The waves glow like the last rays of sunset, rusty orange bleeding into deep crimson, twilight purples pooling into blues so dark they border on black. Faint white lights float like lanterns upon the surface, rolling and bobbing. Beckoning.

Mirae smiles. She has died and moved on to the sea of stars, just as planned. Not the worst end, from what she remembers. Better to die for a cause than in a sickbed. Besides, it seems peaceful here. The breeze is cool against her skin, its brine sharp in her nose. It smells like Farsea, the village of her birth. She steps into the surf, bare feet sinking into the wet sand. Waves swirl around her ankles as though to tug her deeper. She spreads her arms wide to catch the sea spray, feeling lighter than she has in two long years. At last, she can rest.

Dawnbell tolls again, booming and insistent over the ocean's hiss. A strange sound to hear in the afterlife. Mirae frowns, glancing over her shoulder. There are no buildings here. No bell towers. There is only the beach, which stretches some distance before disappearing into a line of gray fog. She turns once more toward the ocean, only to pause as a strange echo reaches her ears. A familiar voice sings from somewhere beyond the fog, a rich alto that starts soft, but grows louder and more resonant.

The sun's begun to rise, the moon has gone away.

Mirae stops. She knows that voice. Those words. "Sefina..."

Open up your eyes and greet a brand new day.

A stinging lump stops up Mirae's throat. If there's anyone she regrets leaving behind, it's her Sefina. She stands ankle-deep in the waves, her previous certainty shaken. Part of her wants to dive into the sea and seek refuge beneath the surface, a reward she's more than earned. Another part longs to follow Sefina's voice into the fog, in hopes of seeing her face one last time.

The breeze stills. Sefina's song dies away. Instead, Mirae hears the creak of oars in the distance. A rowboat cuts across the starry waves, its dark silhouette growing larger as it glides toward shore. A hunched figure wearing a brown cloak pulls the oars, stirring the water in steady rhythm. The rowboat slides to a stop in the shallows, its prow nudging the sand.

1

Mirae glimpses the face beneath the rower's hood. She gasps. "Speaker Yeneri?" Though her old mentor entered Of-Eternal-Sleep's embrace years ago, there can be no mistake. Mirae knows that snow-white hair. That wrinkled brown face. Those dark, glittering eyes.

"Mirae." Yeneri's voice is rough but warm, like the crackle of a log upon the hearth. "It's been too long."

Mirae wades into the shallows, skirts swirling around her legs. She leans over the boat, pulling Yeneri into a tight embrace. Tears burn her eyes, mingling with the sea spray on her face as she breathes in the speaker's familiar scent. Yeneri smells like fresh linens hanging in a warm summer breeze. "I've missed you."

Yeneri smooths Mirae's hair beneath her hand. Her swollen joints seem to lack the stiffness Mirae remembers. "I've missed you too, but why have you come so soon?"

Mirae blinks away more tears. "It's a long story, but I died a noble death. Others will carry on the work I began. I'm not disappointed in how my story ended..."

Wake up! Wake up! Flowers bloom, birds sing. Wake up! Wake up! Good morning, everything.

Sefina's voice rings across the waves, beautifully bright and clear. Mirae lifts her chin from Yeneri's shoulder and glances toward the beach. Pale gray light shines in the distance, reminding her of daybreak on a rainy winter morning. It clears away some of the mist, revealing a faint image. An unfamiliar bedroom, where a figure sits slumped upon a stool.

The edges of the image are blurred, its faded colors nearly translucent, but Mirae recognizes Sefina. Her head hangs forward, wavy brown hair falling about her face. She sits beside the bed, holding someone's hand. Mirae can see their face clearly. It's her own, eyes closed, lips parted. Her body lies still, draped in a thin white sheet.

Mirae wrenches her gaze away. She can't bear to witness anymore. Can't bear to watch Sefina mourn her death. Sacrificing herself for a cause was one thing. Witnessing the consequences is different. She looks to Yeneri, her anchor, the wise one who always knew which path to take in life. "Speaker, am I dead?"

"Not quite yet," Yeneri says. "You should have died, but certain interested parties have requested you be given a choice."

Mirae licks her lips. They've gone dry in the brisk salt air. "A choice whether to live or die?" She isn't sure she wants a choice. Not now, after she's already given so much. Choices are exhausting. It's all too easy to make the wrong ones.

Yeneri nods. Her dark eyes shine amidst the deep wrinkles and folds of her face. "This decision must be yours, but the boundaries of time are fluid here. Fluid enough for you to hear Sefina's side of the story."

At the mention of Sefina's name, Mirae looks back at the sky. The ghostly image of Sefina tucks a loc of hair behind her ear, revealing her pale face and red-ringed green eyes. She leans forward, whispering to the body lying on the bed. This time, when her voice drifts toward Mirae on the wind, it isn't a song. It's a choked, desperate plea.

"Please, Mirae. Remember everything you have to live for, because I'm utterly lost without you."

Chapter One

SEFINA WOKE TO THE sound of gravel scratching the shutters. She rolled over on her sleeping pallet, rising onto her knees to peek out the window. She didn't dare open it all the way or the early morning glare might disturb Great Aunt Adie. Those were the worst days, when she went without breakfast and slogged through chores until sunset. She took extra care to be quiet as she peered through the slats.

The sight of Mirae balanced on bare toes, gripping the damp window ledge, brightened Sefina's mood immediately. Mirae's smile was warmer than the sun and her dark brown eyes sparkled with mischief. Though the slate gray sky offered little more than a drizzle, Sefina felt as though a beautiful dawn had broken.

"Wake up, wake up. Good morning, Sefina!"

Mirae's silvery voice sent a shiver down Sefina's spine. Her skin tingled from the roots of her hair to the tips of her toes. *"Your voice strikes songbirds silent with envy,"* Mirae's father often said, and Sefina agreed wholeheartedly.

Unfortunately, the lovely sound of Mirae's voice carried through the shutters despite her attempts to sing softly. Sefina's pounding heart almost drowned out the final note. "Shhh!" She peeked over her shoulder, then sighed with relief. Great Aunt Adie remained fast asleep in bed, snoring loudly.

"Come out and play," Mirae whispered, peering up at Sefina with pleading brown eyes.

Sefina bit her lip. Her aunt might punish her for sneaking out early, but Mirae's parents always fed her breakfast and their food was delicious. A day full of chores wouldn't be so bad with a full belly. She held a warning finger to her lips, then clambered off her sleeping pallet and crept toward the door.

Great Aunt Adie's snores stuttered as Sefina pushed the door open. She froze, hand hovering over the rusted latch, not daring to breathe. Then the snores resumed. Great Aunt Adie rolled over and buried her face in her pillow. Sefina slipped out into the misty morning, closing the door slowly so it wouldn't creak.

Mirae met her on the gravel path outside. "Let's play on the cliffs, then have breakfast at my house."

Sefina started to say that her aunt had warned her to stay away from the cliffs, but her words died away. Mirae's dimpled cheeks were so round, her eyes so hopeful, Sefina couldn't refuse. "Alright," she said, taking Mirae's hand. Warmth spread through her palm as Mirae's fingers laced with hers. "Let's go."

The dreary sky brightened to pale blue by the time they reached the cliffs. The roar of the waves below was a welcome sound, interspersed with the wheeling cries of seagulls above. Sefina dropped Mirae's hand and stepped onto the nearest cliff, closing her eyes and throwing her arms wide. Cold spray tickled her face and the brisk smell of salt filled her nose. When she opened her eyes, she saw Mirae standing beside her in the same pose. They looked at each other, then burst into laughter.

Mirae sat on the cliff's edge and dangled her legs over the side. Sefina joined her, picking up a loose rock and dropping it into the churning waves. It sank beneath the white foam, causing a faint ripple before disappearing. "Think the rocks like it down there?" Mirae asked, bumping her shoulder against Sefina's.

"I'd rather be a sea rock than a land rock," Sefina said. "It's dark and cool at the bottom of the ocean."

Mirae picked up another rock and lobbed it into the ocean. It splashed through the surface before sinking alongside Sefina's. "You should have been a Sea Child."

"My aunt says Sea Children never bathe in fresh water," Sefina said. "That's why they smell funny."

"I smell better than you!" Mirae threw a handful of sand at Sefina's chest.

Sefina's mouth fell open. She stared at the cold, wet clump as it slid down her shirt, leaving a gritty stain. As she looked up, a thin smirk spread across her face. "You've made a grave mistake," she said, shoving her hand into the sand. "This is my best dress."

Mirae held up her hands. "It was a joke—"

Sefina threw the sand at Mirae's stomach.

Mirae leaped up but didn't brush the sand from her clothes. She crouched for more ammunition and took aim. After that, it was a battle for the ages. They hurled mud and sand until they were covered in filth, then sprinted down the winding path that led to the beach. There, the battle continued amidst the waves. Splashing was much more fun than throwing sand, so they played until Sefina's lungs burned and Mirae started dragging her feet.

When the cold of Sefina's waterlogged dress became too uncomfortable, she staggered out of the shallows to sprawl on the beach, letting the sea lap at the soles of her feet. She stared up at the sky, longing for warm sunshine and wishing the day wasn't rainy and overcast.

Mirae flopped down beside her. "I won, right?"

Sefina snorted but said nothing. Mirae liked to win, and she didn't see any harm in allowing her to think she had, but she had a little pride of her own. "Someday, I'll live in a big city like Stagford and wear fine clothes you won't muck up. Silk dresses with brocade and matching fancy hats."

"Stagford?" Mirae rolled onto her side, propping her cheek on her fist. "Why?"

"My parents lived there, before..."

Sefina's voice trailed off.

Mirae didn't press.

A loud rumble came from Sefina's stomach before she could dwell on those memories. She sat up, attempting the futile task of wiping her hands on her soaked, sand-covered skirts. "Think your parents have cooked breakfast?"

Mirae grinned. "Don't they always?"

They picked themselves up and trudged along the path to town. Sefina licked her dry lips. Mirae lived in a much larger house than Great Aunt Adie's, with four whole rooms and a roof that withstood the weather. The food was better too: fresh-caught fish, warm eggs, and homegrown vegetables. There was even a cabinet of spices from distant lands since Mirae's father was a merchant.

By the time they reached Mirae's house, Sefina's salt-stiffened hair had partially dried. Her dress was another matter. The cold fabric clung to her skin and began to itch. She wrapped her arms around herself, shivering and scratching her elbows while Mirae knocked on the door.

"Mama? Papa? We're hungry!"

Mirae's mother opened the door. She was a beautiful, dark-skinned woman with a heart-shaped face and an easy smile. "What have we here?" she would usually say when saw them like this. "Two big, delicious clumps of seaweed on our porch? Papa, come throw them in the pot. We'll have seaweed soup for dinner."

This morning, Mirae's mother wasn't smiling. She wore her finest dress, a russet orange color with a fitted waist and wide skirt, instead of her usual clothes. Her lips were pressed into a thin line and it took Sefina a moment to place the strange gleam in her eyes. Fear. Mirae's mother was afraid.

"Where have you been?" she whispered, seizing Mirae's arm and pulling her inside. "By the Eight, you're a mess." She grabbed one of two towels that hung outside by the front door for precisely this purpose and began scrubbing sand from Mirae's face.

"The beach," Mirae said, dodging the towels. "Mama, stop!"

Sefina took the other towel, drying herself in silence. Mirae's mother continued muttering as she wiped away the grit plastered to Mirae's skin. "Today of all days, when we have such esteemed company..."

Curious, Sefina peeked through the open door. There was indeed company sitting at the table alongside Mirae's father. Their guest was a woman, perhaps fifty, with pale blonde hair and sharp blue eyes. She wore robes of purple silk, the finest Sefina had ever seen, embroidered with golden thread at the bodice and sleeves. Shiny gold bangles adorned her wrists and gemstones glinted on her fingers. She looked like a queen straight out of a storybook.

The woman's eyes passed over Sefina and focused on Mirae. She rose from her chair with a swish of her robes and approached the open door. "This is your daughter?" she said to Mirae's mother. "The one with the magical voice?"

Magic.

Sefina shuffled back behind the doorframe and chewed her cheek. Great Aunt Adie had warned her not to say such things about Mirae's voice. She claimed it would invite the unwelcome attention of the Eight and one of them might strike her down for such arrogance. As far as Sefina knew, precious few chosen mortals possessed supernatural powers.

But Sefina had always known Mirae's voice was special.

Incredible things happened when Mirae sang. Things that had no other explanation. Like the time Mirae went sailing with her father and called shoals of silver fish to the boat's side. The time Mirae made the saplings in the town square grow into fine young trees when Sefina had lamented the lack of shade. Mirae had kissed her scraped knees countless times only for the cuts to vanish, leaving them good as new.

Sefina stayed silent, drawing herself further into the towel. She had no idea what to make of this wealthy, elegant stranger who showed no fear and said the word 'magic' openly.

Mirae wasn't so meek. "I am," she said without a hint of modesty. "I sing to the sea, the sun, and the flowers. And to Sefina."

The woman's gaze finally landed on Sefina. Embarrassed by the sorry state of her dress and lack of shoes, she forced herself to straighten her posture. The stranger's attention lighted upon her only briefly before returning to Mirae. Sefina tried not to feel disappointed, especially when she noted the covetous sheen in the woman's ice-blue eyes.

"When you sing to them, do they sing back?"

Mirae smiled. Nodded. "Of course they sing back. Even Sefina."

That was true. Sefina sometimes sang alongside Mirae, and more often when she was alone, in hopes she might create a minor miracle of her own. No matter how hard she tried, the waves and sky took no notice of her voice. They remained as distant and timeless as ever. The minor cuts she suffered never healed when she whispered poetry to them. She was, in a word, ordinary.

Sefina looked at Mirae's parents, wondering if they shared her discomfort with this woman's abrupt manner of addressing things best kept secret. They waited in stiff silence, communicating with nervous glances. Mirae's father wrapped an arm around his wife's shoulder as though to comfort her.

"Please, show me," the woman said to Mirae.

"All right." Mirae dropped the dirty towel on the porch, walking past Sefina and into the vegetable garden. Sefina stayed small as the adults followed, lingering behind to see what would happen.

Planted between the vegetable patches were neat rows of flowers. Bee balm, mostly—which tolerated the brisk salt air and made fine poultices—but a few day-lilies as well, not yet ready to open their petals. Mirae stood in front of the day-lilies, folding her hands behind her back and rocking from heel to toe.

As soon as Mirae opened her mouth, the rest of Sefina's world fell away. There was only the ringing glory of Mirae's voice, high and clear as the sweetest silver bell.

> *See the lovely flowers blooming all around.*
> *Flowers that are growing, growing in the ground.*
> *Flowers like the rainbow, every shade and hue.*
> *Orange, red, and pink, with blue and purple too.*

The day-lilies opened as though Mirae were the sun. They swayed in her direction as if straining to hear her better. Sefina's heart swelled.

She knew how the day-lilies felt. She wanted to soak Mirae in much the same way. The thought crossed her mind that she might never have enough of Mirae's voice, or of Mirae herself.

Mirae's last note lingered in the air. Once the final echo faded, she beamed with pride, appearing delighted by the woman's awestruck expression. Sefina's cheeks burned. Great Aunt Adie would chastise such prideful behavior, but Sefina didn't blame Mirae. She'd have given anything to receive that sort of look from a mysterious stranger with so many jewels and such an air of refinement.

"Child, your voice is goddess-given." The woman knelt before Mirae, placing a hand upon her shoulder. Her golden rings sparkled in the rising sun. "My name is Lady Lirath. I live in the city of Stagford. Have you heard of it?"

Sefina often dreamed of Stagford, one of the largest, most prosperous cities in the kingdom of Stelvaine. Her parents had told her it was an inland city, at least a week's journey by cart. How her heart raced to hear it mentioned—simply to know someone from such a wondrous place had graced their tiny village!

"Stagford is where Of-The-Land turned into a white stag and crossed the ford, to show his people where to build their city," Mirae said. "Many Earthfolk live there. Like Sefina."

Lady Lirath continued staring only at Mirae. "Quite right, but Of-The-Land is not the only one of the Eight worshipped in Stagford. Surely you know his sister, Of-Blessed-Dreams."

Before she could think better of it, Sefina spoke. Her own voice surprised her, but the words escaped before she could swallow them. "Of-Blessed-Dreams is the goddess of all things beautiful and inspiring. Song and dance and poetry."

At long last, Lady Lirath turned. A shiver raced down Sefina's spine as Lady Lirath's gaze fixed upon her. She gave a small, tight-lipped smile—nothing like the beaming smile she'd given Mirae, but Sefina's heart soared. "Yes. Of-Blessed-Dreams inspires musicians, dancers, poets, sculptors, storytellers, and all those who create art. She ushers human-made beauty into the world, for what joy is there in life without beauty? What purpose?"

Sefina trembled with delight. What purpose indeed? She had always admired the natural beauty of the sea and sky, but to see a city like Stagford? Her mind whirled with grand buildings, marble statues, gilded tapestries and all manner of wonders. The mere thought overwhelmed her with longing. She wanted to drink it in like the sweetest apple cider.

Lady Lirath turned back to Mirae. Sefina felt the sudden loss of her gaze as though a cloud had passed before her, blotting out all warmth. "My child," Lady Lirath said, "your voice is a gift from Of-Blessed-Dreams. Such wondrous talent requires proper training if you are to reach your full potential."

Mirae's eyes widened. "You would train me, Lady?"

"Yes," Lady Lirath said. "I've spent my entire life honing all aspects of musicianship. My specialty is training voices such as yours. I must admit, I have never heard a child sing quite like you."

Mirae held her head high. "I imagine you haven't."

Sefina swallowed hard. *How can she say something like that with such confidence?* Lady Lirath was a wealthy, glamorous woman from Stagford. Stagford! Surely such a grand city had beautiful voices to spare. Perhaps even other miracle-workers. A pang of longing pulled at Sefina's heartstrings. She would love to visit Stagford, even for a day.

Lady Lirath fixed Mirae with a look of stern disapproval. Her thin lips pulled into a frown and her faint blonde brows drew together in a knot. "You sing sweetly, but your voice is raw. Untrained. Unrefined. You are in desperate need of a teacher, someone to make your voice the best it can be in service to Of-Blessed-Dreams."

Mirae's face screwed up. She stuck out her lower lip and crossed her arms over her chest. "Unrefined? Does that mean bad?"

Sefina stifled a smirk. She wondered if this was the first time in Mirae's life that anyone had scolded her. It wasn't like Mirae had a Great Aunt Adie to yell at her for doing the chores wrong, burning dinner, or making too much noise. Mirae's parents did most of the chores and their house was always full of laughter.

"Unrefined doesn't mean bad," Lady Lirath said. "It means you can become so much better, so much more, with a mentor such as myself. With your parents' permission, I will teach you all I know." She gestured at the day-lilies. "Your voice will grow like these flowers here, into a marvel without compare."

"Yes!" Mirae uncrossed her arms and threw them wide. "Please train me, Lady Lirath. I want to become a marvel."

Despite a brief pinch of jealousy, Sefina shot Mirae an encouraging smile. Mirae was already a marvel in her eyes, but after training with someone like Lady Lirath, she would become nothing short of miraculous. *Someday, she'll be famous throughout the kingdom, and I'll be her very best friend.*

Lady Lirath rose from her crouch, straightening as she turned to Mirae's parents. "I know what I ask for is a great sacrifice. The love parents hold for their children is without measure. But your daughter is no ordinary child. She is goddess-blessed. Her voice and her powers must be trained to reach their full potential and help the greatest number of people. You already know this or you wouldn't have agreed to host me."

Only then did Sefina notice the tears brimming in Mirae's mother's eyes. The stiffness of her father's jaw. He swallowed before speaking. "Yes." His voice grated with pain. "We know."

"May we visit, at least?" Mirae's mother came to stand behind her, resting both hands upon her shoulders and squeezing tight. "I couldn't bear to lose her forever..."

"Of course. I cannot bring you to Stagford with us, or you might distract Mirae from her training, but the Temple of Dreams holds a grand music festival twice a year, in midsummer and midwinter. Those would be excellent times for you to visit your daughter. The temple will provide a stipend, of course. No amount of gold can replace a beloved child, but it will make your lives easier."

Sefina gasped. An invisible fist grabbed her heart, squeezing painfully tight. Lady Lirath was attempting to buy Mirae! To take her away! Her eyes began to burn with tears. *Will I lose her forever? What if I never see her again?*

The same realization dawned upon Mirae. "No." She pulled free of her mother and ran over to grab Sefina's hand, squeezing so hard Sefina almost forgot about the vise around her heart. "I won't leave Sefina! Lady Lirath, you have to stay and train me here in Farsea."

All three adults fixed Mirae with matching looks of surprise. Sefina stood tall, feeling a great swell of pride. Mirae had refused to leave her behind. Never before had she felt so special, so valued. The burning tears receded and her cheeks flushed with warmth.

The wrinkle of Lady Lirath's brow deepened. "You would forgo such an opportunity for this girl?" Her gaze fixed upon Sefina, who shrank under her stare. She'd felt immensely important only moments before, but Lady Lirath's evaluation made her feel small, dirty, and drab in comparison. She remembered she wasn't even wearing shoes and for some reason, that fact seemed very important—and very bad.

Mirae shook her head. "I won't leave Sefina. I won't!"

Lady Lirath stepped closer. "Where do you live, girl? Where are your parents? I would speak with them."

Sefina struggled to speak around the lump in her throat. It felt like her entire face had been set aflame. "My parents got the sweating sickness and went to sleep. I live with my Great Aunt Adie."

Lady Lirath's frown softened into a sweet smile, but Sefina saw the mill wheel of her mind turning behind those icy blue eyes. "An orphan? Tell me, how fares your household? Do you have enough to eat? A warm place to sleep?"

Sefina couldn't find the courage to answer this time. She fixed her eyes upon her muddy feet and shook her head.

Lady Lirath addressed Mirae. "If I permit you to bring your playmate along, will you come to Stagford as my pupil?"

Mirae's hand relaxd in Sefina's. Her stubbornness melted like a spring thaw, as though she'd never been upset at all. "If Sefina comes with me, I'll go to Stagford. Can I please go, Mama? Papa? And you'll promise to come visit us?" She gave her father a pleading look.

Sefina stole a glance at Mirae's parents as well. The sadness etched into their faces was obvious in the tense lines there. It was something Sefina almost envied. Something she would never have again.

"If going to Stagford with Lady Lirath will make you happy," Mirae's mother said with considerable strain.

"Yes, my little love," said her father. "We'll visit whenever we can. Promise."

Though the atmosphere was heavy with grief, Sefina felt the kindling of joy. *We're going to Stagford. Not to visit, but to live there!* Her mind whirled with thoughts of pretty clothes, grand buildings, and important people. She wouldn't receive fancy music lessons, but surely Lady Lirath would find some work for her to do. It had to be better than living in her aunt's shack, with its damp walls and cold dirt floor.

Most important of all, she would be with Mirae. Deep down, that was all Sefina wanted.

Chapter Two

SEFINA PEERED OUT THE window as the carriage crested a gentle hill. She and Mirae had traveled with Lady Lirath and the driver for six days, but their journey was almost over. The frosted glass window—glass! Lady Lirath could afford real glass windows instead of shutters!— offered Sefina a hazy view of the landscape.

A gleaming white wall appeared on the eastern horizon, rising above the endless wheat fields alongside the road. It followed a wavelike pattern that reminded Sefina of seafoam upon sand, while the fields resembled a sun-drenched ocean. She smelled fresh soil and the dust of the road, different than the familiar scents of Farsea, but not at all unpleasant. She craned her neck to see more, taking care not to breathe on the glass.

Mirae showed no such restraint. When Sefina turned to look, she saw Mirae's face and palms were pressed against the window, leaving a fog of breath and noticeable handprints. Mirae wiped away the smudges with her sleeve, but when she turned to Lady Lirath, who sat in the middle of the carriage, her smile showed no remorse.

"Why is that wall wavy, Lady Lirath?"

If Lady Lirath disapproved of the marks Mirae had left on the glass, she refrained from mentioning it. "Why, to use less stone."

Sefina looked through her own window. "Wouldn't a wavy wall need more stones?"

Lady Lirath regarded her with a raised brow. "Clever girl."

A wide smile spread across Sefina's face. It was only two words, but she felt as though she had inherited the world. Lady Lirath—beautiful, refined, wise—had called her clever. Her heart swelled with the praise.

"Under normal circumstances, a curved wall would require more stones," Lady Lirath explained. "However, the wavy shape allowed the stonemasons to build thin. Straight, thin walls are easily toppled, but if their foundations curve, they stand firm against wind and weather."

"What about invasions?" Mirae asked, brown eyes alight with mischief.

Lady Lirath's brows rose well toward her hairline. "No one has invaded Stagford in centuries. Of-the-Land and Of-Blessed-Dreams watch over our fair city personally. Everyone knows Stagford is twice-blessed."

Sefina pondered that as the carriage bumped along the road, stirring plumes of dust behind its wheels. She knew about Of-the-Land, of course. Her parents often told the story of how he raised the bottom of the sea as a betrothal gift for his wife, Of-the-Sky. That gift convinced her to leave her first husband, Of-the-Sea, and give birth to the Earthfolk. Or so her people believed.

Of-Blessed-Dreams, however, seemed to Sefina a far more appealing goddess. She visited mortals frequently, usually while they slept. Through her followers, she inspired miracles of artistic creation. This made her all the more compelling, in Sefina's opinion. She reasoned if she were a goddess, she would consort with mortals too.

They drove a while longer until Lady Lirath bade the driver to stop the carriage before a two-story stone building. The midday sun beat hot upon Sefina's head as she exited on her side, meeting Mirae and Lady Lirath around back. Squinting beneath her cupped hand, she made out a wooden sign above the inn's double doors. It was a white stag's head, glorious golden antlers adorned with moss and flowers.

"White...Horn...Inn..." Mirae said, pausing between words. Sefina looked down, tracing the toe of her shoe in the dust. She'd not yet learned to read, though she'd watched Mirae draw letters in the sand.

Something ached within Sefina's chest as Lady Lirath patted Mirae's shoulder, her many golden rings and bracelets twinkling in the sun. "Well done, Mirae. Come, girls. I've reserved a room for the afternoon."

"What for?" Mirae pointed eastward, where Stagford's white walls had grown taller against the sky. "Stagford's right there."

Lady Lirath clicked her tongue. "For you to bathe and change clothes, of course. You can't appear at the Temple of Dreams in your old clothes with a week's worth of grime on you." She spared Sefina a sidelong glance. "Perhaps more than a week's worth. Come along. We'll soon get the both of you cleaned up."

Sefina followed Lady Lirath inside, feeling like a chastened dog trailing after its master. She'd worn her best dress for the journey, and she'd tried to keep it clean. The fact that it hadn't developed holes yet didn't hide the frayed hems or the stray threads that stuck out of its sleeves.

The inn's entryway was empty of other guests. There was no one else to judge her current state except a young boy who helped the driver with their bags and an older woman behind a counter, examining a ledger book.

"I don't want a bath," Mirae said, her voice bordering on a whine.

Sefina chewed her cheek, hoping Lady Lirath wouldn't scold both of them for Mirae's behavior.

Lady Lirath remained diplomatic, diverting Mirae's complaints before they could brew into a tantrum. "After you bathe and try on your new dress, I'll buy you and Sefina a hot chocolate each. Do you know what hot chocolate is?" She gestured toward the counter, behind which several colorful bottles and flagons stood in a glass case. There was a door as well, which Sefina assumed led to an adjoining kitchen.

Mirae's eyes widened. "I had chocolate candies once. Papa got them from another merchant. They were sweet and bitter at the same time." From the dreamy quality of Mirae's voice, Sefina knew she wanted to taste chocolate too.

"If you shave the chocolate down into a fine powder, mix it with boiling milk, and stir in some sugar, it becomes a delicious drink," Lady Lirath said.

"Okay." Mirae took Lady Lirath's hand, leading her toward the counter. To Sefina's surprise, Lady Lirath allowed it. Sefina followed, wishing her dress had pockets so she could stuff her own empty hands inside them.

After the woman marked Lady Lirath's name in the ledger, they went upstairs. Sefina stood in the hallway, scarcely daring to set foot inside the room. It boasted a large feather bed and matching dresser; not one, but two separate glass windows; and a standing mirror. A tub full of steaming water sat in the middle of the room, accompanied by a wooden stand with various supplies.

"Oh," Mirae said, sounding impressed. "This is so nice! Don't you think, Fina?"

Sefina nodded but didn't speak. Hesitantly, she followed Mirae into the room. She slipped off her shoes by the door so she wouldn't track mud and dust across the floor.

"Go ahead and wash up," Lady Lirath said. "I'll get your new clothes from the carriage."

When she left and closed the door, Sefina's shoulders slumped. She breathed a sigh of relief. Though she admired Lady Lirath greatly, the constant fear of making a mistake in front of her had taken its toll. She felt exhausted, as though she'd been traveling for much longer than a week.

"Come on," Mirae said, stripping off her dress. "You first."

The bath was nothing short of luxurious. Sefina had never soaked in a tub of warm water before, and with Mirae to scrub her back and comb the tangles from her hair, she melted into paradise. She was reluctant to leave when it was Mirae's turn, but wrapped herself in a fluffy white towel and returned the favor.

Mirae soon cheered Sefina up by smearing a beard of bubbles on her face and proclaiming, "There! Now you're Of-Wise-Remembrance."

Sefina laughed and kept the beard on until it dripped down her neck.

Once Mirae was clean, Sefina fixed her hair, sectioning off each coiled lock and rinsing with cold water from a bucket by the tub. Mirae sighed and closed her eyes as Sefina oiled her scalp, only to open them again as Lady Lirath entered the room with a pair of dresses draped over one arm. They both leaped up, Mirae still dripping, in their eagerness to try their new clothes on.

Lady Lirath helped Mirae while Sefina waited her turn, wrapped tightly in her towel. As Mirae's dress fell over her outstretched arms, Sefina gasped. The dress—and Mirae—had to be the loveliest sight she'd ever seen. Its skirt and bodice were a beautiful shade of plum. Eye-catching golden ruffles ran from shoulder to waist, sectioning off the velvet sleeves.

Mirae twirled to show off the artfully crinkled skirts, which floated up past her knees. She posed before the standing mirror, beaming at her reflection. "I love it!" She curtseyed, holding her skirts out like Sefina imagined a lady at court might do.

She stared, equal parts awestruck and envious, until Lady Lirath approached. "Here, Sefina." She offered the other dress, a simple one of white cotton with a pale blue bodice. "I only expected to bring one girl back from Farsea, but I purchased this at one of our stops. It should do well enough."

A lump of emotion formed in Sefina's throat. She wasn't sure which emotions, because there were too many to name, but they made her eyes burn. She took the dress, clutching the soft fabric in her fingers. "Thank you," she said, blinking back tears. She put the dress on, allowing Lady Lirath to lace the bodice.

When Sefina looked in the mirror, she couldn't help but smile. The girl staring back at her looked like a fine young lady! Not as beautiful as Mirae, of course. She'd always been extraordinarily lovely with her dimpled cheeks and bright smile, and her dress was much prettier. Even so, this was the finest outfit Sefina had worn and the smartest she'd ever looked. Joy eclipsed envy as Lady Lirath finished with the laces and placed a hand upon her shoulder.

"There. Don't you look lovely."

Sefina's face split into such a wide smile that her cheeks ached. She descended the stairs at the White Horn Inn to drink her very first hot chocolate with her head held high. She was more certain than ever that Stagford would be the city of her dreams, with a bright and glorious future wrapped like a present within its white walls.

* * * *

While Stagford's shining white walls filled Sefina with exhilaration, the city itself ushered her into a state of awe. She gaped as their carriage passed through the open archway leading to the city's main drag, scarcely daring to breathe lest she interrupt what seemed to her like a dream.

The carriage bounced down a wide cobblestone street, cutting a path through more people than Sefina's eyes could follow. They wore all manner of colorful, stylish clothes, going about their business like bees in a hive. Some stopped to barter at merchant stalls tucked between rows of buildings. Others hurried along the paved walkways, surely on their way to do very important things, Sefina thought.

Most of the buildings were stone, two and sometimes three stories tall. The fancier ones had windows to showcase the goods within. What merchandise! Beautiful dresses and fancy feathered hats filled one store. Another held exotic birds, kittens, and puppies in playpens. That establishment was packed with children, many of whom emerged with cuddly new companions cradled in their arms.

"Can we look in the shops?" Mirae asked. Her face stayed pressed against the window, leaving more smudges.

"May we," Lady Lirath corrected. "You must say...'May we look in the shops,' my dear. No, not today. We must meet with Speaker Yeneri before duskbell. Tomorrow, I'll take you shopping for a few things to keep you comfortable."

Sefina hoped that shopping trip would include her, but bit her tongue in case asking brought disappointment. Instead, she wondered what the Temple of Dreams was like. Would it be as large as the White Horn Inn, or even larger? What about Speaker Yeneri? Was she in charge? Would I get to meet her with Mirael? Though Lady Lirath had no reason to include her, Sefina hoped so.

Those questions and more raced through her mind until Lady Lirath drew her attention. "Look, girls." She gestured out Sefina's window. "Hyron Bridge, where Of-the-Land showed King Hyron the ford that would one day become our city's proudest landmark. Aside from the Temple of Dreams, of course."

Our city. Sefina liked the sound of that.

Hyron Bridge was every bit as impressive as Lady Lirath claimed. Made of the same white stones as the city walls, it was wide enough for ten wagons to drive abreast without skirting close to one another. Several did just that, including their carriage as they joined the flow of traffic and prepared to cross.

The river below Hyron Bridge was broad and sluggish. Its waters swirled in lazy eddies before emptying into a large lake, which sparkled on the left through Mirae's window. It wasn't the same as the sea, but it possessed a similar beauty in its shimmering vastness.

Mirae soon grew bored of the lake. "What's over there?" she asked, pointing out Sefina's window. While admiring the lake, Sefina had missed a significant shift in surroundings on her side. The buildings they passed were smaller, made of mismatched wood like the seaside shacks on the outskirts of Farsea. A few were as run-down as Aunt Adie's. So were the fishing boats that sailed one side of the river. The smell of day-old fish assaulted Sefina's nose even with the carriage window closed. That, she recognized.

Lady Lirath only glanced at the run-down buildings and half-rotted docks for a moment. "Nothing of consequence. A poorer section of Easton. The Temple of Dreams is across the bridge in the plaza between Whiteport and Castletown. You'll find those districts far more pleasant."

Sefina summoned the courage to ask, "How many districts does Stagford have, Lady Lirath?"

"Three," Lady Lirath said, "not counting the plaza and the regent's Green. There's Easton, Whiteport, and Castletown. Here's the edge of Whiteport now."

Whiteport had much finer docks than Easton. The smell of fish lingered, but the boats were bigger, the walkways paved, the streets clear of debris, and the docks showed fewer signs of disrepair. Sefina only glimpsed them for a moment before the carriage made a sharp turn and left the water behind. It entered a wide open space dominated by an enormous white building with towering columns. A giant golden bell tower extended from the domed roof, reaching for Of-the-Sky herself.

"Is that the temple?" Mirae asked, bouncing in her seat.

"Yes," said Lady Lirath. For once, her smile was soft and warm. "Welcome to the Temple of Dreams."

Sefina forgot herself and pressed her nose to the glass. Even from a distance, the Temple of Dreams was nothing less than breathtaking. It was taller than any structure she'd seen and the golden bell tower gleamed in the late afternoon sun. Lush flower beds grew all throughout the plaza and Sefina thought she saw the twinkle of a pond in the near distance.

"Lovely, isn't it?" Lady Lirath said in a low voice.

Sefina turned, expecting to see Lady Lirath speaking to Mirae, but shivered with pleasure when she realized their guardian's attention was on her.

"When the hustle and bustle of the city becomes tiresome, I often find peace and solitude in the temple gardens," Lady Lirath said. "It's the perfect place to rekindle one's creative energies."

Sefina's heart fluttered. "It's the most beautiful place I've ever seen."

Lady Lirath smiled. "I felt the same when I first saw it."

Sefina smiled as well. Even though she wouldn't be learning to sing alongside Mirae, calling such a beautiful place home was a true blessing. It would be a marked improvement upon her former life in Farsea no matter where Lady Lirath put her to work.

At last, the carriage stopped outside the temple. The driver stepped down from the box and opened the carriage door. Mirae hopped out first, not waiting for the driver to offer an elbow. Lady Lirath followed, accepting his arm. Sefina climbed over the seat and clambered down last, pleased to see Mirae waiting for her with an outstretched hand.

She took Mirae's hand, gripping tight as Lady Lirath ushered them up the wide marble steps, pausing briefly to smooth the ruffles on Mirae's dress. "Come now. We mustn't be late." Still, Mirae held onto Sefina's hand. Their fingers remained tightly laced as they ascended the stairs.

The temple's double doors sat on solid wooden frames, with wrought iron designs coiling in relief over twin sheets of opalescent glass. Their color reminded Sefina of the rare chunks of quartz she sometimes found on the cliffs. The designs were so detailed Sefina stopped short to look. Mirae stopped as well, craning her neck to study them.

There were six figures, three on each door. To the far left, Sefina recognized Of-the-Sea, a burly, bare-chested fellow with a wild beard. Beside him stood a slender woman, face tilted up toward the sky. The curls of her hair formed floating, cloud-like shapes behind her. It had to be Of-the-Sky, whose peaceful worshippers isolated themselves in mountain temples, only coming down to bless the lower villages with prayers for rain. On Of-the-Sky's other side stood Of-the-Land, a wiry man with a magnificent pair of flowering stag horns.

The door gave no obvious signs of which god Of-the-Sky favored. Sefina's eyes widened. She'd never seen a temple like this before. Though it boasted no magnificent decorations, Farsea's humble temple placed Of-the-Sea's altar in the center, with Of-the-Sky's directly beside him. Of-the-Land's altar stood on the end of the line, well away from both. It seemed Stagford was a city of differing beliefs.

Sefina admired the other door. On the far right was a thin, reedy figure wearing baggy robes and oversized spectacles. Their gender was purposefully ambiguous. Of-Wise-Remembrance, of course. Holding their hand was Of-Our-Hearts, a voluptuous woman, naked but for the long waves of her hair.

Sefina's face flushed as she averted her eyes from the goddess of love, only to become captivated by the final figure. She was the loveliest of all, a smiling woman crowned with laurels and holding a lyre. Her fingers seemed to strum the instrument as though the iron itself were alive. Sefina almost forgot to breathe. This beautiful figure could only be Of-Blessed-Dreams.

Of-the-Stars, the timeless god whose sight spanned eons, was not depicted; perhaps because they never consorted with mortals. Neither was Of-Eternal-Sleep, though that decision Sefina understood. To depict her openly or speak her name outside her private temples was to invite her attention.

Sefina would have stared longer, but Lady Lirath shepherded them through the doors. They passed through and into the middle of a spacious entrance hall.

Marvelous tapestries in all shades and hues adorned the walls while the domed ceiling bore a stunning tiled mosaic. This also depicted Of-Blessed-Dreams, only in vivid color. Her hair floated around her shoulders and the tiles behind and above her head formed an exquisite rainbow. Her lyre was shining gold, a stark contrast to her white robes.

"It's her," Sefina whispered, squeezing Mirae's hand tighter.

"Has to be," Mirae whispered back.

Like the stag sign outside the White Horn Inn, Of-Blessed-Dreams seemed to watch the goings-on below with wise gray eyes. A pleasant shiver raced down Sefina's spine. It felt as though the goddess were welcoming her home.

A voice echoed through the hall, causing Sefina to lower her gaze from the ceiling. "Well, well. If it isn't my dear Raula, returned from her long journey."

Sefina turned to see a plump, elderly woman with brown skin and enough wrinkles to make the bark of an oak tree envious. Despite her age, readily apparent thanks to her snowy hair and hunched spine, brilliant light danced in her brown eyes. Sefina knew at once that this was no ordinary woman. Who else would dare address someone like Lady Lirath by her first name? She would have bet her brand new dress this was Speaker, leader of the Temple of Dreams. Her heart pounded faster, her stomach full of nervous flutterbugs.

Lady Lirath confirmed her guess. "Speaker Yeneri." She stepped forward, the hem of her purple robes swishing behind her. She took the elderly woman's hands and bowed, touching her forehead to the gnarled knuckles. "My journey was no hardship. In fact, it was a privilege. I have returned with the girl we sought." She released Speaker Yeneri's hands and took Mirae's arm, gently tugging her forward.

Sefina dropped Mirae's hand, feeling the loss of her warm, reassuring grip.

"Hello, Speaker," Mirae said. "That's what I'm supposed to call you, right?" Her dimples appeared on either side of her sunny smile.

Yeneri smiled, causing even more wrinkles and folds to appear on her weathered face. "Good afternoon, young lady. Speaker Yeneri, or Speaker, will be just fine." She offered her hands to Mirae, palms facing up in a greeting between Sea Children. "What might your name be?"

Mirae placed her hands over Speaker Yeneri's. They clasped each other's wrists and squeezed once before letting go. "My name is Mirae."

"A pleasure to meet you, Mirae. How would you like to sing for me? The entrance hall has a wonderful echo."

Sefina glanced at her feet to hide her smile. She was looking forward to seeing Speaker Yeneri's awestruck expression once Mirae sang. No doubt a woman of her years had heard many singers, but no voice could compare to Mirae's. *My best friend is the most wonderful singer in all the world. Probably of all time.*

Mirae broke into song, a children's tune about the eight days of the week and the gods that ruled over each one.

Firstday is for all the stars.
Secondday is for sailing far.
Thirdday is for growing things,
In the summer, fall, and spring.
Fourthday is for rain and sun.
On Fifthday, we love everyone!
Sixday keeps us smart and wise.
Sevenday helps our hearts to fly.
But what of Eightday? Whose to keep?
Our final day is for Lady Sleep.

The final note rang throughout the entrance hall. It carried like ripples on water, filling every corner with the beauty of song. Speaker Yeneri and Lady Lirath stayed silent for a long time afterward. They gaped, awestruck, while Mirae smiled, soaking in their wordless admiration.

Sefina wanted to step forward and squeeze Mirae's hand for a job well done, a song perfectly sung, but didn't dare. Somehow, Mirae had transformed into something far too holy and pure to touch. Even so, her heart brimmed with pride. How privileged she was to claim Mirae as her best friend, a girl who poured such wonders from her mouth!

Eventually, Speaker Yeneri regained her composure. "You have an incredible gift, young Mirae. I must admit, I have never heard a voice like yours. Even the simplest of children's songs is transformed into a treasure for the ears passing from your lips."

Mirae clasped her hands, rocking forward onto her toes. "Thank you, Speaker."

Speaker Yeneri's gaze landed upon Sefina. Her smile fell away in an instant. She froze, unsure what to do while pinned under the speaker's stare. "What about you, young lady? Please, tell me your name and why you've come to the Temple of Dreams."

Though Speaker Yeneri's question was kind and encouraging, Sefina's heart pounded. Her throat went dry. She couldn't find the courage to speak.

Lady Lirath answered for her. "Mirae was reluctant to leave her home without companionship. This girl is her friend and an orphan. Surely we can find a suitable place for her? We always need more workers to keep the temple running for its gifted residents."

Sefina curled her shoulders inward, making herself small. Her stomach churned as she realized Speaker Yeneri had the power to overrule Lady Lirath's decision. They probably wouldn't send her all the way back to Farsea, but they could throw her out of the temple, onto the streets of a strange city. She flinched as Speaker Yeneri spoke in a disapproving tone—but to Sefina's relief, she addressed Lady Lirath.

"You know better, Raula. Of-Blessed-Dreams works her miracles through everyone, especially those who labor for the good of others. She inspires the sweeper to sing in time with the broom and the woodsman to whittle by firelight. She helps the stablehand entertain his friends with stories and blesses the weaver's hands before she begins the humblest of creations. The goddess' light touches every person in the world. That includes this young lady here."

Sefina let slip a quiet sigh of relief. Her heart swelled with gratitude as she decided she admired Speaker Yeneri very, very much.

Lady Lirath dipped her head. "You are right, as always. Forgive me."

"Of course." Speaker Yeneri turned to Sefina. "What is your name?"

Somehow, Sefina found her voice. "Sefina."

Speaker Yeneri offered the backs of her hands. Sefina slid hers beneath, bowing to touch her forehead to Speaker Yeneri's knuckles. They were knotted and bony but possessed surprising strength of grip. "What does Of-Blessed-Dreams inspire you to do when she fills your heart, Sefina?"

Sefina let go of Speaker Yeneri's hands and lifted her head. When she spoke, her voice cracked. "I—I sing, too."

Part of her expected Speaker Yeneri to laugh then. Sefina knew her voice could never compare with Mirae's, which possessed all the warmth and loveliness of a spring breeze, but Speaker Yeneri did not laugh. "Wonderful. Two new singers have graced our temple today. Please sing for me, Sefina."

Sefina's eyes darted toward Mirae, who smiled and leaned forward attentively. Despite the difference in their voices, Mirae always enjoyed listening to her. That gave Sefina the courage to swallow, wet her lips, and take a deep breath. Her first few notes were soft and shaky, but she soon gained volume and confidence, staring all the while at Mirae's face. The echo of the entrance hall was enchanting, making her voice sound far better than usual to her own ears.

Tell me, raindrops, where do you flow?

Why, into the stream. That's where I go.
Tell me, stream, where do you flow?
Why, into the river. That's where I go.
Tell me, river, where do you flow?
Why, into the ocean. That's where I go.
Tell me, ocean. Where do you flow?
Upon all the beaches. That's where I go.

Her last note lingered much like Mirae's had. Definitely better than usual, she decided. Richer and fuller, though she knew she lacked the crystalline clarity Mirae's voice captured with such ease. There was no stunned silence after the echo died, but Sefina's breath hitched as Mirae, Speaker Yeneri, and even Lady Lirath began to applaud.

"I love when you sing that song," Mirae said, stepping over to wrap her arms around Sefina. "It's your best one."

Sefina hugged Mirae, sighing with relief. Only then did she realize her heart was pounding and her hands were shaking.

"You have a wonderful voice," Speaker Yeneri said, catching Sefina's eye from over Mirae's shoulder. "It possesses a different quality than Mirae's, but it has a special spark all its own. With proper training, you will blossom into a wonderful singer and musician."

Sefina pulled back from Mirae's embrace, regarding Speaker Yeneri with narrowed eyes and a furrowed brow. "Really?" Only Mirae had ever complimented her voice and that was only because best friends were supposed to say nice things. She couldn't bring herself to believe such praise. "But my voice doesn't make flowers bloom. It doesn't heal the cuts on my knees. I'm nothing special."

Speaker Yeneri shook her head. "Of course you are, dear Sefina, and so is your voice. How cold and barren the world would be if only one person had talent enough to sing! What would become of duets? Of choirs? Different voices are suited for different songs as well. A single voice, goddess-blessed or no, cannot bring music to the entire world alone. We need many voices, for each comes from Of-Blessed-Dreams. Only you can sing as you do, so you must sing the very best you can, if that is your wish. Do you understand?"

Warmth flooded Sefina's chest, carrying with it tingling exhilaration. It took her a moment to recognize the feeling as pride. Not pride for knowing someone as wonderful as Mirae, but pride in her own abilities. Someone had heard her sing and found it beautiful. Someone believed her voice was worthy of training.

Still, Sefina couldn't help but look to Lady Lirath for her opinion. Her confidence soared when she noted the look of surprise upon Lady Lirath's face. "Your voice is beautiful," she said, bestowing Sefina with a rare smile. "Speaker Yeneri is correct. You have the makings of a fine singer, should you decide to put in the effort. It would be my pleasure to instruct you alongside Mirae."

Sefina beamed. She couldn't believe her ears. *Lady Lirath, my teacher as well? Of-Blessed-Dreams has smiled upon me!*

"Say yes, Fina." Mirae clasped Sefina's hands, squeezing tight. For a moment, Sefina lost herself in Mirae's soft brown eyes, full of affection. "Let's sing together every day."

As always, Sefina couldn't imagine saying no to Mirae. Even if she hadn't longed to be a singer in her own right, she would have agreed merely to please her beloved friend. "Yes, please," she said to Lady Lirath and Speaker Yeneri. "I would love to learn."

Speaker Yeneri clasped her hands before her chest as though to seal the compact. "What a joyful occasion. Not one, but two beautiful voices have arrived at our temple, and on a Sevenday as well. Of-Blessed-Dreams must approve."

Sefina shivered, unable to contain her smile. For the first time since her parents' passing, she felt important rather than invisible, wanted rather than tolerated. Someone other than Mirae had seen her at last.

Chapter Three

"PLEASE, FOLLOW ME," SPEAKER Yeneri said to Sefina and Mirae. "Allow me to show you the temple."

Lady Lirath cleared her throat. "Forgive me, Speaker, but you have many important things to do." Her pursed lips said far more than her words. Sefina's gaze darted down to the shiny new shoes Lady Lirath had provided. Surely playing tour guide to a pair of children would be a waste of Speaker Yeneri's valuable time.

"Nonsense, Raula," said Speaker Yeneri. "It's my pleasure and privilege to welcome newcomers." She smiled at Sefina and Mirae. "You'd like to see more, wouldn't you?"

"I'd love to." Mirae dropped Sefina's hands, bouncing on the balls of her feet. "This place is marvelous."

Sefina's eyes widened when Speaker Yeneri turned to her, expecting a response. She wetted her lips and said, "It's the most wonderful place I've ever seen." She tilted her face to the ceiling, admiring Of-Blessed-Dreams' mosaic. The shimmering rainbow of the goddess' hair floated about her head as though lifted by a playful breeze. Her fingers danced across the golden strings of her lyre. "It's as though I can feel her presence."

Her cheeks burned as she realized what she'd implied. She tore her eyes away from the mosaic and fixed them upon her shoes again. *Speaker Yeneri must think me foolish at best, arrogant at worst. Why would one of the Eight make herself known to me, an orphan who's only just arrived here?*

The sound of footsteps made Sefina's breath catch. Speaker Yeneri's sandals approached and a stiff hand pressed down on her shoulder. Reluctantly, she lifted her gaze. Her palms began to sweat and her face flushed even hotter, but Speaker Yeneri wore a soft expression of approval.

"Of course you feel her presence," Speaker Yeneri said. "Of-Blessed-Dreams isn't an aloof, inaccessible goddess. So long as your heart remains open, she will always be with you, inspiring you to bring beauty into the world."

Sefina stared into Speaker Yeneri's brown eyes, narrowed by wrinkles and heavy lids, but still so warm and kind. Her heart fluttered with the hope that she might find her purpose if she devoted herself to the goddess. Her throat grew tight, but she managed to say, "I will."

"Excellent," Speaker Yeneri said. "First things first. I'll show you our altars so you may worship as you like." She walked to the rear of the foyer, where a stone archway opened into a hall.

Mirae followed, but Sefina lingered a moment, stealing one last look at the mosaic. Her heart ached with a sense of loss, as though she were saying goodbye...but that was ridiculous. It was only a mosaic, no matter how beautifully made.

An expectant look from Lady Lirath sent Sefina scurrying after Speaker Yeneri. Two large, colorful tapestries hung in the hallway beyond, taking up the entire wall on each side. As soon as Sefina laid eyes upon them, she forgot her reluctance to leave the mosaic.

On the left hand tapestry, a majestic white stag with flowering antlers ran through a lush forest. His powerful legs rippled with the illusion of movement. A rainbow of flowers sprang up in his wake, swaying on their stems. The smell of spring blossoms filled Sefina's nose and the distant sound of hooves drummed in her ears. She placed a hand upon her chest, too exhilarated to breathe.

"It's like we're there," Mirae said, equally breathless. She too had stopped to stare at the tapestry, mouth agape.

Speaker Yeneri smiled. "Indeed. Of-Blessed-Dreams grants her followers many talents, including the art of weaving."

"Don't be so modest, Speaker." Lady Lirath peered down her nose at Sefina and Mirae. "These tapestries, along with many others throughout the temple, are Speaker Yeneri's creations. The gift of breathing life through the loom is why she was chosen to ascend to her position."

Sefina stared at Speaker Yeneri with newfound admiration. The woman already struck her as wise and austere, but these tapestries were miraculous. She turned to admire the right hand tapestry.

An androgynous figure in baggy clothes hunched over a wooden desk, writing by candlelight. Judging by the vast library of books that served as a backdrop, this could be none other than Of-Wise-Remembrance. As their hand moved across the page, spidery writing appeared on the yellowed paper. Sefina caught the scent of tallow and old parchment.

This was no trick of the light. There was no mundane explanation. Like Mirae's voice, the tapestries were magical.

"Marvelous," she whispered.

Speaker Yeneri heard her. "They are, but these tapestries aren't really my doing. I'm merely the goddess' hands. Do you understand?"

Sefina nodded, unsure what to say. She glanced at Mirae, who hadn't seemed to hear their brief exchange. "How many miracle workers live here?" Mirae asked Speaker Yeneri. "Are there other singers like me?"

"No singers at present," Lady Lirath answered, "although the temple boasts a world-renowned choir, which I direct. Several instrumental chamber groups as well. We do have a sculptor with unusual talents, and...a young dancer too, yes?" She looked to Speaker Yeneri for confirmation.

"Mistress Jordaine's pupil," Speaker Yeneri said. "Students of all levels come here to develop their talents, not only those with extraordinary abilities."

Sefina swallowed a sigh of relief. She wasn't sure she could bear being the only student without magic, but it seemed those blessed like Mirae and Speaker Yeneri were few in number.

"Here are the kitchens," Speaker Yeneri said, gesturing toward a pair of double doors on the left. "Across the way is the dining hall. You'll have an opportunity to sample our fare tonight. But first, the sanctuary."

Sefina's mouth watered as the smell of fresh-baked bread and roasted meat wafted into the hall, but there wasn't time to linger. Speaker Yeneri and Lady Lirath proceeded to another archway, smaller than the first. An iron gate, without depictions of the Eight, stood open, leading into a dimly lit room.

Mirae entered while Sefina took a moment to gather her courage. The thick, sweet smell of incense filled her nose. She breathed deep, drawing it into her lungs until she felt a warm tingle in her chest.

"Sefina, are you all right?"

Sefina flinched. Lady Lirath was waiting beside the open gate. She entered the sanctuary, avoiding Lady Lirath's expectant stare. Candles in various stages of melt filled the room with flickering light. Seven altars formed a semi-circle along the far wall. Behind each stood a stained glass window, pieced together in exquisite detail.

Immediately, Sefina's gaze fixed on the middle window. It was Of-Blessed-Dreams. Her flowing hair maintained the illusion of motion, much like the tapestries. The golden strings of her lyre quivered as though recently plucked. Flowers, jewelry, scraps of paper, and other small tokens and trinkets adorned her altar, so many that some spilled onto the floor beneath.

The other pedestals bore similar offerings. Of-the-Sea's altar boasted seashells, jars of sand, driftwood, pipes, and fish bones. There was even a necklace of shark's teeth. Of-the-Land's offerings consisted of tied bundles of grain, herbs, small wicker baskets of fruit, and several flower crowns. Of-the-Sky's altar possessed many of the same items, as well as bundles of wool and colorful glass bottles. Her window stood between Of-the-Land and Of-the-Sea, showing no preference.

Sefina examined the other altars in turn, pausing to study Of-Our-Hearts' display. There were a few flowers, bracelets, rings, and other jewelry, but the slab was mostly covered in locs of hair. There were two different shades in each braid, bound tight with ribbon or twine. She'd seen such offerings to the goddess of love before and longed for the day when she was old enough to have a sweetheart of her own.

The image of wavy brown hair braided through a coiled black loc appeared unbidden in Sefina's mind. She blinked, shaking the thought away. Perhaps the incense was muddling her mind. *What a silly idea, two girls being sweethearts!* She would simply choose a boy very much like Mirae once she was grown, although she couldn't imagine caring for a future husband as much as her best friend.

That was all right. As long as she and Mirae spent their lives together, she would be happy. Perhaps they would both live here at the temple when they were grown, performing at concerts, discussing art and literature, wearing the finest clothes and the most expensive jewelry.

"You have an altar for her?"

Mirae's voice, barely above a whisper, intruded upon Sefina's daydream. She turned to see Mirae pointing toward an altar to the far right. The stained glass figure's face was hidden beneath a cloak, each ripple and fold rendered with care. The long, straight hair that flowed over her shoulders hinted her gender was female. In her gnarled hands she held an oar, textured to resemble wood.

"Of course we do," said Speaker Yeneri. "Lady Sleep deserves worship and offerings the same as any other major god. Perhaps more so here in the Temple of Dreams than elsewhere, since she and Of-Blessed-Dreams are sisters. It is good to grow comfortable with the idea of death, since it comes for everyone."

Lady Sleep.

That was one of the kindest euphemisms for Of-Eternal-Sleep. Her full name was rarely uttered, lest the speaker draw her attention. Many feared her, while others revered her in the hopes of extending their lives. Her altar was the most eclectic. All manner of trinkets covered its surface, tokens placed by family members so the sea of stars would accept their departed loved ones.

Sefina wished she had some token to leave for her parents, but their possessions were long gone. Sold to keep her fed, Aunt Adie had said. Sefina suspected that was true. She doubted her aunt had a secret hoard of gold hidden under the floorboards. *In fact, I doubt she misses me at all. She's probably relieved I'm gone.*

"What about Of-the-Stars?" Mirae asked. "I don't see their altar."

Lady Lirath gestured at the ceiling. "There they are, watching over all from their rightful place in the heavens."

Sefina looked up. Though the sanctuary's walls were stone, the ceiling was made of colored glass, illuminated from above by the late afternoon sun. There was Of-the-Stars, a timeless figure portrayed in inky blue silhouette amidst a red and purple sunset. Their body shape and clothing gave no indication of their gender, although they also possessed long hair. Their arms stretched outward, as though to embrace the night itself.

"Perhaps the most timeless and mysterious god," Lady Lirath said. "Some of my favorite compositions feature the eternal dance of the heavenly bodies."

Sefina stared at the mosaic with wide eyes. She looked inside her heart, delving in search of the warmth and familiarity she'd felt beneath Of-Blessed-Dreams' mosaic, but there was no spark. No flicker of recognition. Of-the-Stars was every bit as distant and timeless as Lady Lirath claimed. Sefina looked down again, her shoulders slumping. Though beautiful, this stained glass ceiling stirred nothing within her.

Her heart fluttered as Mirae's hand closed around hers. "This is much grander than the temple in Farsea, isn't it?" she said, not quite whispering, but speaking low so Sefina knew the statement was meant for her. "We've come a long way from home."

Sefina nodded. "Yes...but I think the temple will be good for us."

Her gaze drifted toward Of-Blessed-Dreams' window, backlit by the rich colors of the late afternoon sun. She allowed herself to hope, to truly believe now that they were within the temple walls. She'd traveled a long way from home, but Farsea had never held anything special for her. Not since her parents' passing. Nothing except for Mirae, who'd been kind enough to bring her along on this new adventure. Here, they could start a new life, one that would prove much better than Sefina could have dreamed.

Mirae squeezed Sefina's hand. "Right. I already feel at home here."

Sefina squeezed back. She smiled at Mirae, then at Of-Blessed-Dreams in her window the colors of sunset. The goddess seemed to smile back. "Me too."

* * * *

Freshly scrubbed and dressed in a white nightgown, Sefina stood beside one of two single beds, watching Mirae test the mattress by bouncing on her knees. Mirae's springy curls bounced with her as she fell onto her back, landing with arms and legs splayed like a starfish. She panted, grinning up at the ceiling.

"You shouldn't," Sefina said, hiding a smile of her own. "You'll break it."

"I won't." Mirae rolled onto her side, resting her cheek on her fist. "Have you ever felt a softer bed in your life?"

Sefina tested the mattress beneath her outstretched hand. "It's like a cloud. What if it swallows me up while I sleep?"

Mirae laughed and rolled out of bed. "Come on. Let's push the beds together." She began shoving the bedframe before Sefina could offer an opinion. Not that she minded. She very much wanted to share a bed with Mirae for the added warmth and comfort.

She went to the other bed, pushing it alongside Mirae's. There was a tiny gap between the mattresses, but she doubted it would disturb either of them. These beds were miles more comfortable than her old sleeping pallet.

They climbed into their new single bed, turning the sheets and blankets sideways to share. Sefina couldn't wrap her head around how many there were. First a thin cotton sheet, then a fluffy comforter, and on top of that a handmade quilt. She'd never fall asleep cold again.

Mirae burrowed beneath the covers, poking her nose above the edge. The way her brown eyes danced gave away her hidden smile. "You look like a sand crab," Sefina said, climbing under the covers on her side. She found Mirae's legs with her own, scooting closer for warmth.

"I'm not a crab," Mirae protested. "I'm a marvel, now."

Sefina laughed—because she felt like she was supposed to—but the sting of envy was brief. "You are a marvel." She turned toward the wall, pulling Mirae's arm around her waist and scooting back against her chest. It was their usual method of bed-sharing on the rare nights she'd spent at Mirae's house. "But I'm glad there are only a few marvels here, or I'd never keep up."

"Remember what Speaker Yeneri told us," Mirae said. "Life would be terribly dull if there was only one singer in all the world."

"You're right." Sefina yawned and closed her eyes. "I'm tired."

"Then sleep. That's what the bed's for."

Sefina snorted, but kept her eyes shut. She sighed as her head sank into the pillow. "Good night, Mirae. I love you."

Mirae's arm tightened around her middle. "I love you too, Fina. See you at Dawnbell."

In less than a minute, Mirae had fallen asleep, snoring uproariously near the back of Sefina's head. Her snores relaxed Sefina further—both because she was used to the sound and because it made Mirae seem something less than goddess-touched. She wasn't only Mirae the marvel, but also Mirae the best friend. It made her seem human rather than some divine being.

A smile spread across Sefina's face. Here she was, lying in a fluffy bed that smelled like soap and citrus, in what had to be the grandest temple in all the world. In Stagford, the wonderful city of her dreams. Her new home. She drifted off despite the unfamiliar environment, tired after a long and exciting day.

That night, Sefina dreamed of a silhouette against the night sky, inky black and surrounded by soft starlight. The silhouette embraced her with arms of darkest midnight and said, "Welcome, child. Welcome home at last."

"Who are you?" Sefina asked. "Of-Blessed-Dreams?" She tried to compare the silhouette to the mosaic and the window, but there was no warmth in her chest. No sense of coming home. Instead, she felt as though she were suspended somewhere cold and dark, like the bottom of the ocean.

The silhouette gave no reply. They disappeared, leaving Sefina alone amidst the stars, a strange hollowness lingering within her chest.

Chapter Four

SEFINA'S FIRST MORNING AT the Temple of Dreams began early. No sooner had dawnbell rung than a sharp rap sounded upon the bedroom door. Sefina startled awake, sitting straight up while Mirae yawned and stretched beside her. "Five more minutes," Mirae mumbled, pulling her pillow over her head.

Another knock came, followed by the creak of the door's hinges. Lady Lirath entered, her sharp shoulders and rigid frame filling the doorway despite her short stature. Sefina's heart pounded. She felt the urge to pull the covers up and hide from Lady Lirath's piercing stare.

"Dawnbell has rung." Lady Lirath entered the room, heels clicking upon the stone floor. "I expect you washed and dressed in ten minutes. Lessons begin as soon as you've had breakfast."

Sefina clambered out of bed, smoothed out her nightgown, and scuttled over to the armoire. She found it full of serviceable robes in the correct size. Instead of the royal purple of Lady Lirath's robes, they were mostly forest green, with a few in blue and deep red.

"Green is for daily wear," Lady Lirath said. "Blue for formal occasions, red for concerts." She circled the bed, stopping at Mirae's side and removing the pillow with a flourish. "Ten minutes, Mirae. You will hardly become a marvel without daily practice."

Mirae blinked, rubbing her eyes. "But—"

The sheer force of Lady Lirath's presence offered no room for objection. "Up."

Mirae dragged herself out of bed and trudged over to the armoire. Sefina passed Mirae a green robe, then went to the washroom with an identical robe draped over her arm. She breathed a sigh of relief, glad to be out of Lady Lirath's sight. Whenever those icy blue eyes fixed upon her, she felt as though the woman was peering into her mind.

Sefina stripped and pulled the robe over her head as Mirae entered the washroom behind her, barely swallowing a yawn. "Morning, Fina."

"How can you possibly be tired after all that?" Sefina whispered.

Mirae shrugged. "Just am."

She undressed while Sefina stood before the wash basin, making good use of the toothbrush Lady Lirath had procured for her a week ago at the first inn they'd patronized. Aunt Adie had never been concerned with the state of her mouth, but Sefina had grown fond of the toothbrush.

Once her teeth were clean, she looked around the washroom. "Where's the water bucket?"

"Dunno," Mirae said around a mouthful of foamy paste. A large glob clung to the edge of her lips and began sliding down her chin.

"You look like a rabid dog," Sefina said, then busied herself searching. The cabinets beneath the wash basin were empty except for fluffy white towels and cloths folded in a neat stack. There was a strange porcelain pot in the corner of the room, which she considered investigating, but it looked more like a chamber pot than a water bucket.

It was Mirae who figured out the solution. She fiddled with one of the brass knobs above the basin until a stream of water spilled forth from a matching brass spout. Sefina stared, remnants of toothpaste leaking from her wide open mouth. "How does it do that? Magic?"

"Plummin," Mirae mumbled. She spat into the flowing water, then repeated herself. "It's called plumbing. Papa wanted it installed back home, but Mama said it was too expensive and no one else in Farsea had it anyway."

"Plumbing?" Sefina repeated, testing the word.

Mirae turned the brass knob and the flow of water stopped. "There's a system of metal pipes in the walls and beneath the floor. They bring in fresh water and carry out dirty water."

Sefina was enthralled. She stood alongside Mirae, spat into the basin, and turned the brass knob. There was a soft hiss, then a stream of clear water flowed from the spout, washing the foam of the toothpaste down a tiny drain. She tested the knob several times, turning the water on and off until Mirae stopped her.

"Quit hogging it. I need to scrub my face."

Sefina remembered Lady Lirath's time limit. She wetted a fluffy white cloth, washed her face, and hurried to the door. She stopped short before running into Lady Lirath, whose hand was raised to knock. "Sorry!" She slunk to one side, standing with both hands folded behind her back.

"A young lady does not rush about like a headless chicken, Sefina," Lady Lirath said. "She must always watch where she is going. Mirae, are you quite finished?"

Mirae exited the washroom and stood beside Sefina, though she didn't fold her hands or stare at the floor. "Yes, Lady Lirath."

"Good. Then we shall go to breakfast."

Breakfast was nothing short of decadent. The buffet table boasted fresh fruit; eggs, milk, and cheese; porridge with honest to goodness cinnamon, and much more. There were even pastries, which Mirae wasted no time piling onto her plate. Less bold but very hungry, Sefina took two.

"Take one each next time," Lady Lirath said. "I know this is your first day, but we mustn't overindulge."

"Yes, Lady Lirath," Mirae and Sefina said together.

Once Lady Lirath turned in search of a table, Mirae winked. Sefina suspected she would continue sneaking pastries on a regular basis.

After breakfast, Lady Lirath escorted them to the temple's second floor. They arrived at a heavy wooden door, which groaned in protest when Lady Lirath pushed it open. "This is my studio," she said, ushering them inside.

Sefina peered around the room. It was large and dim, with only one window beside a neatly organized mahogany desk. Thick paisley curtains hung on all four walls. A plush couch and two armchairs with matching patterns sat before a wide stone fireplace. Decorative items stood upon the mantle, the most obvious of which was a shiny silver candelabra.

Warm fingers squeezed Sefina's hand. She turned to see Mirae smiling at her, enthusiasm shining in her bright brown eyes. Flutterbugs filled Sefina's stomach. They were truly about to begin their new lives!

Lady Lirath took the candelabra, lit the candles with a matchbook from her desk, and set it back upon the mantle. The scent of tallow filled the room. "The two of you will share music lessons here every morning and study here in the afternoons, unless you have choir or chamber rehearsals. You will have free time in the evenings, but you must return before duskbell. You are not to leave the temple unless accompanied by myself, Speaker Yeneri, or an approved adult. Have I made myself clear?"

"Yes, Lady Lirath," Sefina murmured.

Mirae bounced on her toes. "Does that mean we can visit the shops?"

"Yes, with prior approval," said Lady Lirath. "But shopping should be the least of your concerns. You want to become a marvel, don't you?"

Mirae squeezed Sefina's hand so tight it almost became uncomfortable. "Yes. More than anything."

"Then we shall begin immediately."

Lady Lirath offered them each a mint from a small porcelain bowl on her desk—to sweeten their breath after breakfast, she said—and the lesson started. Lady Lirath sat in the paisley armchair, which Sefina noticed didn't face the fireplace. Instead, it faced the couch, before which she and Mirae stood.

"First, you must learn to breathe."

Mirae snorted. "I already know how to breathe."

Lady Lirath maintained her cool stare. "Not in the correct way, I'll wager. Sefina, take a deep breath."

Sefina's stomach lurched. She wished she hadn't taken a second pastry. She swallowed, then drew in the deepest breath she could. She held it for several moments, until her chest burned, and the tips of her ears began to tingle. All the air escaped in a loud puff, her shoulders slumping as her lungs emptied.

"Wrong," Lady Lirath said. "All wrong."

Sefina's face flushed. Her eyes darted down to the shiny toes of her brand new shoes. She remained silent, unsure whether to apologize for her unknown mistake.

"Mirae?" Lady Lirath said. "You next."

Sefina heard Mirae inhale a noisy breath. She puffed her cheeks and pursed her lips, and managed to hold the air for a long time before exhaling. Afterward, Sefina caught a glimpse of Mirae's confident smile from the corner of her eye.

Lady Lirath shook her head. "Also wrong. You must breathe down instead of up. Draw the air low into your belly. Do not raise your shoulders or suck into your stomach. Place your palm upon your lower abdomen." She arched an eyebrow. "Well?"

Mirae's brow furrowed, but she did as instructed.

Sefina did the same. Though her hand was on her belly instead of her chest, she was keenly aware of her racing heart.

"Breathe in slowly through your mouth. Fill the bottom of your belly. Keep your shoulders down. Let your stomach push your hand outward."

Sefina closed her eyes. She did as Lady Lirath said, breathing in slowly through your mouth. A flood of air rushed deep into the bottom of her lungs, so much that it almost made her light-headed. Taken by surprise, she let it go in a rush.

"Well done, Mirae. Sefina, try again."

Sefina coughed and tried again. This time, she maintained control. She breathed deep, pulling the room's tallow-scented air all the way into her lungs. She flinched, but didn't cough when she sensed Lady Lirath's presence behind her. Lady Lirath moved quietly and gracefully for a woman with such a resonant voice and commanding aura.

"Behind you," Lady Lirath said, a word of warning before she placed her hand upon Sefina's shoulder. It lighted there only briefly before moving to her stomach, over Sefina's own. "Push my hand outward."

Sefina tried again. Focusing on Lady Lirath's hand allowed her to take in even more air. A smile crept across her face and she opened her eyes. "Like that?"

Lady Lirath returned Sefina's smile. "Better."

Sefina felt suddenly lightheaded and warm. Perhaps it was from all the deep breathing, but she suspected it had more to do with Lady Lirath's approval. Her smile spread as Lady Lirath rose from the kneeling position she'd adopted and headed for the wall left of the fireplace.

Lady Lirath pulled aside one of the heavy paisley curtains to reveal a wooden pegboard that took up most of the wall, upon which a wide variety of instruments hung. Sefina didn't know their names, but they looked marvelous with their curved and brightly polished bodies.

"Oh!" Mirae said. "Are those all yours?"

"Indeed." Lady Lirath lifted a pear-shaped instrument from the pegboard. The deep red hue of the wood resembled a giant ruby, or at least what Sefina imagined a ruby might look like.

Lady Lirath seemed to notice her admiration. "This instrument is called a lute. I shall play a note and you shall match it, sustaining the note for as long as you can. You first, Mirae. Be sure to keep your mouth wide. A nice, round 'Ah' shape." She plucked the lute's strings. A warm note sounded through the room before disappearing into the thick curtains, seeming to sing high and low at the same time.

Sefina listened as Mirae breathed in, then opened her mouth. Her voice spilled forth like crystal clear water from a stream, matching the note perfectly. They melded into a single silvery sound before Mirae's voice faded away. Sefina blinked. For a moment, it was as though she'd been transported elsewhere.

"You have a good ear." Lady Lirath's voice carried the same warmth as the lute. "Again."

They repeated this exercise a few more times. Sefina remained enthralled, so much so that Lady Lirath surprised her by speaking her name. "Your turn, Sefina. If you can do half as well as Mirae, I'll be pleased."

Sefina felt a sharp pinch inside. Like a bee-sting, only somewhere around her heart. She ignored it, unclenching her sweaty hands. When had the room become so hot and stifling? Lady Lirath stared expectantly. Reluctantly, Sefina made eye contact and waited.

Lady Lirath strummed the lute. Sefina listened to the note as it filled the room, trying to catch it in her ear before it disappeared into the curtains. She opened her mouth, but much to her dismay, her voice came out tight and much too low. She pitched her voice higher to match the lute, but not before Lady Lirath frowned.

"Try again. Don't forget the way I taught you to breathe."

Sefina bit her cheek. Her fingers curled back into fists and she had to force herself to open and relax her hands.

Lady Lirath strummed. Sefina opened her mouth.

This time, she overshot and went too high. She found the note in a matter of moments, but Lady Lirath's frown deepened. "Maybe half as well was a generous starting point. Again, Sefina."

Sefina's cheeks burned. Her eyes darted to Mirae, who had always been her most reliable source of comfort. Mirae smiled and lifted her chin, offering wordless encouragement.

Lady Lirath strummed. Sefina sang.

This time, she found the correct pitch. Sefina's relief was so great that she forgot to hold the note for long, but at least it melded with the sound of the lute. Lady Lirath stopped frowning, although she didn't smile. "Acceptable. Again."

They repeated the exercise as Mirae had done. By the time it was over, Sefina's brain felt wrung out like a soap sponge.

As Lady Lirath returned the lute to the pegboard, Sefina checked the candles above the fireplace. The edges had barely begun to melt. She swallowed hard. If this was a fair representation of what daily music lessons with Lady Lirath were to be like, she wondered if she would last.

Chapter Five

SEFINA SHARED TECHNICAL LESSONS with Mirae at dawnbell. There, she learned to support her breath, memorized intervals by ear, and practiced shaping her mouth. Afternoons were equally difficult. While Mirae knew something of reading, writing, and mathematics, Lady Lirath found Sefina's education lacking in comparison. She drilled Sefina on her sums until she dreamt addition and subtraction. Sefina spent hours perfecting her handwriting until her wrist ached alongside her throat.

Lady Lirath was a strict instructor, sparing with praise and exacting in her standards. This propensity grew worse a year into Sefina's training, when she and Mirae began singing duets. At first, duets delighted Sefina. Merging her voice with Mirae's while carrying her own line was everything she hadn't known she craved. Their voices twined to the heavens and Sefina's heart sprouted wings to follow.

But afterward, as Winter walked in her sister Autumn's footsteps, came the critique.

"Breathe deeper, Sefina."

"Support the phrase, Sefina."

"Your high notes are flat again, Sefina."

"Must I remind you every time?"

Lady Lirath often threw up her hands and removed a lute from the pegged wall where she kept her musical instruments. "You will learn to play this," she said, shoving its curved body into Sefina's chest with too much force. "Accompanying Mirae may benefit your musicianship without trying my patience."

Sefina despised the lute, though ample practice sharpened her ear. She improved as both a singer and player, but never fast enough. No matter how hard she tried, she always seemed to lag further behind Mirae.

So it went until a particularly horrible lesson, when Sefina could bear Lady Lirath's criticism no longer. She stood in Lady Lirath's studio one sweltering summer afternoon, surrounded on all sides by stifling paisley curtains and the overpowering scent of tallow. Even on such a hot day, Lady Lirath had not opened the windows even a crack.

Despite the sticky heat, Sefina tried her best. She repeated the same simple warm-up over and over until the notes no longer made sense to her ears.

Breathe from my belly. Push outward. Support the phrase...

Lady Lirath waved for her to stop.

Sefina fell silent, holding her breath.

"Really, Sefina," Lady Lirath said, rolling her ice blue eyes. "Why should I bother teaching you anything at all? Teaching a stone to sing would be more productive." She rose from her chair, turning toward the pegged wall of instruments.

Sefina gripped the edge of her music stand until her knuckles turned white. She inhaled the same stale air as always, her eyes burning with tears. Her gaze remained fixed on the sheet music she hadn't yet been allowed to sing, staring so intently the patterned inkblots became smudged gray smears upon the page.

Humiliation welled within her like dirty rainwater from an overflowing gutter. *I'm not Mirae.* In her heart, Sefina knew that was her failing. *I'm not Mirae, and I never will be for all the wishing in the world.*

"Sefina." Lady Lirath spoke her name sharply, like the crack of a frozen branch underfoot. "Look at me."

Though Sefina knew it would go worse for her if she refused, she couldn't find the courage to lift her head. "I'm sorry, Lady Lirath," she said in her smallest voice.

With an exaggerated sigh, Lady Lirath removed the dreaded practice lute from the wall. "If you insist on wasting my time, you shall accompany Mirae until noonbell. Obviously, you haven't practiced enough."

"But I did!"

The words tumbled out before Sefina could swallow them back. She had—over and over—much more than Mirae in fact, though she'd none of Lady Lirath's praise. Sefina looked to Mirae, who stood to her left before a matching music stand. She bit her lip, hoping Mirae might speak up in her defense. Instead, Mirae offered a wincing look of sympathy and shrugged her shoulders.

It was Mirae's reaction—that helpless reaction, as though nothing could be done about her humiliation—that made Sefina's shame boil over. She shoved her music stand, toppling it with strength she hadn't known she possessed. The stand crashed onto the rug, spilling sheet music at Sefina's feet and causing Mirae to flinch.

"I hate you! I hate you both!" she shouted, tears streaming down her cheeks. Mirae's brown eyes widened until she resembled a frightened deer. That only fed the fire burning in Sefina's belly. *What do you have to be scared of, anyway? Lady Lirath never shouts at you!*

"Enough, Sefina!" Lady Lirath snapped. "You shall apologize to both of us and play the lute for the rest of your lesson. There will be no supper for you, either."

Sefina hardly heard Lady Lirath's words. They were warped, distant. She only saw Mirae, wide-eyed and fearful, yet with a sympathetic wrinkle in her brow. Pity? Sefina couldn't stand to see pity, of all things, on Mirae's face. She ran, barreling through the studio door and into the hall beyond.

The soles of her day slippers slapped upon the stone as she stumbled along. Tears blurred her vision until she scarcely saw where she was going. Swiping her eyes with her sleeve, she ran down the staircase from the second floor and into the grand foyer. People milled about, acolytes and masters of various artistic disciplines, but Sefina ignored them. She blustered past without so much as an apology, stomped down the temple steps, and made a beeline for the pond.

I should throw myself in and drown. Lady Lirath will be sorry then!

But it wasn't only Lady Lirath's fault.

It's Mirae's, for being so terribly perfect. She makes me sound ugly, a crow to her nightingale. If only...

Sefina stopped at the pond's edge, heaving great hiccuping sobs. A stone bench stood a few meters away, shielded by the drooping branches of a willow tree. She clambered onto the bench, hugging her knees and burying her face in her forearms. She wept into her sleeves, struggling to breathe.

When her tears finally ran dry, she lifted her head. She didn't feel any better. If anything, she felt worse. *What if Lady Lirath stops teaching me? What if she throws me out of the temple and onto the streets, to beg with the other orphans at the docks?*

Then Sefina saw the flutterbug. Its opalescent wings shifted between shades of blue and purple as it floated from flower to flower, carried by a gentle breeze. Bitterness welled within her. Even flutterbugs, mere insects, were important. They were Of-The-Sky's blessed messengers. How could such a beautiful thing exist while she was so ugly?

Her hand shot out, snatching the flutterbug from the tree. She wanted something else to hurt. To share her pain. She ripped its wings from its body, throwing them upon the grass. Though the flutterbug couldn't scream, its body writhed. Its torn wings flashed an awful shade of crimson, then froze in that color.

"Sefina!"

Only then did Sefina notice Mirae behind her, a look of horror upon her face. Of course Mirae had searched for her. Of course Mirae had arrived in time to witness such a cruel and shameful act.

Sefina had thought herself cried out, but fresh tears leaked from her eyes. She longed to bury herself in Mirae's arms. Mirae's warm, soothing breath would caress her cheek as she whispered everything would turn out right. But, no. She didn't deserve such comfort.

Mirae strode past her, kneeling upon the grass by the dying flutterbug. She scooped its fuzzy body into her hand and gathered its wings, cupping her other hand over them. Her voice was mournful as she sang, and it plucked Sefina's heartstrings just as her own fingers plucked unwillingly at the practice lute.

Flutterbug, flutterbug,
Floating on the breeze.
Dancing in the flowerbed,
Playing with the bees.
Pick a flower, Flutterbug
Which one will you choose?
Orange, red, or yellow?
Purple, pink, or blue?
Flutterbug, flutterbug
Autumn's here. Fly away!
But spring's around the corner.
We'll meet again someday.

As the final phrase tapered, Mirae opened her hands to reveal a miracle. There was the flutterbug, wings reattached. It flapped, testing its movement, then took to the air, circling several times before landing in Mirae's curly black hair. It remained there like a bejeweled ornament, its healed wings shimmering in a kaleidoscope of colors.

"That was an awful thing to do, Fina." Mirae glared at Sefina with none of the tenderness she'd shown the flutterbug.

Sefina hung her head. What could she say? She had no excuse for harming an innocent creature. "I know."

"Why did you do it?"

She chewed her lip, unable to answer.

Mirae studied her for a long time, as though passing judgment. Then, with all the grace of the goddess who had bestowed her voice, she did exactly what Sefina had longed for. She pulled Sefina into a hug, chin resting upon her shoulder, stroking open hands along her trembling back.

"I love you, Sefina. I always will. You'll remember that, won't you? I'm sorry I didn't stand up for you with Lady Lirath. I could have told her how hard you practiced, but...sometimes, she scares me. I didn't want her to shout at me sd well."

Sefina broke into tears for a third time, only these were tears of relief. Deep down, she believed Mirae. Mirae would always love her, despite her many faults. Even when she didn't deserve it. Mirae had seen her scream and cry and rip the wings off an innocent creature, yet somehow loved her still.

"I love you, too," she whispered, burying her face in Mirae's neck. Her lovely neck, warm and smelling of the sea they'd left behind. Smelling of home.

Sefina didn't know how long they held each other. It seemed to her an eternity, yet never long enough. When Mirae let go at last, the flutterbug remained in her hair. It seemed quite content there, as though it had found the perfect flower to perch upon. Sefina could hardly blame it. If she were a flutterbug, she would make the same choice.

"Promise me, Sefina," Mirae said, fixing her with another stern stare, "that you'll never harm another innocent creature. What you did was cruel. That isn't who you are. You're gentle and kind and you're my best friend."

Sefina answered without hesitation. "I promise."

After that, Mirae was all smiles. All seemed forgiven as Mirae took Sefina by the hand and led her to the pond, urging her to take off her shoes and dip her feet in the water. They searched for the prettiest stones they could find to place upon Of-The-Sea's altar in the back of the temple. It did much to heal Sefina's broken heart.

There they stayed until duskbell, when Mirae finally coaxed Sefina back to the temple. They found Lady Lirath in the entrance hall, awaiting their return. Sefina hung her head, certain Lady Lirath would scold her fiercely. And scold she did.

"Sefina, your behavior today was absolutely unacceptable. You cannot scream and run away when my lessons aren't to your liking. That is something only small children do. You are a young lady, capable of far better comportment."

Sefina kept her eyes fixed upon her shoes. "Yes, Lady Lirath. I'm sorry." As she apologized, Mirae's fingers laced through hers, lending strength and encouragement.

Lady Lirath approached, her heels clicking upon the stone floor. Sefina flinched as Lady Lirath's hand rested upon her shoulder, but it neither pulled nor squeezed too hard. "Look at me."

Reluctantly, Sefina lifted her eyes. To her surprise, Lady Lirath's brow had softened. The usual ice was absent from her calm blue eyes. "Perhaps I was too harsh. I only want your talents to flourish. Do you understand?"

Sefina swallowed a gasp. *Lady Lirath thinks me talented? I can't compare with Mirae...but didn't Speaker Yeneri say many voices are needed to fill the world with music?* "Thank you, Lady Lirath. You're too kind after I've wronged you."

Lady Lirath removed her hand. Sefina found that she missed its weight upon her shoulder. "Come with me. I have something for you. Mirae, you may accompany us."

They took the stairs from the entrance hall to Lady Lirath's studio. Sefina noted that her music stand had been righted and all the sheet music gathered up, leaving no signs of her earlier outburst. Still, her face flushed with shame.

"Wait here." Lady Lirath went to her desk, then returned with a medium-sized bundle draped in purple silk. She passed it carefully to Sefina. "Handle it gently. I spent considerable coin to commission it."

Sefina held the bundle as though it were made of glass. She lifted the silken cover to reveal a lute of polished maplewood. Intricate strands of ivy were carved into its face, lined with silver paint. It was a beautiful piece of work, far finer than Lady Lirath's practice lute, but Sefina's first reaction was stinging disappointment. She despised lutes and everything they had come to represent.

"I know you find the lute tedious," Lady Lirath said, causing Sefina to look up from her gift, "but it is a beautiful and noble instrument. You have learned to play well in a remarkably short time. My intention was never to hurt you, but to teach you a unique skill entirely separate from Mirae. One which allows you to shine while also complementing her extraordinary abilities. Do you understand? I had hoped to give this to you under happier circumstances, but you have earned it nonetheless."

So, this is a reward? Not more punishment? Sefina had never thought of the lute that way before. She repeated Lady Lirath's words in her head, savoring them like the sweetest dessert. *Beautiful and noble...remarkably short time...allow me to shine...*No one had presented her with a gift since her parents' deaths, let alone an instrument so fine as this.

Gratitude won out. "Thank you, Lady Lirath," she said, her voice cracking.

Lady Lirath opened her arms. Sefina entered the protective circle, passing Mirae the lute so it wouldn't become squashed. Though Lady Lirath merely stroked her hair and said nothing more, Sefina understood that Lady Lirath cared for her as more than a mere student, in her own stilted way.

From then on, she found new joy in playing the lute. She never grew to love it as much as singing, but took pride in learning a skill all her own. On good days, her jealousy slumbered when she played, offering precious moments of reprieve. She basked in the glory of Mirae's voice, content to accompany her without a single whisper of resentment.

Yet not all days were good days.

On bad days, the fiery green dragon stirred within her, poisoning her with its breath, choking her heart in its coils. Still, she kept it chained tight. There were no more outbursts during lessons. She learned self-control. Though she never overcame her resentment completely, she managed to keep both Lady Lirath and Mirae in the dark.

Mirae — Seconday

Mirae — Secondday

DAWNBELL TOLLS AGAIN. ITS dull, dreary sound pulls Mirae from Sefina's words as though from a deep sleep. She looks at Yeneri, seated in the rowboat.

"I remember that day," Mirae says. "I could scarcely believe my sweet Sefina would do something so cruel."

"Now you know why," Yeneri says. "Those who suffer great pain often lash out at others, even the innocent."

Mirae flinches as she recalls another memory, one Sefina has not yet recounted. Sefina was not the only one to make that mistake. Her own sins are probably worse in comparison. Didn't she leave when Sefina needed her most? Didn't she blame Sefina for her own frustrations at the temple?

"I apologized," she says, more to herself than Yeneri. The statement is lackluster, far from convincing to her own ears. "I told her I was sorry in the end."

"Apologies mean little without reparations," Yeneri says.

Mirae squares her shoulders. Her decision weighs more heavily upon her than before, like a rain-dampened cloak. "Does that mean I must return? Because I'm so tired, Yeneri. I've given so much of myself to everyone in Stagford. I want to sleep for a thousand years. Have you ever felt that way?"

Yeneri caresses Mirae's cheek, those callused weaver's fingers pleasantly rough upon her face. "In my twilight years. I remained longer than my body and spirit wished because I knew you and Sefina needed me. Yet I have earned my final rest. So have you. You have given more of yourself to others than any young woman should and have done since you were a child. No one, not even Sefina, would think less of you for choosing eternal sleep."

Mirae gazes out across the waves. The vivid oranges and reds have faded, leaving only a deep bluish-purple mass. The pale white stars shine brighter, as though floating closer. They rise and dip in an endless dance, weightless and wondrous to behold. She wades further into the waves to watch them, feeling the sea lap at her knees. The hem of her dress grows wet, swirling around her calves.

Sefina's voice rises out of the fog, then continues in the same soft, soothing way as before. Mirae stops, closing her eyes. *I should hear the rest of the story. Even the parts I would rather forget.*

Chapter Six

YEARS PASSED. SEFINA'S VOICE settled into a rich alto, while Mirae's went high and clear like the sweetest silver bell. Sefina found the new distinction pleasing to her ears as well as her heart. Mirae was the morning songbirds while she was the evening crickets. Proof, in Sefina's opinion, that they were destined to sing together always. That the Eight had somehow ordained it.

Lady Lirath's critiques continued, with Sefina's vastly outnumbering Mirae's. Sefina hungered for improvement, so she took Lady Lirath's words to heart, no matter how harsh. At duskbell, she often collapsed in bed beside Mirae, too exhausted to keep her eyes open—but always found the energy to sing when Mirae asked.

"Sing me a lullaby, Fina," Mirae begged most nights. "I won't fall asleep otherwise."

No matter how strained or hoarse Sefina's voice was, she never refused. Often, she sang the nighttime version of the wake-up song, which she had grown to think of as 'their' song.

> The moon's begun to rise. The stars are on their way.
> So close your heavy eyes until a brand new day.
> Hush now, hush now. Night falls. Crickets cheep.
> Hush now, hush now. Rest your head and sleep.

It became a point of pride that her voice lulled Mirae to sleep without fail. Within a few verses, Mirae would begin snoring. In those moments, Sefina believed her voice might hold special powers after all. Not the power to heal wounds or bring flowers into early bloom, but the power to soothe Mirae, at the very least. That was worth something.

Despite their busy schedules, they always spent Eightdays together, walking the temple grounds or visiting Easton's shopping district during their precious hours of freedom.

One such Eightday, shortly after Sefina turned fourteen, she and Mirae found themselves wandering near the stables. It was a place they rarely visited except when Lady Lirath commissioned a carriage. The day was clear and sunny, with a bright blue sky that reminded Sefina of the ocean at dawn.

"Feel like going for a ride, Fina?" Mirae asked.

Sefina swallowed as she noticed Mirae's mischievous grin, the one that put dimples in both cheeks. "In the carriage? We should ask Lady Lirath."

"No, silly." Mirae nudged Sefina with her elbow. "A ride, not a drive."

"On horseback, you mean?" Sefina hoped not. She'd never ridden so much as a mule, so the prospect of a full-grown steed was intimidating enough to curdle her stomach.

Mirae tossed her tight black curls over one shoulder. "Why not? One of the stablehands can show us how."

Sefina's gut churned, but she suppressed her misgivings and shrugged. "I suppose..."

"It'll be fun, I promise!" Mirae took Sefina's hand, pulling her along at a fast walk.

They soon arrived at the stables, a rectangular building situated some distance from the temple. It didn't take Sefina long to realize why. While she wrinkled her nose, adjusting to the pungent smell, Mirae approached the nearest stablehand. He was a handsome lad around their age, whom Sefina recognized as Trenton, one of the Speaker's students.

Trenton wore a triangular prayer pendant around his neck, though his red hair and freckles were unusual for one of the Earthfolk. As well as being a stablehand, he studied with Speaker Yeneri—not for the traditional sort of weaving, but the weaving of stories and other such yarns.

Mirae offered Trenton a smile, the sort of smile Sefina would have hoarded for herself like gold if she were able. "Afternoon, Trenton. How are the horses?"

Trenton hung his head so his red curls fell in front of his eyes. "Same as always, Miss Mirae." His voice was little more than a mumble.

Sefina wondered why. If it was Mirae's presence that Trenton found intimidating, she couldn't blame him. Despite their long friendship, Mirae had the power to steal Sefina's breath and jumble her words. All these years later, she still made a fool of herself on a regular basis. More often, lately.

Mirae giggled. "Not Miss." She chucked Trenton beneath his chin. He had only the barest scrapings of a beard, so faint as to be hardly noticeable. "Just Mirae."

Trenton peeked out from beneath his wavy bangs. A shy smile spread across his face. "All right. Mirae."

"Are you a skilled rider?"

"I manage," Trenton said.

"You must be, to work here," Mirae said. "Are you good enough to teach us?"

"M-me?" Trenton pointed at himself and stammered, his voice cracking in the way of a young boy who will soon become a man. "Teach you?"

Mirae clasped her hands and rose up on her tip-toes, peering into his eyes. "Please? I've never ridden a horse before."

Sefina chewed her cheek, willing away the uncomfortable burning sensation behind her breastbone. Learning to ride without adult supervision made her uneasy, as did the way Mirae batted her eyelashes at Trenton. She stayed silent, hoping he would refuse since she didn't have the heart to deny Mirae anything.

A blush darkened Trenton's freckled cheeks. Sefina saw the moment he crumbled before Mirae's smile. "Er, why not?"

"Thank you." Mirae hugged Trenton's neck, causing his eyes to pop out. He stared over Mirae's shoulder, opening and closing his mouth like a stunned fish.

Sefina watched his reaction, struck by a cold, dreadful feeling. Logically, she knew a hug for Trenton hardly meant less hugs for her. *So why do I feel like he's snatched something precious from my hands?* She tugged Mirae's sleeve, pulling her away from Trenton. "If we're riding horses, let's pick some."

The sight of a dozen fine horses proved an effective distraction. So enamored was Mirae that she forgot all about Trenton. "They're gorgeous," she said, squeezing Sefina's hand. "Aren't they gorgeous, Fina?"

Sefina savored the feeling of Mirae's warm hand in hers despite its tight grip. "Gorgeous," she echoed, though she wasn't much impressed. The stalls smelled worse than the paddock outside, although the sweet scent of hay offered some reprieve.

"This one's Lightfoot." Trenton placed his hand upon the nearest stall door. A dappled gray mare resided within, facing the rear wall. She seemed content to ignore her visitors and swish flies from her flanks with her tail. "She's a calm old girl. Good for a first ride."

Sefina's fondness for Lightfoot grew once Trenton bridled her and led her from the stall. The mare's large, soft brown eyes reminded her of Mirae's. Lightfoot lipped Mirae's outstretched hand, and her delighted laughter almost convinced Sefina that riding wasn't such a terrible idea. She would go along with anything that brought Mirae such happiness.

"Hold her, please." Trenton offered Mirae Lightfoot's bridle. "I'll saddle her for you, Miss—er, Mirae."

Mirae laughed again as she took the reins from Trenton's hand.

Sefina pursed her lips. Perhaps she'd been wrong about Mirae's happiness always making her happy.

Soon the old mare was saddled and ready. Despite her age, she snorted and stomped her hooves, ready to stretch her legs. Trenton patted her neck to settle her. "Would you like help getting in the saddle, or..." His voice trailed off, but not before Sefina caught a hopeful note.

"I'll give her a boost," she said before Mirae could answer.

Trenton's face fell, but Mirae seemed not to notice. Sefina pretended the same—except for the brief smirk she shot in his direction as she placed one of her hands in Mirae's and the other upon her waist, hoisting her into the stirrups.

"I feel so tall up here," Mirae said once seated in the saddle.

"No shame in being afraid of heights," Sefina said, dreading her turn already. "You can come back down if you want."

Mirae shook her head. "No, I enjoy the view. Trenton, how do I tell the horse to move?"

"A gentle nudge of the heels," Trenton said.

Before long, Mirae and Lightfoot were trotting around the paddock as one. Sefina hovered by the fence, refusing to take her eyes off Mirae in case the worst should happen. In her head, she said a quick prayer to Of-the-Land, father of all animals.

Trenton leaned against the fence's top railing. He seemed far more relaxd while Mirae was occupied with Lightfoot, though he swallowed hard when she waved at him.

At him. Not me.

The thought crossed Sefina's mind that Mirae was probably waving at both of them, but it was too late. Her face flushed and her head swam with a strange, unpleasant lightness.

"Miss Sefina?"

She turned to see Trenton peering at her. Begrudgingly, she admitted he was somewhat good-looking, if one had an interest in boys. He was almost pretty, with his full lips and emerald eyes. Not that she cared about such things. She'd already decided she would never marry. Compared to honing her musicianship, it seemed a waste of time.

"Er, does Mirae ever mention me?" Trenton asked.

Sefina's heart felt as though it had dropped through her stomach and into her shoes. It was clear from his hesitant voice and hopeful eyes what he meant. *What if she finds Trenton's interest flattering? What if she wants to spend her Eightdays with him instead of me?*

She shook off her paralysis. Trenton was waiting, expectant. "She hasn't mentioned any boys to me."

Trenton's shoulders slumped. "Oh." He averted his eyes, staring into the distance. "Does she prefer girls, then?"

Sefina's mouth fell open. This time, she was the stunned fish. She'd never even considered that possibility. As far as she knew, men were supposed to marry women, while women married men. "Two women can marry each other?" The idea filled her with such warmth that jealousy seemed a distant memory.

Trenton rubbed his neck. "I, er—I dunno. You should ask someone else."

Sefina nodded absently, hardly hearing his words. She slipped into a dreamlike stupor as she watched Mirae ride around the paddock, the tight black coils of her hair bouncing behind her. Suddenly, marriage no longer seemed like a waste of time to Sefina. She only came back to herself when Mirae guided Lightfoot to the fence, grinning ear to ear.

"Your turn, Fina."

Sefina swallowed hard. "Maybe I'll learn to ride some other time..."

Mirae shook her head. "Don't be afraid. I'll ride with you. Lightfoot can carry us both. Right, Trenton?"

Trenton coughed into his elbow before finding his voice. "I don't see why not. The pair of you can't weigh more than a sack of feathers."

Sefina was newly intrigued. Riding a horse alongside Mirae, their bodies pressed close. Excitement won out over fear. "If you say so."

Mirae's eyes were too bright and joyful to refuse. "Trenton, help her up."

Sefina didn't object to Trenton's hands as he helped her into the stirrups. They remained chaste and proper, but her thoughts were quite the opposite as she swung her leg over the saddle. The first thing she noticed was the scent of Mirae's hair, warm and floral. She leaned closer, inhaling as she wrapped her arms around Mirae's waist.

When had Mirae's figure become so soft? She was no longer the bony, stick-limbed girl who had run along the seaside cliffs and splashed in the surf. Her hips had a noticeable curve. Her backside fit perfectly into the cradle of Sefina's pelvis. The crook of her neck called for Sefina to bury her nose there.

She couldn't help but wonder how two women engaged in a physical relationship after they were married. Was such a thing possible? How did it work? Her heart hammered so hard she feared Mirae might feel it against her back. Instead, Mirae shifted closer, pressing her back against Sefina's front as she nudged Lightfoot into a walk.

The ride was much less frightening than Sefina feared. The excuse to hold Mirae close filled her stomach with flutterbugs. She ached in ways she didn't understand. She decided that someday, when they were grown and she asked Mirae to marry her, they would own a single horse so they could ride together.

"See?" Mirae said, turning to smile at Sefina. "It's fun."

"Right," Sefina said, embarrassed by the raspiness of her voice.

After several circuits of the paddock, Mirae ended Sefina's bliss by heading back to Trenton. Jealousy reared its horned head as he helped Mirae down from Lightfoot, but Sefina did her best to suppress it. She was the one who had ridden alongside Mirae, after all. She was the one fortunate enough to hold Mirae in her arms. She addressed Trenton politely once her feet were on solid ground. "Thank you."

Trenton's eyes darted down to his boots. "You're welcome, Miss Sefina."

"Yes. Thank you, Trenton," Mirae said, though she wasn't looking at him. She'd glimpsed another horse in an adjoining paddock, a hulking black beast with rippling muscles and a sleek coat that shone in the sun. "Who's that beauty?" Mirae didn't wait for a response before wandering toward this latest temptation.

Trenton tripped after Mirae on both feet and tongue. "Thunder. Still needs breaking in. Stablemaster Horne barely lets me feed him and muck his stall."

Sefina bit her lip, remaining well away from the paddock. "Perhaps you shouldn't, Mirae."

Mirae wasn't dissuaded in the slightest. She climbed the fence, standing with both feet balanced on the bottom plank and bracing her elbows on top. "Here, Thunder," she called, blowing kisses and clicking her tongue. Not quite a magic song, but melodious nonetheless.

Sefina wasn't surprised when Thunder trotted over, flaring his large nostrils. Animals could never resist Mirae, a sentiment she understood all too well.

Trenton stared, eyes wide and mouth agape. "He listened to you," he said, raising his voice above a whisper for the first time.

"Of course he did." Mirae held a hand over the fence. "We'll get along fine. Right, Thunder?"

Thunder eyed Mirae's hand with obvious suspicion. After a tense moment, he dipped his head, pressing his nose into Mirae's palm.

"Good boy," Mirae cooed, stroking Thunder's muzzle.

Trenton gazed at Mirae with nothing short of awe. "Well, I'll be. Stablemaster Horne will never believe me." Sefina recognized the look on his face well enough. Trenton wasn't the first person to admire Mirae, but this time something squeezed painfully inside her chest, like a fist around her heart.

"Come and pet him." Mirae side-stepped along the bottom rung of the fence to make more space, gesturing for Trenton to join her.

The fist in Sefina's chest clenched harder.

Warily, Trenton approached the fence. He extended his hand, inching toward Thunder's neck. Thunder snorted and tossed his head. Trenton stumbled, nearly falling into the mud. He steadied himself at the last moment by grabbing the fence. "I-I don't think he likes me."

"Nonsense," Mirae said. "Look, he's a sweetheart." As if to prove her point, Thunder shoved his nose into Mirae's hand, attempting to convince her to keep stroking.

Though visibly reluctant, Trenton squared his shoulders, preparing for another attempt.

Sefina gritted her teeth. The slumbering green dragon had awakened, coiling itself around her insides. A selfish, evil thought whispered in her mind. *What if Trenton falls? Mirae won't find him so handsome then, his britches sodden with mud, terrified of the animals he works with every day...*

Slowly, Trenton extended his hand toward Thunder.

Mirae nodded her encouragement. Her brown eyes sparkled as she watched him, and Sefina recognized the emotion as happiness. Happiness that Trenton had brought about with his newfound bravery.

Before Trenton could pat Thunder's neck, Sefina coughed. Loudly. At precisely the wrong moment.

Thunder brayed. Mirae hopped down from the fence quickly and gracefully, but Trenton didn't flinch or fall as Sefina had hoped. There was no slipping in the mud, no frightened squealing, nor any other temporary embarrassments. Instead, Trenton froze.

He must have seen Thunder rear up on his back legs. Surely he saw the stallion's front hooves flying toward his face. Still, he didn't move.

Mirae shouted a warning. Sefina wasn't sure whether she cried aloud as well, but a loud scream sounded inside her head.

Then, a wet crunch.

A thud.

A horrible sound like burbling water.

Sefina could hardly bear to look, but when she forced herself, she couldn't tear her eyes away. Half of Trenton's head was caved in, crumpled like a wadded sheet of paper. Blood gushed from all sides of the ghoulish wound and bubbled from his mouth, staining his lips crimson.

A lightning flash of fear shot through Sefina, followed by the cold, dark sensation of growing horror. By the Eight, she hadn't wanted this to happen! She'd never meant to break the promise she'd made to Mirae by the lake, that she'd never harm another living creature. She'd only hoped Trenton would stumble so Mirae wouldn't fancy him anymore.

It was too late. Trenton was little more than a limp heap beside the fence, his face an unrecognizable mass of blood and worse.

Sefina's eyes burned, but the tears wouldn't come. She remained frozen in place, a living statue. *I've killed him. Killed him! Oh, Lady Sleep, take me instead! Trenton's done nothing wrong!*

Mirae dropped to her knees beside Trenton, pulling his ruined, caved head into her lap. Sefina recoiled when she noticed the faint rise and fall of his chest, already beginning to slow. Despite the damage, he was still alive, at least for a few moments. Surely he felt Of-Fternal-Sleep's icy breath on the nape of his neck, waiting to tap his shoulder and lead him to her rowboat and the sea of stars.

But Trenton didn't die.

Mirae sang to him in a tender voice, stroking his sticky curls in spite of the blood. There were no lyrics. She simply opened her mouth, and the most beautiful melody of sparkling notes spilled forth, joyful and mournful at the same time.

For a split second, Sefina's fear and guilt fled. Tears streamed down her cheeks as she listened, spellbound by Mirae's voice. She forgot where she was, who she was, as it poured into her ears, filling her mind with colors she couldn't name.

The song's effect on Trenton was nothing short of miraculous. The flow of blood stopped. The awful dent in his head filled out until it was a curve once more, like an inflating balloon. What Sefina had thought were his final, wheezing breaths evened out. He managed a low moan as his eyes fluttered open.

"Mirae? Wh—what...where...?"

"Shhh," Mirae said, still stroking his hair. "You're all right. I promise."

And Trenton did look all right, aside from the blood all over him. Clearly dazed, but no longer on the brink of death. He tried to sit up, staring down in shock at his bloodstained shirt and Mirae's crimson hands. He touched his own head in disbelief. Though his fingers came away red and wet, no wound remained there.

Sefina's lungs burned and she realized she'd been holding her breath. Though guilt gnawed mercilessly at her bones, she was so overcome by awe that the grinding pain felt dulled, distant. She had witnessed Mirae perform miracles before, but nothing like this. Singing skinned knees better was one thing. Bringing someone back from the brink of death was quite another.

The next few minutes were little more than a blur. Other stablehands came to investigate the shouts. They saw Trenton, covered in blood but uninjured, and listened as he explained how Mirae had saved his life. Lady Lirath and Speaker Yeneri were summoned. Both arrived in short order, Lady Lirath in her fine purple robes and Speaker Yeneri in the homespun tunics she favored.

Trenton repeated his story, with occasional interjections from Mirae. Though she tried to be modest—"I only wanted to help. It seemed the right thing to do."—her voice filled with the golden warmth of pride.

She deserves to be proud, Sefina thought. She saved someone's life, after all. She remained a silent shadow, watching everything unfold, in the middle of the chaos but somehow separate from it all. Not a word passed her lips, though Mirae's eyes darted in her direction several times.

Sefina tried her best to force a smile. To show Mirae some visible sign of how proud she was. Though she was in awe of what Mirae had done, other, darker feelings simmered in her stomach.

You have the power to shape fate to your liking, as though you're one of the Eight themselves. And who am I compared to you? A terrible, selfish girl with no talent, who almost got someone killed today. If you knew, why would you even want my friendship? Or anything more?

In the span of a heartbeat, Sefina's dreams of asking Mirae to marry her shattered into a hundred pieces.

"Perhaps we've kept you shut away in the temple for too long, Mirae."

Speaker Yeneri's voice pulled Sefina out of her spiraling thoughts. She blinked, catching sight of Trenton being borne away on a stretcher—likely to the infirmary.

"It may be time for you to see more of Stagford and its people," Speaker Yeneri continued. "You could be of great help to the sick and injured, particularly those who live by Easton's docks."

Lady Lirath's mouth pulled into an ugly shape. "Speaker, the slums are no place for a young girl!"

"Not so young anymore," Speaker Yeneri said. "She may be your pupil, Raula, but she is blossoming into a woman, one chosen by Of-Blessed-Dreams. There is a great deal of sickness and poverty in that area of Stagford."

Lady Lirath gasped. She began to protest, but Mirae spoke first.

"I want to go," she said, looking between Speaker Yeneri and Lady Lirath. "Lots of Sea Children live by the docks, don't they? Those are my people. If I can ease their suffering, isn't it my duty?"

Lady Lirath pursed her lips. "We are all one people in Stagford. Sea Children and Earthfolk alike obey the Regent and contribute to Stagford's infrastructure, including the temple."

Speaker Yeneri shook her silver head. "You speak from a place of privilege, Raula. The Regent is Earthfolk, as are his courtiers. He tolerates me because my father was Earthfolk, and no one could deny my worthiness after witnessing my ascension. But my mother was a Sea Child. We share little of Stagford's prosperity. Mirae is one of ours. Shouldn't we allow her to serve her own people first?"

Sefina could tell from the wrinkle in Lady Lirath's brow and the tightness of her jaw that she disapproved, but she dipped her head in deference. "Serving those in need is a worthy goal. However, I must insist you allow me to escort her. That area of the city can be dangerous."

"You may accompany her if you wish," Speaker Yeneri said, "but I intend to escort her myself. It's been a while since I visited Easton's docks, no thanks to my sore old bones."

"All the more reason for me to come," Lady Lirath said. "You will need an escort as well, Speaker."

Mirae tugged Speaker Yeneri's sleeve. "Please, can Sefina come with us?"

For the first time, Speaker Yeneri acknowledged Sefina's presence by turning her head. Sefina couldn't blame the Speaker for failing to notice her, not after what Mirae had done, but it stung nonetheless. Once again, she was little more than a shadow to Mirae's brilliant sunlight.

No, don't indulge such envious thoughts. You're lucky Speaker Yeneri doesn't see straight through you and realize what an awful person you truly are.

"Why, of course Sefina can come. It would do her good to see different parts of the city, to become more acquainted with the world. She is also growing into a young woman."

Sefina's heart lifted, both because Mirae desired her company and Speaker Yeneri had allowed it. She shoved down her jealousy and self-loathing and chained them up tight. She would gladly be part of Mirae's entourage. It was a privilege to be the friend and companion of such a marvelous person, even if she didn't deserve it.

"I would like that very much," she said, smiling.

"Then it's decided," Speaker Yeneri said. "Tomorrow, Raula and I will take you both to the Easton docks. There, we shall see what comforts Mirae's voice might bring."

Chapter Seven

AT FIRST GLANCE, THE Easton docks resembled Lady Lirath's unfavorable descriptions. Peering through the carriage window, Sefina observed a rough-looking place with cramped, run-down wooden shacks for buildings and muddy dirt roads instead of paved paths. Fetid water pooled in the lowest parts of the marketplace and the overpowering stench of rotten fish hung in the air.

The residents, however, showed far more life and vitality than their surroundings suggested.

Once the carriage came to a stop, Sefina emerged to see a bustling crowd of shoppers walking the streets. Some pulled loaded carts while others stood behind cheerfully decorated stalls, calling out to potential customers as they passed. The variety of wares within these stalls were even more intriguing. Sefina saw plenty of fish, but also quilts, handmade jewelry, and fresh vegetables.

Mirae took Sefina's hand and laced their fingers. "Incredible," she said in a breathless voice. Her eyes roamed the marketplace as though trying to take in everything all at once. "It's much more crowded than the Castletown shops."

"True," Lady Lirath said, coming to stand beside them. "The northern shops are more spread out. There's less space here."

"Less space, perhaps, but plenty of good cheer and secret treasures to be found," said Speaker Yeneri. Her broad smile caused the wrinkles in her face to deepen like the bark of a tree. Somehow, it made her look all the lovelier. Perhaps it was the twinkle of merriment in her dark eyes as she gestured toward one of the stalls. "Let's have something to eat. I guarantee you'll enjoy it." She headed for the stall, sheltered by a large patchwork quilt of blues and greens.

Sefina took a moment to admire it. Though it wasn't one of Speaker Yeneri's tapestries, she could tell from a distance it was beautiful work.

Mirae tugged her hand. "Come on," she whispered. "The Speaker's fast for an old lady. Look at her go."

Sefina stifled a giggle. Speaker Yeneri hobbled along at an admirable pace with a spring in her step despite her cane. She and

Mirae followed, with Lady Lirath trailing behind like a protective shadow.

"Four slices of eel pie, please," Speaker Yeneri said to the woman behind the stall. She was middle aged and plump, with round cheeks and crow's feet at the corners of her eyes. Her braided hair was wrapped in a colorful red scarf. When she smiled, both cheeks dimpled almost like Mirae's. Sefina thought it was one of the friendliest smiles she'd ever seen. The sort of smile one might offer a close friend rather than a customer.

"Anything for you, Speaker. Coming right up." She turned, bending over what looked like a small, portable stone oven.

"Taela makes the best eel pie in Stagford," Speaker Yeneri whispered. "Probably all of Stelvaine, too."

Sefina's mouth watered. She hadn't tasted eel pie in years, not since leaving Farsea. Mirae moaned and licked her lips, stirring the flutterbugs that had made a home of Sefina's stomach in recent months.

"Eel pie?" Lady Lirath's expression was uncertain, with a furrowed brow and tight-lipped frown. "Is that why you used to visit the Easton docks so frequently, Speaker?"

"Among other reasons."

Taela the pie merchant presented them with four wicker baskets lined in cheap linen. Resting in the baskets were four crisp golden pies, small in size but smelling of heaven. "Here you are. Four pies. Please enjoy them, Speaker. I couldn't possibly charge you—"

"Thank you kindly," said Speaker Yeneri. Sefina didn't miss the gold pieces she deposited on the counter while Taela wasn't looking.

Taela's eel pie was every bit as delicious as Speaker Yeneri claimed. Sefina lingered over each bite, chewing thoroughly despite the instinct to wolf it all down. The light, flaky crust and sweet eel meat deserved to be savored and enjoyed.

Mirae sighed as she ate, pausing only to wipe a crumb from the corner of Sefina's mouth. "Oh, Fina. You're a mess. I love you, you know?"

Sefina's heart nearly burst from her chest. Mirae often declared her love, but lately, the statement had taken on a different meaning. Her stomach somersaulted as Mirae's fingers grazed her lips. She felt the strangest urge to take them in her mouth and bite them. Her heart pounded faster, its rhythm uncertain.

"Now, now," Speaker Yeneri tutted. "Let Sefina enjoy her pie in peace, Mirae."

Sefina blushed, avoiding Lady Lirath's judgmental stare. She'd eaten her pie neatly, though she'd seemed to enjoy it despite her initial skepticism.

The sound of rhythmic shuffling and raised voices caused Sefina to turn her head. A shirtless man with rich brown skin and winding blue sailor's tattoos danced atop a barrel, displaying expert rhythm and balance. His feet moved in a blur while his upper body remained loose and relaxd. A sizable crowd had gathered around him, clapping in time to the dance.

"Wonderful," Speaker Yeneri said. "Nothing like a barrel dance to make one's blood rush!"

Mirae stared, riveted by the sight. Sefina could hardly blame her. The young man's skill was hypnotizing. Her heart sped up every time his feet neared the edge of the barrel, but he never came close to falling.

"May we go and see?" Mirae asked.

"Of course—"

No sooner had Speaker Yeneri said the words than Sefina found herself dragged across the street by her elbow. A gasp rose from the crowd as the dancer performed an expert leap that took him at least six inches off the barrel's lid.

Mirae broke into song, a sea shanty from their childhood days.

> *Oh, we sail by day and we sail by night,*
> *Despite the wind and weather.*
> *The horizon sings within my heart.*
> *We'll follow it together.*
> *Oh, a solid ship beneath my feet*
> *And a strong wind in our sail.*
> *With gracious gifts from Of-The-Sea,*
> *Good sailors cannot fail.*

A hush fell over the crowd. As one, they turned in search of the beautiful voice that had sprung out of nowhere. The man atop the barrel froze in mid-step, an awestruck look softening his features. As Mirae came to the second verse, she let her voice die away, frowning at the enraptured audience.

"Don't stop on my account. Sefina, you know the lower part."

Before Sefina could answer, Mirae picked up the song from the beginning. She joined in, bewildered, fumbling the first few words. Soon, she relaxd into the jaunty tune, put at ease by the familiarity of Mirae's voice. She did indeed remember the lower part after all these years.

By the end of the first verse, they were in their element, hitting every beat in perfect harmony. The man atop the barrel resumed his dance, grinning widely. The crowd picked up their clapping. Pure, wild joy crackled amongst those gathered like the thrill of a lightning storm.

Midway through the second verse, Sefina caught sight of Lady Lirath and Speaker Yeneri. Both appeared pleased, so she sang even more lustily, smiling all the while.

Other voices joined in since it was a well-known song. Some were good, others only fair, while a few were completely out of tune and off-rhythm. Sefina's heart soared anyway. It reminded her of what Speaker Yeneri always said: Of-Blessed-Dreams made every voice unique and precious to lift the souls of all mortals.

They sang until the man atop the barrel was lathered in sweat. He hopped down with a flourish, extending his hands toward them. Riotous applause broke out as Mirae took one hand and Sefina the other. The three of them bowed.

As Sefina straightened, her cheeks flushed with pride and pleasure. She and Mirae had sung during the temple's midsummer and midwinter celebrations, much to the delight of Mirae's parents, but neither had given such an impromptu performance before. She already found herself wondering when they might do so again.

"What wondrous voices," the dancer said, breathless from exertion. "I shouldn't be surprised, coming from two beautiful young ladies."

Mirae giggled. Sefina stared down at her shoes to hide her burning face, which had definitely begun to turn red. As she looked to the ground, she noticed an overturned hat beside the barrel. It was full of copper pieces. She hoped their addition to the dancer's performance would fill his belly for a while. It seemed what little the residents of Easton's docks had, they were willing to share. She reached into her dress pocket for her coin purse, dumping all the silver she'd brought into the hat as well.

Speaker Yeneri hobbled forward as well, tipping in a handful of gold pieces. The dancer bowed before her, taking her bony wrists gently in his hands while she clasped his. Her fingers didn't make it all the way around.

"It's an honor to see you again, Speaker."

"You as well, Brom." Speaker Yeneri let go, patting his cheek. "You know there's always a place for you at the Temple of Dreams. Talent such as yours deserves a home."

"Thank you, Speaker, as always," Brom said. "Your offer is generous, but this is my home and these are my people." He straightened to his full height and tucked back his shoulders. Sefina couldn't miss the pride shining in his dark eyes. He seemed to care a great deal about his home despite how run-down the docks appeared at first glance.

"And I will continue offering whenever we are fortunate enough to meet, although I doubt your answer will change," said Speaker Yeneri. "How is your family? Is everything well with that new wife of yours?"

"With her, yes…" A shadow crossed Brom's face, making him appear older and more world-weary than the young, vivacious man of a few minutes ago. "Our newborn daughter isn't well. She arrived too soon, four weeks ago. I'd rather be home with her, but someone has to put food on the table."

"Of course," Speaker Yeneri said. "May I ask what's wrong?"

Brom frowned, but nodded. "The healer says her heart is weak. She's always cold, no matter how we swaddle her. Sometimes her little hands turn blue."

Speaker Yeneri's gaze shifted sideways, settling upon Mirae. Sefina looked at her, too. She could already guess what Speaker Yeneri would say, and she couldn't deny she was curious to see it happen.

"Brom," Speaker Yeneri said, "if we may impose upon you for a few minutes, Mirae may be able to do something for your daughter. You've already heard her voice…"

"Yes." Brom's lips settled into a polite smile, though Sefina knew he didn't fully understand. "A rare and beautiful one indeed."

"More than you know," said Speaker Yeneri. "Not only does it stir mortal hearts, it has the power to heal injuries. Why, just the other week, Mirae closed a stablehand's head wound before he bled out."

Brom's eyes went wide. "Is that true, young lady?" He crouched down and rested his palms upon his knees, looking at Mirae with hesitant, yet desperate hope. Upon his face, Sefina read his thoughts clearly. He wanted to believe Speaker Yeneri's story, but feared it would end in disappointment.

Mirae lifted her chin proudly. "It is."

"Please." Brom dropped fully to his knees and bowed his head. "Come to my house, I beg you. If you can help my daughter where the healers have failed...even if you can't, a song won't do her any harm."

Mirae reached out, tracing her fingers along Brom's stubbled cheek. "I'll do everything I can. Where do you live?"

While Brom told her, Sefina stole a glance over her shoulder. She wondered if Lady Lirath would disapprove, but instead noted a look of intense focus upon their teacher's face. The line of her jaw was sharper than usual, as though she were clenching her teeth. Her blue eyes sparkled with an emotion Sefina recognized.

Eagerness. She wants Mirae to do this, to become the miracle she discovered in some backwater hamlet. If word gets around that Mirae healed a sick baby in the poorest section of the city, both of them will be famous throughout Stagford. Maybe the whole kingdom of Stelvaine.

Something burned in the pit of Sefina's stomach, but she shoved it down. This wasn't about Mirae's future fame or Lady Lirath's approval. It was about a sick, helpless baby who'd barely started her life. She deserved to enjoy the rest of it. Her own feelings of jealousy were irrelevant.

They accompanied Brom to his house. It was a one-room shack across the street from Hyron Lake, with fresh boards nailed over the worst holes. The interior was small but clean, with scrubbed floors and little dust on the furniture.

Sefina inhaled, picking up the scents of lye and brewing tea. They did a fair job of drowning out the more distant smell of the lake. It almost smelled like her old home in Farsea before her parents died. Colorful hand-woven blankets covered most surfaces, like the awnings she'd admired in the market. Her gaze flicked to Lady Lirath, who had only a slight wrinkle of disapproval in her nose. It seemed even she couldn't find much fault with the humble place.

Brom's wife sat in an old rocking chair by the hearth, holding a bundle against her chest. She was a thin woman with a soft oval face, and a dark blue scarf covered her hair.

"This is my wife, Laru." Brom walked over and placed his hand upon her shoulder. "And our daughter, Sela. Laru, Speaker Yeneri has brought one of her students here to help us."

"My goodness! I wasn't expecting company. Welcome, all of you."

Laru prepared to stand, but Speaker Yeneri waved a gnarled hand. "No need for such formalities, dear. I wouldn't ask a young mother recently out of the birthing bed to kneel for me. Neither would Mirae."

"Absolutely not," Mirae said. "Please, sit down."

"Let me get you something," Laru protested. "Milk or—"

"Please, don't trouble yourself," Speaker Yeneri said. "We've already stuffed ourselves with Taela's marvelous eel pie. Your husband tells us your newborn arrived early."

Laru's smile faded. In her watery brown eyes, Sefina saw a sort of grief she recognized, as deep and boundless as the ocean. "Yes. By Of-the-Sea's grace, perhaps she may grow stronger."

"Perhaps...or maybe he's entreated his sister to help you."

"You mean Of-Blessed-Dreams might heal my baby?" Laru's voice caught, as though she didn't dare hope too hard. Sefina's own heart clenched at the cracked note of her voice.

"Give her to Mirae," Lady Lirath said. "My student has a proven record of healing injuries."

Perhaps, if we're counting my scraped knees as injuries. Sefina watched in silence as Laru passed the bundle to Mirae.

Mirae took the baby, adjusting the blankets to reveal her scrunched face. Sefina had never seen a face so small. The baby's eyes stayed shut and she remained perfectly still in Mirae's arms, without so much as a whine or whimper for her mother.

"She sleeps most of the time," Brom said, hovering near Mirae's shoulder. "I never thought I'd long for a babe's cries, but now, I'd give anything for a loud and boisterous girl."

"A wake-up song, then," Mirae said, stroking the baby's hair. She opened her mouth and their song poured forth, a stream of crystal clear notes that filled the humble shack with light and warmth.

> *The sun's begun to rise, the moon has gone away.*
> *Open up your eyes and greet a brand new day!*
> *Wake up! Wake up! Flowers bloom, birds sing.*
> *Wake up! Wake up! Good morning, everything!*

As Mirae's final note died away, the baby's eyes opened. She looked around, her soft brown irises bleary and unfocused in the way of infants, but clearly alert. She wriggled in her wrappings and began rooting into Mirae's chest.

Mirae returned Sela to Laru, who took her in shaking arms, peering down with a face the picture of wonder. "You woke her?" Tenderly, she unwrapped the baby and stroked her pudgy fists, which began to wave in the air. "Her hands are warm! Brom, feel her skin."

Brom stroked the baby's cheek. Tears leaked from his eyes and rolled down his face to salt his beard. He pulled Laru and the baby into his arms, hugging them tight.

The ache in Sefina's stomach dissolved as she looked at the three of them. Her heart swelled with happiness and more than a little awe. Mirae had performed another miracle, one of her greatest yet. She sidled over and took Mirae's hand. "You did it," she whispered, squeezing. "I knew you would."

"Of course she did." Lady Lirath stepped up behind them, placing both hands upon Mirae's shoulders. "Our beloved Mirae is chosen by Of-Blessed-Dreams herself."

Sefina felt Mirae's arm shift downward as her shoulders sank beneath the pressure, as if she wasn't thrilled by Lady Lirath's touch. She wondered if Mirae would protest, but Brom spoke up, still clinging to his wife and child. "Anything in my power to give is yours, Lady Mirae. My thanks, my service—anything at all…"

"None of that will be necessary." Mirae chewed her lower lip, almost as though she were embarrassed for once. Normally, she preened under such attentions, but something seemed to have come over her, a sort of quiet uncertainty. "It's enough to know I helped someone."

"There must be something," Brom said, almost pleading.

Mirae tucked some loose curls behind her ear with her free hand. "I'd love to watch you do the barrel dance again someday."

"And," Lady Lirath said, "a small donation to the temple—"

"—is not necessary," Speaker Yeneri said, raising her voice. "Our purpose is to serve you." Though she didn't turn and glare at Lady Lirath, the censure in her voice was clear. A strong, steely aura radiated from her bent frame, as though daring Lady Lirath to try again.

Lady Lirath removed her hands from Mirae's shoulders and pursed her lips. She remained silent after that, but Brom and his family were too overjoyed to notice. Little Sela gurgled and wriggled as though she might never need sleep again.

Sefina smiled and exhaled a long breath. Mirae caught her eye, smiling back. In that moment, Sefina felt no trace of jealousy—only pure love and admiration. Mirae had performed a miracle worthy of the Eight and Sefina was unspeakably proud to be her disciple. To be known and loved by one so full of grace and goodness.

They remained at Brom's house until duskbell, accepting a meal of roasted fish as a token of Laru's thanks. As they departed, with full bellies and fuller hearts, Sefina caught Speaker Yeneri slipping more gold pieces into Brom's palm. Neither did she miss his attempts to give them back, only to be rebuffed.

"If you don't need them, give them to some of your neighbors in need of help," Speaker Yeneri whispered, following up with a secretive wink. Only then did Brom accept the gold into his closed fist and bid them goodbye.

Upon returning to their carriage further down the street, Lady Lirath raised her eyebrows. "I must admit, I half-expected to find the groom tied up and our horses gone."

Speaker Yeneri shook her head. "The people here know to whom this carriage belongs. They also know Of-Blessed-Dreams and those who dwell in her temple will provide for them when they're in need. Shame on you, Raula, for suggesting such a thing."

"It only takes one rotten apple to spoil the bunch," Lady Lirath said. "One thief among a hundred good men means stolen horses."

Speaker Yeneri ignored her and addressed Mirae. "You've performed a great deed today, Mirae. The world is full of people like Brom and his family. People in need of help."

"I want to help them," Mirae said without hesitation.

"Of course," Lady Lirath said, "but there may be limits to your abilities that we don't yet know. Also, your education must take priority. There is still much to learn." Though she spoke to Mirae, Sefina suspected the words were for Speaker Yeneri's benefit.

"Let her be yours on Firstdays through Fifthdays, and mine on Sixdays and Sevendays. As always, she shall have Eightdays for herself."

"Sevendays?" Lady Lirath frowned. "With all due respect, Speaker, that day is for—"

"I know whom Sevenday is for. What better way to spend it than to allow Mirae to use the gifts Of-Blessed-Dreams has bestowed upon her?"

The argument ended there, with Speaker Yeneri having the final word. They drove home as twilight descended over the city; an unusually silent ride, considering Mirae was present. Occasionally, Sefina glanced over to see her peering out the window. She gazed back toward the disappearing docks as though she wasn't ready to leave.

Though Mirae said nothing, Sefina understood. These were Mirae's people, whom she hadn't lived amongst for years. The person she loved most was about to embark upon a new path, a new journey. She only hoped Mirae would allow her to share in it sometimes.

* * * *

That night, driven by an invisible force she couldn't name, Sefina crept out of bed while Mirae slept. She threw a scarf around her shoulders to ward off the midnight chill, took an unlit candle from her nightstand, and slipped silently from the room.

Only a few lonely torches still burned at such a late hour. Sefina found the nearest one, lit her candle, and crept along the empty halls toward the back of the temple. She encountered no one else, not even another disobedient apprentice sneaking into the kitchens for a midnight snack, as Mirae often convinced her to do.

She soon arrived at her destination, the wrought iron gate that led into the sanctuary. It was perhaps the only part of the temple she wouldn't be punished for visiting so late, so long as she claimed she was there to pray. The iron doors were kept open and the torches burned at all hours for a reason.

With a glance over her shoulder, Sefina tip-toed through the gate. It was even darker inside the sanctuary, so she lifted her candle higher. Faint light danced across the statues, almost tricking her mind into seeing movement. But, no. The statues maintained their silent vigil. The ceiling of stars above seemed as distant and timeless as ever.

Sefina examined each statue from left to right, pausing to study their lifelike features, before settling on Of-Blessed-Dreams. She approached the altar, admiring the wide assortment of offerings. Sketches, sheet music, whittled wood, and paint-stained brushes filled the stone table, along with the usual flowers and jewelry.

After another furtive glance, Sefina took a feathered quill, dipped it in a mostly empty ink pot, and tore the corner from a scrap of sheet music. She knelt before Of-Blessed-Dreams' altar, gazing up at the goddess' face. Her joyful smile reminded Sefina a great deal of Mirae. The sculptor who had carved her likeness had done so with great love and care.

Sefina swallowed, but when she tried to speak, no words came. Shame stopped up her throat, burning in her eyes as well. She squeezed them shut, blinking back tears. Perhaps she would have to think her prayer instead. She closed her eyes and bowed her head, placing the objects she'd taken on her lap.

Of-Blessed-Dreams? It's me. Sefina. You probably already know that... She worked her lips nervously, only to realize her jaw was clenched tight. She softened it and continued. *You also know what Mirae did today. What she did a week ago.*

She bit her cheek. The dragon she often did battle with wrapped its coils around her heart and choked without mercy.

Why can't I do what Mirae does? Why is she the special one when I'm so...

Terrible.

Selfish.

Ordinary.

There were too many words to choose from.

If I can't be a miracle-worker like Mirae, what is my purpose? Speaker Yeneri says the world needs thousands of voices, but what good is mine? I can't even get through five minutes of Lady Lirath's lessons without doing something wrong.

Sefina waited, but neither heard nor felt any sort of answer. She sighed and opened her eyes, staring down at the paper and quill in her lap. This exercise had been useless. Why should Of-Blessed-Dreams listen to the prayers of a nobody?

She made to stand up, only to stop when she spotted something hanging from the stone slab to her left. Of-Our-Hearts' altar. It was a strand of violet creeper, a beautiful and rare flowering vine which climbed the trunks of trees to find the sun. A well-known symbol of love, for its close dependence on the tree, and also a common ingredient in various medicines and perfumes.

A half-formed thought prodded at Sefina's mind. *Maybe that's my purpose? Few trees have violet creepers, but all violet creepers need a tree. They need something to wrap around and cling to or they'll never find the sun.*

The sense of peace she'd hoped for settled over her at last. All by herself, she might only be an ordinary tree, but as Mirae's friend, she was also host to something far more miraculous. While she remained sturdy in the background, Mirae could cling to her and grow.

Thank you, Of-Blessed-Dreams. Or is it Of-Our-Hearts? I'll always be her tree, and I won't be jealous of her flowers anymore. I promise.

She took the quill and scribbled a small drawing, a tree which looked more like a cloud until she added two lines for its trunk. Around it, she drew a spiral for the violet creeper. Then, she held the paper's edge to the candle. It burned quickly, curling up into black smoke and rising toward the starry ceiling. She would never be a miracle-worker, but she nonetheless had a purpose. That was enough.

As Sefina rose and took up her candle, she glanced at the ceiling one last time. Perhaps it was her imagination, but the pinpricks of light seemed brighter, as though the stars were somehow drawing closer.

A sudden chill washed over her, sending a shiver down her spine. The flame of her candle flickered and dimmed, nearly going out. She pulled her scarf tighter around her shoulders. The warmth and peace she'd felt disappeared, replaced by a strange and hollow numbness that started in the nape of her neck and spread throughout her limbs.

Sefina hurried out of the sanctuary, cupping a hand over the flame of her candle to keep it lit. She set a quick pace, nearly a jog, until she rounded the nearest corner. The chill in her veins dissolved and the flame of her candle grew tall again. She hung her head, exhaling with relief. She had no idea which god had reached out to her in that moment, but she didn't want to know. Probably not one of The Eight, for they were mostly benevolent...

Unless a mortal has been evil and wicked. Did one of them cast judgment upon me?

She hurried away, resolving even more firmly to be Mirae's silent and stalwart support. Perhaps it had been a warning, a glimpse of what would happen if she didn't stamp out her petty jealousy once and for all. Sure that thinking on it would only make it stronger, she forced it from her mind. She crept back to her bedroom, relieved to find Mirae fast asleep, huddled in a ball beneath the covers.

Sefina climbed into bed, cuddling against Mirae's back and inhaling the scent of her hair. She closed her eyes and tried to calm her racing heart. Even with Mirae beside her, it took her several more hours to fall asleep. When she did, it was a light and restless slumber, full of confusing images and even stranger feelings.

Once, she was certain she saw a distant black silhouette against the night sky, or perhaps the rolling surface of the sea. The figure extended its arm toward her, but Sefina turned away and closed her eyes tight, unwilling to face whatever it was.

When dawnbell rang at last, she woke lathered in sweat and even more exhausted than before. However, she managed a genuine smile when Mirae opened her eyes and gazed at her with a soft, sleepy look.

"Morning, Fina. Do you want the washroom first? My arms and legs feel like noodles. I think I slept funny."

"Thanks," Sefina said, but she stayed in bed a while longer anyway, content to lie beside Mirae and wallow beneath the covers. Despite her weariness, today was the day to begin her new growth as a fine, sturdy tree.

Chapter Eight

SEFINA SANG, FIXING HER gaze on an invisible point behind Lady Lirath's head. Observing her teacher's face meant frowns and a furrowed brow, which in turn meant more mistakes. It was a dreary gray Sevenday, one of many Mirae had chosen to spend in Easton rather than lessons. Still, Sefina's voice filled the room with a rich warmth that Lady Lirath had not yet cut off. A good sign.

"Make the high notes float," Lady Lirath said, waving for Sefina to sing through the critique. "Give them a weightless quality. You should know from listening to Mirae."

Sefina tightened her core and expanded her lungs. While keeping her stomach tight, she slowed the flow of air, allowing the notes to resonate within the roundness at the back of her mouth.

"Better," Lady Lirath said. "Continue."

Sefina stole a breath, as well as a glance at Lady Lirath's face. Her frown had disappeared, though a furrow still creased her forehead. She started the next phrase.

Lady Lirath placed a hand upon her desk, drumming her fingers agitatedly upon its surface. "Your eighth notes, Sefina! Make a smoothly running stream of your voice, not the incessant rocking of a ship full of drunken sailors."

Sefina blocked out the paisley curtains surrounding her, the scent of tallow, even Lady Lirath's voice. She sang instead to Mirae, who wasn't there despite her wishes.

The eighth notes flowed like sparkling water from a decanter. Sefina felt as well as heard them. Even Lady Lirath raised a brow. She motioned again, but without her usual impatience.

Encouraged, Sefina built toward the final note. She thought of Mirae's smile. Of the way Mirae made her heart skip and her head float. The peak of the phrase hovered in the air like delicate filigree, shimmering there before tapering into gentle, satisfying silence.

The unexpected sound of applause filled the room. Sefina started, turning toward the door. A middle-aged man with a pale complexion, light blue eyes, and a neat, waxd goatee stood in the doorway. Though his hair was honey brown rather than silver-blonde, his resemblance to Lady Lirath struck Sefina immediately. The similarity was apparent in their gazes, icy and intense.

"Bravo!" His voice was a fine baritone, his smile full of straight white teeth. "Your praise for this young lady's skill is no exaggeration, cousin."

Sefina stiffened, then dipped into a respectful bow. If he had addressed Lady Lirath as cousin, this could be no one but Stagford's regent, Horace Stagford the Third. She'd never met him before, but she knew he attended the temple's solstice festivals. During those performances, she often sang toward the shadowy balconies overlooking the temple foyer, hoping he and the other nobles could hear her.

Lady Lirath stepped away from her desk and bowed to the regent, touching her forehead to the backs of his hands. She lifted her head and smiled a smile of familiarity, becoming far more relaxd. "A pleasure to welcome you to the Temple of Dreams, Horace. Forgive me for failing to meet you. I thought your visit was next week?"

"Think nothing of it." The regent returned Lady Lirath's smile, but his gaze wandered past her shoulder to land upon Sefina. "In fact, the pleasure is all mine."

Sefina kept her eyes down. The regent's leather boots were so brightly polished that they could have reflected his face. A quick glance told her he wore tailored black breeches with shiny gold buckles, a shirt of purple silk, and an embroidered vest. The scent of citrus caught Sefina's nose, momentarily eclipsing the smell of the tallow candles.

"I found myself unexpectedly free and could not contain my curiosity. Word of your miraculous student has spread like wildfire all through Castletown."

Sefina's face burned. *Oh no. Does he believe I'm actually...*

"You must be the lovely and mysterious Mirae." The regent crossed the room to offer Sefina his hands. They were soft, with trimmed and polished nails. She touched her forehead to his knuckles, then looked up into another dazzling smile. Though not quite handsome, he was so well put together that one might easily be fooled into thinking so.

Sefina's stomach sank. It wasn't the first time someone had mistaken her for Mirae only to end up disappointed. "I fear you're mistaken, sir. My name is Sefina. Though I'm not Mirae, I am most fortunate to call Lady Lirath my teacher as well."

"I see." The regent's charming smile remained in place, which lifted him in Sefina's estimation. "Lady Sefina. Yes, my cousin has mentioned you as well. No wonder I was so taken by your voice. You have a rare gift indeed."

A blush rose to Sefina's cheeks. To be addressed as 'Lady Sefina' and praised by someone of such high standing sent a shiver down her spine. For once, Mirae wasn't there to compete. She had the Regent's full attention.

"I'm glad you've come, Horace," Lady Lirath said, "but I fear your visit is in vain. Mirae has accompanied Speaker Yeneri to Easton this afternoon."

The regent's brow furrowed. "That is a disappointment. I so wished to meet her. However, I would hardly call my visit wasted...that is, if your lovely student would do me the honor of performing once more."

Sefina's pulse picked up speed. She swelled with confidence, that morning's critiques all but forgotten. She looked to Lady Lirath, who nodded her agreement.

"Of course. Sefina, sing for him."

Sefina retrieved her lute from its stand beside her foot. She strummed the chords of a seasonal ballad before joining in with the words.

> *Midwinter blows her icy breath*
> *Over hill and dale.*
> *Silent snow drifts gently down,*
> *The season's stark white veil.*
> *But hark! Green sprouts poke from the ground*
> *To hear the bluebirds sing.*
> *The flowers show their faces for*
> *To welcome Lady Spring.*
> *Of-the-Earth has come awake*
> *To greet his youngest daughter.*
> *Their tears to melt the icicles*
> *'Til they are naught but water.*
> *Of-the-Sky's bright golden eye*
> *Beholds their child with pride.*
> *And bids farewell to Winter,*
> *As their eldest stands aside.*
> *For they love all four children,*
> *Each one in equal part.*
> *Each one to their own season,*
> *But always in their hearts.*

Sefina held her breath as the final note faded to nothing. Her gaze darted between Lady Lirath and the regent, searching their faces for some sign of approval. It came in the form of more applause.

"Wonderful!" The regent's tone was bright and enthusiastic. "You have transformed a simple ballad into a rare thing of beauty."

Lady Lirath's lips relaxd out of their usual thin line as a rare smile crossed her face. "Well sung, Sefina."

Her praise made Sefina feel as though she'd downed an entire cup of wine, all warm and tingly from head to toe. Lady Lirath never gave false compliments. Sefina silenced the whisper of doubt that suggested she might do so before someone so grand as the regent.

"Lady Sefina, you should be in concert," said the regent. "Why Raula, you've been hiding not one, but two magnificent treasures from everyone of importance in Stagford!"

"A mistake I shall soon rectify," Lady Lirath said. "A concert featuring my prized pupils is long overdue, rather than simple children's songs at the solstice with the temple choir. I will mention it to Speaker Yeneri. Perhaps such an event would allow you the opportunity to meet our Mirae."

The regent stroked his silky beard between two fingers. "I look forward to it then." To Sefina's shock, he offered her a wink. "We will see each other again soon, Lady Sefina. Until then, best of luck with your musical studies. Not that you need luck with such raw talent."

She placed her lute upon its stand and dipped her head. It was a struggle to summon words amidst such breathless excitement, but somehow she managed. "You flatter me, Lord Regent."

"Stating the truth as I hear it is hardly flattery." With a quick buss to Lady Lirath's cheeks, the regent departed.

"Well done," Lady Lirath said, placing a warm hand upon Sefina's shoulder. It took her a moment to notice the touch, dazed as she was. "Your performance and behavior were exemplary, my dear. I'm most proud of you."

"You are?" Sefina asked, struggling but failing to hide the tremor that threatened her voice.

"You know I only push you because I believe in your potential. My cousin is an expert judge of skill. If he finds you intriguing, all the better."

Something about that word—intriguing—made Sefina's stomach squirm. Her tingling delight vanished, replaced by a frigid sense of dread. "Please, Lady Lirath, speak plainly. What do you mean?"

Lady Lirath adjusted the collar of Sefina's green robe with an affectionate tug. "My cousin seems quite taken with you. It would be an excellent match, in a few years' time."

"Oh." Sefina's heart crumbled. Her pride sank to her shoes. She could no longer trust the regent's appraisal of her musicianship, nor Lady Lirath's. *Stupid, stupid, stupid! How am I supposed to reject someone in such a position of power, especially without disappointing Lady Lirath?*

But Lady Lirath sensed her apprehension. "You're young yet, at seventeen, my dear," she said, tucking a loose loc of hair behind Sefina's ear. "My cousin he may be, but I will not force you to marry against your will. It will be some years before you're ready for a husband anyway—or a wife, if you must make things complicated in your usual manner. In the meantime, I suggest you indulge his attentions so long as they remain innocent. Such a relationship, romantic or not, will only benefit your future."

Lady Lirath's final sentences drifted in one ear and out the other. Sefina remained stuck on the word 'wife' and hadn't listened further. "You would permit me to have a wife?" Her heart hammered against the cage of her ribs. She hadn't realized how much she cared about and feared Lady Lirath's answer before asking the question.

"If no man could make you happy," Lady Lirath said, "I would do my best to find a woman whose social standing and connections would benefit you. More difficult to arrange, but not impossible for someone of my resources."

Sefina threw her arms around Lady Lirath's neck and clung there. She wept, tears of relief rolling down her cheeks. Though Lady Lirath stiffened at first, she relaxd and returned the embrace. "I suppose I have my work cut out for me. No need for tears, my Sefina. You haven't disappointed me in this."

Had she not been so overcome with emotion, Sefina might have thought to inform Lady Lirath that she had no need of assistance. Mirae was her one and only choice. If Mirae wouldn't have her, she had already decided to live her life without a spouse. Nevertheless, it was a heavy weight lifted from her shoulders.

"You should seek my cousin's favor even if you won't have him as a husband," Lady Lirath said while Sefina struggled to stay her tears. "He may yet do you the honor of becoming your patron. We artists are always in need of those."

"Will the Temple of Dreams not provide for me?" Sefina sniffled, her voice rough.

"Of course," Lady Lirath said, "but the temple itself requires ample funding. Someday, when you are in a position of authority here, it will be your responsibility to solicit donations from Stagford's wealthiest. Despite what Speaker Yeneri says, the temple cannot run on music, stories, and art alone. Invaluable though they are, such treasures are funded with silver and gold. The belly cannot eat music as the soul does."

Sefina's mind came to a sudden halt. *A position of authority? Lady Lirath thinks me worthy of such responsibility?* She almost hugged Lady Lirath again. For once, she was glad she'd remained behind rather than venturing into Easton with Mirae. She and Lady Lirath had shared something special in meeting the regent and discussing her future, a future that seemed much brighter than it had earlier that morning.

* * * *

The rest of the day's lessons went smoothly. Lady Lirath was almost complimentary. When Mirae entered their room at duskbell, the hem of her robe stained brown with dried mud, Sefina was all smiles.

"Had a nice day, did we?" she asked, taking Mirae's headscarf and folding it over her forearm.

Mirae yawned, only covering her mouth at the last moment. "A tiring day," she said, flopping backward onto the bed without getting undressed.

Sefina grabbed her wrists, pulling her up into a seated position. "You'll get the sheets dusty."

Reluctantly, Mirae dragged herself out of bed and shucked her clothes, selecting a clean nightgown from the wardrobe.

"Wash your face," Sefina told her.

"Yes, mother." Mirae rolled her eyes but did as Sefina said, leaving the door to the washroom open.

Sefina followed, standing before the mirror and taking up a hairbrush. She did her best not to peek at Mirae's reflection in the mirror. It was a battle she was destined to lose. She couldn't help but steal a glance as Mirae lifted her face from her cupped hands, a droplet of water falling from her full lower lip. Her brown skin had taken on a rich, warm hue in the candlelight.

"What about your day?" Mirae asked. "Was it nice?"

"As a matter of fact it was."

Mirae stole the hairbrush and took over the task of taming Sefina's hair. "Will you tell me about it or gloat over your secrets?"

Sefina snorted. "I keep no secrets from you."

Mirae smirked, showing both dimples. "Then talk."

"Lord Regent Stagford visited the temple today. His purpose was to meet with you, but he overheard my lesson with Lady Lirath and paid me many fine compliments."

Mirae's face puckered in the mirror as though she'd bitten straight into a lemon. "And you believed him?"

Sefina winced. Her mouth opened, but she couldn't summon an immediate response. Mirae's words had cut deep, and she bled anger. She snatched the brush from Mirae's hand, slamming it onto the vanity. "Why should I doubt his assessment? Lady Lirath told me just this afternoon that I'm a singer and musician of rare skill, even if I cannot raise the dead or whatever impossible thing you've accomplished lately."

Mirae's brows knitted together. One of her hands rose, as if to caress Sefina's arm, but she seemed to think better of it. "I didn't mean to insult you, Fina. You're a wonderful singer. I only worry because Speaker Yeneri has told me several things about the Regent. According to her, he's a selfish man who puts himself before the people of Stagford. I was questioning his honesty, not your abilities."

Sefina's anger drained away as quickly as it had flared within her. Perhaps she was overly sensitive. Mirae always recognized and celebrated her talents, mediocre as they were in comparison. It was her own self-doubt that had caused her to lash out, that ever-growing chink in her armor.

She hung her head. "Forgive me. There was no need for me to shout." She offered Mirae the brush as an apology, her gaze still downcast.

Mirae took up the brush and tapped Sefina's shoulder, urging her to face the mirror again. She continued tending to Sefina's hair in silence a while, her strokes gentle, before saying, "You know, my voice can't fix everything. My abilities are limited, as Of-Blessed-Dreams harshly reminded me today."

Sefina met Mirae's gaze in the mirror. Her dark brown irises shone with sadness. She chastised herself for failing to notice sooner. "What happened?"

"A young boy was hit by a carriage today. I tried to heal him, but Of-Eternal-Sleep claimed his soul first. He died in my arms while his parents watched, pleading for me to save him."

The pain written on Mirae's face and threaded through her voice tugged on Sefina's heartstrings. She hadn't considered the downside of Mirae's powers before—that they were limited, perhaps not a perfect solution. Affection swelled within her. She found she loved Mirae even more for this newly revealed vulnerability.

She stilled Mirae's hand, turning to embrace her. Mirae smelled of the sea when Sefina buried her nose in the crook of her neck. Just like always. She felt Mirae give a hitched sob in her arms, then begin to cry against her shoulder. She rubbed circles between Mirae's shoulders, holding her close and hoping it would be enough.

Mirae's tears were only a brief summer rainstorm. She cleared her throat and lifted her head, blinking the last of them away. "Sorry..."

"That's why you asked about my day, isn't it?" Sefina whispered, running her hands along Mirae's trembling back. "You hoped to hear good news."

Mirae nodded, still sniffing.

"I do have some, if you want to hear."

Mirae pulled back, but didn't leave the circle of Sefina's arms. "Please."

"Lady Lirath wishes us to put on a concert. You might not find it as exciting as your work in Easton, but it would mean a great deal to me. Many of Stagford's nobles will be there and Lady Lirath intends to solicit donations for the temple. 'You cannot eat music,' as she says. Perhaps your parents might come?"

A slow smile spread across Mirae's face. "Of course. I love performing with you, Flna. Our very own concert? If such an opportunity fills the temple treasury, all the better, but I would do it for nothing so long as you sing with me."

All of Sefina's sadness, her gnawing doubts, were forgotten. As Mirae had said, any opportunity to sing together was a gift. "What program should we perform?"

"A joyful one," Mirae said. "One to stir the audience's hearts until they can't help but dance and clap."

Sefina laughed. "Lady Lirath might disapprove. I suspect she envisions something formal."

"Something traditional and technically demanding, you mean. Well, Lady Lirath can deal with her disappointment. If this is to be our concert, Fina, let it be our concert. All the stuffy nobles will love it. They'll gladly open their pocketbooks and gold-pouches."

"Perhaps some love songs? Those are always popular." Secretly, Sefina longed for an opportunity to indulge in her secret feelings, especially in a manner that bore no risk. By following someone else's words and melodies, she could pour her passion into something beautiful without fear of rejection.

"Love songs are my favorite," Mirae said.

Sefina almost fainted dead away when Mirae leaned in to kiss her cheek. Mirae's lips were warm and soft, like the brush of sun-kissed flower petals against her skin. If melted gold had run through her veins instead of blood, only to gather in her core and drip from between her legs, she could only imagine it would feel much the same. Her smallclothes were soaked in a matter of moments.

"I—I should lie down," Sefina stammered, taking a step back. Part of her was terrified Mirae would notice her helpless state. Cold sweat ran down the groove of her spine even as her skin burned. "I'm quite tired."

Mirae's brow softened with concern. "Sleep, then. I'll sing you a lullaby tonight, shall I?"

Once they climbed in bed, Mirae sang the same song Sefina usually did. Their song. She stroked Sefina's hair, urging her to rest a cheek upon her shoulder. Sefina obliged, relaxing at the steady thump of Mirae's heartbeat beneath her ear, yet still vibrating with the memory of Mirae's lips.

She closed her eyes and pretended to fall asleep long before she actually drifted off. She knew she would never cross into the land of dreams so long as she was this close to Mirae. She remained awake long after Mirae's head lolled to one side and she began to snore, aching with want, yet overwhelmed by the nearness of their bodies.

I'll find a way to tell you, Sefina pledged as Mirae's snoring evened into slow, steady breaths. *Before the concert.* Afraid as she was, she knew she couldn't keep her feelings secret for much longer. Spun in with the terror of the rejection was a warm thread of hope. Hope that Mirae might miraculously feel the same. *For aren't you always saying you love no one else in the world so much as me?*

Chapter Nine

THE CONCERT CAME TOGETHER before Sefina could process all the moving parts. Speaker Yeneri warmly approved, granting use of the temple foyer and its stage. The date was set for Candlenight, the final evening of summer. After the concert, there would be a feast to bid Summer farewell and hail Autumn's arrival.

Better still, Lady Lirath made no objections when Sefina asked to set the program. When she mentioned love songs, Lady Lirath recommended a lesser-known ballad which told a tale of love between two women. Sefina took the suggestion as a sign of support, one which she found deeply moving.

As the short weeks of summer flew by, she and Mirae polished their repertoire. They rehearsed past duskbell in Lady Lirath's studio, alone in their room, or out by the pond when the weather was fair. Sefina's favorite song became the ballad Lady Lirath had suggested. It gave a voice to all her tender feelings, offering a temporary reprieve from her inner turmoil.

The ballad's subjects had their own struggle. Triss and Isa, lovers from the warring cities of Whitecliff and Greenvale, were separated by a large stone wall. Undeterred, they climbed in the dead of night to meet upon the ramparts. Unlike many tragic ballads of similar mode, this one ended happily. Of-Our-Hearts took pity and tore the wall down, a divine mandate for the cities to end their feud.

Though there were no stone walls to separate her from Mirae, Sefina understood Triss and Isa's longing. She would climb any wall, even the tallest mountains, for a chance to gaze into Mirae's eyes and see her own love reflected there.

Still, as the evenings grew cooler and the trees at the pond's edge changed color, Sefina couldn't find the courage to confess. The words hovered upon her tongue, needing only the slightest breath to send them from her heart to Mirae's ears, yet fear froze her lips. In that terrifying moment, having some small slice of Mirae seemed better than to risk losing all of her.

So went her silent suffering, until that night. The night everything changed.

It wasn't a serious rehearsal so much as a stolen break at the end of a busy Sixthday. Frogs and crickets chirped as she and Mirae sat beneath their favorite willow tree, its flower-laden branches falling around them in a curtain. Mirae serenaded the nighttime creatures while Sefina strummed idle chords upon her lute, following the aimless line of Mirae's melody.

Then Mirae modulated into the ballad's opening. "Cold stone stands before us, a wall between our kingdoms."

Without pausing to think, Sefina sang the answering phrase. "Yet Of-Our-Hearts shows mercy, guiding our love to freedom."

Mirae abandoned her braced position against the willow tree to lie on her back. She rested her head in Sefina's lap, singing up toward her. "Every duskbell without fail, my dearest, I shall find you."

Sefina's breath caught. The first stars of evening were reflected within the dark pools of Mirae's eyes. It was all she could do to sing the next line without losing her voice. "And yet the darkness wanes, the hours far too few."

Mirae braced herself on her elbows, rising closer toward Sefina. "To feel your breath upon my cheek, your lips against my ear. For to whisper words of love, words I so long to hear..."

Sefina's fingers fell away from the lute. She set it aside, sliding a hand beneath Mirae's head to cup the coiled braids pinned behind her neck. She had no idea where her rush of bravery came from, but she barreled on, unable to stop. "With strength of arm and callused hands, no wall shall bar my way. Climbing ever upward to see your face, lovelier than day."

They hovered inches apart. Sefina dared not move. Her thumping heartbeat became a distant echo as her eyes landed on Mirae's lips, full and slightly parted. She wondered if she were trapped in a dream, a bubble easily popped if she so much as breathed wrong.

Mirae rose to kiss her, light as a flutterbug's wings. It was the softest possible meeting of mouths, yet it shook Sefina to her core. It took her far too long to realize she should kiss back. When she parted her lips, Mirae's fingers sank into her hair, sending her into a dizzying spiral. Only Mirae's voice had ever taken her to such heights.

Too soon, Mirae withdrew. Sefina tried to chase her mouth, but Mirae had stolen her breath along with the kiss.

Mirae stroked her cheek with trembling fingers. "You love me, don't you, Fina? Please, say you love me."

With no remaining doubts to still her tongue, Sefina's confession poured forth. "I love you so desperately that I shall never have anyone else."

They kissed again, deeper.

Mirae tasted of warmth and salt, of coming home. Only then did Sefina understand. Such keen-edged craving could never be satisfied, only temporarily sated. She would never have enough of Mirae, no matter how much Mirae chose to give. The realization struck Sefina helpless, yet she couldn't help but surrender.

She had no idea what to do next, other than faint dead away from happiness. Fortunately, Mirae did. She stood and offered Sefina her hand, leading her from the willow tree with a grip so tight it almost hurt. Sefina forgot her lute by the tree and would have left it there if Mirae hadn't reminded her with a whispered word.

They hurried into the temple and through the empty halls with clasped hands. When they reached their room, Sefina's lute ended up on top of the dresser, all but forgotten.

Sefina trembled like autumn's last leaf as Mirae undressed her, but felt no cold. Not even when Mirae lifted her robe, exposing her arms and stomach to the air. Fire crawled wherever Mirae's eyes roamed. Her gaze threatened to devour Sefina whole.

"Fina," Mirae murmured, peeling Sefina's undershirt up and away. A question wavered in her voice, but Sefina scarcely noticed, dizzy and overwhelmed as she was. She would have done anything Mirae asked, obeyed her every command, for the simple joy of knowing she'd pleased this marvelous woman.

Sefina offered no resistance when Mirae walked her into the bed. She sat when her knees hit the mattress, watching Mirae strip off her robe and smallclothes. She could only stare in awe as the last garment fell, too overwhelmed to speak.

The sight of Mirae standing naked before her, the soft slope of her shoulders and rounded hips outlined in gold by candlelight, was Sefina's undoing. She'd seen Mirae naked before, but this was entirely different. This time, Mirae had bared herself with purpose. Sefina understood it for the gift it was.

Mirae joined her on the bed, tipping her onto her back. The brush of her bare skin, so achingly soft, made a pounding drum of Sefina's heart. An echo of the same drumbeat throbbed lower as Mirae's knee slid between her thighs, spreading them apart.

"I love you," Mirae whispered against her lips.

Sefina couldn't find space to respond before Mirae kissed her again, but it didn't matter. She knew what they were to each other. What they would always be. She shuddered, intensely aware of her burning skin—cold and tingling against the air, molten hot where it met Mirae's bare flesh.

Mirae cupped Sefina's breasts, thumbs skimming her stiffened nipples. Sefina sighed encouragement into the crook of Mirae's throat, rising to meet her thigh. Her hips hovered, then began rocking in urgent rhythm. A gasp escaped her throat as she slid along a stripe of her own wetness, painted slick and warm upon Mirae's thigh. Mirae bore down to meet her, cupping Sefina's backside in both hands and urging her on.

Sefina clung to Mirae's shoulders with tight desperation. Mirae was her everything, her anchor through it all. When Mirae's warm mouth found her neck, she came undone, riding an unexpected release with Mirae's lips upon her collar bone and those wonderful hands squeezing her rear, holding her close.

Never before had she reached such heights. The smaller peaks she'd given herself before in the bath—always imagining Mirae's fingers instead of her own—were nothing in comparison, mere ripples rather than a riptide.

As Sefina floated, Mirae's mouth traveled lower, kissing her left breast before taking the sensitive tip. Sefina stiffened as a curious hand cupped between her legs, then relaxd again. It was Mirae, only Mirae. As Mirae's teasing fingers traced her entrance, easing forward, she lost herself all over again. As she gave herself over, she felt no pain—only wonderful fullness. To feel Mirae move inside her was paradise, every curl and stroke divine.

"You're so warm," Mirae whispered against Sefina's chest, her breath a hot pant. Her thumb grazed the aching bud above Sefina's entrance, circling slowly.

Sefina arched and threw her head back, afraid she might melt away into nothing. It was Mirae's words as much as her fingers that granted her second release. To know that one so special as Mirae loved her filled all the empty chambers of her heart. She cried Mirae's name, trembling inside and out.

When Sefina returned to herself, breathing heavily and lathered in sweat, she took note of the tension in Mirae's body. Slick, telling heat pressed against her thigh. She had no idea what possessed her other than instinct, but she grasped Mirae's waist, urging her forward to take a kneeling position.

"Mirae, please."

Though Sefina mourned the loss of Mirae's fingers, she forgot her disappointment as Mirae settled over her. Her outer lips were dark and gleaming, her scent rich, the flavor sharp with salt. Sefina buried her tongue without hesitation, eager to learn it all.

Mirae's low moans filled the room, sweet as any song she'd ever sung. Sefina's heart soared. This melody was for her alone, shaped around the syllables of her name. She worked her tongue deeper, opening wide enough to suck the swollen bundle above Mirae's entrance.

Radiant joy swelled within Sefina's chest as Mirae found release against her mouth, covering her lips and chin in silken heat. Though her hips jerked at the end, Sefina tended to her with all the gentleness she could manage. She kept going until Mirae pushed her head back onto the pillow, begging for reprieve with a glassy-eyed stare.

Mirae stretched out beside Sefina and kissed her. A slow, sure kiss that promised they would share many more nights like this one. Sefina embraced her, shivering atop the covers, simultaneously exhausted and alight with energy.

"How long have you loved me?" Sefina asked Mirae in the darkness.

The candle on the nightstand had long since burnt out, but Sefina heard the snort of Mirae's laughter. "Since always. Haven't I told you so every day since we were children?"

To have confirmation that Mirae had loved her as long as she'd loved Mirae was like a horse-kick to the chest, only far more pleasant. "Why not tell me sooner?"

"I wanted you to come to me." Mirae's voice was unusually hesitant as she cuddled closer against Sefina's side. "But tonight, when I heard you sing, I couldn't keep it in any longer."

Sefina tucked her head beneath Mirae's chin, breathing her scent deep. If she could have existed in such a moment forever, she would have done so without hesitation. "I didn't think I deserved you."

"Never say that again, Fina." Mirae shifted, peering down at her in the faint moonlight that peeked through the curtains. "Never even think it. I decide who is worthy of my love. You've earned it a thousand times over. I can only hope to earn yours in return."

"You already have."

This time, Sefina kissed Mirae first. For once, she believed.

She slept more peacefully that night than she had since early childhood. Her troubling dreams stayed far away, as did her self-doubts. There was only Mirae's warm skin, her steady heartbeat, and her familiar voice as she sang their lullaby.

> *The moon's begun to rise, the stars are on their way.*
> *So close your heavy eyes until a brand new day.*
> *Hush now, hush now. Night falls. Crickets cheep.*
> *Hush now, hush now. Rest your head and sleep.*

Mirae — Thirdday

MIRAE WIPES HER EYES upon her sleeve, her cheeks sore from smiling. Once the flow of tears stops, she remembers Yeneri is in the rowboat...no doubt listening to Sefina's story. She shakes her head, still smiling. "Sorry you had to hear those private details, Speaker. I doubt that was Sefina's intention."

Yeneri's black eyes twinkle, nearly swallowed by the wrinkles around her eyes. "Believe it or not, I remember such passions from my youth. I was blessed with both a husband and a wife at different times, though Of-Eternal-Sleep came for them before you knew me."

Mirae bites her lip to stifle laughter. Of course she knows the old were once young, and many retain the same passions well into their twilight years, but Yeneri was practically a third parent. It's difficult to imagine her partaking in a whirlwind romance, let alone two.

"You know, I've never forgotten the stretch of time when Sefina and I were so happily in love, but it feels so long ago now. Longer than two years. Too long ago to recapture. It's like my childhood home. If I were to return to Farsea, it wouldn't be the same. That version of Farsea lives only in cherished memories."

"True," Yeneri says, "but we make several homes for ourselves during our lifetimes. I, too, long for my childhood home sometimes, just as you long for your childhood love. However, the Temple of Dreams became more of a home to me than even my birthplace. I love it more than anywhere else in the world."

Mirae considers Yeneri's advice. Her childhood romance with Sefina is gone now. There is no way to go back and rediscover that time and those feelings. *But perhaps...perhaps, if I return, Sefina and I can make new memories. We can have a different love. A stronger love.*

She turns toward the pale gray light on the horizon. It's grown brighter since last she looked, as though the sun is rising. Dawnbell tolls a third time, welcoming a new day. A soft smile pulls at Mirae's lips and she takes a single step toward the shore.

The sea of stars disapproves. It pulls at her legs and Mirae realizes the water has risen to her waist. *When did the tide rise so far?* The water feels warmer too, perhaps because of the small motes of starlight swirling around her hips.

Mirae reaches down, cupping a few stars in her hands. They dance as they run through her fingers, flowing back into the sea where they belong. Where she could belong, too. She's dead, after all. Other mortals don't have the same choice she does. It would be unfair, almost like cheating, to take the second chance Yeneri is offering.

"Our love will always exist, won't it? It can't die the way mortals do. Even if I leave, it will still exist. In Sefina's heart and in mine. She'll join the sea of stars someday as well. We can have our new love then, can't we?"

Yeneri nods beneath her cloak. "Your death won't mean the death of your love. Of-Our-Hearts keeps such things alive forever."

Mirae's smile falters. Although Yeneri has agreed with her, she grieves at the thought she'll never see Sefina again. Not in the same way. They'll share no more sweet memories together, no more kisses, no more lullabies.

Though she hasn't entered its embrace yet, she knows the sea of stars is different. It's ancient and timeless. She will meet Sefina there someday, but it won't be the same. They won't be alive. *Am I ready to give up those memories yet to be born?*

Sefina calls out again, her voice warm and full of all the love Mirae remembers from those golden days. She turns toward the light, listening.

Chapter Ten

FOR THE REST OF that glorious summer, Sefina's life was as close to perfect as it had ever been. Her days were long, glowing things, her nights nothing short of rapturous. Mirae hardly left her side, traveling to Easton only on Sevendays. Lady Lirath's lessons became more like dress rehearsals and she gave fewer harsh critiques.

Sefina sang, laughed, and made love with Mirae constantly—beneath the willow tree, a hidden hay bale at the back of the stables, even once in Lady Lirath's studio while she was absent. Sefina considered it a blessing from Of-Our-Hearts that they were never caught, for she and Mirae were insatiable.

Two days before Candlenight, dawnbell heralded another lovely morning. Sefina woke naked in bed, limbs tangled with Mirae's beneath soft cotton sheets. When Mirae's soft brown eyes opened, tinted gold by the light streaming in through the curtains, it felt to Sefina like the true rising of the sun.

Rather than sing a good morning, Mirae rolled on top of Sefina and kissed her. They spent the first part of the morning twined together, clinging to each other until Sefina protested that if they didn't stop, they might not leave bed at all. They dressed, often trading kisses and growing distracted, and only made it to the kitchens well after breakfast.

There they found Speaker Yeneri, making slow work of a bowl of porridge. Sefina couldn't help but notice how her swollen hand struggled to hold the spoon, shaking as she lifted it to her lips. When Yeneri saw them, she lowered the spoon and smiled. "Ah. Mirae and Sefina. A pleasure to see you this fine morning. Where are you bound?"

"To a late breakfast now and nowhere special after," Mirae said. "We'd love to join you, if you'll allow us the privilege."

"The privilege is mine," said Speaker Yeneri. "I got a late start myself this morning." From the twinkle in her eye, Sefina wondered if the Speaker suspected the reason for their late arrival. She and Mirae hadn't told anyone of their romantic relationship, but hadn't taken great pains to hide it either.

Mirae took an empty chair beside Speaker Yeneri while Sefina headed for the kitchen counter. She retrieved two bowls and availed herself of the leftover porridge simmering on the stove for latecomers. "What are your plans for the day, Speaker?" she asked as she ladled porridge into the bowls, sprinkling plenty of cinnamon atop Mirae's portion. "Working on any new projects?"

"My hands ache too much for serious work these days," Speaker Yeneri said. "However, there is a special tapestry I've been meaning to show you."

Sefina returned to the table, setting down the bowls and taking her place at Mirae's side. Mirae stroked her arm in thanks before taking up her spoon and asking, "Special?"

"Yes," said Speaker Yeneri. "It's a very special tapestry, the very one I wove to prove my worthiness for ascension. I keep it in my bedroom, where none may see."

Sefina's eyes widened. She'd often wondered how Yeneri had ascended to the position of Speaker, but no one had ever shared the details. "Ascending involves creating a miracle, doesn't it?"

"Yes," Speaker Yeneri said. "Unlike our wondrous Mirae, the tapestry I wove for my ascension was my first miracle."

"Surely such a tapestry should be displayed," Mirae said. "If it isn't rude to ask, why do you keep it hidden away?"

Sefina pursed her lips. She was of the opinion that it was indeed rude, but said nothing since she'd initiated the conversation.

A shadow flitted across Speaker Yeneri's face, a sign of some old sadness. "It's a choice I make unwillingly. My dearest wish is that someday it may be displayed without consequence. The two of you may live to see my dream become reality."

Sefina's mind raced. What sort of tapestry could stir such strong negative emotions? Did it depict something violent, lewd, or blasphemous? She shoveled porridge into her mouth, hoping Speaker Yeneri would expand upon the subject without her having to pry.

Speaker Yeneri's eyes landed upon her, two glittering black beetle-shells buried in the wrinkled bark of her face. "Tell me, Sefina. You've pledged yourself to Of-Blessed-Dreams, but do you still offer prayers and tithes to Of-the-Land as well?"

Sefina swallowed her mouthful of porridge as quickly as possible without choking. "Yes. I do as my parents taught me before they passed." She shot Mirae a fond look. "I pray to Of-the-Sea as well. I ask him to keep Mirae safe during her trips to Easton. Perhaps I should start tithing to Of-Wise-Remembrance to better remember the repertoire for our concert."

Speaker Yeneri's thin white eyebrows arched. "If you tithe to Of-the-Sea, you should come with us to see my tapestry."

Sefina's heart sank. She'd assumed she was already included, but apparently Speaker Yeneri had intended to show Mirae the tapestry. Still, she was grateful to be included, even as a last-minute addition. "Of course, Speaker. I would be honored."

Once they finished breakfast, Sefina helped Speaker Yeneri stand while Mirae retrieved her cane and dealt with the empty bowls.

"I'm quite curious, Speaker," Mirae said as they began their slow journey out of the kitchen and toward the dormitories. "Your questions to Sefina have only added to the mystery."

Speaker Yeneri's mouth curled into a sly smirk. "Patience. You'll see soon enough."

They arrived at Speaker Yeneri's quarters. Her sewing room was familiar, for though Sefina visited less in young adulthood, she and Mirae dropped by some evenings to enjoy the speaker's spinning of yarns, literally and figuratively. Several unfinished works were stretched across tables and counters, others draped over chairs, and more strapped onto various looms and racks.

On any other day, Sefina would have lingered to admire these works in progress, but Speaker Yeneri shuffled toward the door at the rear of the room. She and Mirae followed, waiting while Speaker Yeneri fished a key from her pocket.

Speaker Yeneri's bedroom was more rustic than Sefina anticipated. Though she could have bestowed upon herself whatever luxuries she desired, she obviously believed the funds were better spent elsewhere. Wooden railings were affixed to Speaker Yeneri's bed frame, so she might get in and out more easily. There was no door upon her dresser, only a patterned curtain, partially drawn to reveal her scant supply of robes.

The speaker saw where Sefina's eyes had wandered. "That's one good thing about being old. People protest less when I don't feel like wearing my vestments...which is most days now. I can out-stubborn the best of them."

By 'them', Sefina knew Speaker Yeneri meant Lady Lirath, but she made a joke at Mirae's expense instead. "You haven't spent enough time around Mirae," she said, shooting Mirae a good-natured grin.

Mirae rolled her eyes, but grinned right back.

"Mirae agrees with me," Speaker Yeneri said. "Don't you, my dear?"

Mirae laughed. "If I were in your position, you wouldn't catch me dead in those old vestments."

Speaker Yeneri's black eyes danced, as though with inspiration or some special secret. "We'll see. Go to the foot of the bed, will you? There's a drawer beneath. Open it."

Mirae opened the drawer while Sefina peered over her shoulder. Inside was only one item, a tapestry, wrapped in silk cloth and folded with great care. Mirae withdrew it and Sefina helped her spread it upon the bed. It wasn't large, only eight feet by five. As they unrolled it, the scent of a fresh sea breeze filled Sefina's nose.

When she saw the tapestry's face, a gasp caught in Sefina's throat. A trio of figures dominated the image, standing upon an oceanside cliff: two men and one woman. All three embraced each other. Rather than remaining in a single stitched position, they seemed to move and breathe like living beings.

One of the men, a handsome dark-skinned fellow with a fine curly beard, kissed the woman's soft white hair. He then turned to gaze adoringly into the other man's eyes. His skin was lighter, his build leaner, but his shoulders spoke of someone used to labor. A pair of stag's horns draped in green moss and flowers sprouted from his head.

Sefina couldn't speak for wonder. It was the most beautiful tapestry she'd ever beheld. Somehow she knew she would never see anything of its like again during her lifetime.

Beside her, Mirae struggled to find her voice as well. "Is that...?"

Speaker Yeneri joined them beside the bed, gazing down at the tapestry. "Yes. It is exactly who you think."

Sefina didn't spare the Speaker a single glance, so riveting was the tapestry. The woman, with skin so pale it almost glowed with translucency, leaned back against the horned man's shoulder. Her hair floated on an invisible breeze, moving more like clouds than normal strands. The taller, dark-skinned man wrapped his arm around the horned man's waist, leaning close as though to murmur in his ear.

"So, Of-the-Sky is married to Of-the-Land after all," Mirae said in an awestruck whisper. "And to Of-the-Sea. All three of them are married to each other."

"That is my belief," Speaker Yeneri said. "Many temples devoted to Of-the-Sky agree, though they rarely advertise this fact when they descend from the mountains to walk amongst Earthfolk or Sea Children. When I wove this tapestry, my mind went to a different place. My hands worked without conscious thought. Of-Blessed-Dreams took possession of me during the long hours I toiled. She must have wished for someone to know the truth of their love."

"Why hide it away?" Sefina asked. "It's miraculous, Goddess-blessed! Such a tapestry might act as a bridge between the Sea Children and Earthfolk. It shows our beliefs need not contradict each other."

"Precisely," said Speaker Yeneri. "Many of those in power would sooner see such a bridge burned than built. The lord regent's grandfather was one such man. When he heard rumors of the tapestry's existence after my ascension, he stormed into the temple and ordered it burned before his eyes. It's only thanks to my old master, a brave and loyal man who entered Of-Eternal-Sleep's embrace some years ago, that it was saved. He foresaw the need for a substitute and worked for two nights straight while I delayed the regent, finishing a beautiful but un-blessed tapestry to serve in place of mine."

At last, Sefina tore her eyes away from the tapestry. The grief on Speaker Yeneri's face was plain, though whether it was for her old master or a world which did not yet exist, she couldn't be sure—a world where such a tapestry wouldn't be burned for heresy, but put on display for everyone to celebrate.

"When I'm Speaker," Mirae said, her jaw set in determination and her voice firm with conviction, "I'll display this tapestry in the entrance hall, damn the consequences." From the upright way she held her shoulders and the fire that blazed in her eyes, Sefina knew she spoke the truth.

She couldn't have loved Mirae more, nor could she have named a better candidate for Speaker Yeneri's eventual replacement. The miracle-worker, the healer, Of-Blessed-Dreams' chosen. Yet the needle of jealousy pierced her heart. *Why not me?* Once more, she was the shadow to Mirae's sun. The woman whose name always came second to people's minds and mouths—even people like Speaker Yeneri, who loved her.

Still, she wrestled her jealousy into submission. It didn't take long, for she and jealousy were well-acquainted. "You'll make a wonderful speaker, Mirae. I'll be honored to stand by your side when you hang the tapestry."

Speaker Yeneri sighed a wistful sigh. "Perhaps you will, Mirae. To display my work thus would be a fitting legacy for the both of us."

Sefina's gaze returned to the tapestry, drawn like a moth to a candle. The weight of its meaning settled over her like a comforting blanket, banishing her envy and replacing it with contentment.

The conflict between Mirae's beliefs as a Sea Child and hers as Earthfolk had never distressed her. Yet this reconciliation of their cultures' core tenets, outside their mutual worship of Of-Blessed-Dreams, was an incredible affirmation. Of-the-Sea and Of-the-Land were husbands, married to each other as well as Of-the-Sky.

She turned to look at Mirae, whose face still shone with stubborn defiance. Her heart melted. *One day...one day, Mirae, you and I will be wives as well.*

The warmth of Mirae's hand around hers pulled Sefina back into the present. If anything could outshine the beauty of such a wondrous tapestry, it was the radiance of Mirae's smile. "I'm holding you to your promise to stand beside me when I hang the tapestry, Fina."

"Of course."

Speaker Yeneri patted Mirae's arm. "Your passion does an old woman proud, my dears. May the Eight make it so."

A sharp knock startled all three of them, causing Sefina to flinch and Mirae's head to whip toward the bedroom door. Sefina grabbed the tapestry and folded it over her forearm, shoving it hastily beneath the top sheet of the bed. A lumpy wrinkle remained, but it passed as an extra blanket.

Speaker Yeneri gave a brief, silent nod before hobbling toward the door. "One moment," she called.

The knocking ceased. Speaker Yeneri opened the door to reveal Lady Lirath, waiting with folded arms and sharp eyes. "Forgive the interruption, Speaker." Her tone seemed annoyed, inconvenienced. "The kitchen staff told me I might find Sefina here."

Oh. Apparently, I'm the inconvenience.

Sefina approached Lady Lirath, leaving Mirae to guard the bunched covers concealing the tapestry. She couldn't help but wonder whether Lady Lirath knew of its existence already, and what her opinion was if she did. Had she been equally awestruck or did she consider it blasphemous? Would she object when Mirae hung it in the entrance hall one day?

"My apologies," she said to Lady Lirath. "Do you need me?" She neglected to bring up the fact that it was an Eightday, her only free day of the week.

"Indeed." Lady Lirath produced a letter from her robes and offered it to Sefina. As she accepted it, she noticed the envelope was made of fine, expensive paper, stamped with an intricate wax seal in the shape of a stag's head. "From the regent," Lady Lirath explained. "I haven't read its contents, since it was sealed and addressed to you. It arrived by courier this morning."

Sefina glanced at Mirae, only to see a frown marring her beautiful face. It made her stomach drop. Hesitantly, she broke the seal and read the letter. The regent's handwriting was flowery but neat. The paper smelled of citrus, perhaps even more so than the man himself.

Lady Sefina,

I eagerly await your concert with Lady Mirae. No doubt it will be a feast for the ears and soul alike! Though our initial introduction was brief, I have been unable to banish you from my mind since that day. Women of such talent and beauty are rare treasures indeed.

I will be honest, I inquired with my good cousin as to whether you might be amenable for courtship. However, she informed me that you prefer the company of women. Therefore, if you will permit, my most fervent desire is to encourage your musical artistry instead.

It would be my honor to make a donation to the Temple of Dreams in your name. In exchange, I ask only a small favor. My mother, who entered eternal sleep some years back, passed on the day before your concert is scheduled to be held. Her favorite song was the folk ballad, 'A Fond Farewell'. I am sure you know of it.

Please, do me the great honor of adding this piece to your program. I would appreciate it immensely. We shall, Eight willing, see each other soon.

With great affection and admiration,

Horace Stagford III

Only after she read the regent's signature did Sefina notice Mirae reading over her shoulder. Her face burned as she felt the wash of Mirae's breath upon her neck. To have unwittingly captured a nobleman's attention was awkward enough without her only love reading such a private letter.

"I assure you, I did nothing to encourage his interest," she blurted out. "I told you, he only overheard part of my music lesson."

Her heart sank when she saw the stormy look upon Mirae's face, the lightning that crackled in her dark eyes. "What business does a middle-aged man have sending letters to a young woman? He must be twice your age!"

"He only wants to be my patron," Sefina protested. Yet it was difficult to believe, no matter how fervently she wished it were true. Such a generous offer should have been an honor, but knowing the regent's offer of patronage was a mere substitute for courtship struck like a sour note.

"Don't worry about the regent's intentions," Lady Lirath said. "I've warned him Sefina wouldn't welcome his advances...though if she did entertain his interest, I fail to see what business it would be of yours, Mirae."

Mirae's fists clenched as she faced Lady Lirath. "It's every bit my business! Sefina is the dearest person in the world to me."

Her sudden outburst of possessiveness filled Sefina's stomach with flutterbugs. To have Mirae express jealousy over her for a change was a heady experience, one which left her dizzy and distracted. It was to Sefina's great shame that she stared at Mirae, admiring the pull of her upper lip and the tension in her neck, rather than attempting to end the argument.

"If that is true," Lady Lirath said, her voice cool and collected as always, "you should encourage Sefina to accept the regent's generous offer regardless of your personal feelings. Such support will benefit her immensely and may improve relations between His Lordship and the Temple of Dreams."

"The temple already has plenty of supporters—"

Lady Lirath rolled her eyes. "Who? The Sea Children in the dockside slums? A few merchants from Easton? Full of heart they may be, but full of purse they certainly aren't."

Mirae straightened to her full height, balling her fists. Sefina couldn't move, stunned by the sight of Mirae lost to such uncharacteristic rage.

Speaker Yeneri placed a soothing hand upon Mirae's shoulder. "Enough. The decision is Sefina's alone, so I trust everyone will give her ample time and space to consider her answer."

Sefina felt a surge of relief at the speaker's words, but her heart kept drumming against her ribs. Her gaze remained locked onto Mirae.

Both Mirae and Lady Lirath offered begrudging agreement by way of stiff nods. "Sefina is a grown woman," Lady Lirath said, "old enough to decide whether my counsel is worth heeding." Her blue eyes met Sefina's and their icy depths made her feel like anything but a grown woman. Under Lady Lirath's stare, she was a little girl again, craving approval.

If that means singing a song for the regent, shouldn't I? For the good of the temple, and to please the woman who has trained and raised me since childhood?

Mirae took Sefina's hand, squeezing far too tight. "As you say, Lady Lirath. Sefina can make her own choices. Now, with your kind permission, we'd like to enjoy the rest of our Eightday."

"A few hours of rehearsal would hardly go amiss," Lady Lirath said. "Your concert is fast approaching."

"Thank you for the suggestion," Mirae said, though her voice dripped with disdain. "Come, Sefina. We should practice."

When Mirae pulled her from the room, Sefina followed, eager to leave Lady Lirath and the argument behind. Mirae led her through Speaker Yeneri's sewing room and into the corridor, hurrying until they'd turned several corners.

The moment they were alone, Mirae backed Sefina into a shadowy alcove by a stained glass window. She transferred her grip from Sefina's hand to her wrists and pinned them to the cold stone wall. A shiver raced down Sefina's spine. She enjoyed the way Mirae's fingers braceleted her wrists, as though she owned them and everything else attached as well.

"The nerve of that man," Mirae said. "How dare he manipulate you with such false flattery?"

Sefina went rigid, torn between anger and arousal. Briefly, anger won out. "I don't appreciate that term, as though anyone who praises my musicianship must only be after what lies between my legs." Yet to see Mirae so furious over someone else's interest made her feel valuable in a twisted way. Before she could think better of it, she kissed Mirae ravenously, like parched earth pleading for rain.

Mirae kissed back with all the ferocity Sefina could have hoped for. When her tongue pressed forward, Sefina parted her lips. A moan escaped her throat when Mirae's grip on her wrist tightened, but Mirae's mouth muffled the noise. "Quiet," she murmured through a string of kisses, "or we'll be caught."

Sefina knew this was her chance to object. To tell Mirae she was too angry for such intimacy, but she did no such thing. She allowed Mirae to bunch her skirts around her waist and slide a hand between her legs.

Mirae seemed to care little for gentleness as she pulled Sefina's smallclothes aside, but neither did Sefina. Their joining felt inevitable. Who was she to resist when she craved the stretch of Mirae's fingers so keenly?

Her head lolled against the wall as Mirae took what she wanted, her eyes fluttering shut despite her efforts to watch Mirae's face. The possibility that someone might stumble upon them set Sefina's heart drumming at double speed, but she found the fear exhilarating. What would they see? Only Mirae's clothed back as she staked her claim.

She bit her lower lip to stifle her cries as Mirae's mouth found her neck, sucking hard enough to leave a large purple mark. Sefina's very core melted as she thought about how she'd need to cover it later, lest someone notice.

"Sing the regent's song if you must," Mirae said, her breath hot and wet against Sefina's throat, "but remember to whom you belong."

Her thumb drew practiced circles in precisely the right spot, and Sefina shattered. Her mouth fell open in a silent scream as her pulse pounded between Mirae's teeth and around her fingers. In that moment, she belonged to Mirae and only Mirae. No one else mattered.

They were in a world of their own making, where not even the gods themselves could reach them, and Mirae was that world's light: a brilliant, burning sun that threatened to consume every part of her.

If the peak Mirae wrung from her shivering body was the pinnacle of bliss, the fall that followed was the opposite. Sefina came crashing back into herself with a sickening sensation of wrongness. Not because Mirae had taken her roughly against a wall instead of softly in their bed, but because Mirae's earlier words haunted her.

False flattery.

Was she so undeserving of flattery? So unworthy of praise and appreciation? Lady Lirath certainly thought so, but Mirae was supposed to be her champion. "Rightly so," such a champion should have said upon hearing the regent's praise. "Sefina is one of the best musicians I know."

Mirae must have sensed Sefina's unease. She withdrew her fingers carefully, keeping her hand cupped in their place. "I'm sorry, Fina. I shouldn't have done that. It's only, the thought of him...and you...I'm every bit yours as much as you are mine, and it terrified me."

"Why are you terrified?" Sefina asked, catching her breath. "I only want you."

"Really?" An uncertain smile spread across Mirae's face. "No one else?"

Sefina lowered her head, burying her nose in Mirae's shoulder. She smelled of sea-salt and flowers, far more pleasant than the cloying scent of citrus. "I notice when a woman is beautiful, but none of them draw me like the moon does the tide. It's always been you, Mirae. Ever since we were children. Surely you know that?"

"I know," Mirae said, her voice low and rough. "But I intend to remind you as often as possible. In our room next time, though."

Mirae made good on her promise several times that day and Sefina thoroughly enjoyed the reminder. Even so, resentment lingered, lurking in a dark corner of her mind. As usual, she refused to let it overwhelm her. She clung to Mirae instead, drinking her in like flowers do the sun.

Chapter Eleven

ON CANDLENIGHT MORNING, SEFINA woke well before dawnbell. Her heart fluttered as soon as she opened her eyes. Rather than lounge in bed and wait for Mirae to sing their song, she untangled her limbs from Mirae's loose embrace. Quietly, she crept to their wardrobe where she'd hung her brand new gown.

It was royal blue silk, one of the latest fashions from Castletown. The collar wrapped high around Sefina's neck but left her shoulders bare in a daring display of skin. She could scarcely believe she was allowed to wear such a thing, but Lady Lirath had purchased it, as she had most of Sefina's possessions. For this event, she'd spared no expense.

Unable to resist the gown's call, Sefina stepped into it. The whisper of silk against her skin felt decadent, so much better than cotton robes. Smiling, she turned to admire herself in the mirror—and gasped at the sight of her reflection.

Sefina rarely took pride in her appearance, but the young woman staring back at her was stunning. The summer sun had brought out auburn highlights in her brown hair. She'd only just left bed, but it washed around her bare shoulders in silky ringlets as though she'd already styled it.

When had her face lost its childhood softness, she wondered. When had the line of her jawbone sharpened and her lips become so full? She had a woman's cheekbones now, without the help of makeup. For once, she felt beautiful, worthy of standing at Mirae's side rather than behind her shoulder.

"Everyone's eyes will be on you tonight, my love."

Sefina turned and smiled at the sound of Mirae's voice. "I doubt that." Faint sunlight streamed through the cracks in the shutters, illuminating Mirae's reclined form upon the bed. The covers draped off her upturned hip to reveal most of her naked body, a lovely landscape of soft brown skin.

Unable to resist, Sefina returned to bed. Mirae rose to meet her, reaching around to loosen the fastenings behind her neck. "No doubts, Fina. You're lovelier than Of-Our-Hearts herself. The mere sight of you will strike the audience silent before you sing a note."

Sefina's cheeks burned. To hear such honeyed words from one as beautiful as Mirae only made them sweeter. For the next hour, the dress lay forgotten on the floor while Mirae showed her just how beautiful she was. She was all smiles the rest of that morning and into the afternoon.

As evening approached, Sefina and Mirae arrived at the foyer to see how the set-up had progressed. During concerts, the domed entrance hall became a theater, with a stone dais for performers and curtain-draped balconies accessible from the second floor. Of-Blessed-Dreams and her long, flowing rainbow of hair watched over it all, as though she too was an audience member.

Volunteers, most wearing green robes, scrambled about the busy space. They spread mats upon the floor for seating and placed vases of flowers upon the dais.

As Sefina's eyes roamed the foyer, tingling warmth spread through her. It blossomed in her chest and rushed to the tips of her fingers and toes. Nobles and merchants throughout Stagford would begin arriving soon, not to mention the regent himself.

Mirae took Sefina's hand. "How are we feeling?"

Sefina's heart flew into her throat and lodged there, pumping far too fast. Suddenly, all she could think about was where she'd be in two candlemarks, standing on the very dais they were admiring.

"Excited." She swallowed hard. "Nervous."

Mirae's brow softened. She squeezed Sefina's hand. "Remember, no one in the audience will pick our performances apart as Lady Lirath does. They're here to enjoy our voices, not listen for our mistakes."

Sefina sighed and relaxd her shoulders. Lady Lirath usually picked her performances apart rather than Mirae's. Nonetheless, the point was well-taken. "How do you always know the perfect thing to say?"

Mirae tucked a stray ringlet behind Sefina's ear. "Because I know you, Fina. I know without a shadow of a doubt that you'll be marvelous tonight."

"Indeed," said Speaker Yeneri, approaching from behind them. "I'm sure both of you will gift us with an incredible performance."

Sefina turned to see the speaker shuffling toward them, gripping her cane in one hand while the other held Lady Lirath's elbow. For once, she wore her official vestments, snow white robes draped about her bony shoulders. Sefina felt a swell of pride. *She actually dressed up for us, even though she detests formality.*

"Joyous Candlenight, Speaker," Mirae said. "Or it will be soon enough. Are you well? You seem tired, if you'll forgive my saying so."

Speaker Yeneri laughed. "I'm always tired. You will be too, once you experience the good fortune of old age."

"Old, but no less stubborn." Lady Lirath narrowed her eyes at Speaker Yeneri. "I urged the speaker to rest until the concert, but she insisted on overseeing the final preparations."

"It's a privilege, not merely my duty," Speaker Yeneri said. "Don't deny an old woman one of the most enjoyable of my responsi—" She turned away from Lady Lirath, coughing into her elbow. Sefina's stomach clenched as the fit dragged on. Eventually, Speaker Yeneri caught her breath. "Apologies. My responsibilities."

Lady Lirath shook her head. "At least choose a mat and direct the proceedings from there. I promise to make sure your instructions are carried out to the letter."

"You always do, dear Raula," Speaker Yeneri said. "Very well. You'll have your way this time. No reason I can't oversee things while seated."

Sefina chewed her lip. Privately, she agreed with Lady Lirath. Speaker Yeneri had pushed herself too hard, if her unsteady bearing was anything to go by. "That seems wise, Speaker."

"There's little left to do," Mirae said, gazing around the entrance hall.

Sefina did the same. While they'd conversed, the volunteers had hung glowing lanterns around the foyer, filling the space with light. Streamers in all the colors of autumn leaves lined the walls above Speaker Yeneri's tapestries. Truly, it was a marvelous sight.

She would have admired the decorations longer, but Lady Lirath waved them away. "Warm up those clever fingers of yours, Sefina—and the both of you should run through your vocal exercises. Be in the southwest corridor half a candlemark before duskbell to make your entrance."

"Yes, Lady Lirath," Sefina and Mirae said in chorus.

Sefina allowed Mirae to take her hand and lead her from the entrance hall.

"She has no idea how clever your fingers can be," Mirae whispered as they made their departure.

Sefina's cheeks flared hot. "Mirae!" She glanced over her shoulder, heart racing at the thought someone might have overheard. Fortunately, no one was nearby.

Mirae laughed that silver laugh of hers and brought Sefina back to their room. There, Sefina retrieved her lute from atop the dresser, sat on the bed, and moved through familiar chord progressions. Mirae donned her concert dress, a sunny yellow in satin with slits up either side. They offered tantalizing glimpses of her calves and thighs when she moved and Sefina soon found herself distracted.

"Problems?" Mirae asked when Sefina hit a wrong note. From the mischievous gleam in her eyes, she knew exactly the effect her appearance had.

"Yellow flatters you," Sefina said.

Mirae sidled up to her, stroking the edge of Sefina's dress near the wrapped neckline. "As blue does you."

A knock interrupted the moment before it could progress. Mirae opened the door to reveal her parents, older and grayer than the last time Sefina had seen them, but beaming and full of happiness.

Mirae's mother embraced Mirae in the doorway, rocking her back and forth while her father wrapped them both in his arms. Sefina didn't miss the tears that glistened in his warm brown eyes, so very much like Mirae's.

"Oh, my baby girl," Mirae's mother said, reluctant to let her go. "Let me look at you." Her hands remained on Mirae's shoulders as she leaned back, taking the sight in. If Mirae had her father's eyes, she certainly had her mother's smile.

"Mama." Mirae averted her eyes, as though to hide tears.

"She's right," said Mirae's father. "You look wonderful." With a caress of her arm, he turned to Sefina. "So do you, Fina. What a lovely dress." He crossed the room and took Sefina into his embrace as though she were his own.

Sefina melted into his arms, inhaling his scent. He'd brought all the best smells of Farsea along with him, and their familiarity caused the knot of nerves in Sefina's stomach to unravel further.

"It's so good to see you," she murmured, hugging him tight.

Mirae's mother took her turn next, holding Sefina for a long time. "How is my other daughter doing? Ready for your concert?"

Sefina's heart glowed. Mirae's parents were always wonderful, including her in their family's good fortune since childhood, when she was nothing but a dirty orphan. "I hope we are. Mirae and I have worked hard these last few months."

"Don't worry if Mama cries during the concert," Mirae's father said. He stood beside Mirae with his arm around her waist, while Mirae rested her cheek on his shoulder. "You know that's how she is."

Mirae's mother sniffed and let Sefina go. "Hush. I'll be much too busy enjoying your beautiful music."

Mirae laughed. "That's what you say every solstice, Mama. And you always cry."

They left the room and went to the southwest corridor adjoining the entrance hall. Mirae's parents lingered a while, which Sefina appreciated, but their presence did cut into what should have been precious warmup time. She ran through the most difficult finger placements silently on the neck of her lute while Mirae and her parents chatted about Farsea, temple life, and the grand feast that would follow the performance.

Eventually, Mirae's parents left to find their seats, leaving Sefina and Mirae alone.

"Of-Eternal-Sleep take me," Mirae said, peeking beyond the curtain that separated the corridor from the hall. "All of Castletown must be here. I've never seen such a crowd, not even in the Easton markets."

Sefina licked her dry lips. The crowd beyond the curtain grew louder, many hushed voices blending into a dull roar like ocean waves. Had so many people really come to hear them sing?

To hear Mirae, a treacherous voice in her mind whispered. The woman with the magic voice. The miracle-worker. As always, she smothered the spark of envy before it could ignite. "I hope they find us worth their time."

Mirae tilted her head and narrowed her eyes, dumbfounded. "Of course they will."

To have such confidence! Sefina envied Mirae's conviction. She clung to what self-assurance she could—her new dress, Mirae's praise...even the Regent's letter, much as it shamed her. False flattery or not, it was the first time someone besides Mirae had praised her musicianship.

A hush fell over the crowd beyond the curtain. The world seemed to hold its breath. So did Sefina, clutching her lute in a white-knuckled grip. Then a loud voice carried through the hall. Lady Lirath could fill any room effortlessly whether speaking or singing.

Somehow, Sefina blocked out Lady Lirath's opening remarks, but then she heard her name. "...my beloved students, Mirae and Sefina!"

Loud applause followed, their cue to emerge from behind the safety of the curtain.

Sefina froze, her feet rooted to the floor. Her vision narrowed to a tunnel, blackness closing in around her on all sides.

Mirae took Sefina's hand. The warmth of her fingers reminded Sefina to breathe. Her vision cleared and she turned her head to see that Mirae was smiling. "We'll be wonderful," she whispered, pulling Sefina past the curtain.

Sefina stumbled along, staring at the large crowd as Mirae led her onto the dais. She could only imagine how the two of them looked: Mirae, smiling and vibrant in yellow; her, wide-eyed and trembling like a deer in a hunter's sights, barely able to put one foot before the other.

But she didn't stumble. Though her hands shook as she adjusted her lute's strap and positioned her fingers on the frets, her muscles remembered. She played the opening chords as though she'd known them all her life. When Mirae breathed in tempo beside her, Sefina inhaled as well.

Their voices filled the hall as one.

The first phrase was pure joy, so perfectly in tune that rich overtones rang up to the domed ceiling and Of-Blessed-Dreams' mosaic. They buzzed in Sefina's ears, resonating with vibrant harmonies. A simple song of praise for Of-Blessed-Dreams became something extraordinary. Something sacred.

> *Sweeter than songbirds my love sings.*
> *Sweeter than wine are her words.*
> *Sweeter than honey from golden hives,*
> *Are the miracles her voice stirs.*
> *Her fingers dye all the colors of dawn.*
> *Her hands carve diamonds from earth.*
> *The rest of the Seven, gods though they are,*
> *For her their own miraculous birth.*
> *And every tale told around a warm fire,*
> *Was her story first, you see.*
> *Bringing good cheer to all who hear,*
> *Making joy through you and me.*

Their final notes faded. Silence reigned. Sefina burned unbearably hot beneath the light of the hanging lanterns, as though she might catch fire and crumble to ash where she stood.

Then, enthusiastic applause! Whistles and cheers!

Mirae took Sefina's hand as she led them in a bow. Sefina scarcely noticed. Instead, her soul floated somewhere high above the stage. Her pounding pulse no longer troubled her. Instead, the heavy thump of her heartbeat brought a pleasant, tingling warmth.

They had done it. She had done it.

The next several pieces went wonderfully. Though the lights surrounding the stage made it difficult to see individual expressions, Sefina sensed the audience's excitement and energy vibrating through the air. Her fingers moved fluidly along the frets of her lute. Her voice sprang forth, twining alongside Mirae's.

Cheers followed every song, each louder than the last. Sefina's confidence flourished. Even Mirae's solo repertoire stirred no envy within her. She stepped back and listened, enraptured not only by Mirae's voice—for she'd long since surrendered to its awesome power—but her striking image in yellow, each captivating movement of her face and hands.

When Mirae sang, she became a brilliant beacon, outshining the sun as the center of all heavenly bodies. Sefina could do little more than allow her heart to orbit such radiance. Yet no part of her protested. This was exactly where she and Mirae were meant to be, doing exactly what Of-Blessed-Dreams meant for them to do.

Before Sefina realized it, they arrived at the program's finale. The love duet. The scorching look Mirae shot in her direction as she sang the opening line stole Sefina's breath so, she barely managed to come in with her part.

> *Cold stone stands before us,*
> *A wall between our kingdoms.*
> *Yet Of-Our-Hearts shows mercy,*
> *Guiding our love to freedom.*

Mirae's voice struck a powerful chord upon Sefina's heartstrings. Despite the ballad's narrative, she wasn't embodying Triss. Sefina wasn't Isa. A shudder coursed through her as she realized the truth. *She's singing to me. Me and only me.*

Sefina struggled to keep from squirming. Invisible flames licked her flesh. Her blood roared in her ears. Her very bones cried out, screaming that she might die if she didn't touch Mirae somehow.

Her fingers fell away from her lute, diligently practiced accompaniment all but forgotten as the instrument dangled from her neck. Instead, she stepped toward Mirae and took her hands, singing directly to her. The audience vanished, as did everything else.

> *Every duskbell without fail,*
> *My dearest, I shall find you.*
> *And yet the darkness wanes,*
> *The hours far too few.*
> *To feel your breath upon my cheek,*
> *Your lips against my ear.*
> *For to whisper words of love,*
> *Words I so long to hear.*
> *With strength of arm and callused hands,*
> *No wall shall bar my way.*
> *Climbing ever upward*
> *To see your face, lovelier than day.*

Sefina barely registered the ballad's climax. The music escaped her, eclipsed by a wave of feeling. Love poured from her mouth and all the while, she never lost sight of Mirae. Her warm, sparkling brown eyes. Her dazzling smile. They were the only two people in the universe, a union of souls somewhere beyond this realm.

> *You are my sun, my moon and stars.*
> *Your very breath sustains me.*
> *You're the altar of my worship,*
> *My hands and lips to praise thee.*
> *Night wraps her cloak around us,*
> *While wall-stones stand as witness.*
> *I pledge to you my undying love,*
> *Sealed with true love's kiss.*

As the final verse faded, Sefina exhaled with a bittersweet sense of loss. The song was over, but Mirae remained her guiding star. Her dress glittered beneath the stage lights, her face aglow with love.

Sefina would have kissed her if not for the intrusion of applause. Though the audience's whoops and cheers energized her, it was nothing compared to the warmth of Mirae's hand gripping her own.

Mirae inclined her head subtly toward the audience, reminding Sefina to bow. They did so, but Sefina refused to let go of Mirae's hand.

It was fortunate Mirae retained some of her faculties, for Sefina found herself empty and hollow after giving everything to the music. When Mirae dropped her hand and approached the front of the stage, Sefina felt the loss far too keenly.

"Thank you all for sharing this special night with us," Mirae said. "It's a night I'll always remember, and I hope you will as well. But before we go—"

Disappointed groans and shouts of, "Encore! Another song!" drowned out Mirae's words for a moment, but she laughed and raised her hand for silence. Eventually, the audience quieted.

"Saying goodbye is always sad, but endings lead to new beginnings. In that spirit, my dear Sefina will serenade you with a farewell song. Please, welcome her warmly! Without her breathtaking talent and exquisite musicianship, this concert would never have happened. She is a constant inspiration to me."

Sefina had intended to sing A Fond Farewell to close the concert, for where else in the set could one put such a song? But to have Mirae announce it as though she approved came as a complete surprise. Mirae had publicly supported Sefina's choice, offering the spotlight in spite of her own resentment.

Somehow, Sefina summoned the courage to take center stage. Her throat was dry, her first note shaky, but once again, muscle memory took over. Her mouth, lungs, and fingers remembered what they were supposed to do.

A fond farewell I bid you,
Be your travels near or far.
We two shall meet again someday
Beneath the same bright star.

Despite her lingering exhaustion, Sefina tapped into reserves of energy and emotion she hadn't known she possessed. The poignant lyrics reminded her of her parents—a decade gone, but never forgotten.

She recalled her mother's voice as she spun stories. Her father's broad shoulders, which he always allowed her to ride upon. The sound of their laughter and the warmth of their embrace.

Oh, the years go on and seasons turn
As is their natural order.
But in golden fields of memory
We remain just as we were.

What would my parents think of my relationship with Mirae? Would they approve? Would it have even surprised them?

Sefina allowed herself to hope that somewhere in the vast ocean of stars, her parents were proud of the woman she'd become. The talent she'd worked so hard to cultivate.

When I reach my own journey's end,
Though we may be far apart,
I will have brought you with me,
Carried safely in my heart.
A fond farewell I bid you,
Be your travels near or far.
We two shall meet again someday,
Beneath the same bright star.

As her final note floated toward Of Blessed-Dreams' mosaic, stunned silence took hold of the entrance hall. She waited, but this time, a smile spread across her face before the applause could begin. She already knew what the reception to her performance would be. Aside from that quivering first note, she'd sung flawlessly and passionately. She doubted even Lady Lirath had found fault with her performance.

But it wasn't applause that followed her final verse. Before it could begin, a sharp cry rang out.

"The speaker is dead! Speaker Yeneri is dead!"

Chapter Twelve

DETERMINED TO SERVE THE speaker even in death, Lady Lirath took charge. Sefina watched, devastated and numb, as Lady Lirath emptied the hall, urging everyone to retire and grieve privately. She shepherded away gawking nobles and instructed two healers to bear Speaker Yeneri to her rooms, where she could rest away from prying eyes.

Sefina found herself standing on the dais steps with Mirae by her side. Several people stopped to wish them well before departing. A line formed as they offered stilted praise and condolences.

Hoping to be rescued, Sefina shot Lady Lirath an imploring look from across the foyer. The stern stare she received in return was clear. *Stay where you are. Do as I've taught you.*

And so Sefina did her best to entertain a seemingly endless line of nobles as they attempted to discuss death, perhaps the world's worst topic of conversation. Her only source of reassurance was Mirae's warm hand, which never left her own.

"What a shame. At the end of such a marvelous concert, too..."

"Speaker Yeneri's death is a tragedy, of course, but she lived a full life. Perhaps she was ready to move on."

"Of-Eternal-Sleep is cruel indeed. Even the best of us cannot hope to earn a reprieve."

Mirae said little, leaving Sefina to do most of the talking. She might have been annoyed if she hadn't seen the tears glistening in Mirae's eyes, threatening to well over. With no other choice, Sefina took her cues from Lady Lirath. If her mentor could muddle through this tragedy with grace and poise, so could she.

"I'm so sorry, Mirae. Sefina."

A familiar voice drew Sefina back from the fog of grief. While her mind was present, her heart returned as well upon seeing Mirae's father. His well-worn features were more pronounced than usual, with a red tinge around his brown eyes and puffy bags beneath. He had been crying too.

A low sob broke in Mirae's throat. She flung herself into her father's embrace, burying her face in his shoulder. Meanwhile, Sefina looked to Mirae's mother, standing one pace behind. She offered a sad, yet somehow reassuring smile. "Of-Eternal-Sleep was kind. The last thing the Speaker heard was your voices. What a peaceful way to enter the Sea of Stars."

Sefina's eyes stung, though she couldn't find it in herself to cry. Not yet. Her heart cracked, but with heartbreak came a much needed release of pressure. She took her first full breath since Speaker Yeneri had fallen asleep. "Thank you. I needed to hear that."

Gently, Sefina pried Mirae away from her father, nodding farewell as they stepped aside. She kept her arm around Mirae's waist until the last noble departed, then heaved a long sigh. She should have felt relief, but all she found within herself was emptiness.

Lady Lirath arrived in time to direct her newfound aimlessness. "Come with me, girls. We must see to the speaker right away."

With a heavy heart, Sefina went to Speaker Yeneri's rooms alongside Mirae. Lady Lirath promised to join them soon. They passed through the speaker's sewing room without stopping to admire the partial tapestries on the looms. Sefina felt another crushing wave of grief when she realized they would remain unfinished forever.

She clutched Mirae's hand as they entered the bedroom. At first glance, Speaker Yeneri appeared as though she'd fallen asleep. One of the healers had draped her with a thin white sheet, but her face remained uncovered. Her eyes were closed, with a peaceful smile on her wrinkled face.

"Perhaps your mother was right. She fell asleep to the sound of our voices after all."

Mirae wept, gazing upon Speaker Yeneri's body in silence. Sefina tried but failed to choke back her own tears. They streamed down her cheeks as she stroked Speaker Yeneri's thin white hair. The room smelled of her, like a sunshine breeze, even at night with the window shut. It made things worse, somehow. Speaker Yeneri would never see another sunrise or feel another breeze on her face.

While Sefina floundered, Mirae dropped her hand and took the speaker's gnarled fingers. From her mouth poured the lullaby she bade Sefina sing each night. A final farewell to the woman who had welcomed them both into her home and made it theirs as well.

The moon's begun to rise, the stars are on their way.
So close your heavy eyes until a brand new day.
Hush now, hush now. Night falls. Crickets cheep.
Hush now, hush now. Rest your head and sleep.

It was the most mournful song Sefina had ever heard. Tears flowed freely down her face, dripping from her chin. If the Eight could weep, surely Mirae's tribute brought tears to their eyes, wherever they were.

The sound of voices brought Sefina back. Mirae's shoulders went rigid and she dropped the speaker's hand. They both turned. What began as low mutters soon became a heated argument, loud enough to carry through the door.

"I tell you, it won't work," said Lady Lirath. Sefina recognized her voice at once. "Mirae's powers measure far beyond those of any mortal healer's, but she cannot bring the dead back to life."

"Asking will do no harm," said another voice, smooth and masculine. "If she could perform such a feat..."

"I wouldn't wish that power upon her or anyone else. Can you imagine being the only person capable of resurrecting the dead? The poor girl's days would be a never-ending parade of weeping parents pleading for her to return their children to them—and that is the most positive outcome I can envision."

"But if she could—"

"While I sympathize with your desire to bring the speaker back, Mirae cannot and should not do so. Speaker Yeneri would object to the mere suggestion."

"Are you sure? From what I hear, the speaker had no qualms about taking the girl to Easton's docks so she might cure the people there of various wretched ailments."

"This situation is entirely different."

Sefina gasped. Surely Lady Lirath and the regent—for she recognized the other voice now—couldn't be having this blasphemous conversation. Speaker Yeneri, raised from the dead? This had to be some horrible nightmare.

Mirae said nothing. Carefully, she lowered Speaker Yeneri's limp hand to the bed and tucked it beneath the sheet. Then she pushed past Sefina and went to the door, flinging it open to reveal a pair of startled faces. The regent's hand hovered in midair, poised to knock.

"Forgive our interruption," he said, putting on a sad smile. "You must be Mirae. Though we haven't had the good fortune of a formal introduction, I know your face from tonight's performance. How regrettable that we must meet under such tragic circumstances."

"Yes," Mirae said, her voice layered with icy disdain. "Tragic."

The regent's smile spread wider, showing all his straight white teeth. "When Lady Lirath told me the speaker was laid to rest in her rooms, I insisted on paying my respects in person. Such a noble woman."

He offered Mirae the backs of his hands, waiting for her to bow and press her forehead to them. Mirae met him stare for stare, refusing the gesture until his smile faltered.

Sefina's heart lurched. Cold sweat sprouted along her spine. She shot Mirae a fearful look, urging her to play along, but Mirae refused to acknowledge her. Her stare remained fixed on the regent, piercing through him like a pin through a flutterbug specimen.

"Why?" Mirae said, neglecting to add the Regent's title. "You've expressed neither admiration nor friendship for Speaker Yeneri before."

Lady Lirath's eyes widened. "Mirae! How dare you address Lord Regent Stagford with such irreverence?"

Mirae turned her icy stare upon Lady Lirath. "Thank you, Lady Lirath, for informing the regent of my decision not to wake the speaker. I would have preferred to voice it myself, but for once we're in agreement. Even if I could raise the dead, Speaker Yeneri would never forgive me for such a violation. Doesn't she deserve to find peace in the Sea of Stars? To drag her soul back to our realm would be wrong." She glared at the Regent, obviously implying that she found him wrong as well.

Lady Lirath said nothing. It seemed she had lost her ability to speak.

The regent narrowed his eyes, but his smile returned, wider and more forced. "You overheard our conversation."

"How could I not?" Mirae said. "You were shouting."

Sefina swayed, overtaken by the chill of fear. Mirae couldn't make such an enemy of the regent if she ever wished to become speaker—a position that was now vacant. She summoned her courage. Lady Lirath had spent years instructing her on the importance of diplomacy as well as musicianship.

"Please, Mirae," Sefina said, placing a hand upon her arm. "Tonight has brought so much shock and grief already. There's no need for anger as well. It's only natural to wish for the return of those we've lost, but no one will force you to do anything you feel is wrong. Allow the regent to pay his respects and trust that Lady Lirath will organize a fine celebration of the speaker's life. Something worthy of her."

Lady Lirath leapt on the opportunity Sefina had laid the groundwork for. "Speaker Yeneri deserves a city-wide celebration for all she has provided Stagford over the decades."

"Agreed," the regent said. His sharp blue eyes softened into something wary and mistrustful rather than brimming with fire and fury. "I will contribute any resources needed, of course. The temple needn't spend a copper."

Mirae's hands balled into fists. She rose to her full height, glaring into the regent's eyes. Her mouth opened.

Sefina took hold of Mirae's elbow and squeezed hard. "Forgive us, Lord Regent. We're quite tired and saddened by the speaker's loss. We should retire for the night. Surely the arrangements can wait until morning."

The regent's expression transformed into one of saccharine sympathy. He frowned, his brow knitting in concern. "Of course, Lady Sefina. I will pay my respects to the speaker with my dear cousin, then take my leave."

"Thank you, Lord Regent. I'm sure we'll have the pleasure of seeing each other again soon, hopefully under more pleasant circumstances."

Sefina dragged Mirae into the sewing room before she could spoil the tentative peace, catching a whiff of citrus as she passed the regent. Lady Lirath inclined her head and held Sefina's gaze for a long moment. Her acknowledgment brought Sefina some small comfort as they returned to their room.

The instant Sefina shut the door, Mirae rounded on her. "What was that?" she demanded, shaking free of Sefina's hold and placing both hands on her hips.

Sefina gritted her teeth. The last thing she wanted was another fight, but Mirae wasn't giving her much choice. "Instead of shouting, you might thank me. Of course the regent's request was horrible, but there was no need to tear into him like a starving street dog. Lady Lirath was already arguing your case for you. Quite effectively, I might add."

Mirae huffed and tossed her hair. "I hardly need Lady Lirath to state my opinions for me. Why are you defending her? If she had a spine, she would have told him off too."

"She was. You know the saying about flies and honey."

Mirae rolled her eyes. "Lady Lirath has a tongue of poison. I see no reason she should curb it around that pompous donkey while giving it free rein upon you."

Sefina flinched. "She's actually been quite supportive these past few months."

"Which hardly makes up for a lifetime of scorn," Mirae said. "But we aren't discussing Lady Lirath. We're discussing how you interrupted me to pacify that...that..."

A hot ball of anger burned within Sefina's chest. "Do you even want to become speaker, Mirae? Because you'll never hold the position with the way you behave, goddess-given voice or no! The regent rules Stagford. How do you expect to run the temple if you make an enemy of him before you've even ascended?"

"With the support of Stagford's people." Mirae's upper lip curled back to reveal a flash of teeth. "The temple belongs to them, not that stuffed shirt. Always has and always will."

Sefina threw up her hands. "You're impossible! There's a difference between being right and being rude. Even Speaker Yeneri, for all the energy she devoted to caring for the poor, never went out of her way to offend the nobles upon whose donations we depend."

"The poor don't need your sympathy," Mirae snapped. "They need respect and common decency, for any of us might be poor but for the whims of the gods. Meanwhile, you're concerned with something as trivial as my rudeness?"

"Perhaps no one bothered to inform you, because they're in such awe of your miraculous voice, but there are social contracts we all must abide by in order for society to function. Contracts which you seem to have no qualms about breaking!"

Mirae took a step back. She gave Sefina a stricken look, her dark brows furrowing above wide, vulnerable eyes. "Is that truly what you think, Fina? That people tolerate my opinions and behavior because of my voice?"

Some of Sefina's anger died away. She heaved an exhausted sigh, pinching her forehead between her fingers. "No, love. I'm sorry. Tonight has been awful."

Mirae closed the distance between them and took Sefina in her arms, pressing a kiss of apology to her temple. Sefina couldn't help but relax at the familiar warmth of Mirae's lips on her skin. "I'm sorry, too. You were only trying to help. I can't hope to become the next Speaker if all the nobles despise me, even if I'm right to despise them. I'm too stubborn for my own good."

Sefina dipped her head, burying her nose in the crook of Mirae's throat. She inhaled Mirae's scent, the floral perfume she wore and the underlying smells of Farsea and home. "I already miss Yeneri," she whispered against Mirae's neck.

"So do I."

They cried and clung to each other for a long time. Only once they'd both exhausted themselves did Sefina allow Mirae to undress her and lead her to bed. She collapsed there, resting her head upon Mirae's shoulder while Mirae stroked her hair. She didn't offer to sing Mirae a lullaby, and Mirae didn't ask. Tonight, that song was for Speaker Yeneri alone, gone to her eternal rest at last.

When Sefina finally drifted off to sleep, her dreams were dark, cold things which offered no comfort at all. She dreamed of a starless void in place of the sky, with a cloaked woman, blacker than black, silhouetted against the chilling nothingness. "Do not weep, child," she said, in a voice that sounded like many mournful people crying out at once. "We gave her the gift of peaceful passage."

We? Sefina tried to ask, but she was frozen. Little more than a block of ice floating within the all-consuming darkness.

"You will understand soon enough."

When Sefina woke screaming, reaching out into the night and covered in clammy sweat, Mirae was there. Mirae, whose palms stroked circles upon Sefina's back to calm her racing heart and soothe her burning lungs. "It's all right, Fina. Everything's all right."

Sefina cleaved to Mirae until there was no space left between them. Mirae held her, murmuring reassurances until she fell into a deathlike sleep without any dreams at all.

Chapter Thirteen

THE DAYS THAT FOLLOWED were dark ones. Often, Sefina found herself walking to Speaker Yeneri's rooms, hoping for conversation or one of her grand tales, only to remember she was gone. Emptiness took up residence within the Temple of Dreams and hollowness lived within Sefina's heart.

While Sefina drifted around the temple like a restless spirit, Mirae spent almost every day at the docks. Sefina suspected she nursed more broken hearts than injuries, so she swallowed her complaints. She wouldn't deny Mirae the chance to help her people grieve the loss of their own.

She had little time to sit with her grief. Lady Lirath soon presented her with an unending list of chores: cleaning out the speaker's rooms, helping to prepare her funeral, and greeting the pilgrims who poured in from beyond the city to pay their respects. Sefina imagined she was a puppet, jumping whenever Lady Lirath pulled her strings, but it was something of a relief to surrender control.

First and foremost, she waited upon Stagford's nobles, most of whom believed it was their right to socialize at the temple under the guise of mourning. Lady Lirath did nothing to discourage them. They flitted about, moving between each other like flutterbugs from flower to flower, repeating the same circular conversations. Sefina lost count of how many times she heard about Lady Tamsin's new racehorse or how the late Lord Goodwin's twins continued to argue over his estate.

A frequent topic of conversation was Speaker Yeneri's replacement. Since Lady Lirath had publicly stated her intention to remain temple treasurer, Mirae was the most popular candidate. In her absence, Sefina found herself barraged by all manner of questions.

"Why isn't Mirae here? Is she in mourning?"

"Has she confined herself to her rooms since the speaker's death?"

From the hungry gleam in their eyes, these nobles hoped this was the case, if only for gossip's sake.

Sefina learned not to mention the docks, for doing so provoked aghast reactions:

"The docks? But why?"

"Such a dangerous place for a young lady…"

"Who knows what manner of ill fortune might befall her there?"

"No," Sefina answered. "She is in Easton, among friends who need her in this time of grief." Better to let the nobles make their own assumptions and imagine Mirae among the middle class merchants. It would set far fewer tongues wagging.

As the days passed, Sefina began to suspect that Mirae wasn't only avoiding the temple, but her as well. Though they shared the same bed and exchanged kisses each morning and night, a great distance seemed to stretch between them. It was a gap Sefina had no idea how to cross.

One brisk autumn day, three weeks after the speaker's passing, Sefina startled awake to loud banging sounds and muttered curses. She rubbed the sand of sleep from her eyes and saw Mirae bustling about their room, emptying drawers and rummaging through the dresser drawers. "What are you doing? Dawnbell hasn't rung."

Mirae straightened from a crouched position, smoothing the wrinkles from her robe. "You cleared out Speaker Yeneri's rooms, yes? Where did you put her ascension tapestry?"

Sefina sat straight up in bed. "On top of the bureau, beneath the extra blankets. I thought it was the least likely place someone might look." Her lips pulled into a frown. "Why? Surely you don't intend to display it now."

Mirae smirked. "That's exactly what I intend to do."

"You can't possibly," Sefina said, throwing off the covers and scrambling out of bed. "I agree that it should be displayed, but wait until you've established yourself as speaker. There will be objections."

Mirae rolled her eyes, turning away to dig beneath the spare blankets. "You sound like Lady Lirath. Who, by the way, has failed to call a meeting where candidates may submit themselves for ascension."

Ah. So that's the reason. You wish to provoke her into handing over the reins of power.

"It's only been three weeks."

Mirae turned, the folded tapestry held tight within her arms. "During which Lady Lirath has taken charge of everything and turned the temple into her own private social engagement." The frustrated furrow in her brow softened and her scowl became a mild frown. "Don't you want change, Fina?"

Sefina sighed. Of course she wanted change, but Mirae's attempt at a power play so soon after the speaker's death would end badly. She went to the wardrobe beside the dresser, retrieving a robe for herself and returning an errant hairbrush and linen shirt to their places as she did so. Mirae had made quite a mess already.

Mirae's gaze followed her, burning in a hot, unpleasant way. "Aren't you going to say anything?"

Sefina pulled the robe over her head and folded her arms. "What do you intend to tell Lady Lirath?"

"That it was Speaker Yeneri's wish to have the tapestry hung after her death."

"A generous massaging of the truth. Be honest. You want to provoke Lady Lirath into beginning the ascension process. Or merely provoke her in general. Don't lose sight of the war for want of a single victory."

Mirae placed both hands upon her hips. "You think bringing our cultures together is a war? How naive of me. I saw it as the right thing to do."

"Stop putting words in my mouth." It took a concerted effort for Sefina not to grind her teeth. "If this is so important to you, let's ask permission. That way, Lady Lirath might view us as collaborators in carrying out Speaker Yeneri's wishes instead of defiant children who don't think of consequences."

Mirae scowled, but dropped her hands to her sides. "Alright. I suppose I don't need to storm the entrance hall and hang the tapestry without warning. Will you come?"

Sefina forced a smile. "Of course."

They went to Lady Lirath's rooms—Mirae, tense and ready for an argument; Sefina, sick to her stomach for fear of the same.

Lady Lirath answered the door in a sleep robe, though its purple silk and tailoring were so fine it could have passed for daywear. Her ice blue eyes shifted from Sefina to Mirae. Something in her cold stare suggested they should have known better than to disturb her so early.

"What brings you here before dawnbell, girls? Somehow, I doubt an invitation to breakfast."

"We're here to fulfill a request from the late speaker." Mirae raised her chin, meeting Lady Lirath's stare with a challenging one of her own.

Lady Lirath arched a single brow. "Oh? Speaker Yeneri left such tasks to me, so far as I'm aware." Her gaze dropped to the bundle in Mirae's arms and stayed there.

"May we come in?" Sefina asked, forcing a polite smile. "Such important conversations shouldn't be held in hallways."

Lady Lirath stepped aside, allowing them entry.

Sefina closed the door, asking Mirae to remain silent with a look. For once, Mirae heeded her. "Before her passing, Speaker Yeneri showed us the tapestry she wove for her ascension—"

Lady Lirath held up her hand. "Say no more, Sefina. You wish to display it, yes?" She addressed the question to Mirae.

Mirae frowned. "As Sefina was saying, Speaker Yeneri wished the tapestry hung upon the event of her death."

"Of course she did." Lady Lirath's irritated countenance changed to something softer. She seemed to stare somewhere beyond them, a sad smile curving her thin lips. It was a wistful look that surprised Sefina with its vulnerability. Then she came back to herself and her expression hardened. "Surely you understand why that cannot happen at this precise moment, though."

"So you know about the tapestry?" Sefina asked.

"Of course, dear girl. I've seen it. Speaker Yeneri kept no secrets from me. I would publicly support what the tapestry depicts, were it not for all the trouble such a controversial message would bring upon our heads during this delicate time."

"Controversial?" Mirae's voice rose in pitch and volume. "Since when have we censored art on the merit of its messages alone? Many works displayed in the temple favor one culture's religious beliefs at the expense of another's. Why should this be any different? Shouldn't the Temple of Dreams host masterworks of all kinds?"

"In theory, yes," Lady Lirath began.

"In practice," Mirae insisted.

Sefina placed a hand upon Mirae's shoulder. Mirae allowed the touch, but her muscles failed to relax beneath Sefina's palm. "Who would object so strongly to the tapestry that it worries you?" Sefina asked Lady Lirath. "In my opinion, it shows a message of peace and unity."

Lady Lirath pursed her lips. "The lord regent's father, my uncle—"

"Who is long dead now," Mirae said.

"Do not interrupt," Lady Lirath said, her voice clipped and frosty. "Obviously, I've failed in my duties as teacher and guardian if the most basic tenets of good manners still elude you."

Mirae had the decency to look ashamed at the reprimand. Her eyes darted down to the floor. "My apologies. Please, continue."

Lady Lirath stepped forward, placing a hand upon Mirae's other shoulder and causing her to look up. "I understand and sympathize with your frustration, Mirae. More than you may realize. But radicals rarely make friends, and friends and their coin are what keep this temple afloat. For once, take my advice. Wait. You do realize how much monetary aid the temple provides your own people, yes? Beyond your healing abilities?"

Mirae bit her lip. When she spoke, her voice held a note of uncertainty. "Speaker Yeneri was always generous with those who live at the docks."

"Extremely so," Lady Lirath said. "Poor Sea Children from that area know they may come here for a hot meal and a clean bed for a few nights. Many attend lectures here to learn reading and writing, so they may better themselves through education and hard work."

"Yes, but—"

"But such things are not free, Mirae." Lady Lirath removed her hand, caressing Mirae's cheek before withdrawing. "Why do you think Speaker Yeneri valued my counsel? Why do you think I intend to remain in my position as treasurer while the position of speaker is vacant? If you want to be an effective speaker, as she was, you will heed my advice."

"But the tapestry—"

"Will not disappear into thin air," Lady Lirath said, waving her hand. "Our Sefina may yet provide the solution you seek."

Sefina blinked. She'd been so intent on their conversation that the sound of her own name surprised her. "Me, Lady Lirath?"

Lady Lirath's gaze fell upon her, unusually warm and encouraging. "Let Sefina convince the lord regent to fund its display once you, Mirae, are settled into your new role. Use his fondness for her and his offer of patronage to make it seem like his idea. He is more progressive than his father and you will meet far less resistance."

It was the wrong thing to say. Sefina recoiled as fire flashed in Mirae's dark brown eyes. Fury radiated from her tense form, charging the air around them. "Such games may amuse you, but they're beneath Sefina and me. We'll leave the playing of them to you."

Mirae shifted the tapestry to one arm and grabbed Sefina's hand, attempting to lead her to the door. Sefina snatched her hand back and stepped away. "Don't tug at me like a dog on a lead. And you always disapprove when Lady Lirath speaks for me. Why are you doing the same now?"

Hurt flickered across Mirae's face, her eyebrows drawing together over her wide, wounded eyes. "You want to court the regent's coin purse, knowing where his real interests lie?"

Doubt gnawed at Sefina's stomach, but she stood firm. "Is it so unbelievable that someone might take notice of my talent? That perhaps I'm better suited to solve a problem that you can't? Whatever interest the lord regent may have in me besides patronage is his problem. The tapestry is ours. Don't you trust me to persuade him within the bounds of propriety?"

Mirae's jaw clenched. "It isn't you I doubt, but this idea is ridiculous. Come find me once you've come to your senses." She whirled and flounced from the room without so much as a farewell, slamming the door behind her.

As soon as she disappeared, Sefina felt the cold, clammy sensation of doubt creep along her spine. She took a step toward the door, already forming an apology, but Lady Lirath held up a hand. "Wait a moment, Sefina."

Instinct told Sefina she should go after Mirae, but wounded pride and practiced obedience kept her rooted to the spot. Hearing Lady Lirath out might give Mirae's temper time to cool. "Not one for compromise, is she?" she said, forcing an awkward smile.

"A massive understatement," said Lady Lirath. "Mirae's heart is in the right place, but her stubbornness blinds her to other, more effective routes. She would trudge in a straight line through knee-deep mud to reach her destination rather than take the subtly winding road."

The way Lady Lirath spoke to her, like a confidant and equal, bolstered Sefina's mood. For once, she was the good and obedient student, while Mirae was the frustrating one who tried their mentor's patience. "What would you have me do? Even I can't convince her to change her mind once it's set in stone like this."

Lady Lirath placed a hand upon her shoulder. "Have you considered that Mirae's talents, while extraordinary, might not make her well-suited to the role of speaker?"

Sefina's brow furrowed. "All speakers must work some public miracle in order to ascend, mustn't they? Mirae has already performed too many miracles to count. Speaker Yeneri always led us to believe that Mirae would follow in her footsteps."

Lady Lirath squeezed Sefina's shoulder. "Do you remember why I taught you to play the lute, Sefina?"

"To accompany Mirae," Sefina said.

"So you would have a skill all your own. You've grown into a remarkable young woman. Your behavior around the nobles these past few weeks has been exemplary. The position of speaker is about much more than performing miracles. That's why we have gods, after all. Sometimes, more human talents are what we truly need."

Only then did the truth dawn upon Sefina—a truth she might have guessed, but for all the years she'd assumed she would always be the second choice. "You think I should be the next speaker?" she asked, breathless with the mere idea. "But I've never performed a miracle."

"Horses may run faster than any man and pull far heavier loads, but they require a well-tempered hand to guide them. Do you understand?"

Heat flashed on Sefina's face—what an offensive comparison to the woman she loved!—yet a greater part of her latched onto the idea. Lady Lirath believed that she possessed enough talent and wisdom to take on the temple's most important role. Never had she felt so seen, so acknowledged.

"I do," she said, struggling to contain her smile. Such obvious gloating would be improper during such a somber moment. "I'm honored that you think so highly of me."

"One thing more," Lady Lirath said. "Not all past speakers performed over a decade's worth of miracles before their ascensions. Speaker Yeneri never wove anything besides ordinary, though beautiful works until the tapestry that earned her the position. Bearing that in mind, I urge you to submit yourself for consideration. Leave the decision in Of-Blessed-Dreams' capable hands. Surely neither you nor Mirae will hold a lasting grudge over one of the Eight's decisions?"

A knot in Sefina's stomach loosened at those words. If Of-Blessed-Dreams chose her as the next speaker, Mirae would find the grace to be happy, as Sefina had faithfully celebrated her accomplishment over the years.

Perhaps Mirae is meant to be a renowned miracle-worker, the temple's greatest treasure and asset, while I'm better suited for the mantle of leadership. And hasn't Mirae given enough of herself already, serving the people at the docks? She'd hate staying at the temple every day, with all the boring nobles clamoring for her attention.

It took Sefina mere seconds to convince herself. She dipped her head, holding herself with all the grace and poise she could muster. "I've always held your counsel in highest regard, Lady Lirath. When the ascension process begins I'll submit myself as a candidate. As you say, the decision is in Of-Blessed-Dreams' hands."

Lady Lirath caressed Sefina's cheek. Though her fingertips were cold, the maternal gesture kindled warmth within the core of Sefina's chest. "Good girl. Now, go and make up with our Mirae. If she offers an apology, I will forgive her outburst. I do admire her motives, though I may disagree with her preference for the blunter instruments of problem-solving."

"Of course."

Sefina departed with a spring in her step and a broad smile, the harsh words she'd exchanged with Mirae all but forgotten. They would reconcile the same as always. Lady Lirath's long-withheld approval gave her confidence she'd never known, as though nothing bad could touch her.

* * * *

Sefina and Mirae danced around each other in the days that followed. Though they shared a bed, they also shared far fewer conversations and casual touches. They made love once, but it was silent and rough—thoroughly enjoyable, but not the reconciliation Sefina had hoped for. She decided to hold her tongue a while longer concerning her decision to submit her candidacy. Surely it wasn't lying by omission if she intended to tell Mirae and was merely waiting for her mood to improve.

A week passed, then two. Slowly, she and Mirae found their way back to each other. Sefina sang lullabies and stroked Mirae's hair. Mirae made fresh eel pie from scratch and presented it to Sefina at lunchtime. Sefina dared hope all would be well again...until the long-awaited notice appeared on the wooden scheduling board in the entrance hall.

They noticed it on their way to relax by the pond. Sefina recognized Lady Lirath's handwriting and paused to read.

In Honored Memory of Speaker Yeneri, Who Has Fallen Asleep Amongst the Stars:

The Temple of Dreams requires a new Speaker. All are invited to submit themselves for consideration. Of-Blessed-Dreams Herself will choose Her Herald, while Master Wiggum the Sculptor; Mistress Jordan of the Dance; and Lady Lirath, Treasurer and First Instructor of Music, bear witness. Come prepared to make an offering to the Goddess, whether it is a performance or work of exquisite craftsmanship, one week from next Sevenday at dawnbell.

May Of-Blessed-Dreams' blessings shine upon us all.

"I wonder how many people will submit themselves?" Mirae mused as she read the notice. "Master Wiggum has a young apprentice. Mistress Jordan has two girls and a boy studying with her, although he hasn't even got a beard yet. Then there's the glassblower and her students...perhaps Trenton may surprise us and tell one of the stories he learned from Speaker Yeneri. Sefina, what do you think?"

A cold stone settled in Sefina's stomach. Now that the notice had been posted, every second she failed to confess felt duplicitous. She plastered on what she hoped was a casual smile and turned away from the notice, toward Mirae. "Actually, I've decided to submit myself."

Mirae's eyes shot open. Her brows rose almost to her hairline. She stared with what looked to Sefina like hurt mingled with disbelief. "What?"

The look of astonishment struck Sefina like a physical blow to the gut. Resentment kindled within her, making her chest burn inside. "Is that so surprising?"

A line creased Mirae's brow and her full lips pulled into a frown. "You've never mentioned a desire for the position before, and Speaker Yeneri...well, she always implied I would take on her role after she passed."

"You were always her favorite," Sefina said, trying and failing to keep the bitterness from her voice. It came out like a keen-edged blade and she saw the way Mirae flinched at its sharpness. "However, Lady Lirath has asked me to submit myself and I've agreed. She says I have a wise, well-tempered nature. She also informed me that Speaker Yeneri performed no miracles before her own ascension. Perhaps I might surprise myself. And you, Mirae."

Mirae's mouth opened and closed several times, like a stunned fish pulled from the water. Then, she laughed. She laughed.

"Fina. Really. You're wonderfully talented in music, clever and kind, and the dearest person to me in the whole world, but my voice sets broken bones and banishes fever. It calls animals to my side and sings gardens into bloom. Do you honestly believe Of-Blessed-Dreams means for someone else to be speaker?"

Blurry tears burned in Sefina's eyes, but she refused to let them fall. "I can't believe you!" Her hands balled into white-knuckled fists. "Your voice may work miracles, but I possess important skills you lack— skills that would make me an excellent speaker. Lady Lirath recognizes this. Why can't you? Are you so blinded by your own self-importance that you can't recognize the talents of those around you? Speaker Yeneri would be ashamed of your arrogance."

Mirae winced as though Sefina had slapped her. The wounded look on her face almost made Sefina take back her words, but it felt perversely good to voice her long-held frustrations.

"I do love you, Fina," Mirae said, her voice soft and uncertain. "I love you more than I can say. I apologize if I've offended you, but Lady Lirath only wishes for you to become speaker because you long to please her."

Sefina clenched her jaw. "'I apologize if I've offended you' isn't a real apology. Why must you assume everyone who admires me has some ulterior motive? Am I your obedient pet, only worthy of praise when I do exactly as you wish? Should I look only to you for approval?"

Mirae narrowed her eyes and fixed Sefina with a scorching glare. "If you're a pet, Lady Lirath holds the other end of your lead. Not me."

Sefina leaned into Mirae's space, fists clenched, shoulders rigid, lips curled into a snarl. "Until you see fit to apologize, you can use that wondrous voice of yours to do your own laundry, style your own hair, and lick your own cunt. You may as well kiss your own ass while you're at it, because I refuse to do it any longer!"

Mirae gasped. "Sefina—"

Sefina stormed off before Mirae could have the last word. Hot tears streamed down her flushed cheeks. Part of her hoped she'd hear Mirae's footsteps behind her, hurrying to catch up and make amends. Another part was relieved when she didn't. She needed to be alone with her anger.

Her feet led her to Lady Lirath's chambers. There was no answer when she knocked, but she'd been given a key years ago. Unwilling to return to their shared room, she removed a spare lute from the pegged wall and sat upon a stool.

She practiced mindlessly, cycling through scales and chord progressions through muscle memory alone. The familiar patterns soothed her.

Mirae never practices like this. Everything comes to her so naturally. She has no idea what it's like to hunch over an instrument, plucking away with callused and aching fingers. She has no idea what hard work and disappointment are.

Sefina wasn't sure how long she practiced. The faint light that filtered through the curtains cast long shadows onto the floor by the time she stopped to stretch her arms and hands. She rotated her wrists, still simmering with rage. She wouldn't share Mirae's bed tonight. Mirae would have no sweet lullabies until she made amends.

She rose to light one of Lady Lirath's tallow candles, but the sound of the door opening distracted her. She turned to see Lady Lirath, whose neutral expression fell into a frown, her forehead creasing with worry. "Sefina? Why are you here so late? It's nearly duskbell."

A stinging lump stopped up Sefina's throat. All that emerged was a broken sob as more tears welled in her eyes. She sniffed, resisting the temptation to wipe her face with her sleeve. Such a display would be unbecoming in front of Lady Lirath.

Though she offered no explanation, Lady Lirath showered her with rare sympathy. She took Sefina into her arms, murmuring into her hair as she wept against Lady Lirath's shoulder. "You and Mirae have quarreled. Nothing else would make you weep so."

Sefina couldn't bring herself to answer. Once the worst of her sobs faded to quiet whimpers, she sniffed again and lifted her head, trying her best to show some composure. "May I sleep here tonight? A pillow and blanket upon your armchair would be more than generous."

"Of course," Lady Lirath said. She patted Sefina's cheek, wiping away her tears. "Would you like a cup of tea? Crying is bad for the throat, you know."

Sefina gave a weak nod. "Yes, please."

Once the tea was brewed, they sipped in silence. Once Sefina calmed, she finally found her voice. "Mirae is displeased by my intention to submit my candidacy. She claims you only encouraged me because I value your counsel. Too much, in her opinion."

Lady Lirath sighed, her hands wrapped around the steaming mug. "Mirae has many difficult lessons to learn, the foremost of which is the management of disappointment. I tried to instill this in her, but I fear Speaker Yeneri, for all I respected her wisdom, has spoiled her."

"She's always gotten everything she wants," Sefina blurted out, tightening her hands around her own warm mug.

"Indeed," Lady Lirath said. "But she loves you dearly, Sefina, in her own way. I stand by what I said the other day. In time, Mirae will see that everyone has their role to play, and yours may very well be speaker. Am I correct in assuming you still wish to submit yourself?"

Sefina nodded, her jaw firm. "If anything, her obstinance only makes me more determined. I need her to recognize my abilities if we're to continue on."

Lady Lirath smiled. "You've always been determined. It's one of your strengths, as is your willingness to heed the counsel of your elders. Don't torment yourself with this spat. Mirae will see the error of her ways."

Sefina remained unconvinced, but allowed Lady Lirath's words to act as a bandage upon her broken heart. She drank in her reassurances like a wilted plant denied life-giving water. By the time duskbell rang, she felt better. At the very least, she was sure of her course. She would submit herself for the role of speaker regardless of what Mirae thought. Mirae would have to make peace with that decision, however much it displeased her.

Sleep scarcely came for Sefina that night. She told herself the reason was Lady Lirath's fireside armchair, but in truth, it was because Mirae wasn't there. She hadn't spent a night apart from Mirae in years. She missed the warmth of Mirae's body and the sound of her snores. Only her wounded pride prevented her from slinking back to their bed. She would return once Mirae apologized and not before.

When she finally stole a few fitful hours of rest, strange and unsettling dreams plagued her mind. The empty silhouette visited her again, a woman of blackest night who blotted out the stars. "Who are you?" Sefina cried. "What do you want with me?"

The woman said nothing, leaving Sefina to shout her questions to the cold, distant stars shining behind its looming black shape. Of course, the stars didn't answer.

Chapter Fourteen

FOR AN ENTIRE WEEK, Sefina avoided Mirae. Mirae made it easy, leaving the temple before dawnbell and returning after duskbell, presumably to visit the docks. When Sefina realized there was no apology forthcoming, she set herself up in one of the spare dormitories reserved for visitors. She gathered her clothes and instruments one morning after Mirae had already taken leave and spirited them away to her new safe harbor.

Every day, hour, and minute she spent apart from Mirae was agonizing, yet every time she imagined Mirae laughing at her ambitions, she felt a smoldering sensation in the pit of her stomach. For once in her life, she wouldn't bend. She would only apologize if Mirae did so first.

Sevenday morning dawned cold, gray, and miserable. A light drizzle drumming upon the window woke Sefina far too early. She'd scarcely slept during the night. The dormitory bed was simultaneously too small and too large without Mirae to share it.

Her legs felt made of lead as she dragged herself out of bed and pulled one of her white concert robes over her head. She'd expected to be nervous on ascension day, but all she felt was sadness. She wanted the role of speaker, but not like this. Without Mirae by her side, she wondered whether her decision was the right one.

She concealed her doubts behind a heavy layer of makeup, powdering her face, darkening her eyes, and painting her lips dark crimson. A stranger stared back at her from within the bathroom mirror. The woman within was beautiful, but her eyes were empty, even with the bags artfully concealed.

Nevertheless, she persisted. Despite her grief, the desire to prove herself burned bright within her heart. That was the fire she relied upon as she retrieved her lute and went to the entrance hall. Though she was well ahead of schedule, she passed the kitchens without stopping for breakfast. She feared anything she forced into her stomach would come straight back up again.

Sefina soon arrived at the same curtained hallway she and Mirae had waited in during their concert. There, she waited with a cramping belly, trembling hands, and heavy eyes. To her warring relief and disappointment, Mirae hadn't arrived.

To drown out her thoughts, Sefina plucked a few faint notes upon her lute. Her fingers walked their way through the piece she'd selected. Rather than singing, she hummed the melody in an attempt to remain quiet, reciting the words only in her mind.

In rosy-fingered dawn and wine-dark seas
In the face of every flower,
And the cool caress of a summer breeze...

A prickle along the back of her neck interrupted her practice. She turned in time to see someone yank their head back behind the nearest corner. "Who's there?" She lowered her lute, taking a step toward the other end of the hall.

As she continued staring, the concealed person cleared their throat and shuffled into view. Though he'd grown a beard in recent months, that fiery red hair and those clear blue eyes were unmistakable. "Trenton? Are you submitting yourself as well?"

"No." Trenton's gaze darted down to his muddy boots. "I drew the short straw."

Sefina allowed her lute to rest from its neck strap, placing both hands on her hips. "Explain yourself. Why are you sneaking around?"

Trenton scratched the back of his neck. "To tell the others how it all turns out. Your and Mirae's bids for speaker. You're the only two who submitted yourselves."

"So you were spying on me," Sefina said.

Trenton nodded, blushing redder than a ripe tomato. "Sorry. I didn't want to, but..."

Sefina sighed. "Are Mirae and I really the only candidates? What about Master Wiggum's apprentice? What about yourself? You could tell one of your stories."

"You couldn't pay me to go up against Mirae," Trenton said, his voice rising. "Not with all the whispers about her and—" He bit his lip as though realizing he'd said too much.

Sefina narrowed her eyes, pinning Trenton with a sharp stare. "What whispers?"

Trenton broke almost immediately. "Some say Mirae sent Speaker Yeneri to sleep amongst the stars...whether by mistake or on purpose."

Sefina's mouth fell open. Mirae, kill Speaker Yeneri? Never! Despite their disagreement, righteous anger toward such rumor-mongers burned within her breast. "Mirae would never do such a thing! She loved Speaker Yeneri like a second mother."

"That's what I told the others," Trenton muttered. "Mirae would never murder no one. At least not on purpose."

"Oh, I don't know," Mirae drawled, startling Sefina as she walked around the same corner. "I can be rather vicious. Don't you agree, Sefina?"

Sefina's mouth went dry. She swallowed, unsure how to respond, struggling to interpret Mirae's expression. Was it bitterness and resentment that creased her brow? Sadness or anger that shone in her dark eyes?

Trenton edged away, his shoulders drooping. "H-hello, Mirae. I didn't mean...uh, I know you'd never...I told them..."

"Just go." Mirae's voice was cold and unyielding as iron, her glare even more so. "I don't care what sort of story you spin for the others. I need to speak with Sefina alone."

Trenton scampered away like a squirrel seeking the safety of its tree. Only after he disappeared did Mirae's gaze land upon Sefina. Sefina stared back. There were purple bags under Mirae's eyes and her normally radiant smile was close-lipped, tight, and forced.

Sefina stayed silent, unsure whether to respond with anger or sympathy. Sympathy won out. "How long have these rumors been floating around?" It wounded her to think of Mirae suffering such slander alone.

"A few weeks." Mirae shrugged, as though being suspected of murder hardly mattered, but the truth of her pain shone in her eyes. Sefina had known Mirae too long and too intimately for Mirae to conceal it from her.

"Before our argument, then. Why keep it secret?"

Mirae made an airy gesture. "What could you have done to stop it?"

Sefina clenched her teeth. "Defended you."

For a moment, Mirae's terse smile softened into something more genuine. "I can hardly envision you in a fist fight."

"With my words, ideally," Sefina said. "What other secrets have you been keeping from me?"

Mirae's jaw clenched. Her smile vanished. "Oh, so now you care?"

The sting of those words almost made Sefina flinch. "Of course I care, darling. Why are you questioning my love for you?"

"Why did you question mine last week? You were all too quick to assume I wanted to see you fail, when it's Lady Lirath and the regent I don't trust. Do you really think I have such a low opinion of you and your talents? Do you really think so poorly of me?"

Sefina shook her head. "You don't understand how you hurt me at all, do you?"

Mirae's glare softened into a look of hesitation and confusion. She started to say something conciliatory, but the moment was interrupted. Lady Lirath pulled back the curtain and poked her head into the hall. "Ah. Both our candidates are here. Wiggum and Jordaine are ready to witness your appeals. Who would like to go first?"

Sefina's heart leapt. So soon? She'd expected more ceremony first, or at least more warning. Perhaps this was less of a performance and more of a secret ritual. She had no idea what to expect other than the knowledge that she would have to sing.

The hairs along Sefina's arms stood up as Mirae's stare left Lady Lirath and returned to her. "Rock, paper, shears?"

Lady Lirath frowned as though she disapproved, but Sefina could think of no better way to decide. She wasn't sure whether she wanted to go first or second anyway. "Why not?"

She and Mirae beat their fists upon their palms three times in rhythm. Mirae threw rock. Appropriate, Sefina thought, considering her stubborn and immovable nature. Sefina threw paper.

Mirae exhaled sharply. "Right then. You first."

Lady Lirath pursed her lips. "Very well. Calm your mind, Sefina, and enter the hall when you are ready." Her pinched expression softened into a brief but encouraging smile before she ducked behind the curtain. Sefina drew all the courage she could from that small gesture, closing her eyes and inhaling deep into her lungs. Her heart drummed faster.

I can do this. Lady Lirath thinks so. My success or failure is in Of-Blessed-Dreams' hands now. That thought calmed her. Either the goddess would see fit to enter her during the performance, or believed she was meant for other things.

"Fina..."

Sefina opened her eyes. Mirae stared at her with a knitted brow and watery eyes, trying and failing to hide an expression of hurt.

Sefina's heart softened. She stepped toward Mirae, resting a hand upon her shoulder. The warmth of Mirae's skin under her palm was familiar and reassuring. "Good luck, Mirae," she said, squeezing once.

"You too."

An apology almost spilled from Sefina's lips then, but the knowledge that Lady Lirath, Master Wiggum, and Mistress Jordaine were waiting nagged at her. There wasn't time now. Perhaps later, once this was over. She withdrew her hand and squared her shoulders, passing through the curtain and into the hall.

Though Sefina knew how the entrance hall looked, felt, and sounded, she felt like a foreigner setting foot in a strange land. Perhaps it was the rectangular table that had been brought to seat the three witnesses: Master Wiggum, Mistress Jordaine, and of course, Lady Lirath. Sefina knew Wiggum and Jordaine, but had never interacted with them for more than a few minutes at a time.

"Candidate Sefina," Master Wiggum said, his wheezing voice amplified by the hall's acoustics. He was old and wrinkled, though not so ancient as Speaker Yeneri had been before her death. His curly white mustache and bushy beard were glorious to behold. "Lady Lirath speaks highly of your talents."

Mistress Jordaine nodded. She was a willowy, middle-aged woman with curly brown hair and an undeniable aura of grace and poise, which somehow remained obvious even while she was seated. "Indeed she has. Please, make your appeal to Of-Blessed-Dreams whenever you're ready."

Sefina's heart pounded so loud she was certain the others could hear. She hadn't expected to perform within seconds, but the judges watched with silent expectation. She spared a brief glance upward, admiring Of-Blessed-Dreams mosaic. Her peaceful smile caused Sefina's heart to slow for a few beats. The nervous burn in her lungs subsided.

All I need to do is submit myself to her. She'll take care of the rest.

As Sefina relaxd, a strange coldness started behind her sternum, spreading through her chest like frost. Her limbs became tingling, leaden weight until she no longer felt them at all. Her heavy heartbeat stopped pounding in her ears, slowing until she couldn't perceive it at all.

Panicking, Sefina attempted to breathe, but a painfully cold wind passed through her lips, drying them out until the edges split. Yet when she sang, her voice was beautiful. It was crystal clear, like a glittering jewel bending and refracting an otherworldly light.

Instead of the song she'd selected, a completely different melody poured from her mouth, accompanied by unfamiliar words.

One to sew diamonds in night's cloak.

Two to push and pull the tides.
Three to kiss each flower and tree.
Four for the winds and clouds of the sky.
Five and six for knowledge and love.
Seven for story and song.
But where is the eighth? The shard of sleep?
In darkness they keep us. Forgotten. Alone.

It was a haunting song with a lonely, wandering melody. Sefina should have been astonished, but just as her body had left her control, her thoughts were no longer her own. She forgot about the entrance hall and her audience as she drifted somewhere apart. Somewhere cold and dark. An endless expanse of nothing.

Where are we? Strange voices moaned in eerie chorus. *Who are we? Let us out! Let us...*

A sharp crack brought Sefina back to herself. Fire raced through her veins as all her missing body heat returned at once. Her heart lurched into its normal rhythm as though she were coming back from the dead. She was Sefina again, but she regained control of her voice only to scream.

Above her, Of-Blessed-Dreams' mosaic split straight down the middle. Debris rained all around as a hundred cracks spread through the ceiling. Sefina threw her arms overhead, but no pain followed. Nothing struck her. She felt only the gentle whisper of dust against her forearms.

As suddenly as it started, the crumbling stopped. Cautiously, Sefina lowered her arms and looked up. Of-Blessed-Dreams no longer had a face. Her warm smile and kind eyes were gone, leaving only bare gray stone. The rest of the mosaic had splintered like a shattered mirror, missing pieces of tile.

Ice gripped Sefina's heart as she beheld the damage. *What have I done?*

Then she noticed the tile had fallen in a perfect ring around her feet. As she realized what had happened, a savage sort of joy washed over her instead. At long last, she'd performed her own miracle! Perhaps a frightening and terrible one, but the haunting song she'd sung and the destruction of the mosaic couldn't be coincidences. Something strange and ethereal had taken her within its grip, something far more powerful than a mere mortal.

Lady Lirath leapt up and rushed around the table. "Sefina, are you all right?" She grasped Sefina's shoulders, attempting to shepherd her away from the mess of dust, plaster, and broken tiles.

Sefina sagged, almost slumping over with sudden exhaustion. Only Lady Lirath's steadying hands kept her upright. Though she tried to say she was fine—better than fine—she couldn't manage a verbal answer. All that came out was a confused whimper as her mind struggled to process everything. Still, a smile crept across her face. She'd done something!

"Eight preserve us," Master Wiggum moaned, pressing an open palm to his chest. "Our Lady's mosaic is ruined!"

"Is she all right, Raula?" Mistress Jordaine asked.

Sefina managed a weak nod. Lady Lirath squeezed her upper arms before turning to address the other witnesses. "Sefina is unharmed—a miracle, though certainly not what I expected."

"You call this a miracle?" Mirae stormed out from behind the curtain, coiled hair bouncing with each step, eyes ablaze. "Sefina could have been hurt! She could have died! And all you want to do is push your own selfish agenda." She rushed over, pushing Lady Lirath aside and taking Sefina into her arms. "Oh, Fina, are you sure you're all right?"

Though Mirae trembled against her, clearly shocked and upset, everything felt strangely right with Sefina's world. Warmth flushed the last of the cold from her limbs. Her heart tripped fast and the smile on her face stretched until her cheeks ached to hold it. She was no longer afraid.

"Did you hear?" She clutched Mirae's sleeves, gazing desperately into her eyes. "Did you see? The song, those words...I've never heard them before in my life. I went somewhere cold and dark and the music poured forth like a wellspring. And the mosaic—"

A frown darkened Mirae's face. She cupped Sefina's cheeks in both hands, resting their foreheads together. "Sefina...I'm sorry, but this is no miracle," she said in a soft voice. "You could have been killed. Our goddess no longer has a face."

Sefina jerked away from Mirae's hands. The words punctured her swelling pride, leaving her empty and deflated. "But—"

"Come," Mirae said, wrapping an arm around Sefina's shoulder. "Let's clean you up and make sure there aren't any scratches or bruises. The witnesses can wait for my appeal."

"Stop!" Lady Lirath stepped in front of them, her shadow stretching over Sefina in the low morning light that filtered through the stained glass windows. "Sefina must stay. This is clearly a sign from Of-Blessed-Dreams. Her song was enrapturing! You cannot deny this simply because you hoped to be speaker instead, Mirae."

Mirae removed her arm, placing herself between Sefina and Lady Lirath. She stood there with stiff shoulders and clenched fists while Sefina's mind whirled. "The girl you raised from childhood was almost struck down and you call it a miracle?" Mirae gestured wildly at the ruined mosaic.

"But I wasn't." Sefina grasped Mirae's elbow, speaking in a breathless rush. "I'm fine. And the song—some strange force took possession of me, pouring the words into my mind and out of my mouth. Isn't that how you feel when you make your miracles? Isn't that the experience Speaker Yeneri described when she wove her tapestry?"

Mirae turned, frowning. "I'm not denying that something unexplainable happened, but it was no miracle. If anything, it was a warning."

Sefina snatched her hand from Mirae's elbow, sucking in a short, sharp breath. In Mirae's drawn brow, she saw complete dismissal—a stubborn unwillingness to acknowledge what she'd done. "You're jealous, aren't you? Lady Lirath was right. You're far too wrapped up in your own self-importance to appreciate anyone else's talents." She placed her palm flat upon her chest, as though it might loosen the growing knot of pain there. "Is it so impossible that Of-Blessed-Dreams might find me worthy? If the goddess believes in me, why can't you?"

Mirae shook her head. "I do believe in you, Fina, but look." She gestured at the mess upon the floor stones. "I know you want and deserve recognition, but not this way. And Lady Lirath is to blame for starving you of all self-confidence in the first place. Don't throw yourself headlong into the ocean because she's kept you thirsty your entire life. I swear, Sefina, it will be the death of you."

"Mirae," Lady Lirath said, "that is entirely inappropriate."

"But am I wrong?"

Sefina stepped between the two of them, clenching her hands together tight. Tears stung her eyes, but she refused to cry. Of-Blessed-Dreams had chosen her. She needed to believe in herself for once. "At least Lady Lirath thinks I could be speaker," she told Mirae. "Unlike you."

Mirae blinked, then shook her head. "Lady Lirath only offers encouragement when you're obedient and useful. Have you forgotten all her harsh words?" Her voice rose, filling the entire hall. "I can't even count the nights I held you while you wept, because she told you that you would never be good enough."

"I am good enough," Sefina declared, with enough force to surprise even herself. "Wise enough to be the next Speaker of Dreams and intelligent enough to decide whose council I value."

Mirae winced. "You value Lady Lirath's counsel over mine? Even after she's been so cruel to you?"

"Right now," Sefina said, in the coldest voice she could muster, "you're the one hurting me, Mirae."

All emotion drained from Mirae's face. It became a blank slate as she squared her shoulders and said, "I see. Well then, I suppose I'm no longer needed here at the temple, am I?"

The words cut deep, all the way to Sefina's heart. Mirae wanted to leave the temple, their home since childhood. The thought of a different Speaker of Dreams was apparently so abhorrent that Mirae preferred to flee rather than stand aside.

"No," Sefina said, forcing the word out like sharp glass through her throat. "I suppose you aren't." Mirae stared at her in stony silence, but she didn't take it back. She couldn't. Her pride wouldn't allow her to surrender the privilege and title she could almost taste.

"Fine," Mirae said. "I'll be at the docks."

Sefina couldn't resist a parting blow. "As you always are these days."

Mirae marched from the room, her spine as rigid as any soldier's. Sefina remained amidst the wreckage of the mosaic, standing in a ring of dust and broken tile. She hoped Mirae would look back, but she disappeared from the entrance hall without another glance.

Tears streamed from Sefina's eyes, rolling down her cheeks. She swayed, nearly crumpling to her knees under a crushing wave of grief and regret.

"There, there, Sefina." Lady Lirath placed a hand upon her shoulder. "None of this is your fault. Of-Blessed-Dreams chose you. Mirae's inability to accept this is her own failing."

Sefina only cried harder at the mention of Mirae's name. Sadness overflowed the bounds of her heart like a river after a rainstorm. There was no barring the flood until Lady Lirath leaned close to whisper in her ear. "Restrain your emotions if you wish to claim the title you've earned. The other witnesses are watching."

A tight lump rose in Sefina's throat as she remembered Wiggum and Jordaine. Her face burned with an embarrassed blush. *If Of-Blessed-*

Dreams truly chose me for this role, I can't let them see me like this—a weak, sniveling child.

Though it required every ounce of her willpower, Sefina wiped her eyes and sniffed back her tears, wrestling her emotions under control. Luckily, she'd had ample practice. She'd spent years concealing her envy, shame, and sadness. She smoothed her wrinkled dress and stepped past Lady Lirath, brushing the worst of the dust from her skirts.

"Forgive me," she said to Wiggum and Jordaine. Both of them fixed her with wide, uncertain stares, shaken after witnessing the mosaic's destruction and Mirae's furious departure.

As Sefina addressed them, it wasn't Of-Blessed-Dreams she channeled, but Lady Lirath. She spoke with all the gravitas she'd observed in her mentor over the years, imitating her better than she could have hoped.

"I apologize for subjecting you to that argument, but I fear it was inevitable. Mirae has left. I remain. I ask not for your consideration or approval, for only Of-Blessed-Dreams can bestow those, but for your support. Should you agree that I'm meant to take on the mantle of speaker, I swear to serve the goddess and her temple with everything I have and everything I am."

After a long silence, Wiggum and Jordaine gave slow nods.

"Your performance was miraculous, if terrifying," Master Wiggum said. "I was in awe from beginning to end."

"Most extraordinary," Jordaine said. "And since Mirae seems to have withdrawn herself from consideration..."

"I am much more than your only choice," Sefina said, staring Jordaine straight in the eye. "I'm Of-Blessed-Dreams' choice. I believe this with all possible conviction."

Lady Lirath smiled. Though Sefina couldn't bring herself to return the gesture, she acknowledged her with a respectful nod. With more bitterness than joy, Sefina realized that she'd finally made Lady Lirath proud. Any pleasure she might have taken turned sour when she recalled how Mirae had abandoned her at her finest moment.

But she couldn't change the past. She couldn't un-speak her harsh words. She couldn't call Mirae back, and a significant part of her didn't want to, even while the rest of her wondered how she could continue breathing. *Mirae is gone. I remain. This is my destiny.*

So Sefina became Speaker of Dreams: alone, wounded, and more broken than not.

Mirae — Fourthday

ANOTHER DAWNBELL, EACH TOLL a muffled sob. Mirae closes her eyes, resting her chin upon her chest. Her tears fall into the waves, mingling with the starry waters. A tight lump of shame sticks in her throat. Her anger had consumed her on that dark day.

The incident with the mosaic had been Sefina's first taste of success after a lifetime of starvation. A rare opportunity to bask in Lady Lirath's approval. To be celebrated. Looked upon with admiration. Weren't those innate human needs, no matter how humble one tried to be?

Yet Mirae also feels the dying embers of anger glow with new life. She'd hurt Sefina's feelings, but she hadn't been wrong. Lady Lirath had pulled Sefina's puppet strings, encouraging her to submit herself as a candidate and proclaiming the mosaic's destruction a miracle. She'd manipulated Sefina at every turn.

Mirae raises her head. "Lady Lirath wanted a speaker she could control," she tells Speaker Yeneri. The waves tug at her dress, threatening to lift her up and carry her out to sea. "Why couldn't Sefina see that? I tried to tell her how special she was, but it was never enough."

"Ah, but you were her lover," says Yeneri, "not her parent or guardian. You had your parents back in Farsea. You felt their love in letters and visits. Sefina had only Lady Lirath—the beautiful, austere noblewoman who saved her from poverty. Is it any wonder she longed for Lady Lirath's approval?"

Mirae turns toward the blue-black sea scattered with cold white stars, unwilling to look at the gray light anymore. "Sefina wasn't a child anymore. She was a woman grown. There comes a time when children realize their parents are flawed. It isn't my fault Sefina never realized that."

Yeneri merely smiles a mysterious smile, the wrinkles around her eyes crinkling at the corners. "Your steps into adulthood were like stepping from a curb into the street. To Sefina, that same step looked more like a cliff. She was afraid of falling."

"I would have caught her," Mirae says. "I would have helped. I...I should have helped more." Regret creeps in like a shadow. She could have stayed and explained herself in a calmer fashion. In private, at the very least, but she'd made a public scene, right on the tail of Sefina's "miracle". Her pride had been stung—

"I was jealous." The truth turns the waves cold around her, sending a shiver down her spine. She wraps her wet arms around herself and chews her lip. "I told myself I couldn't possibly be jealous, because I loved Sefina more than anything. And because I—well, I was always the special one. Then she did something unexplainable and I..."

Fresh tears leak from Mirae's eyes. She had feared, somewhere in her heart of hearts, that Sefina's newfound talents meant hers would be less important. Some subconscious part of her had feared Sefina would cease to look upon her with awe and realize she wasn't that special after all, beneath the miracles.

"I understand now," she says, forcing herself to look at Yeneri. The tear tracks on her cheeks sting in the cold ocean wind. "Sometimes it's better to be kind than right. I didn't only leave because I wished to protect Sefina from Lady Lirath. I also left because I feared she'd outshine me."

Yeneri leans over the side of the rowboat, resting a bony hand upon Mirae's shoulder. "You're only human, Mirae. We all wrestle with jealousy—Sefina especially. If you went back and told her this, she would understand."

Mirae tilts her head, resting her cheek upon the back of Yeneri's hand. "Do I deserve to see her again after I was so awful?"

The sound of Sefina's voice carries across the sea toward her, perhaps in answer to that question. Mirae turns once more toward the distant light upon the shore and listens.

Chapter Fifteen

SEFINA'S NIGHT WITHOUT MIRAE was lonely beyond words. She lay awake in Speaker Yeneri's bed, which Lady Lirath had insisted she claim, staring at shadows upon the ceiling by the light of a lone candle. She burned that candle through the early hours, occasionally turning her head to stare into its dancing flame.

Where had Mirae taken shelter? With those who would care for her, Sefina hoped. Brom and his wife were good friends, as was Taela the pie merchant, and many other grateful residents of the Easton docks. They would certainly take Mirae in after all she'd done for them, but that knowledge was cold comfort.

You're gone. I drove you away.

When dawnbell rang, Sefina couldn't bring herself to leave her bed. She huddled beneath the covers, drifting in and out of bittersweet memories, until Lady Lirath arrived late in the morning. She barged in without bothering to knock, carrying a tray with tea and pastries.

"Get dressed, Sefina," she said, setting the tray upon the nightstand. "The Speaker of Dreams doesn't waste her day in bed."

"All right," Sefina said, but made no move to get up.

Lady Lirath huffed, crossing the room to retrieve Sefina's lute. "If you won't get up, eat and practice in bed," she said, plopping the lute into Sefina's lap. "A single day without practice requires at least two days' recovery, as you well know. I'll inform the temple that you're meditating on your new position, in case you might receive wisdom from Of-Blessed-Dreams or Speaker Yeneri's departed soul. Tomorrow, you must assume your duties."

Sefina only managed a silent nod. That seemed to be enough for Lady Lirath. She left Sefina in peace for the rest of the day and brought her warm broth for dinner. Sefina thought that considerate. Lady Lirath had correctly assumed anything heavier wouldn't remain long in her stomach.

Her second day as Speaker of Dreams was better, if barely. Lady Lirath had to drag her out of bed to be fitted for her vestments. "I'll not have you looking a mess like Speaker Yeneri, may Lady Sleep keep her soul," Lady Lirath said as the seamstress took Sefina's measurements.

"You must wear the proper attire so everyone, temple residents and nobles alike, will accept you in your new role."

Sefina had no energy to argue. Her silence stood as tacit agreement until the seamstress left.

"Now," Lady Lirath said once they were alone, "you'll put on your finest clothes, go to the entrance hall, and receive congratulations from all who would offer you good wishes."

Once more, Sefina obeyed. She remained in a fog as Lady Lirath selected her outfit, a dress of crushed purple velvet, and did her make-up. Unlike Mirae, she didn't know how Sefina preferred it. Still, Sefina offered no complaints as Lady Lirath outlined her lips and eyes too heavily, as though preparing her for the stage. She pinned Sefina's hair up as well, forgetting to leave ringlets to frame her face as Mirae always did. Nevertheless, Sefina had to admit she looked presentable as she studied her reflection in the standing mirror. Drawn and pale, but presentable.

As Lady Lirath led her to the entrance hall, Sefina recalled one of Speaker Yeneri's stories. Garoth the inventor and his automaton, Telos, the iron man which moved of its own accord. The tale was one of Mirae's favorites. For the next several hours, Sefina was Telos. She plastered on a false smile and followed Lady Lirath's wordless commands. If she hadn't had a script to follow, Sefina would have floundered like a fish upon the beach.

She cycled through the same few phrases:

"Thank you so much for your good wishes."

"I'm so honored that Of-Blessed-Dreams saw fit to select me as her speaker."

"I will strive to make Speaker Yeneri proud, may Lady Sleep grant her noble soul rest."

None of the visitors, neither residents nor the nobles who flocked to the entrance hall, dared mention Mirae's absence to Sefina, but she heard whispers as her guests gossiped amongst themselves.

"Where is she?"

"Maybe she couldn't perform a miracle this time."

"I heard she ran away in shame."

"I heard they fought bitterly."

"I heard Mirae shattered the mosaic in her rage!"

Sefina's eyes stung dry as she pretended not to hear. Even the mention of Mirae's name was almost too much to bear.

She soon lost count of the people she spoke with. The line seemed to have no end. Through the entire ordeal, Lady Lirath remained by her side. Whenever Sefina's smile lapsed or her tone of voice revealed a hint of exhaustion, Lady Lirath's hand would fall upon her shoulder, a reminder of how important this performance was.

It took all of Sefina's reserves to reach duskbell, but somehow she managed. Afterward, she mumbled something about soaking in a warm bath, but Lady Lirath shepherded Sefina back to her new rooms, pausing only to smooth out the wrinkles in her dress once they reached the door.

"You will be fine," Lady Lirath said. "Better than fine, my dear."

Sefina squared her shoulders, as though preparing for battle, then summoned her best smile.

Waiting within was the lord regent, hands folded behind his back as he admired an unfinished tapestry on one of Speaker Yeneri's frames. "Pity she never completed this," he said, offering Sefina a brilliant smile. "Like all the late speaker's creations, it is without compare."

"Her hands were goddess-blessed," Sefina said. "Well met, Lord Regent. It is my pleasure to welcome you to the Temple of Dreams this evening."

"On the contrary. It's my pleasure to congratulate you on your new title and position, Speaker Sefina." The regent stepped forward and took Sefina's hand in both of his, giving a friendly squeeze. Sefina managed to hide her surprise, but only just. He hadn't offered the backs of his hands for her to press her forehead against. Apparently, the highest-ranking noble in Stagford considered her a peer now.

Such recognition went a long way toward filling the bleeding hole in Sefina's heart. To receive the approval of someone so wealthy and influential fed some starving place within her. A warm tingle spread throughout her body. She managed her first genuine smile In two whole days.

"Your congratulations are much appreciated. It is my honor to take on the role, though I have large footsteps to fill. On the subject of Speaker Yeneri's tapestries, I had a thought."

Sefina's eyes darted to Lady Lirath, searching for some sign of approval. She offered a subtle nod, so Sefina continued.

"I thought we might arrange an auction for Speaker Yeneri's tapestries. The ones not on permanent display, of course. She kept a great number in her room and it would be a shame to let them sit here, gathering dust. Stagford's nobility would have the opportunity to purchase works of art beyond compare and the temple's coffers will be replenished. We could earmark some of the funds to repair the entrance hall's mosaic."

The regent's eyes brightened. "What a splendid idea. I would part with a generous sum for one of the former speaker's masterworks—or several. No doubt others will feel the same."

"An excellent suggestion, Speaker Sefina," Lady Lirath said. "I shall begin arranging the event at once."

Sefina felt a pang of disappointment within her chest. She'd wanted to arrange the auction herself, a tribute to Speaker Yeneri's memory, but swallowed her words. Though she outranked Lady Lirath now, she didn't want to speak against her before the regent. "The Temple of Dreams appreciates your support, Lord Regent. I have no doubt if you announce your intention to attend, the other nobles will follow suit."

The regent and Lady Lirath both smiled in approval. "It will be my pleasure." After a heavy pause, the regent's smile fell into a concerned frown. "It saddens me, however, to hear that Mirae has left the temple. I fear our relationship began on shaky ground. The former speaker's death was difficult for us all."

Sefina fought to keep her own smile in place. "Yes. I hope that after some time away, Mirae will return with a clear head. She's always loved the temple."

"Perhaps she needs time to overcome her wounded pride," the regent said.

The same thought had crossed Sefina's mind during the past two days, but for some reason, she didn't appreciate hearing it from the regent's lips. Her stomach twisted into an uncomfortable knot. "Perhaps. In the meantime, I have duties to fulfill, while she has her work in Easton. She's always been welcome among the people there."

"Ah, yes. Easton." The regent stroked his honey-brown beard in contemplation. His blue eyes narrowed. "Speaker Yeneri always favored that section of Stagford. I suppose that's why Mirae has made so many friends there."

The regent was by no means a stupid man, but in that moment, Sefina realized something. He was completely unaware of the privilege he possessed, stemming from his wealth and his heritage as an Earthfolk noble. Perhaps he might understand in the barest sense why a Sea Child would seek refuge among her own people, but he would never know the full truth. Why eating familiar foods would no doubt comfort

Mirae. How certain clothes and small but ancient traditions in a Sea Child household could heal a broken heart. Even she, who had lived with Mirae and loved her for years, couldn't know the truth that intimately.

Sefina said nothing of it, merely tucking it into the back of her brain. "Mirae loves the temple," she said. "It will always be her home, if she wishes."

They discussed other subjects for half a candlemark before the regent bade farewell. With a short dip of his head and the usual polite words, he departed, leaving Sefina alone with Lady Lirath.

"You handled yourself well," Lady Lirath said. "This is exactly why I hoped the goddess would select you. I know your heart longs for Mirae's return, but give it time. She may yet overcome her resentment and realize Of-Blessed-Dreams has other equally important plans for her future, in a role that doesn't require so much greasing of wheels."

"I hope so," Sefina said, unable to add any extra energy to her voice. She had nothing left to give that day.

Lady Lirath seemed to realize it too. "To bed with you," she said, shepherding Sefina toward Speaker Yeneri's bedroom. Her bedroom now, though it made Sefina uncomfortable to ruminate on that for too long. "Wash your face and hang your clothes before you go to sleep."

Rather unnecessary parental reminders for a grown woman, Sefina thought, but didn't object. With a whispered, "Good night," she stumbled to bed.

She didn't wash her face, nor did she hang her dress or change into a nightgown. She collapsed into the bed and slept the sleep of the dead, a sleep which was thankfully dreamless.

* * * *

Time slowed to a crawl. A week passed, then two. Sefina wore a forced smile to hide her broken heart. Her laughter was merely the fulfillment of an unspoken social contract. She accepted congratulations with all the grace expected of her, but always felt Mirae's absence.

Each night, she retired to Speaker Yeneri's rooms, unable to sleep except by weeping herself into a state of exhaustion. Though she wore Yeneri's vestments, altered to fit her frame, she felt like an impostor whenever she caught her reflection. The golden stole hung heavy upon her shoulders, the long white robes stifling no matter the temperature.

One gloomy afternoon, a month following Mirae's departure, Sefina sat at Lady Lirath's desk. It was easier to work in Lady Lirath's studio than the departed speaker's room surrounded by the stale yet familiar smell of tallow. A stack of papers sat before her, waiting to be signed and stamped with the Speaker of Dreams' seal. Invitations for the upcoming auction of Speaker Yeneri's remaining works.

Though the event had been Sefina's idea, working through the pile of invitations made her eyes sting. Speaker Yeneri was gone. Sefina would never hear her rich voice carry a story again, nor would she rub liniment into the swollen joints of her hands. She would never listen to Yeneri and Lady Lirath quarrel about whether the window should remain open or closed. She would never see that soft smile buried amidst the wrinkles of Yeneri's face.

Now Mirae was gone as well. Sefina had no idea whether she would return, despite what she told herself. Though she was the most powerful person in the Temple of Dreams, having risen to a station beyond her greatest hopes, she felt utterly alone.

She set her quill in the ink pot and removed the ring that acted as the speaker's seal. It was too large for her fourth finger and too weighty as she held it in her palm. Though she'd worn it for some time, the metal remained cold no matter how long it stayed on her finger. The decoration was a tiny version of Of-Blessed-Dreams' face, with wavy hair and a peaceful smile. It reminded Sefina of the mosaic she'd ruined.

What if Mirae was right? a frightened voice whispered in Sefina's mind. *What if my miracle was indeed a warning?*

No. She couldn't think that way. The strange chill that had entered her body and consumed her while she sang was an act of the gods. She hadn't made it up for attention. She'd been willing to let the goddess choose her own ambassador, but Of-Blessed-Dreams had chosen her. Nothing that followed after was her fault.

Sefina left the ring by the unfinished stack of invitations, rising from the desk and walking to the window. She opened it despite the autumn rain drumming upon the glass, shuddering in the cold breeze and inhaling the scent of wet grass and damp soil. It made her feel closer to Speaker Yeneri. Mirae, too.

The door behind her creaked open. Lady Lirath's sharp voice filled the room. "Sefina, what beneath Of-the-Sky's gaze are you doing?"

"Sorry," Sefina said, shutting the window and turning to meet Lady Lirath. "I only wanted a breath of fresh air."

Lady Lirath waved away the excuse. "You've let the candle burn out," she said, bustling over to her desk to light it once more. "It wouldn't surprise me if you caught cold as well. You must be more sensible."

"Of course."

Conversations with Lady Lirath were like solo performances. Sefina's contributions were little more than accompaniment.

"You were thinking of Mirae again." Lady Lirath's gaze fixed firmly upon Sefina as though to pry the truth from her lips.

Sefina gave no answer. They both knew it was true.

"If she consumes your mind so, take a few hours and seek her out in Easton. Her tantrum has gone on long enough. Perhaps she's ready to make amends and return home. Her support wouldn't go amiss while your position is so new."

Sefina's eyes widened. That wasn't the counsel she had expected. Hope swelled within her. Had enough time passed to soften Mirae's heart? Perhaps only stubborn pride prevented her from returning to the temple. *Maybe if she sees me, she'll realize she misses me and come home.*

"I thought you considered the docks too dangerous for a lady," Sefina said. Though she wanted to go, part of her couldn't help but feel like this was a trap, some sort of secret test Lady Lirath was giving her.

"They are dangerous," Lady Lirath said. "I never approved of the way Speaker Yeneri encouraged Mirae to spend her days there unsupervised, but these are exceptional circumstances. With an appropriate escort, in the middle of the day, it should be safe enough."

Sefina pursed her lips at the word 'escort', wondering whether Lady Lirath meant a large entourage to demonstrate her newly-bestowed station. It wouldn't have surprised her. "I'll assemble one," she told Lady Lirath, already making different plans. Bringing a large group into Easton would upset Mirae—an unnecessary flexing of muscles.

Lady Lirath smiled for the first time since entering the room. "Good girl. Wear your vestments. It will do Mirae no good to remain in denial."

Sefina inclined her head and left Lady Lirath's rooms, exhaling once she was alone in the hallway. For whatever reason, Lady Lirath's presence had felt especially stifling today. She returned to Speaker Yeneri's rooms, removed the golden stole from about her shoulders, and replaced it with a brown cloak. Half her vestments were better than none.

More sensibly dressed, Sefina went to the stables without informing anyone else of her intentions. Thanks to the foul weather, she encountered no one as she tramped through the rain and mud. The only person there was the very one she'd hoped to find: Trenton, toweling off a damp chestnut horse. He turned when Sefina entered, his green eyes widening as she lowered her hood.

"S-Speaker Sefina," he said, his stammer returning in full force.

She held up her hand before Trenton could bow. "Good to see you too. I need a horse. Is one available?"

Trenton stood at attention. "For you, Speaker, always. Where are you bound?"

"The docks," Sefina said.

Trenton's eyes darted, as though he understood what Sefina couldn't say, but made no mention of it. "I'll have a horse ready quick as you like." He led the chestnut into her stall, then saddled a stocky brown gelding with a white star upon his nose. "Will anyone else be going with you, Speaker? How many other horses should I..."

Sefina shook her head.

Trenton coughed. "Just the one, then?"

"Just the one, please. And I'll need you to take me."

This time, Trenton didn't manage any air behind his words. Me? he mouthed instead, pointing at his own chest.

Sefina nodded. "As soon as possible."

A blush crawled across Trenton's freckled cheeks. He hurried to prepare the gelding, then hesitantly offered Sefina his hand. He hoisted her up, keeping his hand upon her waist for the shortest possible amount of time. She pulled her hood back over her head as Trenton hauled himself up with the stirrups, seating himself well in front of her.

Poor Trenton nearly fell off the horse when Sefina wrapped her arms around his waist. She felt guilty, but where else was she supposed to hold on? "Sorry," she murmured.

Once Trenton recovered, he urged the gelding into a trot with a click of his tongue. They rode out into the rain, which had picked up strength as dark gray storm clouds gathered overhead.

It took only a short time to reach the docks. The muddy roads were empty due to the weather. They crossed Hyron Bridge, steering clear of the few carriages that braved the rain. Sefina tried not to look at the churning, swollen waters of the river below. The stench of old fish guts was more difficult to ignore. The delicious scents of Easton's marketplace were muted, failing to conceal it as much as usual.

Trenton stopped the horse beside the main thoroughfare. Standing water soaked the hem of Sefina's cloak as soon as she set foot on the ground. She was grateful she'd worn sturdy boots. "Should I come with you or stay with the horse, Speaker?"

"Sefina, please," she told him. For once, Lady Lirath wasn't around to insist. "Why not stay here? I won't be long." There was only one place Sefina knew to look. If Brom didn't know where Mirae had gone, she'd have to return on a clearer day when more people were out and about in the market.

Trenton stood at attention. "I'll be right here then, Sp—er, Sefina."

She left Trenton holding the reins and hurried through the rain, pulling her cloak around her shoulders. Most of the stalls were abandoned, though a few soggy merchants braved the weather to sell their wares. She passed them, heading for the adjoining street where Brom's home stood. As she turned the corner, she stopped short, her eyes going wide.

Colorful scraps of tapestry and needlework hung in every window. Some were the size of hand cloths, others giant quilts. Here, a fragment of delicate embroidery. There, a hypnotizing geometric design. The display was a gorgeous rainbow amidst the foggy downpour. Sefina couldn't help but stare in admiration.

This had to be for Speaker Yeneri. The dockside residents were celebrating her life and honoring her death months after the fact, in the best way they knew how. It wouldn't have surprised Sefina if some of the works on display were hers as well, gifts for the families here.

Tears ran down Sefina's cheeks, mingling with the rain as she struggled to compose herself. *Yeneri, you would have been so proud to see this.*

Swallowing the lump in her throat, she continued to Brom's home. The shack was in better repair than she remembered. Its roof didn't seem to be leaking, anyway. Warm light glowed from behind the bits of tapestry in the windows. She gathered her courage and knocked.

The door opened. Brom's familiar face peered out and the delighted, high-pitched shriek of a child sounded within. Probably his daughter, Sela. The same one Mirae had saved years ago.

"Speaker Sefina." Brom bowed even though Sefina hadn't offered the backs of her hands. She waved him off.

"Please, don't. I wasn't even sure you'd remember me."

"Of course I remember you." Brom's warm smile and dimpled cheeks put Sefina at ease, but it didn't escape her notice that he hadn't invited her inside. Curious, considering the weather. "You were there the day Mirae made my daughter well again. And you're Speaker of Dreams now, too. Congratulations."

"You can probably guess why I'm here. I'm looking for Mirae." Sefina resisted the temptation to peer past Brom's shoulder, hoping she might catch a glimpse of Mirae inside. "She hasn't been back to the temple in almost a month. I was hoping to speak with her."

Brom's smile slipped away. "I'm afraid I can't help you," he said, his voice low and guarded.

Sefina tilted her head. "Can't, or won't?"

Brom hesitated, then spoke in a hurried whisper. "It would be wrong to betray a friend's confidence, even to one so important as you, Speaker Sefina. She saved my daughter. Please, you must understand."

The poor man looked so upset with his tight brow and intense stare that Sefina couldn't press him further. "Will you give her a message from me, next time you see her?"

"If I see her," Brom said, "I'd be happy to pass along a message."

Sefina's shoulders sank. That would have to be good enough. "Tell her…" What did she want Brom to tell Mirae? How could she boil down her complicated feelings into a single sentence? She worked her lips, then said, "Tell her I miss her and want to see her."

Brom nodded. "Of course, Speaker. If I run into her, I'll tell her."

Sefina forced a close-mouthed smile, all she could manage. "Good. And, here." She reached for the coin purse at her hip, withdrawing a handful of gold. Brom's mouth opened, but she spoke first. "Please, don't refuse me. If your family has no need, as I'm sure you'll insist, perhaps some of your less fortunate neighbors do. Share it with them, or buy enough supplies to prepare a feast. Do it in Speaker Yeneri's memory. It would please her spirit."

Gratitude shone in Brom's dark eyes. "Thank you. She would indeed. I'll gratefully accept this, on behalf of my neighbors and friends, for her sake. Speaker Yeneri's presence is greatly missed here."

"I see that from the lovely display in your windows. A wonderful tribute to a wonderful woman. If you ever need anything, please consider me your friend. I have great affection for the people who live in Easton's docks."

"Thank you. You're most generous, Speaker Sefina."

Despite his words, Sefina doubted Brom would seek the temple's help. He'd never done so during Speaker Yeneri's tenure, so why should hers be any different? Still, she resolved to do her best to support the residents of the docks. It might have been Mirae's stomping grounds, but her responsibility was to the entire city of Stagford, including Easton.

"Have a pleasant evening," she said to Brom. "Stay warm in this awful weather."

Instead of extending the backs of her hands, Sefina offered them sideways. Brom clasped her wrists, and he offered Sefina what she hoped was a genuine smile. "You as well, Speaker Sefina. I promise to pass along your message if I get the chance."

Hollow and disappointed, Sefina turned away from Brom and started down the street, pulling her hood over her head. Halfway to the corner, something compelled her to look back. A prickling sensation on the back of her neck, a slight skip of her heartbeat. She turned in time to see one of the quilts hanging in Brom's window fall back into place.

Sefina's heart ached. Of course Mirae had been there all along. Some part of her had known, but if Mirae refused to come to the door when she'd made the effort to visit in the pouring rain, barging in to confront her wouldn't have done anything to help.

Sefina resumed walking at a rapid pace, boots splashing in the growing puddles, anger gnawing at the edges of her stomach. Before she simmered to the point of tears, she was distracted by a soft tug near her waist. Her cloak's damp hem shifted. Her hand shot out on instinct, only to catch the wrist of a small boy bundled in wet, mud-stained rags. His face was so smudged with dirt Sefina couldn't make out his features, but his eyes were large and round with fear.

"Lemme go!" He tried to yank his hand away with surprising strength, but Sefina held firm.

"Promise not to run away and I'll let you go. I won't hurt you. If you stay, I'll give you something nice."

The boy gawped, jaw hanging loose.

"I'll take that as a yes."

Sefina released the boy's wrist. He peered up at her with blatant curiosity, rubbing a sleeve across his dirty nose. Sefina doubted he knew who she was. Why should a child from the slums recognize the new Speaker of Dreams? Perhaps he'd thought she was a wealthy merchant, lost on such a rainy day.

"What're you gonna give me?" His eyes darted to Sefina's hip where her coin pouch hung. She withdrew the pouch and poured out the remaining coins, offering them in an outstretched hand. The boy's eyes glittered. He snatched them up quick as a flash and stuffed them somewhere in his patchwork pants.

"What's your name?" Sefina asked.

The boy sniffled. "Loma." He hesitated, then offered a sheepish, "Thanks for the money, lady."

"My name is Sefina. If you ever need a hot meal or a warm bed, come to the Temple of Dreams and ask for me."

Loma blew his bangs aside with a puff of air. His brow furrowed, but Sefina didn't hold his distrust against him. From his appearance alone, she could tell life hadn't treated him kindly. Why should he expect her to be any different?

"Right." Loma took a cautious step back, then took off down the street, splashing through a puddle and disappearing around the corner.

Sefina watched him go. There was little to do but return to where she'd left Trenton and the horse. She walked down the street, head hanging low. There were many things she couldn't change, so she resolved to focus on the upcoming auction. Hopefully, it would raise enough coin to keep Lady Lirath proud and support the temple for a long while.

Chapter Sixteen

THE AUCTION OF SPEAKER Yeneri's works started more successfully than Sefina hoped. A swarm of nobles descended upon the temple, dressed in all their dazzling finery. Their clothes spanned the colors of the rainbow and the women wore jewelry that glittered like Of-the-Stars.

Sefina moved among them as though she'd been born to the task. Something within her had shifted since her trip to the docks. Though she missed Mirae fiercely, she wouldn't waste her time waiting to reconcile. All those present addressed her as Speaker Sefina, a title which sent a thrill down her spine. Her vestments were no longer stifling, her stole light as air.

She and Lady Lirath stationed themselves by the entrance, greeting guests and persuading them to part with their coin. A comment here about how much so-and-so had already spent, a whispered word about who was eyeing which tapestry, and the coin purses opened. Sefina began to understand why Lady Lirath preferred her role as treasurer. Money meant power, access to everything she'd been denied as an orphan.

Midway through the evening, the regent found them. Sefina felt his presence before she saw him. A pathway formed through a cluster of colorfully dressed ladies like a breeze bending the stems of wildflowers. Sefina put on a bright smile when she saw him, dressed in royal blue and gold from his shiny hair to his shiny shoes. It wasn't even difficult anymore. As in music practice served her well.

"Good evening, Speaker." The regent offered his hands palms-up, a greeting of equals. A pleasant shiver prickled along Sefina's neck as she took his hands in hers. Neither of them bowed.

"A good evening indeed, Lord Regent."

"Good evening to you as well, Raula. My favorite cousin." The regent offered Lady Lirath his hands next, but this time, he showed the backs.

Lady Lirath touched her forehead to his knuckles. "Are you enjoying yourself so far, Horace?"

The regent withdrew his hands and gave a satisfied sigh. "A marvelous event! The food is excellent, the music lively, and the night young." His gaze returned to Sefina. "This was a splendid idea. It's already endeared you to Stagford's nobility."

Sefina's happiness flickered like a candle in the breeze of an open window. She thought of Mirae and how she would have offered some rude retort, and it filled her with wistful sorrow, but the feeling soon passed. "That was my hope. Tell me, have any of Speaker Yeneri's tapestries caught your eye?"

The regent stroked his beard. "Why, yes. Would you care to see which one?"

"Of course, Horace," Lady Lirath said.

The regent offered Sefina one arm while Lady Lirath took the other. Sefina rested her fingertips upon his elbow. "Come then. I'd be delighted to show you."

He led them through the crowd, which parted before them. Countless stares lingered upon them, but Sefina held her head high. Being the center of attention was far from displeasing now that she'd grown used to it.

The regent stopped before a large tapestry hanging upon the east wall, which told a story Sefina knew well. In the center stood King Hyron, following a white stag with flowering, moss-draped antlers to a ford in the river.

"How good of Speaker Yeneri to weave a tapestry of our city's founding father," said the regent. "This obviously belongs in the ancestral home of King Hyron's descendants. Wouldn't you agree?"

Sefina nodded. The tapestry was indeed a masterwork. Its colors shone by torchlight. The white stag seemed to walk as she looked on, leaving hoof prints in the mud of the riverbank. The river glimmered in a late afternoon sunlight, shifting as though it possessed a real current.

Its lifelike nature reminded Sefina of the secret tapestry. It remained in her bedroom, in the same compartment. *Someday, when the time comes, I'll display it as Speaker Yeneri wanted. Once I'm sure the regent won't misinterpret my actions.*

Perhaps she stared too long at the tapestry, for the regent cleared his throat. "Sefina?" He tilted his head and looked at her, brows drawn together.

Sefina blinked back tears she hadn't even noticed. "Forgive me." She withdrew a handkerchief to dab at her eyes. "I was recalling a memory of Speaker Yeneri. May she find peace in the sea of stars."

"She would be proud of you, my dear," Lady Lirath said with a look of sorrowful understanding. "You've risen to your new role marvelously."

Sefina took comfort in Lady Lirath's reassurances. It eased the ache in her heart to imagine Speaker Yeneri watching over her with pride. "Thank you, Lady Lirath. You're most kind. And you, Lord Regent, have been quite understanding. This tapestry is a wonderful selection. I agree that it belongs in your palace."

"Would a stroll by the lake lighten your mood? You could tell me more about your memories of Speaker Yeneri." The regent adopted a rueful smile. "I fear she never liked me as much as I admired her."

"I doubt that," Sefina lied. "But yes, a moment away from the crowd would be welcome."

She looked to Lady Lirath, who nodded. "No need to worry. I shall see the auction continues smoothly in your absence. Be sure to return in time for your performance later."

"Of course." Sefina bade Lady Lirath farewell, accompanying the tegent outside into the early dusk. Though the air was too cool to be truly enjoyable, a few guests stood on the temple steps and walked about the gardens. The lantern-lit pathway to the lake was far less crowded than the foyer. The moon hung full and round overhead, making the stars seem faint.

"I believe it's not only the speaker you miss," the regent said once they'd left everyone behind. "Tell me, have you heard from your friend Mirae?"

Sefina's eyes widened, then narrowed. Though his tone of voice and understanding expression read concern, she couldn't help feeling wary. Was he fishing for information about Mirae? Does he hope she'll return to the temple, or is that precisely what he fears?

She chose her words carefully. "She has shown no signs of wishing to return, but the temple doors are always open."

"Of course," said the regent. "This was her home for many years. However, I believe things have worked out as Of-Blessed-Dreams intended. You were meant for the role of Speaker while Mirae was meant for other things."

Sefina nodded. "I believe the same. Hopefully Mirae will—"

A startled shout from the Regent cut her off. "What's this?" He dropped Sefina's arm, whirling toward a bush beside the path to grab a shadow crouched behind. The shadow struggled, and Sefina realized it was a child bundled in rags. "Thief!" The regent held the child's arm up into the air, forcing them to stand on tip-toe. "That's what you are, isn't it, you wretched creature? I felt you pull my coin purse."

"Lemmego!" the child cried.

Sefina recognized the voice. It was Loma, the same street urchin who'd tried to pickpocket her at the docks.

She hurried to retrieve him from the regent's unyielding grip. "Loma, this is outrageous! You know better than to play practical jokes on such important guests! If you wish to continue as my student, you will apologize to the lord regent at once."

Both Loma and the regent stared at Sefina with similar dumbfounded expressions, mouths agape, eyes goggling.

"You mean to tell me this...boy...is your ward?" The regent's eyes shifted doubtfully between Sefina and Loma. "Why is he hiding in the bushes and attempting to steal coin purses?"

"Forgive me, Lord Regent. Young Loma wasn't after your coin purse. He's only arrived at the temple recently since the tragic death of his parents, and he's still adjusting to a new environment. Apparently, the street children he used to play with made a game of pulling down each other's trousers. Have no doubt that I shall punish him severely."

Loma nodded frantically, his dark eyes wide with fear.

The regent shook his head in disbelief. "Your ward attempted to pull down my trousers...as a game?"

Sefina stepped behind Loma, placing her hands upon his shoulders. They were unnaturally skinny, with sharp ridges of bone. "Beg the Lord Regent Stagford's forgiveness at once, you wretched boy. Then, return to your room and await punishment. You're banned from the auction and I've a mind to beat you black and blue."

Loma fell to his knees, lowering his upper body to the ground. "Please forgive me. I'm so sorry, Lord Regent! I had no idea it was you."

After a long, tense pause, the regent gave a disparaging wave of his hand. "You shame your generous mentor with such childish behavior. Do you have no respect for the temple or the city's noble peerage? This is hardly the slums Speaker Sefina saved you from. I wouldn't blame her if she threw you back onto the streets with the other dogs."

Loma lifted his head and Sefina caught a glimpse of fire in his eyes. Before he could ruin his chance, she hauled him up by the back of his filthy shirt, with more roughness than she wished.

"Come," she said, dragging him along with her. "I'll find someone to lock you in your rooms until I decide to deal with you. Please, Lord Regent, I beg your pardon on my student's behalf. Rest assured, the boy will regret attempting to embarrass my most honored guest of the evening."

The regent made a show of straightening his clothes. "No doubt you will administer a suitable punishment. Do find me later, Speaker. We have much to discuss."

"Of course. I'll return as soon as I've dealt with this."

Sefina dragged Loma toward the temple, around the main steps, and in through one of the side doors to the kitchens. Several members of the kitchen staff gave them curious looks, but Sefina ignored them, leaving them to the preparation of appetizers as she dragged Loma through the nearest door. She led him into an empty hall and cornered him against a wall between two stained glass windows.

"What an incredibly foolish thing to do! The regent could have thrown you in prison or had you executed."

Loma, who had been smirking in spite of everything, went pale. "Executed?" He gulped. "Er. Thanks, lady. Guess you might've saved my life."

Sefina placed both hands on her hips. "Why were you lurking in the bushes?"

Loma put on a wide-eyed, quiver-lipped look. "You said to come to the temple if I needed a meal or a bed. My parents...they went to the sea of stars last week. It was the sweating sickness."

Sefina frowned, staring down at Loma. He struck her as the type to lie without hesitation, a skill he'd no doubt learned to survive. Still, no child looked, dressed, nor behaved as he did if they had a loving family, a warm home, and enough food. Whether he was telling the truth or not didn't matter.

"My parents died of sweating sickness when I was even younger than you. Come with me. We'll get you situated in the dormitories tonight and begin your lessons tomorrow."

The pitiful look on Loma's face vanished in an instant. "Lessons?" He tilted his head.

"I told the regent you were my student. Since I won't lie to him again, you're my new ward. You'll be given food, clothes, and a room of your own."

Loma folded his arms. "What's the catch? Am I your servant now? Your errand boy?" His mistrust was obvious in his scowl and the rigid set of his skinny shoulders.

"Not at all. These things will be given freely, provided you do your best to learn an artistic discipline. If you show no talent for singing, I'll instruct you in another instrument, or perhaps you may find dance, sculpting, or glassblowing more to your liking. There are plenty of options."

Loma considered this, wrinkling his nose. He scratched his chin. After a moment, his stony expression softened. Not much, but enough. "You mean it?"

"I swear on Of-Blessed-Dreams' holy name. You may also tithe to Of-the-Sea while you live here. I won't force you to worship Of-the-Land. Temple residents may worship whichever gods they wish."

At that pronouncement, Loma grinned. "Right. Where do I sleep? Can I have something to eat? I'm starving!"

* * * *

So it was that Loma of the Sea Children became Sefina's student. He did have a talent for singing, with a clear soprano that almost reminded her of Mirae's childhood voice. He was a hungry student, smart and eager to learn, but his mischievous streak often put him at odds with Lady Lirath.

Though she approved of Sefina taking a student in theory, having not been told about the incident with the regent, she was full of criticism for the boy as well as Sefina's handling of him.

Two weeks into Loma's stay, Lady Lirath dragged him into Sefina's rooms by the ear while he squirmed and cursed. He tried to wriggle free, but Lady Lirath was stronger. She shoved him toward Sefina, causing him to catch his foot on the rug and stumble. "Your ward has been stealing from the kitchens again. This is the third time this week!"

Sefina sighed. Stealing had continued to be a problem since Loma's arrival, though it was mostly food. "Loma, we've talked about this. The temple has plenty of food for everyone. I understand you rarely had enough food when you lived by the docks, but there's no need to steal or hoard here. There will be food tomorrow, and the day after, and so on."

Loma, who had been glaring at Lady Lirath, wilted under Sefina's stare. His shoulders slumped and he folded his hands behind his back. "Sorry, Speaker Sefina," he mumbled, fixing his gaze on the rug.

"Sorry isn't good enough." Lady Lirath placed her hands on her hips, looking over Loma's bowed head and fixing Sefina with an icy glare. Even as an adult, it sent a shiver down her spine. Her eyes almost darted to the floor too, but she managed to hold Lady Lirath's stare. She wasn't a child being punished anymore.

"You must be firmer with him, Sefina," Lady Lirath said. "Since he's already stuffed himself with apple pie, I suggest taking away his dinner. Perhaps tomorrow as well."

Sefina bit her cheek. Loma needed to be punished, but she knew from personal experience that taking away his dinner would only make him more secretive around food. Still, she was reluctant to reject her mentor's advice outright.

"Very well. No dinner tonight or tomorrow. Leave him with me. I'll instruct him in the lute for the rest of the day so he learns his lesson."

Loma shot Sefina a wide-eyed look of betrayal. His mouth opened, but he closed it again, apparently deciding that backtalk would only worsen his situation.

"Very well," said Lady Lirath. "Make sure this doesn't happen again. His poor behavior reflects upon you, Sefina, just as your poor behavior as a child often reflected upon me, but there may be hope for him yet. You improved, after all." She turned and left before Sefina could respond, closing the door forcefully behind her.

"I'm sorry for stealing," Loma said once Lady Lirath had left. "Please don't take away my supper."

Sefina offered him a gentle smile. "I'll never take food away from you, Loma. Just don't tell Lady Lirath. She must think you're being punished. Perhaps you should complain about being hungry within earshot of her later."

Loma brightened, nodding almost gleefully. He clearly enjoyed the prospect of fooling Lady Lirath. "Thanks, Speaker."

"I meant what I said," Sefina said. "There's plenty of food at the temple. I know hoarding food is a force of habit when you've grown up with an empty belly. Trust me, I do. But if you steal instead of taking your portions at mealtimes or asking for a snack, others may be forced to go without that day. Besides..." She gave him a once-over, noting a glob of jelly at the corner of his mouth and a telling stain on his shirt. "Eating an entire apple pie will give you a stomachache. That should be punishment enough."

Loma scuffed his shoe across the rug. "I won't steal pies anymore."

"Or anything else," Sefina said. "I know your tricks."

"Or anything else," he said.

"Good. Now, come sit." Sefina gestured at one of the straight-backed wooden chairs she'd established in the outer room to make it her own. "I'll instruct you in the lute and take you through your chord progressions. Then, I'll send for some dinner for both of us, assuming you aren't too sick to eat."

Loma sat in his chair while Sefina took her own. She withdrew a handkerchief from her pocket, urging Loma to wipe his face clean, then selected one of the beginner lutes from the peg board she'd installed upon the wall. It was identical to the one in Lady Lirath's rooms. She handed the lute to Loma. "Start in the key of C. Play the tonic."

Loma positioned his fingers upon the frets, watching his hands as he worked. The tip of his tongue poked out the corner of his mouth in concentration. He strummed the strings and a decent chord rang out.

"Now, the subdominant."

He took a while to reposition his fingertips, but played the next chord correctly.

"And the dominant."

This he played more confidently, smiling as he did.

"Good. Repeat the progression without looking at your fingers."

Loma tried again, but the second chord went sour.

Sefina shook her head. "Not quite. Again."

On his second attempt, Loma managed the first two chords, but one of his fingers slipped on the third.

"No. Watch me." Sefina lifted her own prized lute from its stand, demonstrating the finger placement. "Again."

They went through the progression several more times, until Loma grew noticeably faster and more comfortable. "How's that?"

"Better," Sefina said. "Now, the same thing in the key of G."

Though she demonstrated several times, Loma found this key far more difficult. He managed the first chord well enough, but the subdominant and dominant escaped him. No matter how many times Sefina said, "Again," he struggled even while watching his fingers, the wrinkle in his brow growing deeper with each mistake.

Sefina noted a growing tightness in her chest. Each wrong note made her jaw clench. Without conscious thought, her voice grew sharper and less encouraging whenever she said, "Again."

Loma shifted uncomfortably in his seat, only watching Sefina's fingers instead of her face. The more mistakes he made, the more determined she became to hear him perform the progression correctly at least once. "Again."

This time, Loma didn't even manage the first chord.

Sefina sighed. "Did you practice yesterday evening like I told you, Loma?"

Loma stuck his lower lip out. "Yes..."

Sefina rested her lute in her lap and folded her arms. "I can't help you improve if you lie to me."

"But I did!" Loma protested. "Let me do it again. I'll show you."

Sefina pushed down her frustration and waved her hand. "Go on, then."

Loma stumbled through the progression several more times, but only seemed to be getting worse. It was a mental block Sefina knew well. The thought that she should have him play or sing something else crossed her mind, but then she thought of her own childhood lessons. *Lady Lirath never let me get away with this many mistakes. It's one of the reasons I perform as well as I do now.*

"Stop for a moment." She rose from her chair and set her lute on its stand, walking over to the desk that had once been Speaker Yeneri's. She removed ten copper pieces from within one of its drawers, then returned to her chair.

"This is a technical method of practice for you to use on your own," she told Loma. "I have ten coppers in my right hand. Each time you play the progression correctly, I'll move one copper to my left hand. If you make a mistake, all the coppers go back to my right hand. Once you've moved all the coppers over, you can move on to something else."

This time, Loma's pout was accompanied by a scrunched nose and an exaggerated roll of his eyes. "Fine."

Sefina felt a flash of heat, but subdued her annoyance. *Lady Lirath would never tolerate that kind of sarcastic response from a student.*

Loma picked up his lute and went through the chord progression. He managed to strike all three chords, if slowly and out of rhythm.

"Good," Sefina said, moving a single copper into her left hand. "Again."

His second attempt was even better than the first.

Sefina moved another copper. "Again."

On Loma's third try, he positioned one of his fingers on the wrong fret.

Sefina passed the two coppers back into her right hand. "All right. Clear your head and start over."

Loma scowled down at the practice lute. "This is stupid," he grumbled, slamming it back down onto its stand. "I'll never do it ten times perfect."

Sefina pursed her lips, then paused to take a deep breath in through her nose, summoning her last reserves of patience. "You will with practice."

"Well, I don't want to! This is stupid! You're stupid!" Loma leapt up from his chair and stomped his foot, inadvertently pulling the rug under his shoe. The sudden jerk caused Sefina's lute to wobble, then tip off its stand, landing hard on the edge of the rug and part of the stone floor.

Sefina gasped. She stared down at the polished cherrywood lute, her most prized possession. Scrapes and scratches marred its body where it had skidded against the stone floor. She snatched it up to examine the damage, her eyes dry but stinging. Her heart sank as she ran her fingertips over the scratches. She could already tell they wouldn't buff out. Lady Lirath's gift was irreparably damaged.

A hard knot lodged itself in Sefina's throat as she looked up at Loma, who had taken several steps back. He trembled, wrapping his arms around himself, but Sefina didn't care. "Speaker...I—I didn't mean to...I wasn't—"

"Enough," she said, tightening her grip around the lute's neck until it dug into her palm. "How dare you be so careless? How dare you address me with such disdain? If you can't bother to learn the most basic of chords, why should I bother teaching you at all? It's like attempting to instruct a rock! Although perhaps a rock might be a better student. At the very least, it wouldn't have ruined my most treasured possession."

Loma flinched as though he'd been struck. His brows pulled together over his wide brown eyes, swimming with tears. He blinked rapidly and gave a loud sniff. "I'm sorry," he said, an uncertain crack in his voice.

Sefina turned away, refusing to look at Loma. Already, she felt the sharp sting of guilt as her own outburst echoed in her head—in a voice quite similar to Lady Lirath's. *Oh no. What have I done?*

"Loma, go to your room," she said, in the most emotionless voice she could muster. "Our lesson is over for today. We'll discuss this when I bring your dinner."

Loma gave a muffled sob. "Y-you mean you aren't sending me back to the docks?"

The question pierced Sefina's heart. Her anger dissolved in an instant. "Oh, Loma." She turned, set her lute carefully upon its stand, and stepped toward Loma, resting a hand upon his shoulder. He flinched but didn't shrug away, staring up at her with swimming eyes. A trail of snot shone on his upper lip.

"Of course I won't send you back. Your home is here now." Sefina took a calming breath, then said, "Please forgive me. You were rude to me and you scratched my lute, but that doesn't excuse what I said to you. The lute is a difficult instrument, as I well know. Lady Lirath often said cruel things to me when I was your age, and I fear I've adopted some of her worse methods of instruction. The fault lies entirely with me."

Loma sniffed, wiping his sleeve across his nose. "What? It isn't your fault, Speaker. I'm just stupid—"

"No!" Sefina tightened her grip on Loma's shoulder. "No, you aren't stupid. You're learning. And I must learn as well, mostly how to be patient. Just as you're learning music, I'm learning how to be a good teacher. In that way, we're teaching each other."

A hesitant smile tugged at Loma's lips. "So I'm your teacher, too?"

"Yes. You have my word that I'll never insult you again. I'm fortunate to have a student like you. Why don't we take a break from the lute and sing together? I'll teach you a new song. Would you like that?"

Loma exhaled deeply, his shoulders sagging with visible relief. "Yes, please. I'm sorry for what I did."

"I know you are. I'm sorry too. I promise never to speak to you that way again."

I won't be Lady Lirath.

Though Sefina couldn't deny that Lady Lirath had made her an exceptional musician, her methods had left ugly marks. Surely there were other, better ways to teach Loma. She would find them, no matter what it took.

"All right. Stand up, then, and get a mint from the desk."

Loma went to the desk and took a mint from the jar, sucking it as he walked back over to stand before Sefina.

"We'll practice some deep breathing first," Sefina said. "Remember to draw the air low into your belly, expanding outward, and don't raise your shoulders."

Loma did so, closing his eyes and placing a hand upon his belly to feel his breath.

"Yes," Sefina said. "Just like that."

* * * *

Later that same night, as Sefina washed her face before bed, a strange feeling overcame her. She wiped the droplets from her chin and stared at her reflection in the mirror, bare of the usual makeup. She listened, but everything within the washroom and her bedroom was silent.

No. The sense of unease was coming from somewhere within her. She couldn't put a name to the feeling. It was like an insistent tug within her brain, as though she'd forgotten something. She struggled to remember as she brushed her teeth, running through everything she'd done that day and everything she needed to do tomorrow. Nothing stood out.

As she left the bathroom and went to bed, about to blow out the candle on the nightstand, her thoughts turned to Loma. Their lesson had ended on a high note, but how was he, really?

Sefina straightened and threw a silk robe over her nightgown, knotting it about her waist and sliding her feet into a pair of slippers. She brought the candle to light her way, crossing the front room and stepping into the hall. It was later than she'd realized. There was no one in the halls as she headed for the dormitories on the opposite side of the second floor.

When she arrived, she heard a telling sound from behind one of the closed doors: muffled sobs. It was Loma's room. Her instincts hadn't led her astray.

Sefina tiptoed to the door and knocked. The sobbing quieted, but Loma gave no response.

"It's Sefina," she said. "I'm coming in, all right?" She waited a moment, then went inside.

The light from her candle illuminated Loma in his bed. He huddled in a tiny ball beneath the covers, clutching his pillow like his life depended on it. He kept his face hidden as Sefina approached, setting the candle upon his nightstand.

"Homesick?" she asked, sitting on the mattress. "I was too when I came to live here."

Loma sniffed, peeking over the edge of his pillow. His eyes were bright red and Sefina didn't miss the shining tear-tracks on his cheeks. When he tried to speak, all that came out was a whimper.

Sefina placed a gentle hand upon his shoulder, urging him to lie on his side. He did so, clutching the pillow to his chest. Once he started to relax, Sefina rubbed circles on his back. She sang the same lullaby she'd used to put Mirae to sleep as a child.

The moon's begun to rise, the stars are on their way.
So close your heavy eyes until a brand new day.
Hush now, hush now. Night falls. Crickets cheep.
Hush now, hush now. Rest your head and sleep.

Gradually, Loma's sobs faded to quiet sniffs, then the slow, steady breaths of sleep. It only took three repetitions of the short verse before he was snoring, sprawled on his back beside his pillow. Sefina slipped it under his head and pulled the blankets to his chin. Loma remained asleep with the slightest of smiles upon his face.

Sefina rose and took her candle, slipping silently away. She lingered in the hall for several minutes, listening at the door in case Loma woke, but no noise came from within his room.

After a while, she returned to her chambers, feeling much lighter. In her new student, she couldn't help but see the child she had once been. Sad, frightened, lonely. But she'd always had Mirae for comfort. Loma had no one.

He won't be alone anymore. I'll teach him to trust me, and someday, he'll come to me when he has a reason to cry.

That was the mantra Sefina lived by as the months passed. Though Loma fell into trouble from time to time, usually for sneaking out on Eightdays to play with his friends at the docks, he no longer stole. He attended every lesson with a big smile. He improved rapidly, until even Lady Lirath begrudgingly admitted the boy had talent.

Sefina missed Mirae terribly, but found new purpose. Devoting herself to Loma's wellbeing and education lessened the pain, especially at night. When her bed became unbearably lonely, she snuck into Loma's room. She told him stories passed down from Speaker Yeneri and sang their lullaby before she tucked him in.

In that way, she maintained some small connection to Mirae, and to her own past.

Mirae — Fifthday

DAWNBELL AGAIN. THIS TIME its notes sound silvery and cheerful to Mirae's ears. She smiles at Yeneri. "Sefina, taking a student of her own. Wonderful. I know the boy, too. He caused all sorts of mischief at the docks. Poor Sefina must have had her hands full with such a boisterous pupil."

"You weren't always an easy pupil yourself," Yeneri said. "I remember dragging you unwillingly to lessons on sunny summer days. And all the bugs, birds, and rodents you tried to keep as pets! You always cried when I set them free."

Mirae grins. She'd undoubtedly tried Yeneri's patience as a young girl, but the speaker had never once gotten cross with her. Not like Lady Lirath—although Sefina had taken the brunt of their teacher's abuse, enduring her foul moods like a young sapling bending to avoid being snapped by the storm.

"How did you do it?" she asks Yeneri. "How did you always stay so calm and loving?"

"The same way Sefina is doing, through constant awareness and years of practice. Anger is an easy emotion. Patience is learned. Keep your mind and heart open and you will learn it, too."

Mirae tilts her face toward the sky, an inky black sea extending forever upward. Unlike the waves, it has no stars. In the emptiness, she imagines Sefina instructing Loma. Sefina guides his fingers upon the frets of a lute, helping him strum a new chord.

"I won't see her teach if I join the sea of stars," she says, softly. "I'll never take students of my own. Lady Lirath may have treated us harshly, but if Sefina can take her techniques and pass them along without the same cruelty..."

"She will," Yeneri says. "Whether you return or not, Sefina will always be a teacher. The skills Lady Lirath passed down to the two of you won't be forgotten. Her students will pass it down to their students, and so on until the end of time. It is an ancient and unbroken chain in which even Lady Lirath is an important link."

Mirae lowers her gaze to the dark, shining sea. It's almost as black as the sky now, so black she can hardly discern the beach. The waves have risen to her shoulders, leaving only her head and neck above water.

"I don't have much time left to decide, do I?"

Yeneri nods. The gesture tells Mirae more than words. Time may be fluid while she's adrift in the sea of stars, but her chance to return is slipping away.

But she isn't ready to decide. She needs to listen to Sefina a bit longer. She has questions that need answers—not only the current state of things in Stagford (although that is admittedly on her mind). She needs to know why Sefina came to save her, not once but twice. She needs to know that Sefina will be all right without her.

The thought of returning to the world, with all its people and problems, leaves her weary down to the bone, but returning to Sefina, and only Sefina? That, she might summon enough strength to do.

Chapter Seventeen

THREE MONTHS LATER, SWEATING sickness descended upon Stagford. One day, everyone moved freely throughout the city, buying merchandise, chatting in the streets, going about their lives. The next, everyone hid away in their homes, afraid to venture outside. A black cloud of despair swallowed Stagford, bringing barren streets, shuttered windows and hushed whispers.

Following Lady Lirath's advice, Sefina set strict rules for the temple residents. No one was permitted to leave except to purchase supplies. Strangers were denied entry for any reason. This broke her heart, for they had to turn away a growing number of people each day, most of whom had lost their livelihoods as the sickness spread.

Sefina gave away what food and supplies the temple could spare, but couldn't offer refuge. She was the Speaker of Dreams, and the temple had to be her first and only priority. It went against everything Of-Blessed-Dreams and her temple stood for, but it was the only way to keep her charges safe.

For a short time, anyway.

Before long, the infirmary was full of sweating, feverish patients with clammy skin and rattling lungs. Those tending to them often fell ill themselves, forcing other, inexperienced people to take on their duties until they recovered...if they recovered. Too many closed their eyes and never opened them again.

With more sick people springing up every day, Sefina decreed that everyone must wear scarves about their faces as the Sea Children did, with pouches of herbs sewn inside. Everyone spent a great deal of time sewing these scarves. Sefina herself contributed, though her sewing skills were barely adequate despite Speaker Yeneri's attempts to teach her the basics. These scarves were distributed among the temple residents and given freely to all those who came to their doors.

Unfortunately, Loma failed to take the massive changes in stride. He was accustomed to slipping away on Eightdays to visit his old stomping grounds. Though Sefina convinced him to wear his scarf with several stern lectures, she couldn't keep him indoors.

The worst of it was part of her didn't want to succeed. Loma often returned with news of the docks—and Mirae. It was as though he knew Sefina would be less angry if he shared the latest gossip.

"Mirae is trying to heal everyone," he told her during one of the early weeks, after she caught him climbing in through his bedroom window. "But there are too many people asking for help. They say her voice gave out yesterday and she can't sing at all today. Twice as many died today as yesterday."

Sefina sighed, folding her hands in her lap. She laced her fingers, staring at them as though they might provide answers, but her mind was already elsewhere.

Oh, Mirae. Surely you blame yourself for all this death. She recalled a night many years ago when Mirae had confessed her inability to save a young boy run over by a carriage. *What a torment, telling parents you can't heal their children, informing children their parents have passed on.*

She raised her head, fixing Loma with her most serious stare. "You mustn't go out again. I know you're worried about your friends, but think about how they'd feel if they got you sick? Think about how you'd feel if someone in the temple got sick from you?"

Loma stopped in the middle of changing his dirty shirt for a clean undershirt. "I didn't think about that." He left the old shirt on the floor and crept over to the bed, sitting by Sefina's side. "I wanted to make sure my mates were all right. That they had enough food and scarves."

Sefina sighed. She wrapped her arm around Loma's shoulder, pulling him against her side.

"Don't!" Loma said, jerking away. He stared at her with round brown eyes full of fear. "I could get you sick."

Sefina forced a smile. "You won't. Of-Blessed-Dreams protects me. But just in case, go wash your hands and face."

Loma shot her a narrow, skeptical glance. "Does the goddess really protect you, Sefina?"

Sefina swallowed down her guilt and said, "Of course. Someone has to look after the city while the gods are busy, don't they?" The lie tasted like ash in her mouth, but Loma had already lost two parents. He was so young. He didn't need to fear losing another guardian. Not yet.

Loma's brow softened. "Okay," he said, as though he were afraid to believe her. He scampered into the washroom and Sefina heard the hiss of running water as he scrubbed his hands.

"Your heart is in the right place, Loma," she said from her place on the bed. "The temple will give whatever we can to the people who come to us for help. We just can't let anyone in or out for a while."

"Even the Sea Children?" Loma called.

"Of course," Sefina said. "Especially anyone who lives at the docks. The cramped quarters there mean the sickness has taken hold faster."

Loma emerged from the washroom. He regarded her with a tired, drawn look that made him appear several years older. "That's not what I heard."

Sefina raised a brow. "What did you hear?"

"That the Sea Children brought the sickness here on our ships. That we get sick because we're poor and dirty, and we should keep to our own part of the city so we don't get everyone else sick."

Sefina went over to Loma and placed both hands upon his narrow shoulders. "We all must stay in our homes so the sickness will slow, but the rest is blatantly untrue. Earthfolk who say that are cruel and hateful, or badly misinformed by someone they trust. Sickness doesn't care who you are or who you worship. When it comes, everyone suffers."

That wasn't true, of course. Stagford's nobles could afford clean water and shelter, have extra supplies delivered to their lavish mansions, and pay for good doctors to tend them when they fell ill, but that wasn't what Loma needed to hear.

Loma looked up at her, his brow drawn and his eyes crinkled. His face was easy to read. He clearly wanted to believe even though his common sense was telling him otherwise.

"Besides," Sefina said, "the Sea Children have Mirae. That means Of-Blessed-Dreams is looking out for them, too. The docks are a hard place to live, but Of-Blessed-Dreams won't let your people suffer."

A hopeful smile spread across Loma's face, softening his worried expression. "I'll stay here. Even though it's boring."

"Boring, am I?" Sefina gave him one last squeeze before letting her arm fall. "Well, you'll have time to practice." She nudged her elbow into his side.

Loma gave a bark of laughter. "No fair!"

Sefina knew an invitation when she heard one. She wiggled her fingers ominously as Loma wrapped his arms around his midsection to protect himself. She leaned over and tickled him, finding some solace in the sound of his giggles. He was only a child, after all. Eight willing, he would grow up tall and strong, and the year sweating sickness overtook Stagford would only be a distant memory.

* * * *

Loma stopped sneaking out on Eightdays. Soon, he was the least of Sefina's problems. To her shame and frustration, many residents of

Upper Easton, Whiteport, Castletown, and The Green failed to take the same precautions the temple required. They assumed the squalid conditions at the docks were responsible for the sweating sickness and claimed to be immune.

They were wrong.

Soon, all sorts came to beg for assistance at the temple doors. Wealthy merchants and even nobles. Sefina refused them entry while offering all the supplies they could spare—but Lady Lirath's opinion changed.

"We must protect our own," she said, "but Lord Talisen is a good friend of the regent. Surely we can make an exception?"

"We have some of the best healers in Stagford here at the temple. It would be wrong to deny Lady Melis treatment."

"Sefina, will you have these scarves delivered to Castletown at once? They're in short supply."

They argued several times a day, but more often than not, Sefina unwillingly submitted to Lady Lirath's judgement. Her shame grew, but she had been Lady Lirath's student for many years. Lady Lirath had raised her. Saved her. Encouraged her to become a leader she'd never thought she could be. How could she say no?

She kept the nobles outside the gates, for that was her line in the sand, but occasionally lent out extra supplies and a few of the temple healers, since the numbers in their infirmary had at last begun to dwindle. Lady Lirath had a way of looking at Sefina that made her feel like a young girl, unqualified to make such important decisions.

It came to a head in the middle of the night, several months after the onset. Sefina woke to a loud banging upon her door and the urgent sound of Lady Lirath's voice. "Sefina, wake up and get dressed. You're needed in the infirmary at once!"

Sefina was out of bed in an instant. She threw a robe over her nightgown, threw a scarf around her neck out of habit, and hurried to answer the door. "What is it?"

Lady Lirath's visage was far paler than usual. The faint yellow light from the candle she held made the upper half of her face appear thin and gaunt. There were visible bags beneath her eyes, a state she would never appear in while there was anyone around to see. "There's an emergency. Come with me."

She turned away, leaving Sefina to hurry after her.

They arrived swiftly. Lady Lirath strode into the infirmary without knocking, nearly bowling over an exhausted looking healer in full headscarf. Sefina pulled up her own scarf and murmured an apology, circling around the healer as she followed Lady Lirath's rapid stride.

Lady Lirath pulled aside a curtain to reveal a sickbed. A gasp caught in Sefina's chest. The Regent lay limp atop the thin covers, a folded cloth covering his forehead. The white sleep shirt he wore was yellowed and damp with sweat. It clung to his chest, which rose and fell with an awful rattle to his breaths. Even through Sefina's scarf, the smell of sick, stale sweat was staggering.

"You must do something," Lady Lirath said, grasping Sefina's hand. Fear shone in her pale blue eyes, ringed red at the edges as though she'd been crying.

Despite Sefina's growing frustration with Stagford's nobles and their entitlement, she felt sorry for the regent. His gaunt face and skeletal frame were painful to witness.

"What would you have me do?" she asked Lady Lirath. "You've already brought him here against my orders." She struggled to keep her voice calm as a frown pulled her lips.

"Sing," Lady Lirath said, pleading.

Sefina's eyes widened. Lady Lirath had never pleaded with her before. She always demanded. "Why me? I've never healed anyone with my voice before. Only Mirae has—"

"Mirae isn't here," Lady Lirath insisted, squeezing Sefina's hand tighter. Her fingers were strong as steel and just as cold. "You are. You performed a miracle at your ascension. Your voice often soothes people to sleep. I've heard you do it for Mirae and even that troublesome ward of yours. Even if you can grant him a short reprieve from his pain..."

"But—"

"Please," Lady Lirath said. "This is the regent of our city. He's the most important person in Stagford and my cousin. You must ease his suffering. Imagine the political chaos and upheaval that will descend upon us if he dies. Things are terrible enough."

Grudgingly, Sefina admitted Lady Lirath was right. The regent's death would cause considerable unrest during an already tumultuous time. *What harm can I do him now? Even if my voice can't heal him like Mirae's, some decent rest might do him good. And a lullaby will hardly make him any worse.*

She lowered her scarf and opened her mouth, but couldn't sing the lullaby she used for Mirae and Loma. It wouldn't come. She cleared her throat and tried again.

The moon's begun to rise,
The stars are—

Her voice cracked on the second line. She licked her lips, stealing a nervous glance at Lady Lirath. It seemed silly to feel stage fright in a situation like this, but the pounding of her heart and the sweat sprouting on her skin were undeniable signs. "This won't work." Sefina's eyes darting down to avoid her mentor's inevitable look of frustration and disappointment. "I'm no miracle worker. We should find Mirae."

"Mirae isn't here," Lady Lirath repeated. "You must try again. You're the Speaker of Dreams, Of-Blessed-Dreams' voice in this realm. Let her decide whether a miracle will happen tonight or not."

Sefina sighed, then lifted her chin and squared her shoulders. She looked at the regent instead of Lady Lirath, watching tense lines of pain pull at his pale, sweaty face. She inhaled, choosing a different lullaby. It felt wrong somehow, singing that particular song to the regent.

The sun has set behind the hills.
The evening is quiet and still.

Ice flooded Sefina's veins. Her skin went numb. Each breath drew biting frost into the bottom of her lungs, as though she were standing outside in the dead of winter. The crackling hiss of the regent's breaths went silent. There was only the sound of her own voice. Though soft and low, it swelled to fill the entire room.

Each little star is shining bright.
Peace drifts on the air tonight.

Blackness closed in around the edges of Sefina's vision, creating a tunnel of white light until all she saw was the regent's face. She was a mere conduit as the lullaby poured freely from her mouth, a gateway for something so far beyond herself that she couldn't begin to describe it.

Now climb in bed and rest your head.
And dream your pretty dreams

The regent exhaled. His breathing slowed, the unsettling rattle nowhere to be heard. The strain on his face softened as his chest rose and fell in a peaceful rhythm.

Sefina came back to herself, wincing as warmth flooded her stiff limbs. She felt as though she'd plunged into icy water and only just managed to clamber out, stinging from the sudden change in temperature.

Lady Lirath, who had been staring at her in stunned silence, seemed to return to reality as well. "Change him into a dry shirt," she ordered the healer, who had stopped in the middle of the room while Sefina sang. As she glanced in his direction, she noted his eyes were still wide with awe.

"Right away," he said, hurrying to a set of drawers and rummaging within.

Sefina turned back to the regent, scarcely able to believe what she'd done. Had she healed him or merely helped him sleep peacefully? That seemed more plausible. Maybe he would feel better in the morning...or maybe he would die during the night despite her efforts. Though an otherworldly power had possessed her, she couldn't bring herself to call the experiment a success.

Lady Lirath, however, was thrilled.

"I always knew you were special, Sefina," she said, throwing her arms around Sefina's waist. Sefina accepted the hug, too bewildered to protest. Her mind raced as she stood awkwardly in Lady Lirath's embrace. If she had healed the regent, that meant she had a duty to heal as many people as possible.

Sefina suddenly understood how Mirae must feel, enduring a fraction of the weight she'd carried since early adolescence. The knowledge that you and only you could make the difference between life and death wasn't nearly as exciting a realization as Sefina had expected. In fact, she shuddered with rising fear.

Nevertheless, she remained in a chair outside the infirmary with Lady Lirath, waiting for news of the regent until pale light peeked through the windows and the silver notes of dawnbell rang out to welcome a new day. She waited silently, tense as a wire, because she had to know. Had she truly performed a miracle? Had she been wrong all these years, thinking herself ordinary?

As the sun rose, the healer came to fetch them. The Regent's curtain had been pulled aside to reveal that his eyes were open and clear. "Water," he said, his voice crackling like a hearth.

Sefina noted a pitcher of water upon the nightstand and filled the empty cup beside it, offering it to the regent. He drank deeply, allowing some of the water to run from the corners of his mouth in his eagerness.

"Are you well, Horace?" Lady Lirath asked. "How do you feel?"

Horace cleared his throat, responding in a stronger voice. "Yes, by the grace of Speaker Sefina's voice."

Sefina's stomach churned. Her throat tightened and she had to force out her response. "Thank the Eight, my lord, not me. A full night's rest often helps the sick feel well again."

The regent propped himself into a seated position. Sefina blinked in surprise. It seemed he'd already recovered a significant amount of strength in order to move so freely. "You're far too modest, Speaker Sefina. I heard your sweet voice in the midst of a terrible fever. Afterward, I felt cool and numb to all my pain. You healed me—and I'm thrilled to say so, since that spoiled child refused to attend me when I summoned her."

"Mirae refused you?" She wished she could say she was surprised. Though Mirae considered it her duty to heal anyone and everyone, it was just like her to turn away the most powerful man in Stagford for approaching her with such entitlement.

The regent's face, which had regained some of its rosy color, darkened further with anger. "I sent four different messengers to bring her to The Green, but she sent them all back, claiming she was needed at the docks, where the plague runs rampant. Such audacity! Does she fail to realize it has spread from the slums she so cherishes to Upper Easton and Castletown? People there are dying in droves while she does nothing to stop it!"

"Please, Horace," Lady Lirath said, motioning for him to lie back down. "You mustn't overexert yourself."

Sefina's shoulders stiffened. She clenched her jaw. Refusing the regent's 'summons' was one thing, but refusing people because they didn't live in the docks? That didn't sound like Mirae at all.

"Forgive me, but you must be mistaken. Mirae and I may have gone our separate ways, but she's a good person. She would never let such suffering spread if she had the power to stop it. It's possible her voice has given out. I've heard rumors of that happening before."

The regent huffed. "That isn't what my messengers told me."

Sefina looked to Lady Lirath. "Tell him. You raised Mirae from childhood. She'd never stand by while a plague took our city."

Lady Lirath shook her head, taking Sefina's hands in hers. "I fear you think too highly of her, my dear," she said, patting the back of Sefina's hand as though to comfort her. "Mirae is too stubborn for her own good. She cares about the Sea Children more than any Earthfolk. Her refusal to help our people in Castletown hardly surprises me."

Those words cut deeply, but Sefina realized further argument was pointless. Lady Lirath and the regent would continue to think poorly of Mirae no matter what she told them. She reclaimed her hands and smothered her anger, as she was accustomed.

"Let us speak no more of Mirae, then. I struggle to believe my voice possesses the same power as hers…" She swallowed around a growing lump in her throat. "But I see little harm in trying to help others. As you said, Lord Regent, people are dying. If Mirae cannot or will not work in Castletown, I suppose I must."

The regent's frown transformed into a dazzling smile. "Thank you, Speaker Sefina. You are truly Of-Blessed-Dreams' voice in the mortal realm. I knew from the moment I met you that you were extraordinary. Will you come to The Green and reside there with me for the time being? I shall set aside a portion of my castle for an infirmary, where you may tend those in need."

Sefina hesitated, drawing her hands close to her stomach and lacing her fingers. She wanted to curl into herself and disappear. If she had discovered some sort of latent power to heal the sick, or at least ease their suffering, she had a duty to use it. However, in accepting the role of Speaker, she'd promised to care for the temple and its residents first.

"It would be most generous of you to maintain an infirmary in your castle, but I'm afraid I can't stay there. My home is here. I have an obligation to Of-Blessed-Dreams, her temple, and her followers. Instead, I'll come at duskbell and sing for as many as I can. Is that an agreeable compromise?"

A shadow of disappointment flickered across the regent's face, but he banished it in less time than it took Sefina to blink. His unsettling smile spread wider. "Then I shall be pleased to see your lovely face every evening, even while half-hidden behind a scarf."

Sefina's face grew unpleasantly hot. The compliment sent a cold trail of sweat down the groove of her spine. She resisted the urge to shudder as she turned to Lady Lirath. "Will you look after the temple for a few hours each night while I'm gone?"

Lady Lirath rested a hand upon Sefina's shoulder. "Of course, dear girl. It would be an honor."

So it was that Sefina visited The Green every night at duskbell. True to his word, the regent housed the sickest nobles and some fortunate city folk on the lowest level of his castle, in what had once been a grand dining hall.

Sefina sang to them individually. She sang to them in groups. She sang until her voice became a hoarse croak like a summer frog by the lake. She sang so long and often that she often failed to finish before dawnbell, and the only sleep she got was on the carriage ride back to the temple, where she sang some more for any residents who came down with sweating sickness.

Sometimes, her patients improved. They woke feeling strong and well-rested, no longer drenched in sweat, able to eat and drink without expelling everything.

Sometimes, they died anyway.

Sefina looked on, a grave witness as elderly people like Speaker Yeneri passed on. She saw parents die, leaving behind orphaned children. She saw children die, leaving behind devastated parents. Her heart bled constantly, but she learned to keep it hidden from everyone. She couldn't show her grief, or her patients might lose hope.

In the rare moments her mind wasn't foggy with grief or exhaustion, she hoped her voice brought those who joined the Sea of Stars some comfort. Though she couldn't heal in the same effortless way Mirae did, it quickly became apparent that she could reliably put someone to sleep and ease their pain.

She sent the worst cases to Of-Eternal-Sleep that way, with closed eyes, steady breathing, and peaceful smiles while their families said goodbye from a safe distance. She considered it a smaller miracle than those Mirae performed so reliably, but an important service nonetheless.

Secretly, she hoped Mirae was proud of her. She hoped Mirae might hear of the good she tried to do, even though it was for Stagford's wealthier residents. The falsehood she had initially told Loma became truer and truer by the day. Sickness loomed large over everyone, a shadow that didn't care whether one was rich or poor, young or old, good or evil. It claimed whoever it wished in its icy claws, no matter how hard she fought to keep it at bay.

Chapter Eighteen

THE LONG DAYS AND longer nights stretched into weeks, then months. Despite Sefina's efforts, sweating sickness spread to every corner of Stagford. The regent released a proclamation: no one was allowed in or out of the docks. They were to remain under strict quarantine. No exceptions.

Loma informed her of this one Eightday at duskbell when he knocked upon her door. "Sefina," he said, jogging into the room without an invitation and letting the door slam behind him. He unwound his scarf from around his head and shoved it into his trousers pocket. "Did he tell you he was going to do this?"

Sefina looked over the sheet music she'd been studying and set her lute upon its stand. Upon seeing Loma's wide eyes and furrowed brow, she rose from her stool. "Who is 'he' and what did he do?" she whispered. Her voice had given out earlier that day, so she'd drunk some tea with honey and decided to wait an hour before going to The Green.

"The regent." Loma rocked on his toes as though unable to stand still. "His guards almost caught me. They've surrounded the docks, stopping everyone who tries to leave."

Sefina placed her hands on her hips, fixing Loma with her sternest stare. "You mean you snuck out again? I thought we'd come to an understanding."

"This was an emergency," Loma said. "I heard about it from Trenton and had to see for myself. The regent's guards are crawling all over. I heard one of them tell the merchants it's a lockdown. No one in or out so they don't spread the 'Sea Child Sickness' to Whiteport and Castletown."

Sefina clenched her jaw. She should be frustrated with Loma, but found she was far angrier at the situation. Sweating sickness had already taken root in Easton, Castletown, and The Green weeks ago. Encouraging residents to stay in their homes was one thing. This was something else, punitive rather than precautionary.

"Has the regent locked down Whiteport and Castletown?"

"No." Loma shook his head. "A merchant asked that same question. One of the guards shoved him to the ground and the other one kicked him 'til he couldn't stand." His gaze darted down to the carpet, as though he were trying to banish the memory.

Sefina's heart picked up speed. "Please tell me you didn't get involved." The mere thought of Loma in an altercation with the regent's guards made a line of cold sweat break out along her hairline.

"No," Loma said. "People don't see me unless I want them to."

Sefina exhaled deeply. "Thank the Eight for that." She summoned what remained of her broken voice, pitching it low and firm. "But this is the last time, Loma. I mean it."

Loma stuck out his lip. "I wore my scarf the whole time. I didn't pass within two yards of anyone."

"It isn't just sweating sickness anymore. If the regent ordered his guards to close the docks, they could catch you trying to return to the temple. I won't see you thrown in a cell because some guard with his head up his own rear end doesn't believe you're my student. Do you understand?"

Loma stopped his nervous rocking. His shoulders slumped. "Oh," he said. Just one word. Oh.

"It's all right." Sefina stepped forward, folding Loma into her arms. He entered them willingly. "You'll be safe here. And know that I won't stand for this. I'll speak to the regent tonight. Unless he makes an example of those guards and treats all sections of the city equally, I'll refuse to come to The Green."

Loma's head snapped up. "You can't." He clutched the sleeves of Sefina's white robe, clinging tight. "The sick people there need you."

Sefina ignored the stab of guilt in the pit of her stomach. "That's why the regent must listen."

"What if he throws you in a cell? What if I never see you again?" Loma's hands shook, but he squeezed tighter. Terror shone in his wide brown eyes.

Sefina's heart ached. In that moment, she understood that she was truly all Loma had. And so she lied. She lied to ease Loma's fears, for he was still so very young, and didn't deserve to carry such a heavy fear.

"Don't worry about me." She stroked his hair, offering him her gentlest smile. "I'm Of-Blessed-Dreams' voice in the mortal realm. She's chosen me to care for the Temple of Dreams, the city of Stagford, and everyone in need that I meet. She won't let anything happen to me, because she needs me to do her work, remember?"

Loma stared straight into Sefina's eyes, as though searching for the truth within them. "You promise?"

Sefina nodded and opened her arms. Loma fell into them, burying his face in her shoulder. She rubbed circles upon his back the same way she did while putting him to sleep each night before she left for The Green. Loma squeezed her so hard with his skinny arms that it almost hurt. Still, Sefina let him hug her as long as he wanted, pretending not to notice the quiet sobs he tried to stifle.

"I promise," she said aloud, blinking back tears of her own. "Now then. Shall I make you some warm tea before I leave tonight?"

Loma drew back, wiping his nose on his sleeve. "Yes, please."

Sefina withdrew her handkerchief and offered it to him. "Here, don't ruin your shirt. I'll make your tea." She turned, then hesitated. "Has there been any news of—?"

She didn't need to finish the question. "Mirae is tired, but well," Loma said. "She's staying with Brom and his family. Every day, no matter what, she visits the sickest people and sings for them. Sometimes, they get better."

Sefina understood what Loma didn't say. Miraculous as it was, Mirae's voice couldn't stave off Of-Eternal-Sleep when it was someone's appointed time. A truth she'd also learned of late.

As she boiled water for more tea in the fireplace, Sefina allowed her anger to boil as well. Fear had been at the forefront while Loma explained what he'd seen and heard, but her knuckles went white as she gripped the kettle's handle far too tight.

She'd indulged the regent's ego and his unsettling compliments. She'd done everything he asked, even coming to his castle every night.

Now, this.

She'd been proud of herself for tolerating him thus far, considering it her solemn duty to cooperate with the city's foremost leader, but her dark thoughts gathered like storm clouds. When they sounded, they were eerily similar to Mirae's voice.

There's no good reason to quarantine the docks and nowhere else. No good reason for guards to assault a merchant for asking a reasonable question. The regent hasn't done anything to stop his peers from calling it the 'Sea Child Sickness'. Not a single denouncement. All the while he sits in his castle, playing the generous benefactor to other nobles and their children, while I put in all the effort.

At first, Sefina had liked the regent for his compliments and attention. Then, she'd tolerated him for the sake of Lady Lirath and the temple. Now, this. *You were right all along, Mirae. I should have seen it sooner.*

* * * *

That night on the carriage ride to The Green, Sefina tried to decide what she would say to the regent. Her mind, however, was flooded with thoughts of Mirae. *Are you eating enough? Getting enough sleep? Probably not. What would you tell the regent in my place? The unbridled truth, I'm sure.*

She wrapped her arms around her elbows beneath her cloak, longing to hold Mirae just one more time and smell the familiar scent of her hair. It had been almost two years, but Sefina recalled Mirae's face as clearly as ever; her wide smile, dimpled cheeks, and tightly coiled cloud of black curls.

Do you look different now? Perhaps your face has more lines. Perhaps your eyes are older and wiser.

Even after Trenton halted the carriage and escorted her into the castle, Sefina remained in a sad, wistful mood. Realizing she was in no state to speak with the regent and suspecting he was asleep, she resolved to confront him at dawnbell. She made her way to the refurbished dining room, where a sickbay full of people waited in need of her help.

As she entered, the smell struck her nose—seeping through her scarf and into her skin. Sweat, urine, despair. No matter how many times she encountered them, there was no getting used to them. There was only enduring them.

Then came the wash of low moans and whimpers, all down the endless rows of cots. She pretended it was a restless night wind. It was the only way her mind and heart could cope during the long hours between dusk and dawn.

Worst of all was the invisible weight of death. It hung in the stagnant air, reminding her of the choking tallow in Lady Lirath's studio. The sensation was of being smothered on all sides. She steadied herself, drawing from a dwindling well of determination and perseverance that seemed emptier by the day.

That night, Sefina saw Mirae's face in every person she sang for. One young woman shared Mirae's kind brown eyes, another her elegant brow. This old man had dimples like hers, that young boy the same warm red undertones in his bronze skin.

One little girl looked so like Mirae had as a child that tears welled in Sefina's eyes. Or perhaps she didn't resemble Mirae much at all, but she was missing her left front tooth—the same one Mirae lost early by falling from the branches of a tree.

"Speaker," the little girl said as Sefina sat by her cot, "do you know any stories?" Her whisper carried a distinct lisp that melted Sefina's heart.

"Stories? Of course." She attempted to speak cheerfully, fighting the soreness and strain of overuse. "But would you rather hear a song? It might help you feel better."

The girl shook her head weakly upon her sweat-soaked pillow. She was painfully thin, more skeletal than human. "A story, please. My parents always tell me—" She broke into an ugly, hacking cough that jerked her whole body.

Sefina winced in sympathy. A persistent gaze warmed the back of her neck, and she glanced sideways. One of the castle healers looked at her as he passed with an armful of blankets. He caught her eye and shook his head sadly before going on his way. Though not a word passed between them, Sefina understood. The little girl's parents had already gone to the Sea of Stars.

Knowing that, she couldn't refuse. "All right, but did you know some songs are stories as well?"

The girl worked her dry lips a moment before whispering again. Her voice was little more than a frayed, trembling thread. "Really?"

"Yes. Would you like to hear one?"

She managed a weak nod.

Sefina sat up straight, inhaled deep into her belly, and sang. A comfortable numbness descended, starting in her chest and spreading outward through her veins. Though she chose the words of the song, controlling each note with deliberation and care, strange but familiar energy swelled within her. She'd gradually learned to maintain some awareness of the real world while submerging herself in the cold, icy darkness.

Once there was a bright young girl
Whose name was Luralu.
Her smile shone like a polished mirror.
In fact, she looked like you!

Now Luralu set out to sea
In an old rowboat called the Leaky Lee
To catch some fish for dinner
For her mam and brothers three.

Song of Stars

The waves were tall as oak trees
And the sky a stormy gray,
But Luralu sailed bravely on
To where the fishies play.

As Sefina sang, the girl's eyelids drooped. A soft smile spread across her face. Her crackling breaths came slower.
Sefina lowered her voice to a soft croon.

She held her net beside the boat
And flashed that big bright smile.
She said, Come jump into my net,
So we can play a while.

Now all the fishes big and small
Were hiding from the storm,
But when they heard young Luralu
They found her in a swarm.
They jumped alongside Leaky Lee
And into the net—one, two, three!
But Luralu felt guilty,
And she set them all back free.

She headed home with a heavy heart
For now there was no supper.
Her mam and brothers three
Would go to bed a hungered.

The girl lay still beneath the covers, as though she couldn't hear Sefina at all. She stopped for a moment, swallowing around a hard lump in her throat. Warmth began returning to Sefina's cold, heavy limbs, but then the girl's eyes cracked open. Though she didn't speak, she shifted her tiny hand toward the edge of the bed.

Sefina took her hand and placed it back upon the bed, stroking the girl's knuckles with her thumb as she resumed singing.

But as she sailed back to the dock,
The fishes followed near.

They filled her net with oysters
And all began to cheer.

Thank you, thank you, Luralu,
For freeing us today.
Share with us the bounty
From deep beneath the bay!

So Luralu said, "Thank you too,
We shall eat well this evening.
She took the oysters straight back home
To find her brothers weeping.

The girl's hand went slack. Her breathing slowed until Sefina could no longer hear it.

Oh Luralu, how cruel of you,
They wailed in raucous chorus.
We thought we lost you out at sea
While catching dinner for us!
Luralu held up her net
And showed them all the oysters.
Never would I leave you three,
Now cook these up for mother.

Sefina felt the girl leave. She departed with a peaceful sigh like whispering wind.

They ate and ate 'til it grew late
Stuffed full of oyster stew.
They gave a cheer and said, Here here!
For the brave, kind Luralu!

Sefina squeezed her hand, then let go. There was nothing more to be done. There was no sudden, jarring return to her body this time, but she wanted to crawl out of her own skin anyway. Her throat was a painful knot and tears rolled down her cheeks. She brushed the girl's damp hair away from her forehead before she rose to find the healer.

Someone would take her away for burial while she washed with lye soap and steaming water.

As Sefina stood, she looked at the girl one last time, hoping she had found her parents amongst the Sea of Stars. Perhaps this was as Of-Blessed-Dreams and Of-Eternal-Sleep willed, but if it was, she hated them as she had never hated the gods before.

She swallowed her sorrow and wiped her eyes with her handkerchief before stopping the nearest healer, an older woman with graying hair and a hunched posture. "The young girl in that bed has passed. Did she or her parents tell you her name?"

The healer closed her eyes a moment, as if to compose herself. "Sonya. She told me."

"Sonya," Sefina repeated. She would remember. Someone would remember.

* * * *

Shortly before dawnbell, Sefina scrubbed herself raw with lye soap, changed scarves, and marched up the grand staircase to the second floor. She prepared herself for a long wait only to find a butler standing at attention outside the regent's study. It seemed the regent had gotten an early start that morning.

Sefina strode up to the butler and summoned her most superior voice. "Is the regent awake? I must speak with him."

The butler bowed, maintaining his stoic expression. "Allow me to inquire, Speaker."

She offered a stiff nod. "Please, do."

The butler opened the door, his coattails swishing behind him as he slipped into the study. Sefina waited in the hall, maintaining her rigid posture, trying to ignore the cold trail of sweat that ran down her spine. Her every muscle screamed exhaustion, but she'd promised Loma. She was one of the only people in Stagford who could address the regent as a peer. It had to be her.

After a short while, the butler returned. "The regent will see you, Speaker." He held the door open and made a flourishing bow, ushering Sefina through. She strode inside and didn't stop until the door clicked shut.

The study smelled of leather-bound books and parchment, with more than a hint of familiar citrus perfume. Sefina was glad of her scarf, for she'd come to loathe the scent. The regent sat behind a polished mahogany desk, quill in hand. He set the quill aside and rose from his chair, making no effort to pull up the scarf that hung beneath his chin.

"Speaker Sefina? What an unexpected pleasure." He offered a syrupy smile to go along with his honeyed words. "How are things progressing in my infirmary?"

Sefina swallowed around a lump in her throat. Thoughts of the little girl who'd left for the Sea of Stars flooded her mind. Her gap-toothed grin. Her small, limp hand. Sefina smothered them and held the regent's stare. "Much the same, Lord Regent. Some patients improved. Many others entered Lady Sleep's embrace."

The regent frowned, stroking his waxd goatee. "I'm sorry to hear that of course, but who are we to challenge the will of the gods?"

Once more, Sefina was glad of her scarf. It meant she didn't have to force a smile. "We privileged few still possess some influence. Which is why I must ask; why have you quarantined the docks?"

The regent's smile vanished. He removed his hand from his chin. "Isn't it obvious? The sickness has ravaged the slums with no signs of stopping. Surely you understand that we can't have it spreading to Castletown."

It took an effort of will for Sefina to relax her shoulders and uncurl her shaking hands. She pictured the surface of the temple pond on a still night, smooth as polished glass. She needed to remain calm. "Why not quarantine Castletown as well? To my knowledge, no one there has been confined to their homes."

The regent offered her an even more saccharine smile. "The people of Castletown are responsible. I have no doubt those who are ill shall remain in their homes."

Sefina took a step forward. "Are you implying those who live in the docks aren't as responsible?"

The regent's smile faltered at the corners, but only briefly. It was so subtle that Sefina doubted anyone who hadn't been taught by a master of social etiquette like Lady Lirath would have noticed. "Sefina, I know you have a soft spot for the Sea Children, but not all of them are as well-educated and socially aware as your former friend Mirae. Unfortunately, poverty breeds ignorance."

Sefina curled her lip. She no longer bothered smoothing out her voice. "I would hardly call them ignorant. The use of scarves to prevent the spread of sickness comes from their culture, after all."

The regent sighed, then turned to shut the curtains at the window behind his desk. The orange glare of the early morning sun disappeared, leaving the room much darker. Only a tallow candle on the desk provided a steady source of light. When he turned back, his brow was deeply furrowed.

"There have been rumors," the Regent said, circling the desk to meet Sefina on the other side. "Some residents of the docks are unhappy with the current state of affairs in Stagford."

Sefina rolled her eyes. "Forgive me, but everyone is unhappy with the current state of affairs."

The regent's nostrils flared slightly. "You're deliberately misunderstanding me and I don't appreciate it. These rumblings of dissatisfaction will do no one any good. It isn't as if I can banish the sickness myself or make more food and medicines appear out of thin air. I'm only mortal, after all..."

From the way the regent's voice trailed off, Sefina knew exactly what he was thinking. Who he was thinking of. A hot ball of anger smoldered within her chest, but she chose her words carefully. "You believe armed guards patrolling the streets are the answer?"

"If you have a better solution, do feel free to share it with me."

"Remove your guards. Let them fish again. Send what food you can. Hungry bellies breed resentment. We could spare more from the temple orchard—"

The Regent shook his head. "Speaker. Your impulses are generous as always, but certain people are just looking for an excuse. The sweating sickness has given them one. It is my duty to protect Stagford, even from itself. Especially in times like these."

Sefina opened her mouth to argue, then closed it again. From the steel edge that flashed in the regent's blue eyes, she already knew she wouldn't succeed. Not only was he determined, but he was also paranoid. Tightening his grip. She needed to find another way.

"Very well, Lord Regent. You've heard my advice, but the decision is yours. Unfortunately, my influence is confined to the Temple of Dreams."

"I don't find it unfortunate." The regent's face softening. He placed a friendly hand upon Sefina's shoulder. Resisting the urge to flinch tested even her tight control. "You are a credit to this city, but allow me to worry about this. You have enough burdens to bear, spending your days looking after the temple and your nights here."

Sefina removed the regent's hand with a brush of her own. "Then I suppose that the temple is where I should return. I'll leave Stagford's safety in your eminently capable hands." She turned and left without waiting for a farewell. She threw open the door, brushed past the startled butler, and stormed toward the stairs, her mind already racing.

The temple doesn't have much to spare, but if the Regent refuses to loosen his fist, someone has to make up the difference. It's what Speaker Yeneri would do. It's what Mirae would want.

Chapter Nineteen

WEEKS PASSED WITH ALMOST unbearable slowness. Each day seemed to last a hundred years at least, while night time passed in a feverish blur. Sefina ate little and slept less, for there always seemed to be some emergency.

Thanks to the secret deliveries she'd organized, the temple garden ran out of healing herbs and the orchard was picked clean of fruit. She attempted to barter for more supplies, but everything for sale in Whiteport and Castletown's markets was exorbitantly priced. There wasn't enough food to go around, especially not fish, for the docks remained quarantined.

The temple ran short of blankets next, then cots, and finally scarves. Sefina resorted to using the least valuable of Speaker Yeneri's tapestries. She enlisted Loma's help in cutting one apart to repurpose as extra scarves, though they tried their best to preserve individual pictures in each fragment. She imagined Speaker Yeneri would understand and perhaps even appreciate the noble purpose her art served.

Worst of all, Sefina heard less news of Mirae. She was forced to rely upon secondhand whispers, mostly by eavesdropping during her nightly rounds at the regent's palace.

The news was always grim.

"Did you hear?" a healer at the regent's castle whispered to another one muggy evening, having not noticed Sefina's approach behind him. "An entire block in Castletown has come down with Sea Children Sickness. The regent's guards had it cordoned off earlier today, but they opened it again by evening."

The second healer sighed and shook her head. "I'd never speak ill of our lord regent, but that block should have remained isolated. A single day won't make much difference."

Sefina's jaw clenched. So much for the regent's honeyed promises.

"The guards at the docks must not be doing their jobs," the first healer said. "If they were, that block wouldn't have needed cordoning. Or if that Mirae decided to heal everyone instead of sitting on her ass in Easton..."

Mirae? A shiver ran along Sefina's spine. She edged closer to the wall and tried not to breathe too loud, lest the healers notice her and stop conversing.

"I heard her voice gave out again," said the second healer. "It's been three days, last I heard."

"Hmph. That'll stop her slandering the regent for a while."

"Enough, Henrick. People have reason to be angry. The sweating sickness isn't the Regent's fault, but fear stokes harsh words in all of us. I've heard you complain about the Regent yourself when there was less bread to go around three summers ago."

"Well, I wonder if she's even a true miracle worker. Didn't she grow up alongside the speaker at the Temple of Dreams? Maybe Speaker Sefina was the one making miracles happen? We've seen her work wonders here, after all…"

Sefina decided she'd heard enough. She cleared her throat and stepped away from the wall. "We're almost out of soap," she said as the healers tried to look innocent, standing tall like soldiers on parade. "Is there more?"

The second healer bowed at the waist instead of touching her forehead to Sefina's hands, which she neglected to extend. That custom had died in recent months. "I'm afraid not, Speaker Sefina. There should be more tomorrow morning…if the extra shipment from Easton arrives as planned."

Sefina ignored the growing tightness in her chest. She had no doubt the soap was needed in Easton more. "I'll keep my distance as much as possible, then. When I return to the temple, I'll see how our own supplies are faring. If we have more than we need, I'll send it here with the usual carriage."

The first healer, Henrick, stared at her with glowing admiration. "You truly are sent by Of-Blessed-Dreams, Speaker Sefina."

Sefina fought the urge to shift uncomfortably beneath his gaze. She couldn't forget what he'd said before, that Mirae was a fraud, not to mention calling sweating sickness the 'Sea Child Sickness'. In the end, she could no longer bite her tongue.

"Thank you, but you're wrong about Mirae. Of-Blessed-Dreams may have chosen me as speaker, but Mirae possesses more raw power than I could ever dream of. Wherever she is, I know she's doing her very best to help those in need."

Henrick cleared his throat. "Well. Since you know her, I'm sure you're right, Speaker." He started to adjust the scarf around his face, then caught himself and lowered his hand, straightening the hem of his shirt.

"This sickness will end someday soon," Sefina told the healers. "The Eight won't see our entire city destroyed."

The second healer smiled. Though Sefina couldn't see her mouth move, she recognized the gesture in the eyes. "I believe you. Until then, it's up to us. Let me check upstairs and see if there's any extra soap we've forgotten about." With another bow, she departed with Henrick behind her.

Sefina watched them go, then prepared to move on along the line of cots. A wave of dizziness overcame her, causing her head to swim and her vision to blur. She swayed, bracing her forearm upon the wall.

She shook her head to chase away her exhaustion. Her throat felt rough as sandpaper and her chin dipped as though her head were filled with rocks. Though she hated to admit it, she knew she had no more to give that night. With one last look at the long line of beds, she turned and left, her heart as heavy as her limbs.

Slowly, she made her way outside, pausing a moment upon the castle steps. She lowered her scarf, allowing the early morning breeze to caress her face and taking her first real breath in hours. It was cold and damp and smelled of wet earth, but lovely all the same.

She closed her eyes and pictured Mirae in her mind: braided hair, warm brown eyes, dimples and all. The memory of Mirae's face was often the only comfort to be found these days.

Once she summoned enough strength in mind and body, she pulled up her scarf and dragged herself toward the stables, where her usual carriage waited. Trenton sat atop the driver's box, wearing a scarf with a fragment of unicorn over his mouth. Part of Speaker Yeneri's repurposed tapestries.

"Good morning," Sefina said as Trenton hopped down from his seat to open the carriage. Normally, Sefina would have politely waved away such close contact coming straight from the infirmary, but she felt so faint that Trenton's arm was a welcome offer.

"You look like you might keel over, if you'll forgive my saying so, Sefina."

"I'm hardly surprised. What time is it?"

As if to answer her question, dawnbell rang as she settled in the carriage. The sky beyond the window remained a dark gray while faint raindrops drummed on the carriage roof.

"Time to get you home, I think." Trenton closed the door, pulled his hood over his bright red hair, and climbed up on the box. He urged the horses into a brisk trot. The gentle rock of the carriage and the soothing sound of rain swiftly bore Sefina off to sleep, as though she were adrift in Of-Eternal-Sleep's boat.

When she opened her eyes again, it was to Trenton's face hovering in her field of vision. The upper half, at least. His brows were knitted with concern. "Sorry to wake you, but you'll be much more comfortable abed instead of dozing in the carriage."

Sefina managed a weak smile behind her scarf. "No time for that, I'm afraid. I have far too much to do today. Perhaps I can steal a short nap this afternoon."

"Sefina!"

In the distance, Sefina caught sight of a short, bundled figure sprinting down the temple steps, taking them two at a time. Even shouting from a distance, she recognized Loma's voice right away. "What is it?" she asked, hopping out of the carriage to meet him.

Loma skidded to a stop, crouching with hands on knees and panting for breath. "The regent—here! Got a bunch of guards, too."

Sefina's blood ran cold. From the fearful, wide-eyed look she glimpsed beneath Loma's hood, she knew something was very wrong. "Where?"

Loma pointed.

She ran in that direction, scarcely noticing the rain had become a downpour as she tripped through the muddy grass to reach the path. Her shoes and the hem of her robes were covered in filth and the fabric soon clung to her skin, but she didn't care.

At the top of the steps she saw them: eight guards in plate armor, which would have been shiny if not for the mud on their boots and greaves. One carried the regent's standard, a white stag's head mounted upon a golden triangle. The others carried short swords.

Sefina stormed up to them and tried to enter the temple. "Stand aside. Where is the regent?"

The nearest two guards closed ranks in front of her, standing shoulder to shoulder. Though they made no move to raise their weapons, the threat was clear.

"Sorry, Speaker," one of the guards said. His voice was polite but distant, devoid of emotion. "You're to wait here until the regent returns."

She glared at the guards. "Excuse me? This is my temple!" She threw out her hands as though to encompass the entire temple grounds. "It doesn't belong to the regent and never has in all its centuries of existence. As the voice of Of-Blessed-Dreams, I'm not subject to any mortal leader's whims."

"Not a mere whim, I fear." The regent emerged from behind the pair of guards. They stepped apart, allowing him through. He wore his usual finery, a forest green doublet overlaid with a rich brown cape embroidered in gold. The scarf around his face was a pure, crisp white. His brows drew close together as though in deep concern, but his blue eyes were as icy as Lady Lirath's ever were on her worst days. "This pains me, Speaker, but I must ask. Has Mirae sought refuge in the temple?"

Sefina shook her head, stunned. The rain poured down in a torrent, soaking through her hood and dampening her hair, but she was numb to it all. "What? Why?"

"Please." The regent made no move to leave the cover of the temple doorway. He locked eyes with Sefina, sending a chill across the back of her neck that had nothing to do with the weather. "Do not be difficult. Is Mirae here?"

Sefina squared her shoulders and lifted her chin. "No. I haven't so much as spoken with Mirae since her departure two years ago."

The regent sighed. "I wish I could believe you, Speaker. Though I will admit, my guards have found no trace of her yet, but if she is here, they will find her. Do not think you can hide her away."

"What reason has she to hide?" Sefina pushed through the soreness and pain in her throat until her voice cracked with effort and anger. "You behave as though she's committed a crime!"

"I sincerely regret to inform you that she has." The regent's voice took on a note of saccharine pity. Sefina didn't trust it in the slightest. "I have it on good authority that Mirae is responsible for the sickness ravaging our city. Witnesses have come forward claiming she cursed them, a misguided desire to purge the Earthfolk from Stagford. She's no miracle-worker, but a witch. Perhaps she has stolen her power from some minor godling rather than acting as a vessel for Of-Blessed-Dreams or the Eight."

Fear, sharp like a knife, lodged in Sefina's heart. "Never! Mirae would never do such a thing—and you know as well as anyone that the sickness is worst at the docks!"

The regent folded his arms. "Perhaps, but Mirae heals her own while the Sea Child Sickness races through Castletown. Don't you find it suspicious that the sickness started around her, after she left the temple and came to reside in the slums?"

Tears of anger welled in Sefina's eyes. They rolled down her cheeks, mingling with the rain. "I won't hear another word against her, not from you or anyone else. Take your guards and leave my temple at once!"

"Do calm down, Speaker." The regent gestured to one side, indicating the hall behind him. Sefina noted a cluster of eavesdroppers huddled past the large double doors. "People are listening. Surely you don't want your own residents running around like headless chickens?"

Headless. Sefina's stomach twisted. Was that how the regent intended to deal with Mirae? She looked to the temple residents. Their pale, frightened faces urged her to do something, for their sake and Mirae's.

She knew what Mirae would do—tear into the regent with the blade of her tongue. She also knew what Lady Lirath would do—kowtow to the regent and attempt to pacify him. She inhaled through her wet scarf and relaxd her shoulders.

"Forgive me," she said, drawing upon every lesson Lady Lirath had ever taught her. "You must understand that Mirae is my childhood friend, so I find these accusations of witchcraft impossible to believe. However, I see that you must uncover the truth. Allow me to provide an escort. You may search the temple and see for yourself that Mirae is not here."

The regent shook his head. "No escort, Sefina." She didn't miss the fact that he neglected to use her title. "I want to trust your change of heart, but—"

"My people are frightened by this unexpected intrusion," Sefina said. "An escort will calm their fears and convince them to cooperate."

"Hmm." The regent made as though to stroke his beard before realizing his scarf was in the way and rubbing the opposite shoulder instead. "Provide us with an escort and we'll commence our search. For your sake, I hope you were honest with me."

Sefina turned and waved at Trenton, who had remained at the bottom of the steps to watch the proceedings. "Trenton, come here."

He bounded up the slick steps. "Yes, Speaker?"

"Accompany the regent and his guards as they search the temple. Allow them access to every room, no matter how small, but please dissuade them from throwing things about and disturbing the furniture. That will only frighten everyone." She looked to the regent as she said this and he nodded in begrudging agreement. "Now, I need to retire to my rooms and wash, since I just came from the castle infirmary. I'll join you afterward, Lord Regent. Is that agreeable?"

The regent nodded again. "I'm pleased to see you've come to your senses. I feared you might try and stop me."

Sefina narrowed her eyes. "Make no mistake. I believe wholeheartedly in Mirae's innocence, but hiding her away helps no one. Once you find her, she may prove her innocence to you herself."

"I fear you will be disappointed, my dear. Nevertheless..." The Regent inclined his head, then addressed his guards. "Search the temple from top to bottom. If she's here, we'll find her."

The guards tromped in, their heavy metal boots tracking mud all over the tile floors. Sefina's skin crawled and she scratched her arms through her sleeves. She felt as though she were being violated in some way, with enemies crawling about her home, but there was no time. Once the guards began their search, she hurried past the search party and up to her rooms.

Barely pausing to close and bolt the door, she made a beeline for the hidden drawer concealed beneath the bed frame. There was no telling what the regent's guards might do to the tapestry hidden within. She bundled it in her arms and carried it into the sitting room, glancing about in search of a hiding place.

The most obvious location was behind an existing tapestry. Several prized pieces hung upon the walls, having escaped the scissors. She picked one of similar size, a beautiful scene of Sea Children fishing in Hyron Lake beneath the bustling bridge. She took that tapestry down as quickly as possible and set about hanging the other. The three gods depicted smiled at her in their lifelike way, as though they knew she was attempting to protect them.

"Sefina?"

A sharp bang sounded upon the window. Sefina nearly dropped the corner of the tapestry she'd been attempting to hang. Loma's face pressed against the rain-streaked glass. She set the tapestry down to open the window. "Loma, you mustn't climb up to the second floor windows! I've told you, you could fall."

Loma clambered over the sill to stand before Sefina, not even bothering to argue against her chastisement. "Soon as I met you outside, I snuck over to the docks. Sorry, I know I'm not allowed out anymore, but I thought I could warn Mirae. Tell her they were coming."

His eyes darted down to his muddy shoes as though in shame. "I was too late. Got there just in time to see a brawl in the streets. Some of the dockside guards found her. They wrestled her into a carriage. Plenty of folks didn't like that, so they started throwing rocks and bricks, whatever they could get their hands on."

Sefina's stomach sank like a stone. She could picture what had happened afterward. Surely the guards had beaten those brave people into submission before hauling Mirae away. She was in the regent's clutches now, whether he knew it yet or not.

She took a shaky breath. Closed her eyes. Smothered her fear. Although her heart still hammered fearfully against her ribs, she'd had ample practice. *One thing at a time, Sefina. Mirae would hate to see this tapestry destroyed. Hide it, then make a plan.*

"Here, help me hang this tapestry," she said to Loma. "We must hide it from the regent, although I hope he stops his search once he learns Mirae is in custody."

Loma looked up at her with wide eyes. "What about Mirae?"

"Let me worry about her. First, the tapestry."

Loma shuffled over to help. When he saw what the tapestry depicted, he gasped. "Wait...is that...?" His eyes darted as he tried to take it all in at once.

Sefina nodded. "I intended to show you one day soon. There will be time for explanations later."

Loma blinked, then closed his gaping mouth. He pulled a chair over to the wall to help Sefina hang the tapestry, followed by the less 'offensive' fishing scene. As Sefina stepped back to check their work, she noted that nothing looked out of the ordinary. The top tapestry stood out slightly from the wall, but she doubted the regent's guards would notice.

"Thank you," she said to Loma. "I need one more favor. Find Lady Lirath for me. We need to talk about Mirae."

"No need." The door opened to reveal Lady Lirath, holding a key in her outstretched hand. A worried expression clouded her face. She closed the door and placed the key in her pocket. "Leave us, Loma. I must speak with Sefina in private."

Loma's eyes darted between Lady Lirath and Sefina.

"Go and wash up." Sefina gave his shoulder a gentle tap. "You're drenched and covered in mud."

Loma looked as though he wished to protest, but a firm nod from Sefina sent him scurrying out through the door and into the hall, his wet shoes slapping upon the floor stones.

Once he was gone, Lady Lirath bolted the door. "Mirae is to be beheaded tomorrow. Horace told me himself. I'm not supposed to tell you."

Sefina's breath caught. Her heartbeat felt faint and distant. A silent roar filled her ears, splintering her thoughts in the face of blinding fear. She almost felt as though she were in the cold, dark place she visited while singing, only infinitely more terrifying.

Mirae. Silent. Cold. No longer breathing. She couldn't imagine it. She refused to imagine it. A world without Mirae was hardly a world at all. Finally, after a tight, pained breath she said, "What? But she hasn't had a chance to prove her innocence!"

Lady Lirath shook her head. The furrow in her brow deepened. "Horace doesn't care. He believes he needs someone to blame for the sickness that's all but destroyed our city. Mirae is convenient."

"A scapegoat, you mean," Sefina snapped. "At least you see it, too. What will we do?"

Lady Lirath's clear blue eyes took on a wet sheen, no longer cold as ice, but watery with unshed tears. She waited for a beat of silence and lifted her chin as though to compose herself. "There is nothing we can do. Horace is the regent. We are his subjects. I only told you in order to prepare you for the worst."

Sefina's fear boiled into white-hot anger. She squared her shoulders, glaring at Lady Lirath. "You intend to do nothing? Nothing at all? Don't you remember when Mirae was your favorite student? She may as well have been your adopted daughter! How can you stand by and allow your own cousin to execute her? Have you no love left for her in your heart at all?"

Lady Lirath flinched as though Sefina had struck her. "Of course I love Mirae. I never stopped loving her, not even when she left—"

"Then for once in your life, show it!" Sefina's voice broke. "Help me! If you're content to watch an innocent woman beheaded for a sickness no mortal can control, when she's done nothing but try and help, I shall have nothing to do with you anymore. I'll disavow you completely, and you'll lose two daughters forever instead of just one."

Lady Lirath's jaw dropped. Her mouth hung open, and she gaped like a stunned fish scooped into a fisherman's net. After several tense seconds, she closed her mouth, lowered her eyes, and nodded.

"Sometimes you're much wiser than I am, my Sefina. Regent or not, I can't let Horace do this."

Through the storm of anger and fear that raged within her, Sefina felt a flicker of pride. For once in her life, Lady Lirath had listened to her. As the tension between them subsided, she took a calming breath.

"Very well. Heed me for once, and I'll tell you how you can help me save her."

Mirae — Sixthday

DAWNBELL SINGS ACROSS THE ocean, but Mirae scarcely hears its soft tones. She remains silent, lost in thought. The waves lap her neck. Lady Lirath claimed to love her like a daughter, even after all these years.

That should make her angry. It should make her rage at the unfairness of it all—that this woman, who had hurt her and especially Sefina so deeply—should claim to be driven by love. Love enough to defy her cousin and help Sefina attempt a rescue.

But it doesn't. Instead it makes her feel strangely warm within the sea's cold embrace.

Yeneri seems to understand Mirae's thoughts. She settles back in the rowboat with a deep sigh. "Love is not only for the perfect and good. All mortals must love someone or something, even those who are harsh and cruel. They love in a broken way, like themselves, but they do love."

Only then does Mirae realize she's crying. She sniffs, swiping at the tears that roll down her cheeks with a heavy, salt-stiffened sleeve. Though she wishes she didn't, she loves Lady Lirath while hating her at the same time. She understands better why Sefina remained by Lady Lirath's side through all the abuse.

"What do I do with this? How do I move forward?"

"By loving in a better way," Yeneri says. "Whether you choose to live or die, love in a way that nurtures. You know healthy love from your parents, from Brom and his family, from Taela and all the people of the docks. They welcomed you into their lives and loved you as their own."

Mirae drifts back in time, remembering warm fires and good food. Loud stories and laughter, some she told herself. The happy squeal of children jumping through mud puddles. The scent of Brom's soap, of Laru's fresh linens, of Taela's delicious eel pie. The best she's ever tasted.

Then, she thinks of Sefina.

She bites her lower lip until it throbs. "My love for Sefina wasn't always healthy, was it? I adored her, but..." It's hard to force the words through her stinging throat because a lump of shame has all but stopped it up. "Sometimes, I tried to control her. I told myself she was mine and mine alone, just as Lady Lirath did. I expected her to follow my lead—"

"Not always," Yeneri says. "You encouraged her to sing the regent's requested song at my final concert, even though it hurt you to see her indulge his whims."

"Yes, but other times...other times, I could have loved her better. I should have loved her better."

"We can always love each other better. It's the trying that's important."

Mirae draws a shaking breath of brisk sea air, as though to pull Yeneri's words all the way down to her heart and keep them there forever. "I'll try."

Yeneri smiles, the many crags in her face standing out even more. "Good. Now, listen. Sefina is almost finished."

Chapter Twenty

SHORTLY AFTER DUSKBELL, TRENTON drove an old wooden cart across the city plaza and up the wide cobblestone path that led to The Green. Sefina rode in the rear, crouched alongside a human-sized marble statue donated by Master Wiggum, thanks to some artful persuasion from Lady Lirath.

A white sheet covered Sefina and the statue. Even so, she held her breath when the cart stopped at the castle's outer gate. She pretended she was made of marble as well, listening as Trenton addressed the guards on duty.

"Good evening, sir and madam. I'm here to—"

A gruff voice interrupted him. "Turn around, lad. The Speaker isn't needed in the infirmary tonight. Regent's orders."

Trenton coughed. "I'm not here with the speaker or I'd have brought the good carriage. This here is a statue the regent commissioned from Master Wiggum. I was supposed to deliver it this afternoon, but...I'm sure you've heard things at the temple were a bit out of order today."

Sefina tensed. Though she couldn't see the guards, she heard the skepticism in their voices.

"A statue, eh?" said the second guard, a woman with a voice even rougher than the man's.

"Waste of coin if you ask me," said the first guard.

"It was paid for months back, before supplies here ran so low," said Trenton. "The speaker insisted I deliver it today no matter what. I think she wants to stay on the regent's good side."

"Smart of her," said the second guard, "since the witch loses her head tomorrow."

"Aye," said the first. "That should put an end to the Sea Child Sickness. I'll be glad to get rid of this damned scarf."

Sefina ground her teeth. *Stay silent. Stay still.*

Trenton coughed louder. "Me too—ahem. Excuse me."

"Let's have a look at the statue, lad," said the second guard.

Sefina's heart leapt into her throat as the sound of footsteps drew closer to the cart. She stopped breathing entirely. If the guards discovered her, she'd have no choice but to try and sing them to sleep—and there was no guarantee they wouldn't subdue her first.

Trenton coughed a third time, a nasty, alarming fit that went on for several seconds.

"Don't be an idiot, Berta," the first guard said amidst Trenton's hacking coughs. "The boy might have come down with it." To Trenton he said, "Go along, lad, and be quick about it. Tell someone in the palace that statue needs scrubbing top to bottom in whatever way won't damage it. No offense."

"None taken," Trenton rasped. "I'll be straight back."

A wave of relief washed over Sefina as Trenton clicked his tongue, spurring the horses into a walk. The heavy gate groaned open and the carriage pulled through into the palace grounds.

It took Trenton a few minutes to find a shadowy place alongside one of the carriage paths. He hopped off the driver's seat and hurried around to lift the sheet. The first thing Sefina saw was his pale face, his brow crinkled with worry beneath his wavy red bangs. "You can come out now, Sefina. No one's around." He hesitated, his gaze darting side to side, then added, "Please, be careful. I'll be devastated if something happens to you."

Sefina climbed out of the cart and gave Trenton a tight hug. His arms wrapped around her to return the embrace, strong and sure. *When did he become such a solid, reassuring figure of a man instead of the scrawny boy I grew up with?*

"I will," she whispered in his ear. "Wait here for me. I won't be long." She released Trenton with one last squeeze and snuck off into the night. As she'd hoped, The Green appeared deserted. The only light came from the moon, a mere sliver of faintly glowing gray in the dark sky.

She crept behind trees, stone fences, and artfully trimmed topiaries. Thanks to the months she'd spent coming and going from the regent's castle, she'd memorized the layout of the ground floor. With soft steps and shallow breaths, she approached a side door that usually remained unlocked for the removal of waste from the scullery.

A lone woman was washing dishes when Sefina nudged the door open. She looked up from a sink full of suds, her eyes widening in surprise above her scarf. "Speaker? What are you—"

Sefina lowered her own scarf and sang, keeping her voice low and soothing.

The sun has set behind the hills.
The evening air is quiet and still.

By the end of the first couplet, the woman's eyes began to droop. She yawned, swayed, and staggered over to the nearest chair, slumping down and tucking her chin against her chest. "Speaker...you shouldn't be here..." Her mumbling trailed off into quiet snores.

Sefina felt only a brief pinch of guilt as she hurried into the kitchens adjoining the scullery. This was to save Mirae's life, after all. Hopefully they would be long gone by the time the woman woke up and alerted someone.

She slunk out of the kitchen and into the castle's shadowy halls, searching for the entrance to the dungeon. Though no one had ever told her where to find it, there was only one door she knew of that always remained locked and bolted. It was this door she decided to investigate first, peeking her head around the nearest corner to check if the way was clear.

It wasn't. Two guards stood at attention on either side of the door. Like the guards who had overturned the temple earlier that day, they carried short swords, though they wore no helmets. No scarves either, the fools. Sefina ducked back around the corner, then began to croon the same lullaby.

The guards swayed like cattails caught in a gentle current. One yawned, then both slumped in on themselves, leaning against the wall beside the door. The first began snoring uproariously while the other dropped his sword to the floor with a clatter.

Sefina froze, but after waiting for several tense moments, it seemed no one was coming to investigate the noise. She hurried over to the guards, retrieved their swords, and searched them. One had a ring of keys upon his belt, which she unfastened. It took some trial and error to find the right one for the door, with her heart pounding like a drum the whole time, but eventually she heard a telling click.

She opened the door to reveal a set of steep, stone steps. A lone, ghostly torch burned at the bottom of the stairs, but there didn't appear to be anyone else waiting below. She hurried down the steps and stopped before the torch.

A narrow corridor ran in both directions, with barred cells on either side, but no more guards to watch them. All those she could see were empty. She'd been prepared to sing any prisoners to sleep, but it seemed anyone else arrested recently had been tossed in the city jail, or perhaps moved there so Mirae might be isolated.

Having no idea how to use the swords, Sefina hid them in the shadows along one wall, then debated which way to go. The stone corridor and its empty cells looked the same in either direction. Her heart sank. *Where are you, Mirae? How will I find you? What if you aren't here at all and the regent's hidden you away somewhere else where I can't reach you?*

Before despair could creep in, a song sprang to Sefina's lips unbidden. She hadn't sung it in years, but remembered the words as well as her own name. It surprised her as it poured forth, a lonely question in the darkness. "Cold stone stands before us, a wall between our kingdoms..."

She waited a moment, afraid Mirae hadn't heard. Afraid Mirae couldn't, or wouldn't, answer. Then—oh, then!—Mirae's clear, sweet soprano filled the dungeon with its power and Sefina's heart with hope. "Yet Of-Our-Hearts shows mercy, guiding our love to freedom."

Sefina ran in the direction of Mirae's voice, singing with everything she could muster. "Every duskbell without fail, my dearest, I shall find you."

"And yet the darkness wanes, the hours far too few!"

Sefina rounded a corner and there she was. Older, thinner, sadder, but Mirae's sparkling brown eyes were the same as always. Her voice, too. If anything, it was more beautiful and resonant than ever.

Sefina raced to Mirae's cell, completely forgetting the keys she'd stolen. Mirae was there to meet her, scarf already lowered, reaching through the bars to grasp her hands. "You came. Oh, Fina, I hardly dared hope..."

Sefina cut her off with a kiss. Their mouths met between the cold metal bars. Oh, how she'd missed this! How she'd longed for Mirae these past two years—and here she was, smelling and tasting the same, her lips moving against Sefina's in a familiar dance.

Only the growing need for air forced them apart. Sefina stared at Mirae in wonder, blinking back tears of joy. Through the watery blur, she noticed a shadow around Mirae's left eye. A red cut beside her lip. A scrape upon her shoulder where the sleeve of her dress had torn.

"By the Eight, what have they done to you?"

Mirae managed a faltering grin. "Nothing too horrible, yet. Suffice to say I didn't come quietly."

Sefina gave a choked laugh. "Of course you didn't." She fumbled for the keys in her pocket, flipping through them in an attempt to find one that matched the iron lock upon the cell door.

"Fina, wait."

Sefina scarcely heard Mirae. She turned the correct key and rushed into the cell, flinging herself into Mirae's arms. She buried her nose in the crook of Mirae's neck, inhaling the familiar scent of the sea in her hair. Her trembling lips found Mirae's throat while Mirae's hands rubbed circles upon her back.

Mirae cupped the back of her neck, urging her to look up. In her glistening eyes, Sefina saw the same longing she'd suffered for two long, lonely years. When Mirae kissed her again, she knew nothing else. She forgot where they were and what she'd come to do. They may as well have been in their old room at the temple as Mirae walked her back into the nearest wall.

A hot string of kisses followed, then hitched skirts and heavy breathing. Heat bloomed in Sefina's core at the first touch. She gasped as Mirae's hand slid beneath her smallclothes. She was already slick and sensitive, her body keen to re-learn this means of connection.

Mirae's fingers moved as though they'd never forgotten her. As though they'd never been apart at all. Sefina tensed, then shuddered as two of them pushed inside, with Mirae's thumb falling into place above.

She tried to swallow her cries, but failed. Her only saving grace was Mirae's mouth, which caught every one of her moans and scarcely allowed her room to breathe. She didn't mind. The only thing she wanted to breathe was Mirae anyway.

Sefina rocked her hips faster, tugging Mirae's lower lip with gentle teeth. Mirae's fingers curled more firmly at their old signal, and Sefina found her bliss all at once, fluttering and pulsing.

She wasn't prepared. After two long years, her release had only taken an instant. She should have been embarrassed, but she was too far gone to feel anything but relief. She surrendered and rode the waves, bucking in and out of rhythm as she clenched around Mirae.

Mirae didn't pause. She didn't even slow. Her fingers pumped faster, pulling still more pleasure from Sefina's shaking body. It was all Sefina could do to kiss Mirae back and keep her skirts bunched in her trembling hands. She longed to reach for Mirae, to let her hands roam the familiar landscape of her back and shoulders, but Mirae was relentless.

Sefina reached another peak right on the heels of the first. She stiffened for a single heartbeat, then relaxd as warmth spread from her lower belly to the tips of her fingers and toes. She nearly screamed, but Mirae smothered her cries, slowing her fingers at last. She kept her hand cupped between Sefina's legs long after, breaking away to nuzzle the crook of her neck.

"I missed you," she whispered.

Sefina scarcely had breath to answer, but by the time she finally stopped quivering, she was freshly determined. She pushed Mirae away, only briefly mourning the loss of fullness. She reversed their positions, dropping her skirts and lifting Mirae's. For once, Mirae obeyed. She held her skirts up as Sefina pulled down her smallclothes, burying her face between Mirae's thighs without hesitation.

She whimpered the moment her tongue slid through Mirae's heat. How could she have forgotten this taste, salty and sweet at the same time? How had she survived two years without it? Why hadn't she remembered how warm and silky Mirae was beneath her tongue? She swept the flat of her tongue everywhere at first, selfishly seeking more of Mirae's taste.

"Fina..." Mirae's hand pressed upon her head, fingers weaving into her hair. "Please."

Sefina allowed the gentle redirection. She drew Mirae's clit between her lips and sucked, instinctively remembering the right pace and pressure. After that, bringing Mirae release became her only goal. She cupped Mirae's backside in both hands, urging her to rock forward. Mirae took the invitation, stroking Sefina's hair all the while.

"Oh, Fina. Fina—I love you."

Warmth blossomed within Sefina's belly again—not desire, but something softer. After everything they had been through, together and apart, Mirae still loved her. Then Sefina fluttered her tongue just so, the way she'd done so many nights before, and Mirae spilled into her mouth, tugging her hair as though in need of a lifeline.

Sefina sighed as a surge of slick heat ran into her mouth and down her chin. Only when she was certain Mirae had nothing left to give did she withdraw, smearing kisses across both shimmering thighs. She hadn't had nearly enough, but the feel of cold stone beneath her knees reminded her where they were.

She stood, wiping a hand across her mouth. "Mirae, we need to leave. We'll continue this back at the temple."

Mirae pulled up her smallclothes and dropped her skirts. A frown darkened her face. "I'm sorry, Fina. I can't go with you."

Sefina stopped adjusting her own clothes. "What?"

"I can't leave. Not now."

Sefina stared, slack-jawed. Finally, she frowned and shook her head, certain she'd misunderstood somehow. "The regent intends to behead you tomorrow. Of course you're leaving." She took Mirae's hand and pulled her toward the open cell door.

Mirae stood firm despite Sefina's tugging. "I know." She ran her thumb softly over Sefina's knuckles, then reclaimed her hand. "Sefina, you've led a very different life than me these past few years, but try to understand. My people are dying in droves—not only from sweating sickness, but the regent's fear-mongering. He's taken all our supplies. All our medicines. Confiscated our fish to feed Whiteport and Castletown. His guards keep everyone shut away in their homes while the other districts roam free as though the plague can't touch them."

Tears burned in Sefina's eyes. "How will your death fix any of that?" she cried, her hoarse voice echoing from the stone walls. "You are your people's savior. If you're executed, you would be abandoning them as well as me!"

Mirae's shoulders slumped, but she kept her chin raised even as her soft brown eyes welled with tears. "I'll truly become my people's savior once the regent tries to execute me. My friends in the docks won't tolerate it. They'll rise up in righteous anger and things will finally change."

"You can't know that." Tears burned hot trails down Sefina's cheeks. "Please, Mirae. You'll die if you stay." Her voice cracked. "We've wasted two years apart. Don't throw the rest of our lifetimes away too."

"I know, but I'm so tired, Fina. So unspeakably tired." Mirae's body seemed to close off, her shoulders curling in as though she were decades older. Even the tired lines at the corners of her eyes and mouth seemed deeper.

Sefina tried to speak but couldn't. She longed to take Mirae in her arms and spirit her away somewhere they could safely rest. She understood Mirae's exhaustion all too well. "I know exactly how you feel, but if you come with me—"

Mirae shook her head. "No, Fina. I've felt too many children die in my arms and seen too many orphans weep for their dead parents. I've watched husbands lose their wives and mothers their sons. My voice wasn't enough." She took a tight, shallow breath. "I wasn't enough."

"No one can be everything to everyone. Not even you." Sefina grasped Mirae's shoulder. When Mirae's own hand rose, Sefina half-expected her to brush the touch away. Instead, Mirae's fingers curled tight over hers, urging her hand to stay.

"If I'm beheaded, I can be enough to inspire my people to end the regent's tyranny." She swallowed, her lips trembling as she tried and failed to smile. "My final wish was to say farewell to you."

Sefina snatched her hand back. "You can't be serious. If you refuse to live for me, live because you're Of-Blessed-Dreams' voice on this earth! We both know the truth. I may have coveted the role of speaker, but I'm nothing compared to you."

"No." Mirae shook her head, wide brown eyes welling with tears. "Don't you understand? You're everything. Everything, Fina. You're full of talents and wonders all your own. I—" She paused to wipe her eyes with her sleeve. "I'm the one who stands in awe of you."

Sefina could scarcely breathe. How long had she waited to hear those words? How long had she spent dreaming of the day Mirae would view her with the same overwhelming sense of wonder she herself inspired? But it was wrong. All wrong.

She clenched her jaw and bent to retrieve the keys she'd dropped when Mirae first kissed her. "If I'm so wondrous, then listen to me for once in your life. Come with me. We have to leave now." She tried once more to lead Mirae away, placing both hands upon her shoulders in order to steer her from the cell. "I have no idea how long the guards upstairs will sleep, but I can sing to them again—"

Mirae stood rooted to the floor. She took Sefina's hands, gently prying them away from her arms to hold them. The keys were unpleasantly cold between their palms. "Fina. My last wish isn't only to say goodbye. It's to apologize. I've been a fool. My anger toward Lady Lirath should never have been greater than my love for you. I should have swallowed my pride and stayed. Maybe then our story would have a different ending."

Sefina stumbled back. Her chest shook with barely stifled sobs as fresh tears rolled down her face. "You're still such a selfish brat! Dying only benefits you. It won't save your people, but you and your voice still might."

"Of-Blessed-Dreams will choose another miracle worker," Mirae said. Her voice went low, barely a whisper. "She lends her power to whomever she chooses, including you."

Sefina's hands balled into fists. Her chest burned with anger and grief and too many emotions to name. "Of-Blessed-Dreams might choose another miracle-worker, but you're irreplaceable to me. Does that count for nothing?"

Mirae sighed. "You're right. Allowing myself to die is selfish. But it will be the first selfish thing I've done in a very long time." She took a cautious step forward, one hand hovering as though uncertain whether another touch would be welcome. "Kiss me again before you go, Fina. Please. I'm begging you."

Sefina shook her head, taking another step back even though to pull away from Mirae was agony. "No. I won't kiss you until I've saved you. If you refuse to leave with me now, I'll save you at your execution, whether you want to be saved or not."

Mirae offered one last smile, a tender smile of farewell. "We shall see what the Eight will."

"I don't give a damn about the gods or your rebellion! You'll see my will tomorrow." Sefina tossed her hair and turned, storming out of the cell with squared shoulders and a fire in her chest. As she fled, Mirae began to sing. Softly, sweetly, sadly.

"A fond farewell I bid you, be your travels near or far."

The cell door clanged shut behind her, a discordant note amidst Mirae's mournful ballad.

"We two shall meet again someday beneath the same bright star..."

She would not, could not listen. She couldn't look back lest she crumple at the sight of Mirae's face. She fled from Mirae and her voice, tears of despair running freely down her face. The set of her jaw, however, remained hard with resolve.

Mark me, Mirae. I won't allow you to go peacefully to your death. I love you too much and too desperately to let you go again.

Chapter Twenty One

THE NEXT MORNING WAS cold and gray. Of-the-Sky wept in a light drizzle as though grieving what the morning would bring. Sefina dressed in dark trousers, a loose shirt, and a drab brown cloak. They were Mirae's, shoved to the very back of the wardrobe. Years later, they still smelled like her.

With dry eyes and a righteous flame in her heart, Sefina left her rooms, drawing the cloak tight about her shoulders. She brought nothing save for a few coins in her pocket. She didn't know what dawnbell would bring, but she was determined. Mirae wouldn't become a martyr while there was breath enough left in her body to fight.

Sefina left the temple alone and on foot. Unfortunately, she didn't remain alone long. Several temple residents walked down the wide front steps at the same early hour, shuffling along in groups and whispering amongst themselves.

"Do you think she'll sing death upon the Regent when he gives the order?" asked one of Jordaine's young pupils, a boy just beginning to sprout peach fuzz upon his chin.

"I hope she does," said a tall, willowy girl beside him. One of his classmates. "Tearing apart the Temple of Dreams with his brutish guards. How dare he?"

The boy rubbed nervously at his neck. "What if he chops off Mirae's head and Of-Blessed-Dreams unleashes something even worse than the sweating sickness upon Stagford?"

Sefina hurried on, ducking beneath her hood so no one would see her face. It was easy to blend in with the crowd without her vestments. Remaining unnoticed became even easier when the stream of people from the temple fed into the large, milling lake of onlookers overtaking the plaza.

It took time, effort, and more than a few mumbled apologies for Sefina to fight through the crowd. She seethed with impatience, wishing she'd come earlier. It seemed half of Stagford had risen before dawnbell, eager to witness Mirae's sentence. Some carried blankets and baskets of food as though they were on their way to a pleasant Eightday picnic.

As Sefina squeezed her way closer to the podium, she realized 'eager' didn't apply to everyone. Sea Children in colorful scarves surrounded the old, scarred wooden platform. Unlike the chattering crowd behind them, they spoke only a few hushed words to each other. Some carried hefty wooden planks, fishing hooks, gutting knives, and bits of water-hardened rope with knots tied in. They didn't shout or brandish these weapons, but kept them lowered. Watching, waiting.

Sefina felt their righteous anger crackle in the air around them like a lightning storm. She understood better why Mirae had believed her plan would work. She was more their speaker than Sefina herself had ever been. No doubt they would storm the podium should the regent go through with his plan. She stared at the chopping block for a long moment, then closed her eyes.

You're the kindling, my love, just as you wanted. You've fed the flames of rebellion. Now let me save you.

The high, brassy notes of a trumpet blasted over the early morning mist, heralding the arrival of the regent and his entourage. Sefina swallowed through a tight, dry throat. The sound made her heart pound faster.

Several people began muttering.

"Bastard's here early."

"Can you see her?"

"Not yet. Wait, look there!"

Sefina craned her neck, struggling to see through the crowd. In the distance, she saw a small form flanked by a score of guards, with more tramping behind. As the form drew closer, Sefina caught a glimpse of the person's face. It was Mirae, both wrists bound behind her back. Mirae, with a rough burlap sack over her head, concealing her from view. Her Mirae.

The guards separated into parallel lines, forcing the crowd apart. Some carried spears, using the handles to shove people back. Others carried drawn swords, which caught the first gleam of the rising sun on their silver blades.

Down this makeshift pathway walked the regent, head held high, his blood red cloak swirling behind him. His golden circlet glinted upon his brow. Though Sefina couldn't see his piercing blue eyes from such a distance, she pictured them all too easily, cold and full of hate.

The regent ascended the steps of the podium, three guards at each shoulder. A hush fell over the crowd as he stopped behind the execution block. When he spoke, his deep baritone carried an impressive distance.

"People of Stagford, a blight has descended upon our city. However, there is no reason to fear. I've ferreted out the source of our woes and she stands here before you today!" He made a sweeping gesture. Two guards began to drag Mirae up the steps by her elbows.

She stumbled.

Sefina's heart skipped a beat. Cold sweat ran down along her spine.

The guards hauled Mirae up and dragged her onward, shoving her onto her knees before the executioner's block. Another figure emerged from the regent's entourage, a man dressed in a black cape and hood that concealed his face. He carried a polished ax in one gloved hand while waving the other, acknowledging the rising cheers of the crowd.

Sefina struggled to breathe. She could scarcely bring herself to look at the awful implement, knowing who it was intended for.

The regent made another flourishing gesture. The crowd fell silent once more. "This woman, Mirae, is no miracle-worker. She is a witch, siphoning power from some dark source. She is the one who brought this plague upon us, and I swear to you, it will end with her!"

Cheers and boos filled the plaza, such a raucous roar that Sefina could scarcely hear herself think. She drew in a terrified breath as she realized her voice would never rise above such a din. She'd planned to sing the regent and his guards to sleep, her voice being the only weapon at her disposal, but not even Lady Lirath could match such volume.

Still, she had to try. There was nothing for it but to get closer. She shouldered through the crowd, swimming against the current in an increasingly desperate effort to reach the podium.

Then the current shifted. Others began pushing toward the podium, rolling toward it like waves chasing each other to the shore and bearing Sefina with them. These were mostly Sea Children, but a number of Earthfolk as well, shouting as they tried to climb the sides of the podium.

The guards circled in upon them from either side. Breaking dawn stained the sky red as wooden planks clashed against short swords. Swinging ropes thudded against metal breastplates. Sefina tripped over the end of one guard's spear and fell to her knees in the churning mud.

Her eyes darted, searching for an escape from the fray. Amidst the chaos, she met a pair of wide brown eyes. A burly man with blue sailor's tattoos sprawled across his bare chest shoved his way toward her. He offered Sefina his hand, his grip swallowing hers, and hauled her back onto her feet.

Heart hammering, legs still shaking, Sefina gestured to the podium. The man nodded. He gripped her by the waist and lifted her up, nearly tossing her onto the podium. A few brave souls had managed to climb up alongside her, but they were met with fierce resistance.

As Sefina clambered onto her hands and knees, she saw a guard's blood-stained sword plunge through a man's chest mere feet away. Another woman had wrapped a rope around the nearest guard's neck, pulling it tight as his face turned blue. He fell, shaking the boards of the platform beneath him and nearly upending Sefina again. She scrabbled, her hands slipping through a spreading pool of blood.

The stench of sweat and iron filled Sefina's nose. Her vision swam with fear as she hauled herself away from the blood, but then her eyes found Mirae. Mirae, who knelt calmly upon the podium despite the chaos, as though content to wait for death. Sefina clambered toward her, ducking beneath the point of a spear and crawling over another fallen body.

Ten feet. Five. Three. She could see Mirae's torn dress and dirt smudged shoes now.

"Skip the ceremony," the regent bellowed from somewhere above. "Do it now!"

But the cloaked executioner had already fallen. He'd dropped his wicked-looking ax, clutching a hand to his shoulder as blood wept from between his fingers. He scrambled back and away, seemingly in no condition to obey.

Sefina grasped the edge of the execution block, using it to haul herself upright. She tore the burlap sack from Mirae's head with bloodstained hands. Mirae's cheeks were smudged with dirt, a frayed cloth gag stuffed in her mouth. Her eyes—those dear, sweet brown eyes—met Sefina's, not the least bit fearful, but strangely soft and affectionate.

"Fine, I'll do it myself!"

Sefina whipped around to see the regent storming past the bleeding executioner, shoving aside his guards and drawing his sword. The blade swung toward Mirae in a glittering arc. Before she could breathe or even think, Sefina threw herself over Mirae.

No fear. No doubts. No hesitation.

Splitting pain pierced her chest. Icy metal, burning and freezing her insides. Heat flooded her throat as blood bubbled out her mouth and down her chin. More blood seeped through her shirt, pleasantly warm at first, then swiftly turning cold.

Mirae's eyes hovered somewhere above her. Beautiful, but pained. Shining with sadness.

In spite of everything, Sefina smiled. Dawnbell finally tolled as she sank into darkness, a low, distant farewell.

* * * *

When Sefina opened her eyes, Mirae was gone. So was the podium. The regent, the guards, the sword that had run her through: all gone. She stood upon a barren beach of black sand without another soul in sight. The sky above was pitch black, but dancing stars swarmed in the sea below. Countless white lights bobbed and twinkled to the gentle hiss of the waves.

It was the most beautiful, peaceful place Sefina had ever seen. "So, this is the Sea of Stars," she whispered into the loneliness. "Seems like a nice place to spend eternity."

Sefina lowered herself onto the sand, stretching out upon her back as she and Mirae used to when they were children. Though the sky held neither sun nor moon, the sand felt sun-kissed, warm and soft against her skin. She closed her eyes and rested her palm on her chest. There was no more pain. Her wound had closed as though it was never there.

So this was what it was to die. Quite nice, actually. Much nicer than expected. Sefina felt as though she might fall asleep on the beach while the starry waves lapped at her feet. The water was as warm and welcoming as the sand.

The tide rose quickly, creeping past Sefina's ankles to dampen her trousers. It didn't bother her. The pull of the sea was like a welcoming embrace she never wanted to leave...

The sun's begun to rise, the moon has gone away.
Open up your eyes and greet a brand new day!

Mirae's voice called out, a plaintive gull cry above the vast shore. Sefina opened her eyes. White-hot pain stabbed her chest as though the regent's sword had pierced her all over again. Then, as suddenly as it appeared, the stabbing sensation vanished. Mirae's voice sang on, high and clear and beautiful, drowning out the soothing hiss of the waves breaking upon the sand.

Wake up! Wake up! Flowers bloom. Birds sing.
Wake up! Wake up! Good morning, Sefina!

"Well?" said a different voice from somewhere above Sefina. It was a woman's voice, lower than Mirae's, with a heavy note that Sefina immediately interpreted as exhaustion. "Will you wake up?"

Startled, Sefina pushed herself into a sitting position. Standing before her was a woman wreathed in darkness, with cold, brilliant stars for eyes and a silver crescent smile reminiscent of a waning moon. Graceful tendrils of shadow floated behind her like strands of long raven hair.

"I know you," Sefina said, breathless. A familiar cold raced along her limbs, fighting off the rising tide's warmth. Hesitantly, she rose to her feet. "You're the one who visits my dreams."

"'I', if you wish to use that term, am no one," said the woman. "Once, I was part of someone. Now, I am a mere fragment. A single shard of a whole that is no more."

Sefina's eyes widened. A series of events spun through her mind, some long-forgotten. Her strange dreams. Her uneasy communion with an otherworldly being before the temple's altars. The cold, dark numbness she felt whenever she sang people to sleep.

"Are you Lady Sleep?"

"No. Not in the way you mean." The woman's voice pitched several octaves higher and lower, spanning multiple layers as though a whole group were addressing Sefina through a single mouth.

"We were once Of-The-Stars. Long ago, our siblings failed to watch over your realm on their assigned days. We made up the difference, but the work was too much for one, even a goddess. So we...divided ourselves."

The glowing white stars of the woman's eyes flickered like dying candles. Her crescent smile faded. "Our plan did not work." Her voice returned to a single thread once more. "Now, 'I' am simply a long-forgotten echo."

Sefina stared up at the woman, struggling to make sense of this revelation. Each answer only led to more questions, but she managed to voice only one of them. "Are you the source of my power?"

"Yes," the woman said. "Your Mirae is Of-Blessed-Dreams' avatar in the mortal realm. Thus, she was...observed. We also observed. While watching her, we saw how hard you tried. How you threw yourself into your music with a passion and determination we had never witnessed before.

"So we followed you. We wanted to see what you would do. What you were capable of. When we saw how badly you wanted to help your people, 'I' lent you what remained of my power. We have always been helpers first and foremost, even before we were separated."

A tight knot formed in Sefina's chest. *Someone was watching me all these years. Someone who wanted me to succeed.* "I wasn't blessed," she murmured, her heart swelling with pride. "You picked me."

"We are no longer a god, but some of our former power remains. 'I' was the copy meant to watch over Of-Eternal-Sleep's day. Eightday. Restful sleep and peaceful passage were all I could give you. Sometimes, rest is enough to make a difference."

Sefina hung her head. She knew the other side of that coin. "The others...we eased their pain. That means something."

"After witnessing such pain, do you still wish to return? Will you choose to see Mirae again? Or will you go to your own rest?"

Sefina opened her mouth, but found she couldn't speak. *Do I wish to return to a world of pain, hate, and bloodshed, knowing that world also holds Mirae? Mirae, who has always been my world in and of herself?*

Once more, Mirae's clear soprano broke through the silence of the dark and desolate beach.

> The sun's begun to rise, the moon has gone away.
> Open up your eyes and greet a brand new day!

Fresh energy coursed through Sefina's limbs, tingling like blood returning to her veins. She squirmed with discomfort, curling her toes in the wet sand. She loved Mirae's voice more than the sun, moon, and stars, but why wouldn't it leave her alone, just this once? A large part of her longed to close her eyes, lie down, and slumber beneath the waves where nothing and no one could harm her...

No. No! Sefina's fears rushed back in a wave. Drowning her, stealing her breath. Mirae! She'd left Mirae gagged and bound with the regent and his guards! "Please, let me go back," she pleaded, peering up at the woman who had once been part of Of-The-Stars. There was no longer any question of rest. If there was any way to return and save Mirae, she would do it without hesitation.

"Our sister wishes to intercede for you," said the woman. "Our other sister, the one I was created to assist, has delayed her claim on your soul. You may return, should you wish."

Tears welled in Sefina's eyes, mingling with the sea spray upon her cheeks. "Thank you," she said. "For everything."

The woman nodded. "Follow Mirae's voice. Once you've returned to the land of the living, the rest is up to you."

Sefina bowed once, then turned and fled without a backward glance, following the sound of Mirae's voice. Her heart pumped as she splashed through the shallows. Burning pain pierced through her chest, but she ignored it. At the tideline, she broke into a stumbling jog, fighting through the endless dunes of black sand. The sand sifted beneath her feet, causing her to sink into the dunes. It was as though they were trying to stop her, swallow her up. Still, she struggled on.

A faint light shone in the distance, peeking over the horizon opposite the starry sea. It was pale gray at first, but from that gray came all the colors of the rainbow, as though breaking through a thick fog. Beautiful blues and purples yielded to soft oranges and pinks, all the shades of a miraculous sunrise. They grew brighter and brighter until finally—the sun, blazing and glorious, shining so bright that Sefina raised a hand to shield her eyes.

* * * *

Sefina's eyes shot open. She drew a sharp breath into her lungs—not the salt of a sea breeze, but the hard tang of iron. Blood flowed everywhere, metallic and pungent, soaked completely through her shirt. She was wrapped in Mirae's arms, shielded from the raging storm of battle. A ring of Sea Children had surrounded them, standing shoulder to shoulder, bloody but determined to fend off the regent's guards.

"Fina." Mirae kissed Sefina's sweat-damp forehead, stroking her hair away from her face. Her gag had fallen beneath her chin and her smile shone with such tenderness that tears burned in Sefina's eyes. The image of Mirae's face blurred above her, but she never lost sight of that smile.

"Mirae?"

"I knew you'd come," Mirae whispered. "Please. Forgive me." Her arms went slack around Sefina and she fell, slumping onto the blood-soaked podium.

Sefina tried to cry out, but her throat cracked and her voice broke. She reached for Mirae instead, shaking her by the shoulder. "Mirae?" No response. She kept shaking, desperate. "Mirae!"

Mirae remained limp. Her chest rose and fell with shallow breaths, but her eyes remained closed. With harsh clarity, Sefina realized what she had done. In bringing her back to life, Mirae had...

The stomping of heavy metal boots and loud, angry shouts reminded her where they were. She could do nothing to help Mirae while the brawl continued.

Please, Of-The-Stars, help me! Help me save her...

A mind-numbing cold crawled through Sefina's body, freezing her limbs even as an outside force compelled her to rise. She stood with jerking movements, raising her arms and turning toward the roiling mass of the crowd beyond the podium.

Blackness closed in around her eyes, leaving only a pinprick of white light above her. It pierced through the center of her forehead like an arrow, but instead of more blood, a wordless song came pouring out her mouth.

She didn't know the melody. Certainly she'd never learned it from Lady Lirath, nor any music book she'd ever studied. It was a harsh, wailing thing like the winter wind, freezing Sefina's lips as it blew past them. Her voice rose louder and louder, a tumultuous thrum vibrating through her entire being.

All other sights and sounds vanished, snuffed out completely. There was only Mirae, lying sprawled at her feet. Unmoving.

When the final note of the final measure of the final phrase died away, Sefina returned to herself with sudden, snapping force. She gasped for air, shaking violently as she became herself again. The echo that was Of-The-Stars had departed as quickly as she'd appeared.

Sefina blinked through cold, watery tears, then wiped them away with her sleeve so she could look around. Mirae remained unconscious at her feet—breathing, but barely. Sprawled around her were the regent and his guards, their eyes closed fast in sleep. Drool ran from the corners of their mouths, their jaws hanging slack.

Sefina heaved a sigh of utter relief. Perhaps she couldn't sing Mirae back from the dead or rain destruction down upon the regent's men, but this was enough. It had to be enough.

She looked next upon the crowd that surrounded the podium. It too had gone eerily still and silent. Almost everyone was fast asleep. They lay in piles, slumped against each other, even on top of each other.

The only sound aside from the moaning wind and the faint sprinkle of rain upon the ground were a few soft snores.

Still shocked by what she'd done, Sefina knelt beside Mirae, preparing to carry her somewhere safe. After that, she had no idea what she would do. Care for her? Find a healer? Try to bring her back?

"Speaker Sefina?"

Sefina paused, glancing toward the voice. Hobbling up the steps was an old woman with weathered umber skin and almost as many wrinkles as Speaker Yeneri once had. Sefina recognized her hands, which she'd watched fold delicious slices of eel pie into greasy wrapping paper.

"Taela?"

"What happened?" Taela asked. "I was trying to get away from the worst of the fighting, then everyone fell asleep!"

Sefina's brow rose. "Taela, are you deaf?"

Taela nodded. "Aye. Have been for years. Read lips these days, mostly. Helps when my friends sign."

So she didn't hear my song. That's why she's awake. Sefina spared another glance at the crowd. A few people milled about, as though unsure what to do.

"Taela," Sefina said, "will you sign a message for me?"

Taela straightened, standing a little taller despite her bent and withered frame. "Depends on the message, Speaker."

"Tell them...tell the Sea Children who are still awake and any Earthfolk who resent the current state of affairs to tie up the guards. Do with the regent as you will. I won't decide his fate. I'm taking Mirae somewhere safe to see if I can wake her."

Taela's eyes darted toward Mirae, still lying limp in Sefina's arms. Then, she nodded to Sefina. "I'll do that." She hesitated, then said, "She missed you fiercely every day, you know. Never said so outright, but I knew. She'd get this far-off look and I'd know her thoughts were with you."

Sefina's heart clenched. She tightened her hold on Mirae, but managed a weak smile. "Thank you."

She left Taela to address those who remained, only watching the old woman's gestures from the corner of her eye. Her focus returned to Mirae and only Mirae. She slid both elbows beneath Mirae's arms and tried to drag her. When that didn't work for more than a few paces, she wrapped Mirae's arms about her neck and re-bound them with the fallen gag, slipping both elbows underneath her knees.

With slow, plodding steps, Sefina carried Mirae down the podium steps and through the field of fallen bodies. It must have taken a hundred years. Only the faint thump of Mirae's heart against her back and the soft breath against her ear kept her sane. A short distance from the podium, Trenton found her, his eyes widening and his steps quickening when he saw them.

"Sefina—is that Mirae?" He rushed over, his hands flitting about both of them as he tried to decide on the best way to help.

"Trenton. Why aren't you asleep?"

He grinned. "Plugged my ears with cotton. I had a feeling you or Mirae might sing, and who knows what could happen then."

Sefina returned his smile. "Have I told you lately how smart you are?" She ducked her head, removing Mirae's arms from around her neck and sliding her hands beneath Mirae's shoulders. "Here, take her feet. We'll bring her to the stables. Then..."

Then, she didn't know. If any of the regent's forces remained, they might search the temple. Returning there seemed unwise. They needed somewhere isolated. Somewhere quiet.

She had no idea why she thought of the White Horn Inn, but as soon as the idea dawned, she knew it would do nicely. They had rooms aplenty, and no one else knew its significance—that she and Mirae had visited as children on their first day in Stagford. "I'll look after her at the White Horn Inn. We should be safe there."

Trenton, the dear man, did everything he could to help. He took over carrying Mirae completely when Sefina's limp arms could take no more and placed her carefully in one of the carriages when they reached the stables. It was he who drove them to the inn just outside the city, while Sefina sat in back with Mirae, counting her breaths and watching her face for any signs of consciousness.

There were none. Mirae lived, but remained dead to the world. Her eyes didn't even twitch behind their closed lids.

"Please," Sefina whispered, "wake up. You can't leave me now. Not after everything..."

Her pleas had no effect at all.

By the grace of the gods, they arrived at the inn without incident. Trenton purchased a room with the coins Sefina had brought with her that morning. Together, they spirited Mirae in through a side door and up the stairs, making sure no one saw them. They laid her down in the room's only bed, atop crisp white sheets. There was drying blood on

Mirae's hands and the sleeves of her dress—likely Sefina's own—but otherwise, she appeared uninjured.

"Thank you, Trenton," Sefina said, gripping his hands tight in hers despite the blood and grime all over them both. "I owe you everything. Please, do me one last favor?"

Trenton smiled, his green eyes gentle and kind as always. "Of course, Sefina."

"Fetch water and some cloths from the innkeeper. I'm going to clean her up."

"You should consider washing up as well," Trenton said. "And changing shirts."

Sefina grimaced as she looked down at her blood-soaked shirt. That would have to be the first order of business. After that, all she had left at her disposal was hope.

Mirae — Sevenday

SEFINA'S VOICE SPEAKS FROM somewhere beyond the shore of black sand.

"It's been a week since then, Mirae. Eight days. I've scarcely left your side, not even to eat or sleep. You slumber on despite everything I've tried. I've sung to you. Talked to you. Bathed you. Poured hot broth into your mouth, coaxing you to swallow. Opened the window so you can hear dawnbell and duskbell and smell the evening breeze.

Please, Mirae. Please. I know you're in there somewhere, clinging to life in spite of everything. Please come back. I'm utterly lost without you."

Mirae doesn't look toward Sefina's voice, the shore, or the hazy light in the distance. She floats on her back, staring up at the pitch black sky. In one hand, she clutches the edge of Yeneri's rowboat, feeling the grain of damp wood beneath her fingers.

Her time has come. She must choose. Yeneri need not tell her again.

She thinks of the people she couldn't heal. Hundreds of faces, young and old, one blurring into the next. She has heard more final breaths and felt more hearts stop beating than any mortal should. The ghosts of the dead, all the souls she failed, surround her as the waves do, threatening to drag her into the depths of despair.

How can I return to life while they remain trapped here? How can I go on with the weight of their lives and deaths upon me?

Yet she also thinks of Sefina, weeping by her body, drowning in grief. Sefina, who overcame death and denied eternal rest for her sake. Her heart can't bear it.

She died while saving me. To choose death now would be like spitting in her face.

"Please, Yeneri. I don't want to choose. I'm too tired to choose."

Yeneri peers over the edge of the boat, looking down at her with sorrowful black eyes. "I can't choose for you, Mirae. You must decide. Life or death?"

Mirae can't speak. The waves roll beneath her, ready to carry her away as soon as she lets go of the boat, yet the gray light on the beach grows brighter as she turns her face toward it.

"One thing more," says Yeneri. "A warning, should you wish to return instead of slumbering here. It will cost you something precious. Of-Eternal-Sleep does not let souls, even souls blessed by Of-Blessed-Dreams, escape without payment."

Mirae's breath hitches. A spark ignites in her mind. "You...you aren't Speaker Yeneri, are you?" She studies Yeneri's face, but sees nothing amiss. It's exactly as she remembers, down to the last wrinkle and the color of her teeth.

Yeneri shuts her eyes for a moment. "She has been one of my beloved children for some time. I commune with her soul, which resides in my domain. Thus, I can put her thoughts into words."

Mirae shudders. Of the Eight, Of-Eternal-Sleep is by far the most frightening. However, the goddess has been nothing but kind and indulgent. She cannot bring herself to be afraid. She tilts upright in the water, bringing her other hand to grasp the edge of the boat. "I miss you. Her. I think about her every day."

"I know, child. You will see her again. The only question is, when?"

"If you are Of-Eternal-Sleep," Mirae asks, "why let me return at all? Why let Sefina return?"

Of-Eternal-Sleep tilts her face toward the sky, a look of fondness softening the face she has borrowed from Yeneri. "Of-Blessed-Dreams is more than my favorite sister. We are the two youngest and have always been inseparable, like you and Sefina. She asked a favor, which I chose to grant. You are her voice in the mortal realm and she is not finished with you. Yet she also knows how exhausted you are. She won't force you to live after all you've endured, unless you also wish it."

Time is running out. She must choose. "You mentioned a price to be paid. What price is that?"

"A steep one," says Of-Eternal-Sleep. "In exchange for your life, I shall take your voice."

Mirae's throat closes. She forgets how to breathe. *My voice? No! Anything but that!* For an instant, even Sefina's life seems a smaller price to pay. Her voice is her. It has returned countless people from the brink of death. Is her own life worth more than theirs? Who is she without her voice? Certainly not Of-Blessed-Dreams' avatar. She will not only be mortal, but ordinary.

Powerless.

Worthless.

No. Not worthless. Sefina wasn't worthless before, was she? All those people I healed. Were they worthless?

Mirae's throat opens again. She exhales, clearing her fear-fogged mind. No. Her first instinct was wrong. Sefina is worth so much more than any magic voice. The life they might have together is worth more.

Perhaps this could even be a blessing. An easing of her burdens. She will grieve the loss of her voice for the rest of her life. This she already knows, because she needs music with all of her soul. It nourishes her like nothing else. It brings joy and comfort to many. And yes, it makes her extraordinary. She will miss all those things.

But.

If she can't sing the sick well, make the animals come, or coax flowers into bloom, the burden weighing upon her will be lifted. If she gives up her voice, the loss will be a blessing as well as a curse. She might not be a miracle worker, but she will no longer be responsible for the wellbeing of an entire city. Sefina has always been better at shouldering such burdens, anyway.

I could help her. I could be her support, as she was mine for so many years. To her, I'll always be extraordinary. Is that enough?

Her answer comes like the breaking of dawn in spring, warm and full of promise. She has no desire to return to her old life. It was lonely, wearisome, and made her feel far older than her twenty years, but if she returns—when she returns—it need not be to that same life. When she returns, it will be to Sefina. She will exchange the role of miracle-worker for the humbler, but far sweeter role of wife.

That is, if Sefina will have me.

"Of-Eternal-Sleep? I've chosen."

"What have you decided?" The goddess's voice is no longer old and rough like a gravel path, but rich and smooth. Still, it retains a trace of Yeneri's inflection in the broadness of the vowels, as though some part of their connection remains.

"Please, send me back to Sefina. For a while, anyway. The two of us will join the sea of stars when you decide we've earned our rest."

Of-Eternal-Sleep straightens, sitting taller in the rowboat. Long, lustrous white hair spills free of her hood, flowing over her shoulders. Her eyes brighten, glowing with ethereal white light. "Are you certain? Of-Blessed-Dreams won't think less of you for choosing rest."

"Thank you, but no. I'll live the rest of my life with Sefina, however long that may be."

Of-Eternal-Sleep extends her hand over the edge of the boat, no longer gnarled like an old tree branch, but strong and smooth. Mirae grasps firmly, allowing Of-Eternal-Sleep to help her into the rowboat.

The goddess's hand is cool, but without the stiffness she's come to expect from corpses. It grips her forearm and hauls her over the side, helping her sit on the opposite bench.

Of-Eternal-Sleep lets go and takes up her oars. Her lips curl into a soft, mysterious smile. "Give Sefina my regards. She's stolen several souls from my shores after their appointed time, but I can't say I'm unhappy about it. Nor your own interference, for that matter."

Mirae smiles back at the goddess. "Thank you."

She turns toward the shore, gazing at the pale gray light. It grows larger and larger, spanning the horizon behind the beach. Other colors stretch their pastel fingers across the sky: purples, pinks, and blues give way to oranges, reds, and yellows, just like a sunrise. Dawnbell tolls one final time, singing its joyful song louder than any time before.

A tear trails down Mirae's cheek. She wipes it away with a damp sleeve, still smiling.

Sefina. I'm coming home.

Mirae — Eightday

MIRAE OPENS HER EYES to soft golden sunshine and Sefina's worried face. There are purple crescents beneath her eyes and blue shadows live in the hollows of her cheeks, but it's still her Sefina, the most beautiful woman in the entire world.

The woman who is her entire world.

"Sefina."

Her voice is a cracked, broken shadow of its former glory, but still capable of speech. A twinge of loss squeezes Mirae's heart, but the smile that dawns upon Sefina's face, her look of wide-eyed wonder, more than makes up for that. She'll mourn the songs she'll never sing later. Right now, she wants to rejoice in being alive.

"Mirae!" Sefina surges out of the chair where she's no doubt kept vigil, throwing herself upon the bed in her eagerness to take Mirae into her arms.

Mirae welcomes her, wrapping Sefina in a weak embrace, inhaling the scent of her hair. Tears of joy spring to her eyes.

"Can't...believe...you got yourself stabbed for me." Every word hurts, but she will adjust. She must.

Sefina laughs, drawing back only far enough to stare at Mirae in bewilderment. "I can't believe it took you eight days to wake up. You've always had a tendency for tardiness, but this is ridiculous."

"Sorry."

"What can I fetch for you? Food? Water?" Sefina starts to leave the bed, but Mirae tightens her hold, refusing to let go. She never wants Sefina to leave her side again...which might be a bit of a problem, later.

"You. Only you."

Sefina settles back down, stroking Mirae's hair beneath a trembling hand. It's just as Mirae remembers, back when they shared a bed and Sefina sang her to sleep each night. "At least drink some water. Your throat sounds terribly dry."

Mirae's smile falters, but she steels herself against grief. "My voice. It's gone, Fina. Forever."

Sefina's hazel eyes widen. "What do you mean, gone?"

Mirae shakes her head. "I gave it to Of-Eternal-Sleep as payment. The cost of your life was mine. The cost of my life was my voice. I met her, Fina. She was there, as real as you are, rowboat and all."

Sefina's jaw drops. She stares at Mirae, stunned, then says, "Well. That puts my story about meeting an echo of a dead god to shame."

"I heard you tell me," Mirae says. She's getting used to her new whisper, now. "Losing my voice isn't all bad. I can't sing, but that means the entire world isn't on my shoulders anymore. I'm free to be with you. We can be 'us' again. If you still want me, now that I'm no longer a miracle-worker."

Sefina squeezes her so tight that it's hard for Mirae to breathe. "Of course. Haven't I always told you I'd never love anyone so dearly as you?"

Mirae breathes the largest sigh she has ever sighed in either of her lives, old or new. Despite choosing to return, a small part of her had feared Sefina would reject her. She should have known better. Sefina's love has never wavered, not even after her departure from the temple...

Oh. The temple. If she intends to remain by Sefina's side, that means she must return, but is it safe to do so? "What happened to the regent?" she asks, afraid of the answer, but needing to know. "How is Stagford?"

Sefina's brow furrows. "Tense. Uncertain. After Trenton and I took you from the plaza, they...the dockworkers beheaded the regent. He's been dead and buried a week now. The nobles cry for justice, but Lady Lirath has done her best to quell their anger for now. She's convinced some that the regent was unfit to govern, considering how poorly he handled the sweating sickness."

Mirae nods. She had thought, perhaps even hoped, that might come to pass. "Stagford needs a new leader. Someone who will put the people first."

"Yes," Sefina says. "I must admit, I've been neglecting my duties as speaker in order to remain with you, so I'm not fully apprised of the situation. Trenton and Loma bring me news, and food as well, but I've remained here since you fell asleep."

"Then you'll neglect them no longer." Mirae sits up, though it causes her heart to pound harder than it should and sweat breaks across her brow. Still, she manages. Her head feels much better upright, her voice a bit stronger. "The temple is your responsibility. So long as you want me, I'll stay by your side. Your duties are my duties. Wherever you go, whatever you do, I'll follow."

Sefina strokes her cheek, gazing upon her with watery eyes. "I couldn't ask that much of you."

Mirae takes Sefina's hand, lacing their fingers, gripping as though they're her lifeline—because they are. It was Sefina's hand as much as Of-Eternal-Sleep's that pulled her back into the boat and returned her to the land of the living.

"You could ask for the moon and the stars themselves, Fina, and I'd give them all to you. I won't be your accompaniment, as you were forced to be mine for so long, but I'll be your harmony."

Sefina kisses her. Softly at first, then with greater passion. Their shaking breaths mingle together, warm lips seeking each other out. It is perfection. Sefina fills Mirae's lungs with new air, her heart with new hope, and her mind with dreams of the future. She has chosen well and wisely. This is only the first of many kisses. The first of many shared mornings.

The start of a new song.

Their song.

Together.

About Rae D. Magdon

Rae D. Magdon is a writer of queer and lesbian fiction. She believes everyone deserves to see themselves fall in love and become a hero especially–lesbians, bisexual women, trans women, and women of color. She has published over ten novels through Desert Palm Press, spanning a wide variety of genres from Fantasy/Sci-Fi to Mysteries and Thrillers. She is the recipient of a 2016 Rainbow Award (Fantasy/Sci-Fi) and a twice-nominated GCLS finalist (Fantasy/Sci-Fi). When she isn't working on original projects, she spends her time writing fanfiction for Mass Effect, Legend of Korra, The 100, and Wynonna Earp.

Connect with Rae online

Facebook: Rae D. Magdon

Tumblr: https://raedmagdon.tumblr.com/

Twitter: Rae D. Magdon

Email: raedmagdon@gmail.com

Cover Design By : Rachel George
www.rachelgeorgeillustration.com

Note to Readers:

Thank you for reading a book from Desert Palm Press. We appreciate you as a reader and want to ensure you enjoy the reading process. We would like you to consider posting a review on your preferred media sites and/or your blog or website.

For more information on upcoming releases, author interviews, contest, giveaways and more, please sign up for our newsletter and visit us as at Desert Palm Press: www.desertpalmpress.com and "Like" us on Facebook: Desert Palm Press.

Bright Blessings

www.ingramcontent.com/pod-product-compliance
Lightning Source LLC
Chambersburg PA
CBHW051128020726
47501CB00005B/1407

* 9 7 8 1 9 5 4 2 1 3 4 7 0 *